DEADLY COAST

A Thriller By

R. E. McDermott

Published by R.E. McDermott

Copyright © 2012 by R.E. McDermott

ISBN: 978-0-9837417-3-2

For more information about the author, please visit
www.remcdermott.com

Layout by Guido Henkel, **www.guidohenkel.com**

In Memoriam
Rita McDermott Mayer
1942 - 2002

Sister, Aunt, Friend, and
Wordsmith Extraordinaire

Acknowledgements

With this second book, I owe thanks to many of the same people as I did for the first. My wife Andrea was, as always, first reader and sounding board. Our sons Chris and Andy and daughter-in-law Jennifer provided support and comment, and my old friend Dennis Wright volunteered once again as an early reader, as did Theo Mandopoulos. As an aside, I would also like to thank Theo's wife, Ada, for helping me choose a Spanish translator for my first book, *Deadly Straits*.

New to the team were Barbara and Anton Elsborg, who spotted some early inconsistencies and helped me ensure my Brits spoke like Brits. Also in the UK, Terry Watson and Simon Swallow helped educate me on the role of insurers in ransom situations. Apologies to both gentlemen for stretching the facts a bit to suit the demands of the story.

As always, friends and former colleagues from the marine industry were generous with their time and support. Captain Ken Varall read an early draft and flagged time and distance inconsistencies. Captains Bill Abernathy, Dave Fath, and Jay Lemon in the US, and Captain Jeff Thomas in the UK gave unstintingly of their time to share their experiences transiting Suez and to provide other details that enriched the story. Special thanks to Captain Bob Cameron for introducing me to Jeff in the UK, and also to Kurt Larsen of the American Bureau of Shipping for clarifying a point on current standards in drillship construction.

Finally, I'd be remiss if I didn't mention the publishing professionals to whom I owe a debt of thanks. Peter Gelfan of The Editorial Department did his usual fine job of finding the weak spots in the story and then helping me strengthen them. Eagle-eyed Neal Hock once again mercilessly purged the manuscript of typos, misspellings, and grammatical errors. And if an ordinary picture is worth a thousand words, then the covers of the talented Jeroen ten Berge must be worth many times that. Once again, he nailed the essence of the story exactly with his great cover.

Over a hundred readers of *Deadly Straits* volunteered to read the advance review copy of *Deadly Coast*. Space prevents me from mentioning each by name, but you know who you are and you have my profound thanks.

Any errors made, despite all this excellent help and support, are mine and mine alone.

Thank you for taking a chance on a new author. I sincerely hope you enjoy *Deadly Coast*. If you do, please consider the other books in the Tom Dugan series listed at the end of this book. And if you'd like to be notified when I release a new book, please consider signing up for my mailing list at this link.

PROLOGUE

PINGFANG COMPLEX TEST GROUND
UNIT 731
EPIDEMIC PREVENTION RESEARCH LAB
HYGIENE CORP
JAPANESE IMPERIAL ARMY
HARBIN, CHINA - 20 JUNE 1944

Shiro Ishii struggled to suppress his impatience as the last of the fifty *marutas* was led blindfolded into the test area and bound to one of the stout upright poles. He regretted the waste—a dozen subjects would have sufficed, but he wanted to impress. He lowered the binoculars and turned to his visitor, a man in the field gray uniform of a Waffen SS colonel, adorned with the crested serpent insignia of a medical doctor.

"That's the last of the marutas, Doctor," Ishii said. "It won't be long now."

The German grunted and continued to peer through his binoculars at the circle of poles and a pair of Japanese medical technicians fussing over a device in the center of the circle. He lowered the binoculars and turned to his host.

"I'm unfamiliar with the term. Does *maruta* mean 'test subject'?"

Ishii smiled. "In a manner of speaking. It means 'log.' As you can see, our complex is quite large, and we can hardly publicize the nature of our work, so the curious are told the facility is a lumber mill." Ishii's smile widened. "And what does a lumber mill process but logs? In fact, a number of the overly curious have themselves become logs."

The German smiled politely as Ishii turned his attention back to the distant circle just as the two technicians started toward him in a run. They crossed the five-hundred-meter separation and came to stiff attention in front of him, bowing deeply. He returned their bows with a shallow bow, and then barked at them in Japanese, sending them to a control panel. Ishii turned back to his guest.

"We're ready, Doctor," he said.

"You're sure we're safe here?" the German asked.

"Quite sure." Ishii pointed to telltales, streaming from a pole in the light wind. "We're well upwind. Now please watch closely. It will be over quickly."

The German nodded and raised his binoculars as Ishii gave orders to the technicians and then peered through his own field glasses. Ishii saw a small puff of smoke in the center of the distant circle as his technicians triggered the device, and began a running commentary for his visitor's benefit.

"Efficient distribution is dependent on the delivery device. For this test, we're simulating delivery by artillery shell, with each maruta twenty meters from the point of impact. The gas inhibits the central nervous system, producing cardiac and respiratory arrests. The effect is immediate and near one hundred percent lethal, even in very small doses."

Ishii paused his narration and watched through the binoculars as the test subjects stiffened and strained desperately at their restraints before collapsing like rag dolls, hanging from their posts by tethered hands. Within five minutes, all were dead. Next to him, the German lowered his binoculars and spoke.

"Very efficient. But what of residual evidence?"

"None," Ishii said. "Unlike earlier agents, the gas causes no burning or scarring. Victims appear to have died of natural causes, as you'll see during the autopsies. Of course, the enemy will know you've used gas, but proving it is a different matter. We've used the gas extensively here in China against both military and civilian targets for several months without problems." He smiled. "Of course, the world cares little about the Chinese."

The German appeared skeptical. "That may be true, but I hardly think we can use gas in the European theater with impunity. I remind you that, unlike Japan, Germany is a signatory to the Geneva Convention."

"And if Germany is defeated, what will your fellow signatories make of your efforts at Dachau, Auschwitz, and elsewhere?"

The German stiffened.

"I mean no disrespect, Doctor," Ishii said. "But there's a time for propaganda and a time for truth. We both know this war isn't winnable. The Allies have taken Rome and established a beachhead in Normandy, and your cities are being bombed into rubble. And here in the Pacific, we've been on the defensive for months. Last week, American bombers based in India destroyed the steelworks at Yawata. With American air power increasingly able to reach Japan, the situation is grave."

"Such defeatist talk is bordering on treason!"

"I didn't say we're defeated, merely that we can't win—a different matter entirely. Besides, what I'm proposing has approval of the highest authority in both your government and mine. Hardly treason."

"And what *are* you proposing?" the German asked.

"A fighting retreat to our respective homelands, using *every* weapon at our disposal to convince the Allies that invading our countries would result in unacceptable casualties. We can't win, but perhaps we can avoid losing. But we must act together. If either of our countries fall, the other must face the Allies alone. Japan leads the world in chemical and biological weapons development, and it's in our best interests to share those weapons with Germany."

The German nodded and Ishii turned and gave more orders before turning back to his guest.

"My men will wait for the gas to dissipate and move the marutas to the morgue for the autopsies. It'll take an hour or so. May I offer you lunch? We've a great deal of work this afternoon, and I wouldn't like to approach it with empty stomachs."

HEADQUARTERS
UNIT 731
EPIDEMIC PREVENTION RESEARCH LAB
HYGIENE CORP
JAPANESE IMPERIAL ARMY
HARBIN, CHINA - 23 JUNE 1944

Shiro Ishii sat at his desk and stared down at the plain, thin folder. Such a simple container for the last best hope of Imperial Japan. *Operation Minogame* was neatly hand printed on the cover, beside a TOP-SECRET EYES ONLY stamp. Everything in the folder was handwritten as well—details so sensitive that no clerical personnel were allowed to see them, regardless of security clearance.

Ishii looked up at a soft knock on his door, and slipped the file into a desk drawer before calling for the visitor to enter. Seconds later, Dr. Yoshi Imamura stood before Ishii's desk, bent at the waist in a deep bow.

"So, Imamura-san. Did our German guest get away safely?" Ishii asked.

"Hai!" Imamura straightened from his bow. "He left an hour ago, Ishii-san."

Ishii nodded. "And do you think he suspected?"

Imamura looked thoughtful. "I don't think so. Why would he? Your presentation was very logical and convincing."

Ishii smiled. "Thank you, Imamura-san. Is the shipment prepared?"

"As you ordered. Everything crated and ready. It'll be taken by one of our destroyers to our submarine base at Penang and transferred to a German U-boat for the trip to Germany."

"And have you given thought to who will accompany the shipment?"

"I have," Imamura said. "Honda and Sato are the best candidates. They've both worked with the agent extensively and know enough of the plan to deflect any of the Germans' questions."

Ishii nodded. "I agree, Imamura-san, with one addition. You'll join them."

Blood drained from Imamura's face. "Forgive me, Ishii-san, but is that the... best use of our resources? I've many other projects under development here and—"

Ishii cut his underling off. "None remotely as important as this, Imamura-san. You have time to brief a replacement on your other projects."

"But Ishii-san, I—"

Ishii's face clouded. "Imamura-san. You will go. It is the will of the emperor!"

"Hai!" Imamura cried, and bowed deeply.

UNTERSEEBOOT U-859
ARABIAN SEA, OFF OMAN
28 AUGUST 1944

Imamura lay sweating in the narrow bunk, cursing his inability to sleep and dreading the moment he'd have to surrender even the scant comfort of the bunk to Sato. Space was at a premium in the U-boat, and the three Japanese were allotted a single bunk they occupied in eight-hours shifts, spending the remainder of each interminable day trying to keep out of the crew's way—a difficult task in the cramped confines of the submarine.

The boat smelled of unwashed men, and the *gaijin* submariners' diet produced a body odor unpleasant to Japanese sensibilities in the best of circumstances—in the congested U-boat it was overpowering. Worse still was the ever-present smell of diesel exhaust as the boat ran submerged at snorkel depth. The Germans took it in stride, but Imamura had been plagued with headaches since the second day out of Penang, and bouts of nausea caused by the unfamiliar diet sent him to the cramped and complicated common toilet with increasing frequency.

His mood brightened as he heard the rumble of ventilation fans and smelled a faint hint of fresh salt air through the miasma of the sub. They had surfaced! He crawled from the bunk and joined Sato and Honda, faces lifted to the nearest ventilation register like hungry pups nursing.

Korvettenkapitän Johan Jebsen stood in the conning tower of *U-859*, binoculars pressed to his eyes as he cursed under his breath and scanned the moonlit horizon. He cursed the luck that had seen *U-859* make two combat patrols without a single kill, and wondered if that had motivated his superiors to strip his boat of all but six torpedoes to turn it into a carrier of mysterious cargo. He cursed Allied air cover that forced him to run at snorkel depth during daylight at six knots. But mostly he cursed the fact that his rather liberal interpretation of his current orders had come to naught.

He was tasked with getting his cargo and passengers to Germany, but nothing precluded kills en route if the opportunity presented itself. He'd swung farther and farther north in pursuit of just such an opportunity, with no results.

Jebsen lowered his binoculars and heaved a sigh as he looked over the calm surface of the sea. The full moon was bright enough to make the horizon visible and the slight lightening in the eastern sky signaled the coming day. He had perhaps an hour of darkness left and then he would submerge and head south, thoughts of a kill forgotten. He started at the voice of the lookout beside him.

"Herr Kapitän, I have a ship. Two points on the starboard bow!"

Jebsen jerked up his binoculars and peered in the direction indicated. Sure enough, visible on the western horizon was a ship.

"Excellent! A straggler from some convoy, no doubt. Good work, Müller!"

Jebsen lowered his glasses and glanced again at the eastern horizon. The ship was steaming at a right angle to his own course. He could never overtake her submerged, but it would soon be daylight. If the ship saw him too early and got off a distress call, he was well within range of shore-based aircraft. Still, he'd be approaching the target from out of the rising sun and could probably sink her before she even saw him. Beside him, Müller seemed to sense his indecision, and Jebsen read disappointment on the man's face. His crew needed a victory.

"Well, Müller," Jebsen said, "what say we go hunting?"

"Jawohl, Herr Kapitän!"

Jebsen returned Müller's grin and ordered flank speed.

It took well over an hour to close to torpedo range, but Jebsen's timing was perfect. The rising sun was just above the horizon and felt good on the back of his neck as he approached the ship, hidden in the glare. He studied it in his binoculars. An American Liberty ship, ugly but utilitarian. He could just make out the name SS *John Barry* on the bow.

Jebsen wasted no time in taking his shot. He fired two torpedoes from the forward tubes, his heart in his throat as the twin tracks sped away from *U-859*. The bridge watch on the Liberty ship must have seen them as well, because the ship started a desperate turn toward the sub to present a smaller target. But it was too little, too late, and the *John Barry* had hardly started the turn when both torpedoes slammed into her starboard side. The sound of the explosion carried through the water, and Jebsen didn't even have to report success before the cheers of his crew echoed up from the open hatch. Across the water, he heard the strident clanging of the ship's general alarm bell and the moan of her whistle sounding abandon ship.

Minutes later Jebsen stood off the sinking Liberty ship and watched as the crew launched lifeboats and tossed rafts overboard. The ship was well down by the bow and sinking. He was debating another torpedo to hasten the process when he heard the drone of an approaching plane.

"Dive! Dive! Dive!" he screamed into the voice tube, and the loud *ooh-gah, ooh-gah* of the dive klaxon filled his ears. He watched Müller disappear down the hatch as the sea washed over the foredeck, and took a last nervous look astern at the British plane lining up for a run. Jebsen followed Müller down, closing the hatch behind himself and spinning the locking wheel. As soon as they were submerged, he'd make a drastic course change and dive deep. He prayed it wasn't too late.

Imamura stumbled to the cramped toilet, oblivious to the submariners' cheers or anything else but his own cresting nausea. He got there barely in time, and steadied himself against the bulkhead as he leaned face-down over the stainless-steel bowl. It was a long and gut-twisting ordeal, punctuated by dry heaves, leaving him trembling and sweat-soaked just as the terrifying sound of the dive klaxon filled the sub.

The deck tilted at a crazy angle, slamming him against the bulkhead. Imamura recovered and wrestled the toilet door open a second before a powerful explosion rocked the sub. The lights failed, plunging him into a pitch-blackness filled with the terrified cries of dying men. He felt water on his feet, then his knees. Rising pressure sent ice picks of pain into his ears, and he groped his way down the corridor as water rose above his head. He swam underwater, moving blindly and banging his head and limbs on unseen obstacles. Then suddenly he was free.

Imamura spotted light above, and kicked for all he was worth. He surfaced in a patch of diesel oil, the noxious smell ambrosia now, mixed as it was with breathable air. The sea was littered with debris, and he pulled himself up on a sizable piece of wood he recognized as the wardroom table.

CHAPTER ONE

LONDON, UK
PRESENT DAY

Dugan awakened slowly as the erotic dream faded, leaving him with a throbbing erection. Anna lay naked in the crook of his arm, pressed against his side, and he could just make out her sleeping face in the moonlight leaking around the window blinds. He smiled and suppressed an impulse to stroke her cheek, fearful of waking her.

"You awake?" she mumbled into his chest.

"And so are you, I see."

Anna lifted her head. "I could hardly be anything else, now could I? You've been poking me with that bloody thing for half an hour. And what ungodly hour is it, might I ask?"

Dugan turned to peer at the glowing face of the alarm clock. "Four thirty."

"Bloody hell! Why did I have to fall in love with a morning person," Anna groused, as she rolled on top of Dugan and nibbled his ear. "But since we're both awake, I think one good poke deserves another. Don't you, Mr. Dugan?"

Dugan responded with kiss, just as his cell phone vibrated on the bedside table. He turned his head to stare at the phone.

Anna sighed. "Go ahead and answer it. No one is calling with trivial news at this hour. Even if you don't take it, you'll be distracted." She kissed him and smiled. "And I do want your full attention."

Dugan reached for the phone. "Dugan."

"Thomas. This is Alex. I need you to join me in the office as soon as possible."

"What is it? Are Cassie and Gillian—"

"No. No. They're fine. But *Phoenix Lynx* has been taken by the bloody pirates."

"On my way," Dugan said.

OFFICES OF PHOENIX SHIPPING LTD.
LONDON, UK

Dugan paced the windowed wall of Alex's spacious office, oblivious to the magnificent view of the Thames below in the dawn's light. The knot of his tie hung loose at his neck and the sleeves of his dress shirt were rolled to his elbows. He glanced at Alex, slumped morosely at his desk, and like Dugan, unshaven. Anna, sitting in a chair across from Alex, appeared unruffled. But Anna could look calm—and gorgeous—in a hurricane.

"Right, then," Anna said, glancing at a yellow legal pad in her lap. "Why don't we go back over what we know and put together a plan of action?"

Dugan saw Alex nod a weary affirmation, and he moved away from the windows to the chair beside Anna's.

"Notifications," Anna said. "Who do we need to call?"

"The International Maritime Bureau in Kuala Lumpur already knows," Alex said. "I'll ring the underwriters as soon as they open. Beyond that, we should begin notifying the crew's families. They should hear the news from us first and know we're doing all we can to get their loved ones back."

Anna nodded. "I'll get a contact list from HR as soon as someone comes in." She looked out the window at the lightening sky. "There are always some early birds down there, so I suspect we'll see someone within the hour. What about the ransom?"

"Fifteen million is pretty stiff," Dugan said. "Thank God for the hijacking-and-ransom policy. I just hope those guys don't drag out the negotiations too long. How does that work, Alex?"

"W… we don't have coverage any longer, Thomas," Alex said. "I'm afraid I dropped it two months ago."

The color drained from Dugan's face. "You *WHAT*?"

"I dropped it," Alex said. "Premiums had risen into the millions. We just can't afford it—no ship owner can in this market. It's not like a year ago when premiums were reasonable and freight rates high after the Panama closure. Since the global economic meltdown, we barely cover costs."

"So you just dropped it? Just like that? No discussion? No joint decision?"

Alex's face colored. "Yes, I suppose I did. But let's pretend for a moment that I had come to you two months ago and solicited your opinion. Would you have studied the issue and given me an opinion, or would I have received the standard Tom Dugan 'I'm the technical guy. You take care of all that financial stuff' response?"

Dugan glared, then sighed.

"You're right," he said. "I would've left it to you anyway, so I guess the point is moot. But where does that leave us on the ransom? How about the P&I club?"

Alex shook his head. "No help there. If there's a pollution incident arising from the hijacking, or crewmembers are killed or injured, protection and indemnity will cover liability, but they won't pay a penny toward ransom."

"So we're screwed."

"Not completely," Alex said. "Hull and machinery insurers might contribute to a ransom, as will the cargo insurers. Both will suffer smaller losses from a ransom than by declaring the ship and cargo as total losses. But that means protracted negotiations not only with the pirates but between themselves, as each seeks to minimize their contribution."

"God, I hate the thought of paying off these bastards, no matter who does it," Dugan said. "Are you sure there's no other option, Alex?"

"None that I can see," Alex said. "None of the Western naval forces will consider a rescue attempt if the crew is under pirate control—it's too risky for the hostages."

"What about your people, Anna?" Dugan asked. "Any help there?"

Anna Walsh, in addition to being Dugan's significant other and holding down a cover job as his secretary, was also a senior field operative with the British Security Service (MI5), currently tasked with maritime threat assessment.

She shook her head. "The official view of these hijackings is that they're a strictly criminal activity. As such, they aren't considered a threat to national security. In fact, you should be thankful the government isn't involved."

Dugan looked puzzled. "What do you mean?"

"What she means is, for Her Majesty's Government to get involved, terrorism must be at least suspected," Alex said. "And if terrorism is involved, the payment of ransom becomes illegal. As much as I dislike the thought of paying off these people, I wouldn't like the option precluded."

Dugan turned at the sound of activity coming through the open door.

"Sounds like people are starting to arrive," Anna said, rising. "I'll pop down to HR and get that contact list."

Alex nodded. "I'll get off emails to the insurers, and follow up by phone as soon as their offices open. Thomas, when Anna gets the contact list, could you begin notifying the families. I think it imperative that they hear the news from senior management first. We must reassure them we're doing all we can."

Dugan grimaced. "Those aren't calls I ever wanted to make, but yeah, OK."

By noon Dugan was finished—and emotionally drained. He'd started in the Philippines, where it was early evening, alerting the families of the unlicensed crew. From there he'd moved to various European countries where most of the officers lived.

By the time he'd made a few calls, word raced ahead of him along the informal and mysterious networks that connected a ship's crew and their families, regardless of nationality, and soon his calls were expected. Some reacted with stoicism, long accustomed to the possibility their loved one might one day fail to return. Others reacted more emotionally. Dugan listened to them all, for as long as they needed him to listen, then left them with a special number and the address of a dedicated website Anna was setting up to provide information.

He checked the time and did a mental calculation. Early morning in Virginia. Jesse would be at his desk. Dugan made another call.

"Maritime Threat Assessment, Ward speaking."

"Jesse. Tom Dugan."

"Tom! How the hell are you?"

"We got problems, Jesse. *Phoenix Lynx* has been hijacked by Somali pirates."

"Christ! I'm sorry. Is there anything I can do?"

"I don't know. *Is* there anything you can do? We don't seem to have many options at the moment," Dugan said.

"Well, admittedly I can't do much. There aren't any links between the pirates and terrorists—"

"I think I've heard that speech from Anna, but it's nice to know MI5 and the CIA are on the same page," Dugan said. "Though, frankly, I'm getting a little tired of you intelligence folks apologizing. When the shoe's on the other foot, it seems Alex and I bend way over to help you out."

Silence.

"What's eating you?" Ward asked, at last. "I just got to the party here. I don't think I deserved that."

Dugan sighed. "I'm sorry. I guess I'm wound a bit tight. It hasn't been a fun morning. But you're right. You didn't deserve that. What can you do?"

"I can share intel, if I stretch the point. Are there any US nationals involved?"

"Just me," Dugan said.

"I meant in danger," Ward said. "Our resources are spread thin as it is."

"Yeah, I get the picture, but at least keep me posted on whatever you have, satellite imagery or whatever, OK?"

"Will do," Ward replied. "What's the ship again?"

"*Phoenix Lynx.*"

"Being held where?"

"I'm hoping you can tell us," Dugan said. "The pirates knew enough to disable the AIS before they diverted the ship to Somalia."

"OK," said Ward. "I'll check the birds. She shouldn't be too tough to find; the various pirate clans tend to use the same anchorages. And I do have limited assets on the ground there. But Tom, she's not a US-flag ship, so I'm really off the reservation here. If I get any push back from up the food chain about expending resources—"

"I understand," Dugan said. "I appreciate whatever you can do."

"OK. I'll get back to you."

Dugan hung up and stared at the crew contact list. He ran his hands through his hair and said a silent prayer he'd never have to work his way down that list to deliver even more tragic news.

CHAPTER TWO

US-FLAG SHIP
M/T *LUTHER HURD*
AT ANCHOR
PORT SAID, EGYPT
SUEZ CANAL NORTHERN TERMINUS

Captain Lynda Arnett sat on the sofa in her office and glared at the brightly colored cartons of cigarettes stacked high on the coffee table. "This pisses me off," she said through clenched teeth.

"Can't say as I blame you," Chief Engineer Jim Milam replied from the chair across from her. "They don't call it the Marlboro Canal for nothing; *baksheesh* is the name of the game here." He nodded to the towering stack of cigarettes. "And I have a suggestion. Better put most of that stash out of sight in your credenza, and just leave a few cartons out at a time. There's going to be a steady stream of 'officials' knocking at your door, from the pilot to the rat inspector to the frigging dogcatcher. If they see all that, they'll get greedy."

Arnett sighed. "Good point," she said, rising to gather an armload of cartons and carry them to her desk. Milam followed her with the rest. Arnett squatted behind her desk and stacked the cartons inside the credenza as Milam handed them to her, one by one, until the space was full. Arnett closed the cabinet and rose to face him.

"That should do it," she said. "Any more advice, Obi-Wan? What about this Charlie Brown character? I've been ignoring him, but he called three times on the VHF while I was anchoring. I wish the damned agent communicated as well."

Milam shrugged. "Your call, Captain, but Vince Blake and other captains I've sailed with usually let him on. Thing is, we'll be swarmed by these guys selling trinkets or whatever, and it's tough to keep them off, short of injuring them, and then there'd be hell to pay. Vince always figured Charlie Brown at least seemed to manage the swarm, and establish a sort of half-assed controlled chaos. And besides," Milam added, "rumor is this guy has a lot of lower-level officials in his pocket. All it takes to lose our position in the next convoy is a little delay here or there. It's happened before."

"OK, so you're telling me a 'normal' Suez transit means the ship's going to be swarming with Charlie Brown and his gang of thieves, a bunch of line handlers, the useless Suez searchlight 'electricians,' and an unknown number of bogus officials. And I get to be the friggin' cruise director and pass out smokes. Is that about the size of it?"

Milam grinned. "Almost. You also get the blame if anything goes wrong."

"Christ," Arnett said. "Captain Blake picked a great time to get appendicitis."

"Look, Lynda, I've sailed with Vince Blake for ten years, and he thinks you're up to it, and so do I. We both told Hanley that on the sat-phone before the chopper took Vince off at Gibraltar." Milam grinned again. "Besides, you're the only one with a master's license."

"Yeah," Arnett said. "For a whole month. I need a lot more experience as chief mate before I'm ready for this. I wanted—"

"You wanted to be totally prepared so you could do a remarkable job and no one could say you were promoted fast because you're a woman. And now you're terrified you're going to screw up, and people will say that anyway."

Arnett glared at Milam, then her face softened. "Well, yeah."

Milam shrugged. "News flash. Some guys are going to say that regardless, so screw 'em. Lynda, we've been shipmates four years, and you pull your weight and then some. Better than most of the candy asses in the fleet that'll be complaining."

Arnett smiled. "Well, thanks for the vote of confidence, Chief, but frankly I'm surprised Hanley didn't relieve me here in Suez. I was looking forward to going back to chief mate."

"Ray Hanley's not stupid," Milam said. "He's the most hands-on, unmitigated, pain-in-the-ass control freak you ever want to meet. If the city's patching a pothole in the street outside his office in Houston, Ray is probably out supervising. He knows exactly who you are and figures there's no point in wasting airfare to bring out a relief when he's got a perfectly good captain in place." He smiled. "Also, I reckon he's crunched the numbers and figured that even with the remaining mates splitting extra watches and collecting overtime, he's still saving money by sailing a mate short once you figure vacation pay and benefits."

"I'm not sure whether to be flattered or pissed," Arnett said.

"Go with flattered," Milam advised. "If Hanley didn't think you were up to it, he'd relieve you in a heartbeat."

Arnett shrugged. "Well, flattered or pissed, there's nothing much I can do about it. Which brings me to this little turd the agent sent an hour ago." She picked up a piece of paper from her desk and handed it to Milam. His eyes widened as he read.

"Son of a bitch," Milam said. "The Egyptians aren't going to let the security team board?"

"That's what it says," Arnett said. "Seems arms and ammunition aboard a merchant vessel are a violation of 'law number 394 for the year 1954.' I guess the new government's decided to dust off the old law and enforce it. They turned our security team back at the airport."

"So where will they board?" Milam asked. "No matter how eager Military Sealift Command is to get this jet fuel to Diego Garcia, I doubt they'll want us sailing past the Horn of Africa without security. I'm not too keen on the idea myself."

Arnett shook her head. "Egypt was our best shot. But we'll have a US Navy escort from the southern end of the canal at least through the Gulf of Aden. Maybe MSC can work something out with the navy." She sighed. "One more thing over which I have zero control."

US-FLAG SHIP
M/T *LUTHER HURD*
AT ANCHOR
PORT SUEZ, EGYPT
SUEZ CANAL SOUTHERN TERMINUS

Arnett looked down from the bridge wing and drummed her fingers impatiently against the wind dodger, watching the chaotic scene on the main deck below. Stan Jones, the newly promoted chief mate, was scurrying about with a clipboard, trying valiantly to do a headcount as people left the ship to board multiple boats jockeying for position at the bottom of the accommodation ladder. The "official" personnel—petty officials, line handlers, and searchlight electricians—asserted privilege and bulled their way down the crowded accommodation ladder through hordes of Charlie Brown's vendors descending with bundles of unsold inventory and whatever they'd been able to steal while aboard. Here and there on the accommodation ladder, violent arguments ensued as a few of the vendors got far enough down the accommodation ladder to toss their bundles to comrades in the waiting boats and then turned to force their way against traffic, back up to the ship for a second load. Charlie Brown watched from his place near the gangway, smiling benignly and offering no assistance whatsoever.

Elsewhere on deck, Milam and one of his engineers were helping the deck gang discourage other late-arriving vendors from trying to board. Arnett watched as Milam and a seaman unhooked a homemade ladder from the ship's side and let it splash into the water, earning them curses and shaking fists from the Egyptians in the boat below. *Please, God! Get these people off my ship!* Arnett prayed, as she took it all in.

She turned and glowered as Akil Shehadi, the ship's agent, limped out of the wheelhouse toward her, clipboard in hand. The limp was of recent origin, a result of miscalculation. Assuming a female as young and attractive as Arnett had risen to her current rank by unprofessional means, Shehadi had decided to try his luck. His tender application of a hand to her ass had been rewarded by the significantly less tender application of her knee to his balls. From the man's gait, the impact of the lesson was still being felt.

Shehadi stopped a safe distance away and displayed his crooked teeth in an unctuous smile. "Almost done, Capitan Arnett. I require one more signature."

Arnett grunted and held out her hand, and Shehadi extended his arm to hand her the clipboard, keeping his distance. She suppressed a smile and the impulse to inquire as to the state of his testicular health, then signed the form and returned the clipboard.

"That it?" she asked.

"Yes, Capitan. But I was wondering. Do you think it would be possible for me to have a few more cartons of—"

Arnett froze him with a look.

"Perhaps not," he said. "Forgive me for asking, and may Allah grant you a safe journey."

Arnett nodded, and as Shehadi limped back into the wheelhouse, she turned back to the scene on the main deck, relieved the chaos was abating. The last of the Egyptians were going down the accommodation ladder, and as if by some silent signal, the late-coming vendors that circled the ship were moving off to other prey. Soon she saw Shehadi appear on deck, limping forward to accompany Charlie Brown down the accommodation ladder. She smiled as Charlie Brown stepped into the last boat and she saw the bosun begin to raise the ladder.

Thank you, God. She lifted her radio to order Stan Jones forward to stand by the anchor.

Ahmed Chahine, aka Charlie Brown, stood in the launch and watched as the stern of M/T *Luther Hurd* receded into the distance. Relief washed over him in waves. He was done now. His family was safe, and the men who had threatened them were gone. And he had been careful—no one could ever connect the men with him. He didn't know who they were—nor did he wish to. What you don't know, you can't be forced to tell, and that was best for everyone.

CHAPTER THREE

Ali Ismail Ahmed, aka Gaal ("The Foreigner"), crouched in the bow of the boat as it circled *Phoenix Lynx* to the cheers of the Somalis lining the big ship's rail. The daily arrival of the *khat* boat was a much-anticipated event, a break in the pirates' otherwise boring existence. He looked back at the boat's cargo of the narcotic leaf, wrapped in damp cloths to preserve freshness and packed into plastic bags, and sent up a silent prayer to Allah for his good fortune. Catching a ride on the khat boat was a stroke of luck. He had quite a sales job before him, and it would be infinitely easier if the pirates were in a good mood.

He worried again about his potential reception. Despite his embrace of jihad, al-Shabaab, the local al-Qaeda affiliate, had been wary of his American roots. He hoped the pirates would be more welcoming.

His musings were interrupted by the bump of the boat against the ship's side, and the pirates lining the sloping accommodation ladder began to clamor for khat. Smiling broadly, Gaal passed bags of the narcotic leaf to the men at the bottom of the ladder, who passed them hand-over-hand up to the deck of the ship. When the last bag had been delivered, he nodded to the boatman and trailed the happy pirates up the ladder.

Gaal hung back a bit, fearing a challenge as he followed them aft to the deckhouse, but the khat-obsessed pirates didn't look back. Reassured, he closed the distance, and entered the deckhouse on their heels. The passageway was thronged with more pirates, but they parted willingly to allow passage of the khat bearers, Gaal among them now. Through an open doorway of what must be a mess room, he glimpsed hostages, hollow-eyed and fearful.

Knowing Zahra would have appropriated the best quarters for himself, Gaal separated from the group at the central stairwell and pushed through the door. He mentally rehearsed his pitch as he climbed the stairs.

Zahra Askar leaned back on the sofa in the captain's quarters—now his own—and transferred the wad of khat leaves from one cheek to the other with his tongue.

"Forgive me if I'm skeptical of your sudden change of heart, Gaal," he said in Somali. "But your activities aren't unknown to me. For months you've been proclaiming your allegiance to al-Shabaab and holy jihad, and now you ask to join us. Surely you know those fanatics consider our business, and any money flowing from it, *haram*. Now, why would an enthusiastic jihadist decide to join a forbidden business to earn tainted money? You can understand my confusion."

Gaal shrugged. "Al-Shabaab isn't what I thought. The same rigid philosophy that leads them to declare your operation haram makes me suspect because of my origin. I assumed my knowledge of the enemy would earn me a prominent place among them, but they use me as little more than an errand boy. I can't help being born in belly of the Great Satan, but because of that, I will never be a true brother in their eyes. I realize that now."

Zahra seemed to consider that, then shifted the wad of khat again and smiled. "Then perhaps we can offer duties more in tune with your abilities." He gestured to a chair and turned to a small man seated beside him. "Omar, offer our guest some khat."

The small man glared as Gaal took the offered chair, then tossed a plastic bag on the coffee table. Gaal nodded and extracted a stem of khat leaves.

"So you're American," said Zahra, as Gaal stripped the leaves, rolled them into a ball, and popped it into his cheek. "I suppose your English is very good."

Gaal nodded. "I speak without accent. Or more correctly, with an American accent," he said around the wad in his cheek. "I could interpret."

"I'm the interpreter," Omar said.

"Our only interpreter," Zahra said. "We could use another."

Omar's scowl deepened, and Zahra moved to defuse the situation. "In time, of course," he added, looking at Gaal. "For the moment, Omar here is handling all our needs quite well. And you could hardly expect to *start* as interpreter. You must work your way up—first holder, then attacker, perhaps first attacker if you have the courage. After that..." Zahra shrugged. "We'll see."

"I don't trust him," Omar said. "He's a spy from al-Shabaab."

"It's precisely because that's such an obvious possibility that it's unlikely," Zahra said. "The jihadists are fanatics, not stupid. If they wanted a spy, they'd corrupt someone already in our midst."

"I could be useful if you do take an American ship," Gaal suggested. The Somalis shook their heads in unison.

"Far too much trouble," Zahra said. "Now, when the Americans or the Western navies catch us at sea, they take our weapons and free us. Even if they catch us during an attack on some foreign ship, they're very careful to avoid killing us. They just send us to Kenyan prisons." He smiled and rubbed his thumb against his forefinger. "And with proper placement of a little cash, we're soon home.

"But if we take many Americans, that may change," he continued. "The Americans will come with guns to kill us. Then maybe we kill the hostages, and soon we'll have American drones looking for us and bombs falling on our heads. All because the Americans don't understand business." He shook his head. "It's much better to stick to capturing ships with Filipino and Indian crews. The insurance pays to get the ship and cargo back and no one causes trouble, even if we do kill a few crewmen. It is foolish to capture an American ship."

"What of the *Maersk Alabama*?" Gaal asked.

Zahra smiled. "I didn't say there weren't fools among us. I can't control the actions of others."

Gaal nodded, and Zahra turned to Omar. "Give him a chance to prove himself. Put him to work."

Omar glared before standing and motioning Gaal to do the same. "Come with me. The cook can use a helper. We'll start you gutting goats."

OFFICES OF PHOENIX SHIPPING LTD.
LONDON, UK

"This is useless," Dugan said. "Jesse gives us intel and then says we can't use it? What the hell good does it do us if we can't share it with our negotiators?"

Alex nodded and sighed. "I admit it's disappointing. The insurers aren't very forthcoming. One gets the impression they're haggling among themselves. I'd hoped if we could offer them insights into how the pirates were reacting to their counters, we might play a larger role. "

Anna appeared impatient. "I don't think either of you appreciate just how far Ward has his neck stuck out on this. He's re-tasked assets to help us on his own authority. If those assets are compromised, he could be in serious trouble. The least we can do is cover his back."

"We don't even know what his assets are," Dugan said. "How can we compromise them?"

"By seeming to know more than we should," Anna said. "If the insurance blokes doing the negotiating begin to seem clairvoyant, the pirates may well suspect a leak. And if they start looking, they may well find it."

"OK," Dugan said. "But the intel is still useless unless we can act on it. How do we do that without screwing Jesse?"

"We vet the information carefully, sharing only things that have an impact," Anna said. "And *only* if I can invent some plausible source that doesn't compromise Ward's assets."

"Sounds easier said than done," Alex said.

"Perhaps not," she said. "Phoenix is a British company. There is no official government involvement, but suppose I chat with the insurers and imply there is? That might buy us a bit more participation in the negotiating process. We can then selectively share intel and vaguely attribute our source to MI5 involvement and monitor and control how the information is used." She smiled. "And, of course, I'll also threaten them with charges under the Official Secrets Act if they deviate so much as an iota from our instructions regarding use of the information."

Dugan smiled. "God, you're a devious woman."

"And whose neck is stuck out now?" asked Alex.

M/T *LUTHER HURD*
GULF OF ADEN
SOUTH OF BAB-EL-MANDEB

Arnett took a last look at the chart and walked from the chart room to the wall of windows at the front of the bridge. Night was beginning to fall, and she set her coffee cup on the windowsill and raised binoculars to watch ships on the sea around *Luther Hurd* melt into pinpoints of red, green, and white lights—lights that revealed not only their positions, packed close to transit the narrow waters of Bab-el-Mandeb, but also their courses. She heaved a relieved sigh as those courses diverged, every captain taking advantage of the greater sea room of the Gulf of Aden to spread out.

"Come left to zero-eight-eight," she said to the helmsman.

"Come left to zero-eight-eight, aye," the helmsman parroted, and Arnett watched in the gathering gloom as the big ship's bow swung to port.

"Steady on zero-eight-eight, Captain," the helmsman said a moment later.

"OK, Green. Put her on the mike," Arnett said.

"Put her on the mike, aye," said Green, as he transferred steering control to the autopilot, or "Iron Mike," and stood watching the course heading for a moment to make sure the autopilot had engaged.

"Helm's on the mike at zero-eight-eight, Captain."

"Helm's on the mike at zero-eight-eight," Arnett confirmed. She took a sip of her coffee and shuddered. "Did you make this friggin' coffee, Green?"

Green's grin was a flash of white in his dark face. "No ma'am. That was Gomez."

Arnett shook her head. "Well, I don't want to hurt Gomez's feelings, but while he's on lookout, would you please pour it out and make a fresh pot. And if you see Gomez even look at the coffeepot again, please break both his thumbs."

Green's grin widened. "Yes, Captain," he said, and headed toward the coffeepot as Arnett turned back to the window. She looked up as Stan Jones walked in from the bridge wing.

"We're getting close," Jones said. "Where the hell's the navy?"

"We're two hours from the rendezvous, Stan," Arnett said. "I wouldn't start worrying just yet."

Despite her reassuring words, Arnett shared Jones's concern. Something seemed off somehow. A feeling vague and undefined, shared but unspoken. Whether it was the Egyptians' refusal to board the security team at Suez or running into dangerous waters with a new, untested skipper, she couldn't tell. But she felt it. The crew had been twitchy for the whole four-day Red Sea passage, Jones most of all.

"They should have met us at Suez," Jones said. "Especially after the security team was a no-show. Just watch, this is all going to turn into a big clusterfu—"

"*Luther Hurd, Luther Hurd*," squawked the VHF. "This is USS *Carney*, do you copy? Over."

"Well, I guess your worries are over, Stan," Arnett said, moving to the radio.

"*Carney*, this is *Luther Hurd*," she said into the mike. "We copy five by five. Nice to hear from you. We were afraid you didn't love us anymore. Over."

She heard a chuckle on the other end. "Negative that, *Luther Hurd*. We've been waiting with bated breath. Understand you did not receive houseguests at your last stop. Do you require boarders? Over."

Arnett considered the offer. Extra people had a way of disrupting the routine of a working ship. "I am considering your last transmission, *Carney*. What are your orders? Over."

"I'm to stay with you to the discharge port, keeping you in sight at all times. Your cargo is required soonest. Over."

"In that case, *Carney*, then negative boarders; repeat, negative boarders. You should be able to scramble assistance if needed. Is that affirmative? Over."

"That's a roger, *Luther Hurd*. Though you've broken my Marines' hearts. They heard your chow was outstanding. Over."

Arnett laughed. "Get us to Diego safe and sound, and I'll have Cookie put together a big feed. Over."

"Roger that, *Luther Hurd*. We have you on the scope and will maintain station one mile on your bow. USS *Carney*, out."

Mukhtar knelt with his three men, facing the stern of the ship and Mecca beyond, as they prayed the *Maghrib*, the sunset prayer, in the dim glow of the electric lantern. They couldn't see the setting sun, but Mukhtar had carefully inscribed prayer times on a scrap of paper and checked his watch faithfully. When they finished the prayer, he rolled up his prayer rug on the aluminum floor plates of the ballast tunnel walkway and watched his men do the same. He'd yet to make his own *hajj*, and the four-day voyage down the Red Sea in the belly of the great ship took him as close to the holy city of Mecca as he'd ever been. He felt a twinge of guilt that here, so close to the Holy of Holies, he was compelled to pray in such filth.

He'd done all he could, of course. Even though his men had complained, he'd forced them to walk far forward in the pipe tunnel, almost to the bow, to relieve themselves in the bilge. He'd realized his mistake on the second day. The ship was trimmed by the stern, and condensation on the ballast piping and tunnel bulkheads fed a tiny but constant flow of water into the tunnel bilge. Only millimeters deep as it trickled aft to the bilge wells, it was sufficient to carry stale urine and fecal matter a meter below the walkway where he perched with his men. By the third day, the tunnel reeked of human waste; so much so, Mukhtar worried the smell might carry to the main deck almost twenty meters above.

Nor was that the only problem. The cavern-like tunnel, running the length of the ship along the keel, was the perfect hiding place—hard to access, seldom visited by the crew, and far enough below the waterline that the flow of water against the hull kept it cool. But *cool* in the Red Sea was a relative concept, and soon the rank smell of sweat and unwashed bodies mixed with the effluvium wafting up from below.

To pray in such conditions was an abomination, and he'd compensated as best he could, diverting ever more of their limited water supply for ritual ablutions and ending each prayer session with an entreaty to Allah to forgive their transgressions and to bless their mission with success. It was in Allah's hands, but as he watched his men move listlessly in the dim light, he struggled to suppress his doubts.

Hiding in the American ship until its closest approach to the Somali coast had seemed an easy thing on paper, but who could foresee these conditions? Minutes had turned to hours as the men crouched in fetid blackness, saving the lantern batteries for prayer and mealtimes. At first they'd passed the time reciting and discussing Quranic scripture in the dark, but they were fighters, not scholars. Discussion turned to other things, and then stopped altogether.

The men became fixated on food and water; so much so, Mukhtar felt compelled to guard their limited stores of both. They were near mutiny, and he was increasingly uneasy leaving them alone, even for his nightly twenty-meter climb up the ladder to the main deck to take a GPS reading through the open hatch.

Mukhtar was pulled back to the present by a sudden change in the pitch of vibration in the steel hull, a change he'd come to understand signaled a major course adjustment. He nodded to himself as he felt the ship turn to port, and realized the significance. Last night's GPS reading had them just north of Bab-el-Mandeb, and he'd been waiting for a sign they'd moved through the narrow strait into the Gulf of Aden.

The men had sensed the change as well, and turned toward him, every face a question. Mukhtar ignored them and pulled the last water bottle from his pack. Less than a liter remained. They were not as close to home as he would have liked, but he could delay no more.

He straightened and handed the bottle to the man beside him.

"One swallow and pass it on," he said. "We save the rest to cleanse ourselves this evening before *Isha'a*." Mukhtar smiled at his men's expectant looks. "We strike tonight, when everyone except the bridge watch is asleep."

"Allahu Akbar," murmured his men in unison.

CHAPTER FOUR

Mukhtar squatted in the darkness on the starboard bridge wing, his left shoulder pressed against the wheelhouse bulkhead, and his senses heightened by a rush of adrenaline. He felt the rhythmic throb of the engine through the steel at his feet and heard the soft breathing of the man squatting behind him. The others were similarly deployed on the port side, waiting for his signal.

He rose until his eyes just cleared the bottom of the waist-high side window of the wheelhouse. The helmsman and the watch officer had their backs to him as they stood side by side, leaning on their elbows on the forward windowsill and gazing out at the ship's bow. They appeared to be chatting, and even without the night-vision goggles, he would've been able to make out their silhouettes in the soft glow of moonlight. Good, the ship was on automatic pilot. Should something go awry, he wouldn't have to worry about veering off course and alerting any escort.

The sudden thought of an escort chilled him. The plan called for the infidels to be subdued silently, but fire discipline was always a challenge with the mujahideen, and their weapons were not suppressed. The flash and sound of gunfire would carry a long way over water, and it wouldn't do to alert either the sleeping crew or an escort before he was prepared. Mukhtar sank back into a crouch and reconsidered his plan to rush the wheelhouse from each bridge wing.

After a time, he smiled, and motioned for his man to follow as he duckwalked forward, staying below the wheelhouse windows. He stopped a few feet aft of the open door into the wheelhouse and pulled a spare magazine from his pants pocket. He turned to see his underling nod in understanding and follow suit. Mukhtar held up three fingers for a silent countdown, and they lobbed the magazines in unison, away from the wheelhouse, which struck the steel deck with a sharp metallic clatter.

As expected, the watch officer came to investigate, intent on reaching the source of the sound farther out on the bridge wing. He moved through the open door with the helmsman on his heels, both playing small penlights on the deck in front of them. The pirates let them pass, then rose as one from the darkness to press the muzzles of their weapons against the backs of the seamen's heads.

"Move or make a sound, and you're dead," said Mukhtar.

Arnett hadn't had a decent night's sleep since she'd watched the chopper carry Vince Blake away at Gibraltar. Sleep came in patches, punctuated by weird dreams, the latest of which was unfolding behind her twitching eyelids. In it, she watched helplessly as Charlie Brown and thousands of his minions sailed off with *Luther Hurd*, leaving her adrift in the lifeboat in her underwear. She screamed curses, and then jerked awake in the dark—wakened by a sound that shouldn't be there.

She lay panting in the twisted sheets, trying to get her bearings and straining to hear what had wakened her, rewarded only with the distant throb of the engine and the familiar sounds of a ship at sea. She debated getting up, then decided against it. She wouldn't be a nervous pain-in-the-ass captain that didn't trust her people. The watch would call if she was needed, and she needed rest. She'd almost convinced herself that was going to happen when her phone buzzed.

"Captain," she answered.

"Captain," said the third mate, "I need you on the bridge."

"OK. Be right up," Arnett said, rolling out of bed.

Arnett pushed open the door from the central stairwell and made her way across the chart room, her path illuminated by the dim red lights of the chart table. She stepped through the curtains onto the darkened bridge, taking care to close them behind her, and then stopped a moment to let her eyes adjust.

"I'm here, Joe," she said. "Give me a minute to get my night vision and—" The smell hit her first—the sickening odor of an unwashed body and excrement. Before she could react, strong arms encircled her, pinning her own arms to her sides, as she was pulled close to that unwashed body. Then her training kicked in.

At five foot two, 120 pounds dripping wet, and determined to make her way in what was still very much a man's world, Lynda Arnett had carefully selected interests. Chief among them was martial arts. Rather than resist, Arnett tensed her legs and forced her back into her captor's chest. She sensed his surprise and a slight loosening of his grip, and still in the circle of his arms, she spun violently to the right, raising her right arm to deliver a savage elbow strike at the place where his head should be. There was a sharp pain as her elbow struck teeth, mitigated by the satisfying feel of the teeth giving way and arms releasing her as her attacker spewed unintelligible curses. She stepped back, still night-blind, and stumbled through the dark toward the general alarm.

Then the night exploded in stars, and she felt, rather than saw, the deck rising up to meet her face.

Mukhtar pocketed the leather-covered sap, and squatted over the motionless woman. He felt her pulse at the neck. Strong and steady—she'd have little more than a headache. Which was more than he could say for his second-in-command. He looked over to where the man stood, florescent in the night-vision glasses, holding his face.

"Are you injured, Diriyi?" he called, as he bound the whore's hands with a plastic restraint.

Mukhtar heard the sound of spitting and a soft click as something hard and small hit the deck. Diriyi's reply came as a wet, lisping rasp. "The bitch broke my teeth. I'll kill her!"

"Not yet," Mukhtar said, as he felt Arnett's pockets and extracted a key ring. "I'll stay here and guard the bridge. You take her master key and the other men and secure the rest of the crew. Enter their quarters and take them while they sleep. Leave each bound and gagged in their room for now. Start on the top deck and work your way down to neutralize the officers first. If you must kill anyone, use your knives. Now hurry!" He rose, and pressed the key ring into Diriyi's hand.

Arnett drifted back into consciousness, her head throbbing and a tightness enveloping the right side of her face as her flesh swelled from the savage blow she'd received. She couldn't see, and she fought down rising panic as she attempted to touch her aching face and couldn't. The panic worsened as she attempted to speak and couldn't open her mouth.

She forced herself calm and tried to assess her situation. She was sitting on the deck with her back against a bulkhead. Her hands were bound be-hind her and something sticky covered both her mouth and eyes—duct tape, she guessed. Light leaked around the edge of her blindfold, so she knew it was daytime, and from the sounds around her, she knew she was on the bridge. It sounded like her attackers had released Joe Silva to con the ship.

The VHF squawked. "*Luther Hurd, Luther Hurd.* This is USS *Carney.* How do you copy? Over."

"What do they want?" asked a foreign-accented voice.

"I don't know. Probably just a communications check," Silva said. Arnett heard the terror in his voice.

"Answer it and get rid of them," said the foreign voice. "And do not attempt to warn them, or first the whore dies, and then you."

"I'll try," said Silva, "but the captain's been talking to them. They may be expecting her."

Something hard pressed into Arnett's temple and she heard the foreign voice from just above her. "Do it," the man said. "And be convincing, or the whore dies."

"This is *Luther Hurd, Carney*," she heard Silva say. "We copy five by five. Over."

Joe Silva had been in the States for most of his forty years—a US citizen for thirty—but there was still a ghost of his native Brazil in his speech, evidently enough to draw interest.

"*Luther Hurd*, this is *Carney*. Please identify the speaker. Over."

"*Carney*, I'm Joe Silva, third mate of *Luther Hurd*. Over," said Silva, his accent becoming more pronounced due to stress.

"*Luther Hurd*, stand by. Over."

The radio fell dead for over a minute, then squawked again.

"*Luther Hurd*, this is *Carney*. Is Captain Arnett available? Over."

Arnett could hear the panic in Silva's voice as he addressed their attacker.

"They want to talk to the captain! What do I do?"

"Make some excuse to delay," ordered the foreign voice. "Then break communications."

Arnett heard Silva sigh and then key the mike.

"*Carney*, this is *Luther Hurd*. I must call Captain Arnett to the bridge. She will contact you soonest. *Luther Hurd*, out."

"Understood, *Luther Hurd*. We will stand by. USS *Carney*, out."

Arnett felt strong hands in her armpits as she was hoisted to her feet and pushed forward. She stumbled a few steps and felt the chart-room curtain brush her face as she was pushed through it. Rough hands seized her arms again, and she sensed she was being held between two men, her attackers having apparently learned not to underestimate her. The body odor was mixed with a shit smell that was overpowering and nauseating, and she thought of her taped mouth, visions of strangling on her own vomit flashing through her mind.

She flinched as duct tape was ripped from her eyes and mouth, and blinked in the light as her eyes focused on the scene around her. The chart room was crowded. Two men held her against the chart table, and another stood across the room pointing an automatic weapon down at Joe Silva and

Gomez, a young ordinary seaman on his first trip to sea. The terrified crewmen had been forced to their knees, and Gomez's hands were bound behind him. Silva's hands were free, but he looked almost catatonic from fear. In the middle of the small space stood a fourth man, very much in charge. The men were all black, armed, and of medium height and indeterminate age. They were dressed very much like the vendors that swarmed aboard at Suez.

Mr. In Charge smiled as Arnett's eyes watered in the unaccustomed light, and a tear rolled down her cheek.

"Ah, the whore captain cries," he said in accented English. "Did we upset you?"

He said something in his own language, drawing laughter from the pair holding her and a grin from the man across the cabin holding her crewmen. A grin somewhat spoiled by missing front teeth.

Arnett smiled back at the man across the cabin. "Nice teeth, asshole," she said.

The man scowled and started for her, then stopped at the upraised hand of the man in charge.

Now she knew at least two of them spoke English.

Mr. In Charge moved in front of her.

"My name is Mukhtar, whore," he said. "But you will call me master. In a few moments, you will radio your navy friends and convince them everything is in order, or you will live to regret it. Any questions?"

"Yeah. Would you assholes like some deodorant? I've got some in my cabin."

Mukhtar's fist flew back, then he stopped.

"No," he said, "I must not damage your mouth. I want you to speak clearly on the radio. Diriyi," he called over his shoulder to the man with the missing teeth, "show the whore we mean business."

Without hesitation, the man raised his weapon to Gomez's head.

"No!" shouted Mukhtar. "Use your knife."

Toothless nodded and lowered his weapon to dangle from a shoulder strap, and whipped a knife from his side. He jerked Gomez's head back by his hair and sliced the young seaman's throat in one fluid motion, and bright arterial blood sprayed forward onto the deck. Toothless released him, and Gomez toppled forward, face-down as blood pumped from the wound and puddled in a spreading pool. Beside him, Joe Silva blanched, and dark stains of blood from the spray dotted his face in stark contrast to his skin. He trembled in wordless terror, trying to speak, but his mouth opened and closed soundlessly, like a fresh-caught fish in the bottom of a boat.

Shock coursed through Arnett, followed by rage. There was no training now, just undiluted hatred. She struggled to escape, but her captors were prepared and held her tightly. She aimed a kick at Mukhtar's groin, but he sidestepped.

"You bastard," she screamed. "I'm going to kill you!"

"I don't think so," he said, then turned to his underling. "Diriyi!"

Toothless moved toward Joe Silva with the knife.

"Wait!" screamed Arnett.

Mukhtar turned back toward Arnett and smiled. "Will you cooperate?"

"Let the crew go," Arnett said. "You have me and the ship. That should be enough for whatever you plan."

Mukhtar came close and grabbed her chin, putting his face inches from her own. "Listen to me, whore, because I will tell you once. What I 'plan' is of no concern to you, and you are in no position to negotiate. I can kill you all in five minutes, much sooner than any help can arrive, and I will do so if I must. My men and I are not afraid to die, and in fact, assume we will, so there is no threat you can use against me. Whether or not we complete our mission is the will of Allah, but you should hope for our success as well. It is the only way you and these other infidels will survive. Now, will you cooperate?"

Arnett glared at him. "Yes," she said at last.

Arnett lay face-down on the chart-room settee, bound hand and foot and once again blindfolded with duct tape. Mukhtar kept her there, always within sight, allowing her to use the bridge toilet and having food brought up sporadically. From the sounds around her, she knew he'd released at least a few crew members to run the ship, their good behavior guaranteed by threats against their shipmates.

It was hard to judge the passage of time, but she'd been hauled to her feet to participate in three more communications checks, so she figured they'd been running at least a day or so. She felt dull and lethargic, drugged by failure, racked by doubt, and denied any visual stimulation. She tried to keep herself alert, but monotony and fatigue overcame her at times, lulling her into fitful sleep. Sleep full of dreams of Gomez, a kid just out of high school and on his first big adventure. She remembered his eagerness to please, and the unmerciful but good-natured teasing he got from his shipmates, herself included.

And she remembered her big mouth had gotten him killed.

Tough-talking, take-no-shit-from-anyone Lynda Arnett. She'd always been proud of that image, and the respect that came with it. But someone else had paid the price, and she was determined no one else would die for her pride. So each time the *Carney's* captain used the word *storm* in their conversations, she'd worked *good weather* into her response, signaling that all was well aboard *Luther Hurd*. And each time she'd been tempted to respond with *bad blow*—the prearranged signal to alert *Carney* she was under duress—she thought of young Gomez lying on the deck. She saw no way *Carney* could intercede without getting more of her crew killed, and she couldn't take that chance.

She roused at the sound of several people moving through the chart room, some of the steps hesitant, like those of blind men in unfamiliar surroundings, mixed with the more confident footfalls. The sound moved away onto the bridge, and despite her situation, she took comfort in the sound of a familiar voice coming from that direction.

"Get your goddamn hands off me," said Jim Milam.

She flinched at the sound of a blow, followed by a moan.

"Get the woman," she heard Mukhtar say, and moments later she felt the restraints on her ankles being cut. She was hauled to her feet and half dragged onto the bridge, where Mukhtar ripped the tape from her face and stood waiting for her eyes to adjust.

Chief Engineer Jim Milam stood on the bridge, his hands bound behind his back, with what looked like a small horse collar sprouting multicolored wires around his neck, held down by straps under his armpits. The cook, the bosun, and a seaman stood beside him, similarly bound and outfitted with the strange collars.

"Take them to the top of the wheelhouse," said Mukhtar to Diriyi, in English for Arnett's benefit. "Bind one to the rail at each corner." He smiled at Arnett. "That should keep them far enough apart to allow us to detonate them one by one."

"Just a minute, Mukhtar! You said—"

"Silence," screamed Mukhtar, as he backhanded her. Caught off guard, and with hands bound behind her, she stumbled backward and lost her balance, crashing to the deck in a heap.

Milam started toward Mukhtar, to be folded over by a rifle butt to the midsection.

"Take them up," said Mukhtar, jerking his head toward the door to the bridge wing, and Diriyi towed the still-gasping Milam toward the door. The other two terrorists herded the three bound seamen in their wake.

Mukhtar grabbed a handful of Arnett's short hair and hauled her to her feet.

She twisted her head and glared at him. "What're you going to do?"

He ignored her question and dragged her to the steering stand. Holding her with one hand, he fished handcuffs from his pocket and locked one cuff around the storm rail on the steering stand. He moved behind her, and she felt his gun at the base of her skull and heard the soft click of a switchblade opening.

"I am going to cut your hands free," Mukhtar said, pressing the gun harder to her skull. "I want you to handcuff your right hand to the steering stand. Move slowly. Try any of your tricks and your whole crew will die. Understand?"

Arnett nodded, and she felt the blade between her wrists, slicing through the plastic cable tie like butter. She wanted desperately to rub her raw wrists, but did as ordered and cuffed herself to the steering stand. She heard the slightest sigh of relief from behind her.

He was afraid of her. Despite her circumstances, the realization brought a small thrill of satisfaction and a ray of hope.

"Now," said Mukhtar, "place steering in manual and come right to a new course of one-eight-zero degrees."

Arnett did as ordered, without bothering to repeat the course back to him. A mile or more ahead, she could see the stern of the USS *Carney*, moving out of view to port as the bow of *Luther Hurd* swung due south.

"What are you doing?" Arnett asked.

"What I'm doing is changing our destination," Mukhtar said. "Very soon I'll be showing your navy friends they can do nothing about it."

The words were hardly out of his mouth when the VHF squawked. "*Luther Hurd, Luther Hurd*, this is USS *Carney*. Why have you changed course? Over."

"There they are now," he said. "The show is about to begin."

CHAPTER FIVE

Dugan gazed at Alex Kairouz across a conference table littered with sandwich wrappers, the debris of a working lunch.

"For Christ's sake," Dugan said. "It took the insurers ten days just to agree on a five-million counter on a fifteen-million ransom demand? While our ship and crew are rotting in some Somali shithole? What's the matter with those guys?"

"I'm afraid feeding them intel may actually be working against a speedy conclusion," Alex said. "They haven't said it in so many words, but I'm increasingly of the opinion the insurers see this as a golden opportunity to drive the ransom as low as possible, with a possible knock-on effect on future ransom demands."

"Then we need to explain to the insurers that our intel is a perishable commodity," Dugan said. "I'm sure there's a limit to Jesse's patience."

"And mine," Anna added. "Given the nature of my involvement, I'm not keen to see this drag out either. I'll drop some veiled threats to the insurers that Her Majesty's Government would like this concluded expeditiously."

Alex sighed. "Well, there's nothing more we can do now. The counter has been made. We just have to hope it isn't so low that it's angered the buggers and hardened their position. I'm anxious to hear from Ward on that point."

Dugan's cell phone vibrated on the table, and he glanced at the caller ID. "Speak of the devil," he said.

"Jesse," said Dugan. "We were just talking about you. Any word—"

"We? Are you with Alex and Anna?" Ward asked.

"Yeah, they're right here."

"Best put me on speaker," Ward said. "They'll want to hear this. And check your email."

Dugan activated the speaker function, placed his phone in the middle of the table, then pulled his laptop over and opened his email. "Go ahead, Jesse," he said. "You're on speaker and I'm opening my email. I see one message from you with an attachment. Looks like a video clip."

"That's it," Ward said. "Yesterday an American flag ship, M/T *Luther Hurd*, carrying a full cargo of jet fuel for Diego Garcia was hijacked off the Horn of Africa. There were—"

"As in the Panama *Luther Hurd*, the Hanley new build?" asked Dugan.

"The same," Ward said.

"But how could that happen?" Alex asked. "Surely, given the cargo and destination, there was a security presence."

They heard Ward's sigh through the speaker. "It's easier to show you than tell you," Ward said. "Play the video clip. But be warned, it's tough to watch."

Anna and Alex moved around the conference table beside Dugan, as he opened the video. They saw an aerial view of a ship in the distance, taken from an aircraft. The ship loomed larger as the camera closed on it, and then the camera circled the ship, making it obvious it was footage taken from a helicopter.

The ship was underway, but no one was visible on deck or on the bridge wings. However, there were four men on the flying bridge, standing by the handrails at each corner of the wheelhouse. The camera zoomed in to show the men bound to the handrails, each with a strange collar around his neck. As the camera panned over them, the men stared up at it, their terror obvious.

"Wh… what are those collars?" asked Alex.

A light began blinking on one of the collars, and the man wearing it screamed and tugged at the restraints binding him to the handrail, attracting the attention of the cameraman, who zoomed in closer still. There was a flash and the man's head disappeared, to reappear tumbling through the air. It landed on the main deck below, as the headless body collapsed to sit on the deck, torso held upright by wrists bound to the top handrail. The three other men looked dazed, the closest covered with his shipmate's blood, then all began to scream and tug at their bonds. The cameraman held focus on the ship, but the ship began to fade into the distance as the chopper beat a hasty retreat.

Dugan stared at the screen, blood drained from his face, the pencil he'd been twiddling snapped in half. Anna suppressed a strangled sob, and Alex sat wordless, moving his mouth as if trying to speak but not producing a sound. Dugan spoke first.

"The bastards," he said through clenched teeth.

Ward's voice came from the speaker. "That was filmed by a chopper from *Luther Hurd*'s escort, the USS *Carney*. The hijackers didn't even issue a warning until they'd killed the first guy to prove they meant business. Only then did they contact *Carney* on the VHF and order the immediate withdrawal of the chopper. The chopper withdrew, of course, and the hijackers informed *Carney* they would execute a crewman every thirty seconds if *Carney* violated a buffer zone of five nautical miles."

"If *Luther Hurd* had an escort, how the hell did the pirates get on in the first place? And wasn't there a security force onboard as well?" Dugan asked.

"There was supposed to be a private security team onboard," Ward said. "But since the revolution last year, the Egyptians haven't been very accommodating. Last week they began to enforce a 'no security team, no weapons' ban on merchant ships in Egyptian waters. My guess is that wasn't a coincidence, and it left the ship wide-open for the hijackers to stow away at Suez."

"What's the navy doing now?" Dugan asked.

"What can they do?" Ward said. "After the hijackers decapitated the crewman, the *Carney* pulled back and shadowed the *Luther Hurd* at the specified five-mile distance. We're dispatching more ships to the area, as are the UK and several NATO allies. Based on her current course, it looks like she's headed for Harardheere, where your own *Phoenix Lynx* is being held."

"Bloody hell," Anna said, now recovered. "Does it get any worse?"

"Unfortunately, it does," Ward said. "The hijackers must have had a camera of their own mounted to film the decapitation. It's starting to show up on several radical Islamic websites."

"Radical Islamic websites?" Dugan said. "Aren't we dealing with pirates?"

"I was coming to that," Ward said. "Al-Shabaab, the al-Qaeda affiliate, has taken credit. They've issued a statement via al-Jazeera, refusing any monetary ransom, and a list of terrorists they insist be freed. The list includes the names of over a hundred dangerous terrorists held in a dozen countries. The logistics alone of dealing with that many jurisdictions make it an impossible demand on its face, even if anyone was inclined to free terrorists. They claim they'll kill all the hostages and blow up the ship if their demands aren't met."

Dugan buried his face in his hands, then looked up. "OK. We understand, Jesse. Where do we stand?"

"I'm scrambling to get in front of this new situation, which leaves you without help, I'm afraid. I need to focus all my resources on al-Shabaab."

"Understood," Dugan said. "But could you try to get the pirates' reaction to the five-million-dollar counter before you pull out?"

There was a prolonged pause. "I don't think you understand, Tom. This is a game changer," Ward said.

"What do you mean?"

"I mean that Somali piracy just became unambiguously linked to terrorist activity, and the US, the UK, and many other countries have a clear policy of refusing to negotiate with terrorists. That includes allowing ransoms to be paid by US or UK citizens or companies."

"But they're different groups," Dugan said.

"Not to the general public," Ward said. "Public perception drives politics, and politicians make policy. Homeland Security is notifying US ship owners and insurers as we speak. Anna can check on her end, but I'll be very surprised if the Brits aren't doing something similar. It's always been a gray area, and rightly or wrongly, this pushed it over the line."

"Agent Ward," Alex asked, "are these public pronouncements or private notices to the owners and insurers? At any given time, the pirates hold over a dozen ships and several hundred crewmen, all the subject of negotiations. There's no telling what impact such a public pronouncement would have on the safety of the hostages, but I suspect the pirates will murder a few just to test the governments' resolve."

"That's been considered," Ward said. "For the moment, the notifications are verbal and no statements will be issued. Owners and insurers are free to continue talks, but no money can change hands. At least, that's what US owners are being told. But it's moot for us. The only US ship being held is the *Luther Hurd*, and Hanley's not talking to anyone, except calling me every thirty minutes to scream in my ear."

"So what you're saying is that we're screwed and there's not a damn thing we can do about it. Does that about cover it?" Dugan asked.

"Look, Tom. I'm sorry about—"

"We understand," Anna said. "But unless you've something else, we should ring off and check things from our end before someone lets the cat out of the bag."

"No. That's it," Ward said, and they said their goodbyes.

Anna looked at Alex. "I'll ring MI5 HQ if you'll contact the insurers."

Alex nodded, reaching for his phone, and Dugan stood to pace in front of the windows. He was not reassured by the bits of overheard conversation. Anna finished first, and Dugan sat down again, as they both waited for Alex to hang up. When he did, he didn't look pleased. He motioned for Anna to go first.

"Right," she said. "Long story short, HQ basically confirmed what Ward told us. Ransoms are prohibited and they're in the process of notifying owners and insurers. We're on the list to be notified, but they're starting with the major insurers first. No public announcement and no prohibition against talking to the pirates, but no money can change hands. What'd you find out, Alex?"

"Much the same. Our insurers intend to drag out negotiations as long as possible. From what they said, it seems all the major insurers are taking the same approach. I suppose no one wants to worsen an already horrible situation." Alex sighed. "In retrospect, I suppose our low-ball offer puts us ahead of the game. We can't have the buggers agreeing to a ransom we can't pay."

"How much time do you think we have before the pirates figure things out and it starts to get ugly?" Dugan asked.

"God alone knows," Alex said.

CHAPTER SIX

M/T *Phoenix Lynx*
At anchor
Harardheere, Somalia

"How many did we lose?" Zahra asked, leaning on the bridge-wing rail as he gazed at *Luther Hurd* in the distance.

"Four holders from here onboard," Omar replied, "including Gaal." He shifted the ball of khat to his other cheek and spit over the side, as if the American's name left a bad taste in his mouth. "Not that it's a great loss. He wasn't even a competent cook's helper. I can't imagine how he thought he could be an interpreter."

"And from our core group ashore?"

Omar hesitated. "That's more troubling. Five more holders—"

"Forget the holders! Any fool can be a holder," Zahra said. "Did we lose any attackers?"

Omar nodded. "Three."

Zahra stifled a curse and looked out over the anchorage dotted with captive vessels. He said nothing for a long moment, then shifted his gaze farther seaward, at the two American warships and those of half a dozen other countries, all drawn here by the presence of the *Luther Hurd*. He turned back to Omar.

"What're they doing, Omar? Al-Shabaab is full of fanatics, but they're not fools. Why, after months of declaring our business haram, have they decided to take it up themselves?"

"I don't know," Omar said. "But they've been recruiting for over a week now, and not the standard 'join the jihad and earn a place in Paradise,' either. They're promising holders twice the going rate and offering *four times* the going rate for attackers. In both cases, with half as cash in advance." He shook his head. "We can't compete with that. All the groups are losing men to them. Clan loyalty is keeping most groups together, but everyone has some men without strong clan ties, and they're flocking to the al-Shabaab operation."

"But that's just it," Zahra said. "There is no 'al-Shabaab operation.' They've captured one American ship, murdered crewmen, and drawn half the warships in the region to our doorstep. That isn't an 'operation.' It's insanity."

Omar hesitated. "There's more, I'm afraid."

Zahra sighed. "You're full of good news this morning. What is it?"

"Something strange is going on with negotiations. I was surprised when the initial counter on *Phoenix Lynx* was so low, but thought it a negotiating tactic. But I've been talking to interpreters for the other groups, and now I'm not so sure. They all tell me that their negotiations have slowed. In fact, one group was within days of finalizing a ransom amount and the ship owner and insurer suddenly raised objections to the terms of the deal. Terms agreed weeks before. It seems like a concerted effort to stall. What's it mean?"

Zahra glared out across the water at the *Luther Hurd*. "It means the fanatics have complicated our lives, and that negotiations will be more difficult." He sighed. "We must become more aggressive, both in pressing our ransom demands and acquiring more hostages to enhance our bargaining position. It will be best if we can coordinate our efforts and move quickly. I will contact the other leaders."

He shifted his gaze to the warships. "Perhaps, in a strange way, the fanatics have done us a favor. The more warships that collect here, the more freely we can operate out of the other ports and at sea. And Omar, find out more of the fanatics' plans. Pick out one of our most loyal men to defect to al-Shabaab." He turned and smiled. "Tell him he can take the fanatics' money, but not to forget where his loyalty lies."

M/T *Luther Hurd*
At anchor
Harardheere, Somalia

Mukhtar stood beside Diriyi on the bridge wing of the *Luther Hurd*, staring across the water at the *Phoenix Lynx*, three miles away.

"You were right, my brother," Diriyi said, as he gazed in the opposite direction, seaward toward the line of warships. "More arrive every day. But how can you be sure they won't attack?"

"On the contrary," Mukhtar said. "I'm quite sure they will, but not immediately. The killings make them wary, and as long as we don't force their hands with more executions, they'll talk." He smiled. "The Americans like to show the world how reasonable they are before they murder the faithful. They'll talk and talk, and meanwhile, their Navy SEALs will find a sister ship and familiarize themselves with every detail. Then they'll build a mockup and plan the attack meticulously, and count themselves very clever to have bought the time to do so. And *Inshallah*, by the time they attack it'll make no difference." He placed a hand on Diriyi's shoulder. "I'm counting on you to buy me at least two weeks—four would be better. But if you sense attack is imminent, kill as many of the hostages as you can, then save yourself. Go ashore on some pretext and leave our new recruits to face the Americans' wrath."

"As you order," Diriyi said. "I think my job is less difficult than yours. Are you sure our other recruits can be relied upon?"

Mukhtar shrugged. "They're motivated by dreams of wealth, which will buy their loyalty as long as needed. Besides, we've no choice. The faithful are few, and none of us have experience attacking ships. It made little difference with this one, because we got aboard and attacked by surprise in the middle of the night. But our next attack will be very different." He paused. "Which brings me to my next question. How's recruitment going?"

"We're almost ready. I've screened twenty experienced attackers, including two first-boarders, and begun to send them north to Eyl in twos and threes to avoid arousing the infidels' suspicions. Their satellites and drones are snooping everywhere."

"Good, good," Mukhtar said. "Holders?"

Diriyi snorted. "Holders we can have without number at the wages we're promising. Each day brings another boatload. I'm going to start turning them away."

"No. Bring them aboard and arm them to the teeth. The more armed men the Americans see aboard, the longer they'll delay and plan."

"All right," he said. "A few more then, but remember, every man aboard means more food and khat we must bring from shore. And with nothing to do, the men quarrel." Diriyi sighed. "I think I'd prefer to face death at your side than manage this pack of greedy and unruly children."

"And I'd prefer to have you there, my brother," Mukhtar said. "But none of the other faithful has enough English to deal with the Americans."

"Which reminds me. The boat this morning brought our runaway American back to us. I suppose the promise of cash was more alluring than faith."

"Gaal? Do you trust him?"

Diriyi shrugged. "He's a fool, like all these American jihadists. They all come impressed with their own sacrifice, and most are so squeamish they faint at the sight of a little blood. And then they expect us to make them leaders. " Diriyi spit over the side. "I didn't trust him before he deserted us, and I trust him even less now. I have him under guard, but it just occurred to me that his language skills might be useful."

Mukhtar stroked his chin. "You may be right, and even if you're wrong, he's expendable. But he's an unknown. We must test him somehow."

"But how?" Diriyi asked.

Mukhtar smiled. "I have an idea. Bring Gaal to the captain's office. And have someone bring up the woman."

Gaal's mind raced as, hands bound behind him, he was half dragged up the stairs toward an upper deck. At D-deck, he was tugged into the passageway and hustled toward the captain's office. He tensed involuntarily as Diriyi released his arm and pushed him through the open door.

Mukhtar stood in the middle of the room, and kneeling before him was a slight figure, head concealed by a pillowcase. The kneeling figure was dressed in the khakis of a ship's officer, and the diminutive frame and body shape left no doubt the captive was female.

"Ah, Gaal. You've come back," Mukhtar said in Somali. "So you find the promise of cash more alluring than that of Paradise."

"A believer may serve Allah in many ways, Mukhtar. I wish only to use the skills I've acquired in His service."

Beside him, Diriyi scoffed. "From the others who arrived with him, it seems his most recently acquired skill is gutting goats."

Mukhtar smiled at Gaal. "Not a skill in short supply, I'm afraid, but still, you may be of some use. Of course, given both your background and your recent betrayal, your loyalty is very much in doubt. As I'm sure you understand, we will require some proof of your renewed commitment."

Gaal nodded, but said nothing.

Mukhtar inclined his head toward the kneeling woman as he drew a Glock from his belt. "This whore is one of your former countrymen. I want you to kill her." He paused, as if he just remembered something. "Ah. But what am I thinking? We must watch her face while you do it." Mukhtar ripped the pillowcase off the woman's head.

The woman looked up, confused and blinking in the light. There was duct tape over her mouth. Mukhtar leaned down and spoke in English.

"You are about to die, whore. I would allow you some last words, but I don't care to hear anything you have to say."

Then he straightened and faced away from Gaal as he pointed the Glock down and racked the slide. He turned and held out the gun to Gaal, butt first.

Behind him, Gaal heard the click of a spring knife and felt cold steel against his wrists as Diriyi sliced through the plastic restraints.

"Kill her," Mukhtar ordered, thrusting the Glock at Gaal.

Gaal hesitated for an instant before taking the gun and pointing it between the woman's eyes, inches from her head. He said a silent prayer to Allah for her soul and pulled the trigger.

OFFICES OF PHOENIX SHIPPING LTD.
LONDON, UK

Dugan sat before his open laptop and steeled himself. Anna and Alex flanked him at the conference table on either side, just out of range of the laptop webcam.

"Thomas, you don't have to do this alone. I'll join you on the call," Alex said.

Dugan shook his head. "We agreed I should be the point of contact for the families, and based on the emails and voice mail, some of them already hate my guts. I may as well continue as the face of the company until my credibility is completely shot." He smiled wanly. "The way things are going, that won't be much longer. Then you can come in as backup."

"I think 'hate' is a bit harsh," Alex said. "I'm sure most of the families realize we're doing all we can."

"Are you?" Dugan asked. "Well, I'm not, and who can blame them? The friggin' pirates are calling them on their loved ones' cell phones, spreading the lie that we're stalling to save money, and all I can respond with are lies—yes, the negotiations are progressing... no, I can't discuss the negotiations... yes, we're hopeful of a breakthrough at any time. Christ! I'm beginning to hate myself."

"Still," Alex said, "are you sure a group video call is wise?"

"Hell no," Dugan said. "But it can't be any worse than individual phone calls day after day. It'll be intense, but at least it'll be over faster than having the same conversation twenty-plus times."

"And wise or not," Anna added, "we can hardly call it off now. We've had the time posted on the family website for three days, and I emailed the families the call-in number yesterday." She glanced at her watch, then at Dugan. "And speaking of that, you've got five minutes."

Dugan nodded and focused on the laptop. "Might as well open it up now," he said, moving the mouse. "So people can sign in and we can start on time."

He opened the conference call and watched as caller names popped up on the participant list. A few little squares of video flashed on the screen as some participants joined in video mode, but most preferred to listen and watch unseen. At the scheduled time, Dugan opened the call.

"Hello everyone, and thank you for joining the call. As I've told you previously, negotiations are progressing. The insurers' negotiating team is in daily contact with the pirates. I'm afraid I don't have anything substantial to report, but our best information is the crew is healthy and—"

As Dugan spoke, another square of video flashed onscreen, freezing him mid-sentence. A man sat restrained in a straight-back chair, a car tire draped over his neck. It was Luna, the bosun of the *Phoenix Lynx*. The tire glistened wetly, and as Dugan watched, hands appeared to upend a gasoline can on Luna's head, the liquid soaked him and his clothes. The hands withdrew as an accented voice narrated.

"We have been patient long enough," the voice said. "Phoenix Shipping is not bargaining in good faith. This is a small preview of what will happen if our demands are not met promptly."

A lighted match came sailing into the video, and Luna burst into flames, his tortured screams blaring from the speakers until they were cut off abruptly as Dugan ended the call.

Dugan was still trembling with rage fifteen minutes later. "How the hell did they get on our call?"

"I suppose we might have anticipated it," said Anna. "We know they've been calling the families to put pressure on us. I suppose somehow they found out about the private website and monitored it. When we posted the call time, they must have intimidated one of the families into producing the call-in number."

Alex nodded, his jaw clenched. "So we provided the audience for their barbaric exhibition. The question is, what do we do? If the families were distraught before, I can imagine their state now."

"There's nothing we can do about the families now," Dugan said. "I doubt any of them will believe a word we say anyway. We've got to do something to solve the problem, because this is going to get worse—much worse."

"I agree," Alex said. "And it's not just our ship. The insurance chaps tell me things are breaking down across the board. Apparently, some groups are copying al-Shabaab and adding a demand for the exchange of their own men captured at sea. That's *in addition* to monetary ransom. That and the fact that no money is flowing mean discussions are becoming more acrimonious."

"Exchanges? Christ! Why the hell is that an issue?" Dugan asked. "Most captured pirates end up in Kenyan prisons and back in Somalia before the ink's dry on the paperwork. It's a joke."

"Not entirely," Anna said. "Captured pirates are increasingly being bound over for trial in Yemen and especially neighboring Somaliland. And given centuries-old animosity between the clans in what are now Somali and Somaliland, Somali pirates aren't going to escape from a Somaliland prison quite so easily."

Dugan shrugged. "That doesn't seem to have made much of a difference so far, and this is going to end badly. I think we all know that. Sooner or later, the US Navy or Special Forces or someone is going to take back the *Luther Hurd*—public opinion in the US won't allow anything less. But there are hundreds of other captives, on two dozen ships scattered up and down the Somali coast, and when the *Luther Hurd* is free and the money dries up, you know what's going to happen."

Alex looked distressed. "Perhaps all the navies acting in concert—"

"Can what?" asked Dugan? "Mount a simultaneous rescue operation of two dozen ships? If that was going to happen, it would have happened months ago. Hell, Alex, no one was willing to take that risk when there were a few crews held captive and rescue was possible. No one's going to step up to the plate now that hundreds of lives are at stake. I doubt even the US would risk attacking the *Luther Hurd* if there was an option. These al-Shabaab assholes are clearly out to provoke a confrontation, and will murder as many crewmen as necessary to get one."

Alex sighed. "You're right, of course. As much as we all hated paying these murderers off, ransom was the only practical recourse to safeguard the crews. I shudder to think what will happen now that we can't give them what they want."

Dugan nodded. After a moment, he spoke.

"Suppose we do give them what they want?"

"What? How, Thomas? The government isn't going to allow ransom. What else do we have they want?"

Dugan smiled. "Oh, we don't have it yet. And they don't know they want it yet. But they will, they will." He glanced at his watch. "Let's take a little cab ride. I'll fill you in on the way."

EMBASSY OF THE REPUBLIC OF LIBERIA
FITZROY SQUARE, LONDON, UK

Given the nature of the visit, both Dugan and Alex had prevailed upon Anna to absent herself. As he looked around the richly appointed conference room, Dugan wondered if he should be here himself. A question made moot by the arrival of the Honorable Ernest Dolo Macabee, Foreign Minister of the Republic of Liberia, who bustled in and took a seat opposite them across the table.

"May I offer you some refreshment, gentlemen?" he asked. "Coffee? Tea? Something stronger?"

Dugan looked at Alex, who shook his head.

"No, we're fine, Mr. Minister, thank you," Alex said. "And thank you also for seeing us on such short notice."

Macabee made a dismissive gesture. "Not at all, Mr. Kairouz. I'm just glad you caught me in London." He smiled. "And I'm always happy to see you and Mr. Dugan. I always find our discussions agreeable."

To say nothing of profitable, thought Dugan.

"Now," Macabee said, "how can I be of service?"

Alex glanced at Dugan again, seemingly hesitant, and then began.

"We'd like to discuss the issue of piracy," he said. "Specifically in Somalia."

Macabee nodded as he leaned back in his chair and steepled his fingers. "A serious issue. Not only in Somalia but increasingly in West Africa as well. We, of course, decry these barbarous acts, and are fully supportive of international efforts to end the blight of piracy wherever it exists."

"What we'd like, Mr. Minister," Dugan said, "is some clarification of the Liberian position regarding the penalties for piracy and enforcement of anti-piracy laws. The Liberian statutes seem a bit..." Dugan smiled. "Shall we say, vague."

The Liberian returned his smile. "I think of them as flexible, Mr. Dugan. After all, no law can anticipate the circumstances of every incident." He shrugged. "Alas, the point is moot. My poor country lacks resources to enforce criminal laws on an international basis. But what, may I inquire, is your interest?"

Dugan looked at Alex, who extracted a small notepad from his breast pocket, scribbled a figure on it, and slid it across the table to Macabee. The Liberian picked up the pad and peered at it at arm's length, before fumbling in his shirt pocket for a pair of half-lens reading glasses with expensive tortoiseshell frames. He donned the glasses and stared down his nose at the note.

51

"Your interest is quite… substantial," he said at last.

"And available for deposit in the offshore bank of your choice," Alex said.

Macabee smiled. "Once again, Mr. Kairouz, how may I help you?"

"As Mr. Dugan indicated," Alex said, "we'd like to know your country's position on piracy."

Macabee's smile widened. "My dear Mr. Kairouz, what would you like it to be?"

CHAPTER SEVEN

Alex pecked at the keyboard, studying the spreadsheet as Dugan and Anna looked on.

"Are we going to have enough?" Dugan asked.

"It's tight," Alex said. "Between Macabee and the projected costs of the operation, we'll consume our entire cash reserve, to say nothing of loss of the ship. I've got to find some contingency funds somewhere." Alex sighed. "And then hope like bloody hell I can convince the insurers to make us whole later."

Dugan nodded, as Anna spoke.

"Not to change the subject," she said, "but what about Ward? Have you filled him in on this bloody insanity? If not, I'm going to have to, I'm afraid. Besides, he has the best intel, presuming he's inclined to share instead of having you two locked up as dangers to yourselves and others."

"I'll call him later," Dugan said, "after I've—"

"Now, Tom. Or I will," Anna said, holding up her cell phone.

Dugan glared at her, then sighed and punched Ward's number into the phone on the conference table.

"On the speaker, please," Anna said sweetly, and suppressed a smile as Dugan jabbed the speaker button.

"Are you nuts?" Ward asked, ten minutes later.

Dugan looked at Anna. "I get that a lot."

"Seriously," Ward said. "You can't go around making up your own laws, even if it is the high seas."

"They're not our laws," Dugan said. "They're laws of the sovereign Republic of Liberia, and *Phoenix Lynx* and well over half the hostage ships fly the Liberian flag. It's all legal."

"Laws you influenced and—"

"Give it a rest, Jesse," Dugan said. "The US and UK and every other nation tries to influence other countries' policies all the time. How else did corrupt shitholes like Yemen and Somaliland become so cooperative about taking captured pirates when no other countries want to get involved?"

"Those were *government-to-government* deals, and you know it. Not greasing some minister's palm."

Dugan scoffed. "Which means there were a few more layers and some fancy bookkeeping involved before the money got in some minister's pocket. The US probably paid about a hundred times what we did, so there'd be a bit left to spread around to make the common folk happy. I think you're just pissed because we're better at this than you bureaucrats."

"Dammit! You're jeopardizing an ongoing operation."

"Am I?" Dugan asked. "As I see it, our failure won't hurt you a bit, but if we're successful, it will damn sure help you. On the other hand, a rescue op on the *Luther Hurd* alone, followed by the continuation of the ban on ransoms, leaves over three hundred seamen in the hands of very pissed-off pirates. Isn't that about the size of it?"

Ward didn't answer, and the silence built.

"Look, Jesse," Dugan said, "I know you're doing what you have to do, and no one wants to see you get *Luther Hurd* back more than I do. But what I'm proposing won't hinder that at all. And as I see it, it's our only chance at getting everyone back. All I'm asking is that you provide us as much intel as possible."

Ward still didn't speak, and Dugan began to think he'd hung up.

"Anna?" Ward said, at last.

"Here," Anna said.

"What's your take on this?" Ward asked.

Anna sighed. "My take is that Tom and Alex are both certifiable, but that doesn't mean they're wrong. I can't see any other solution."

"All right," Ward said. "I guess when you get right down to it, everything they're proposing occurs well beyond the jurisdiction of either the US or UK anyway, so there's not a damn thing we can do about it. I'll tell you what I know, such as it is."

"Great," Dugan said. "We can start now. What can you tell us about their organizational structure?"

"Best we can tell," Ward said, "there are between fifteen hundred to two thousand active pirates, divided into gangs, roughly along clan lines. The gangs form alliances and work together as necessary, but that changes relatively frequently. For your plan to work, you'll have to spread your net pretty wide. I have a chart that shows the various clan relationships. I'll email it to you."

"Thanks," Dugan said.

Alex spoke for the first time. "Agent Ward? Did I understand you to say there may be as many as two thousand pirates at sea?"

"No, two thousand total," Ward said. "And I emphasize that's an *estimate*. Ninety percent of those guys are holders, with the rest attackers. They're sort of the rock stars of pirates, for want of a better term. They've had some military training. They take all the risks and get much larger cuts of the ransom. Also, each group has a first-boarder, the first one aboard the ship. He gets an even bigger cut of the ransom, and sometimes a bonus."

"Basically, the varsity," Dugan said.

"Yeah," Ward said. "Evidently they're arrogant pricks. They're excused from holding duty and spend their off time ashore, chewing khat and bragging. A lot of them have escaped from Kenyan prisons or been caught at sea and disarmed and released. They're pretty contemptuous of the Western navies, but seem terrified of the Russians."

"Understandable," Dugan said. "I doubt the Russians worry overly much about due process."

"They don't care about bad press, either," Ward said. "That's pretty much the sum of my intel on the pirates."

"You left out the most important point," Dugan said. "Time?"

"Honestly? Not a clue. But as long as al-Shabaab isn't murdering people, the navy's holding off to refine rescue plans. The more complacent and sloppy the pirates get, the better for us." Ward paused. "But understand this, Tom. If an opportunity presents itself, we'll take it. In two minutes or two months, and regardless of what's going on with *your* plan."

"I wouldn't expect anything else. Thanks for the help."

"You're welcome," Ward said. "Now you can return the favor. You know Ray Hanley, right?"

"I doubt there's anyone in the industry who doesn't. Why?"

"Because he's been crawling up my ass daily about the lack of progress of getting his people back, supplemented by calls from what seems like every elected official in the great state of Texas. I also have it on good authority that he's inquiring about Somali interpreters and airstrips in Kenya and Somalia." Ward sighed. "He's about to do something stupid and there's nothing I can do about it. He's a force of nature."

"And you're telling me this why?" Dugan asked.

"Because your harebrained plan is orders of magnitude better than whatever harebrained plan he's concocting," Ward said. "And yours has the added advantage of taking place a long way from my plan. Let's invite him to your party."

"He's not exactly a team player, Jesse. He doesn't want to lead the band, he wants to *be* the band. Besides, why join us? Our focus isn't *Luther Hurd*."

"No, but I can sell it to him as a necessary diversion, and if I don't do something, he'll screw things up for both of us," Ward said.

"I don't know," Dugan said, "Hanley can be—"

"Agent Ward, this is Alex Kairouz. Tell Mr. Hanley he is most welcome to join us." Alex shot Dugan a pointed look. "And tell him to bring his checkbook."

Ray Hanley, force of nature, arrived in London the very next morning on a nonstop redeye from Houston, all five foot seven and 180 pounds of him. He sat now at one end of the conference table, an unlit cigar jammed in the corner of his mouth, as he glared at the speaker phone in the middle of the table. Dugan sat at the opposite end of the table, and Alex and Anna flanked them on either side, all listening to the latest intel update from Ward.

"And there's been a huge increase in traffic out of Eyl as well as Garacad and Hobyo, all main pirate ports," said Ward's voice from the speaker. "It's beginning to look like some sort of major pirate offensive, and it's very unusual for them to be coordinated to this degree."

"What does that have to do with anything, Ward?" Hanley asked.

Ward's exasperated sigh was audible through the speaker. "I don't know, Hanley," he said. "It may have an impact, so I think we need to stay on top of it."

"Maybe this 'offensive' is what the *Luther Hurd* snatch is all about," Dugan suggested, ignoring Hanley. "To draw Western naval presence to a high-profile target and clear the field for more hijackings."

"Except that al-Shabaab and your regular pirates don't get along," Ward said. "Make no mistake, it's the terrorist angle that's drawing all the official attention. If *Luther Hurd* had been hijacked by garden-variety pirates, I'm sure the US Navy would be there alone." He paused. "No, al-Shabaab is doing this for their own reasons. The others may be taking advantage of it, but that's just a sideshow."

Hanley interjected himself back in the conversation. "Well, whatever's causing it, having the damn pirates out in force will help our operation."

"Ah… I don't think I want to hear about that," Ward said.

Anna smiled and reached across the table to the speaker phone. "Goodbye, Jesse. And thank you," she said, and disconnected.

Dugan looked down the table at Ray Hanley. "I think you need to tone down the attitude, Hanley. Ward is helping us, after all."

Hanley took the unlit cigar from his mouth and smiled. "He works for the government, and that makes him a bureaucrat in my book. And I have a standing policy of never cutting a bureaucrat any slack. They shovel BS on a daily basis, and you have to question everything that comes out of their mouths."

Anna stiffened.

"Present company excepted, of course," Hanley added. "Besides, Ward brought it on himself. He wasn't telling me a damn thing about what was happening on *Luther Hurd* until I forced his hand by putting out feelers for Somali interpreters and intel on airstrips and whatnot."

"That was a ruse?" Alex asked.

Hanley snorted. "Of course it was a ruse." He looked around the table. "Y'all think I'm a dumbass? I know I can't mount a rescue operation on my own. And those murdering al-Shabaab bastards don't want a ransom, and the government wouldn't let me pay it if they did, so the navy's the only option. I just wanted Ward to let me in on the plan, which he did." Hanley smiled. "He even told me about your little party."

Dugan looked puzzled. "If you got what you were after, why join us?"

"Plan B," Hanley said. "I didn't have one. I figure if the navy boys screw the pooch and there's anyone left alive on *Luther Hurd*, y'all's plan is my only shot at getting them home. Besides, we need to do something about these damned pirates."

There was a lull in the conversation, broken by Dugan.

"Right. Where were we when Ward called? Oh yeah," he said, looking at Alex. "Where do we stand with the Liberians?"

"They're set to expedite the flag change on Mr. Hanley's *Marie Floyd*, and to issue letters of marque for both *Marie Floyd* and our own *Pacific Endurance*." He smiled. "There was a bit of delay, since no one in the Liberian Ministry of Transport had ever *seen* letters of marque and reprisal. I had to get our solicitors to dig out the history books and cobble one together. However, they assure me everything is quite legal." He smiled again. "All according to recently enacted statutes."

Dugan nodded and turned to Hanley. "How about your end?"

"*Marie Floyd* is eastbound, in the Arabian Sea. I got word to her this morning to divert to Muscat, and I reckon she'll be there inside of two days."

Hanley shrugged. "It's not too tough to change from US to Liberian flag. It's going the other way that would be a problem. Besides, between y'all greasing things on the Liberian side and my Washington contacts pushing on my side, there won't be any trouble. Of course, everyone sort of figures I've got a screw loose, paying to reflag a ship that was already on her way to scrap."

"We're happy to have her," Alex said. "Odds are much better with two ships."

"I've still got doubts if we can do it, even with two ships," said Hanley.

"We'll have to," Dugan said. "We can sacrifice two old, tired ships, but remember it's a long shot as to whether the insurers are going to make us whole. We have to survive this financially, come what may."

Hanley nodded as Dugan continued. "What about the riding crew? You sure these guys are up to it? Maybe I should get some of my—"

"Dammit, Dugan! Give it a rest," Hanley said. "I been using Woody and his boys for twenty years. They can do everything we need done, and they're bringing all the electronic gear with them. Besides, I left 'em my plane so they could fly straight into Muscat." He looked at his watch. "They're already on the way." He looked back up at Dugan. "You let me worry about my boys, you just worry about these friggin' Russians of yours."

"Look, Hanley—"

"Gentlemen," Anna said, "and I use the term loosely. Do you think you two could stop comparing penises long enough to allow us to finish our discussion?"

Dugan and Hanley looked indignant. Alex suppressed a smile and changed the subject. "Speaking of planes, Thomas, when are you leaving for Muscat?"

"Tomorrow morning," Dugan said. "I'll use the time before the ships arrive to start rounding up material. I don't want to stay in port any longer than necessary."

CHAPTER EIGHT

M/T *LUTHER HURD*
AT ANCHOR
HARARDHEERE, SOMALIA

Mukhtar and Diriyi stood on the main deck and gazed down at the boat bobbing at the foot of the accommodation ladder.

"Remember," Mukhtar said, "drag things out as long as possible. Take a hard line in negotiations, but do nothing to provoke the Americans into a premature strike. They'll expect us to kill more hostages, so do the unexpected. If absolutely necessary, release one or two of the lowly crewmen, but make sure that before they go they see the others with the collars around their necks. They'll report that to the Americans, and perhaps it'll reinforce their indecision. Then—"

"I know, my brother, I know," Diriyi said. "We've discussed this many times. Don't worry. I'll buy you your time, Inshallah."

Mukhtar smiled. "Forgive me, my friend. I know you will." He changed the subject. "I should be in Eyl in two days. The rest of the men are already there, and the boats are ready."

Diriyi nodded, and embraced Mukhtar. "May Allah protect you."

"And you as well, my brother," Mukhtar said, returning the embrace before moving down the sloping accommodation ladder to the boat.

Diriyi stood on deck watching the boat move toward shore. He gave one last look and smiled, as he turned to walk back toward the deckhouse. He'd do all that he'd promised and more, but first he had a score to settle and wagging tongues to still. He could hardly maintain control of this rabble when they whispered behind his back, calling him the Toothless One or He Who Was Beaten by a Woman. No, he must put things right, and quickly.

He entered the deckhouse and moved down the passageway to the crew lounge. Men sat squabbling over the dregs of the previous day's khat, a few wilted leaves of diminished potency, as they awaited the arrival of a fresh supply. He spotted the American at a table near the door, and nodded.

Arnett drifted in and out of consciousness. The darkness of the windowless storeroom was complete, and she'd lost all sense of time. The stench of stale urine was overpowering, and even now, hours or perhaps days later, her cheeks burned with shame. She remembered the muzzle of the Glock, inches from her eyes, and the abject terror. She remembered the click of the striker on the empty chamber, the terror yielding to confusion, and then the wonderful realization that she was alive. She remembered her soaked crotch and the shame of having wet herself, and the laughter of her captors. But most of all, she remembered the face of the bastard that pulled the trigger.

They'd dumped her in the storeroom shortly thereafter, still bound hand and foot. She'd been ignored since, without food or water, a blessing of sorts, since she had no access to a toilet. The hunger was bearable, but she was severely dehydrated, her tongue thick and swollen in her taped mouth. It was becoming increasingly difficult to tell dreams from reality, and images of Glock muzzles, Gomez, and the *Luther Hurd* sailing away flashed through her mind like an insane slide show.

She jumped involuntarily as the dogs on the watertight door disengaged with squeaks and thumps, and blinked in the sudden harsh glare of the overhead light.

Diriyi looked up as Gaal stepped into the room, the woman over his shoulder. He ordered Gaal to dump her on a table at the far end of the room. The men all looked up, interest on their faces, in anticipation of a break from their boring routine. Diriyi walked to the table and glared down at the woman. She lay on her back, her bound hands beneath her. She was totally helpless, but there was hatred in her eyes as she returned his glare. *We'll soon have that out of you,* Diriyi thought. He turned to his men, who had begun to gather around.

"This, if you can believe it, is what the Americans call a ship's captain," he said in Somali, and nodded at the laughter that followed. "This shameless whore, who doesn't even cover herself properly, would think to order men about. And what's most fantastic, these Americans follow those orders like small boys." He paused to let his words sink in, gratified at the sounds of disgust coming from scattered voices.

"But what's to be expected of infidels who keep unclean and dangerous animals like dogs as pets? And like a dog, even a woman can be treacherous to the unprepared." Diriyi smiled, displaying his missing teeth. "And I'll admit that I was unprepared when the bitch decided to bite." All of the men were laughing now, won over by Diriyi's admission.

"Like an infidel dog, this whore must learn her master, so I'm going to take her now in front of you. And when I'm finished, I'll take her to my cabin and have her many more times every day, until I grow tired of her.

After that, you may have her. There are many of you and but one of her, so I suppose you'll have to use your imaginations to arrive at the most efficient combinations." He gave them a gap-toothed smile. "But I'm sure you'll think of something. Do try to make sure the bitch's heart is still beating when we sell her back to the Americans."

Diriyi finished his monologue to cheers, as the mob pressed close to watch. He ripped open the woman's shirt, popping buttons and shredding cloth to expose bare skin and a bra. He reached in his pocket for a switch-blade, and the woman's eyes went wide as he slid the blade beneath the center of the bra. It yielded, exposing small but well-formed breasts. Diriyi was moving to slice the plastic tie on her ankles when a voice spoke behind him.

"But like the infidel dog, Diriyi, this woman's unclean," said Gaal in Somali. "She reeks of piss and sweat, and is unworthy of your dick. Better to wash the whore and take her slowly, rather than take her like this and pollute your manhood."

Diriyi glared at Gaal. "What do you think you're doing?" he asked in English.

Gaal smiled for the benefit of the mob, and answered in the same language.

"Stopping you from making a mistake," Gaal replied, his bantering tone in contrast to his words. "There are over forty men here, with only khat to pass the time. There are no women but her, and now you've promised her to them. Do you think you're going to be able to control them if you take her in front of them? Their blood's up, and she won't survive. And then what'll you do when the Americans demand proof that everyone's unharmed?" Gaal ended with a raucous laugh, as if he'd just told Diriyi a great joke.

The men grew quiet, their confusion palpable, and Diriyi smiled and stepped back, his nose wrinkled in mock disgust. "It seems our friend Gaal is right," he said in Somali. "The whore is filthy! Let's be thankful he didn't spend so much time among the Americans that he lost his good sense." Diriyi turned to Gaal. "Take the whore to my cabin and wash her. I'll be along shortly."

Gaal moved to the table, but the others made no move to return to their previous activities. Diriyi had worked them into a mob, and tension lingered, an ill-defined and unspoken threat. Then came the bellow of a hand-held air horn, announcing the arrival of the khat boat. The muttering morphed into shouts of joy as the men rushed out to bring the drug aboard.

Arnett lay on the table as the men rushed out. She was bare to the waist, and felt not shame but white-hot rage. She'd been biding her time, waiting to kick Toothless in the face the moment he cut her ankles free. Then she heard the voice. An American voice. Coming out of the other one, the one that tried to shoot her. A traitor! And he was discussing her like she was a piece of meat.

Traitor bent over the table to pick her up, and she jackknifed at the waist, sitting up and using her neck muscles to deliver a head-butt. The pain of teeth biting into her forehead was dulled by the pure joy of striking back, and she tried to swivel on her butt to sink her bound feet into his gut.

But Traitor was too fast and delivered a vicious openhanded slap, driving her once again onto her back, as he cursed her. Blood leaked into Arnett's eyes from her cut forehead, but not before she saw him step back, blood streaming from his mouth.

On the other side of her, Toothless erupted in laughter.

"She likes to take teeth, this one," Toothless said in English. "How do you like the bitch's sting, American? Did you too sacrifice teeth to the jihad?"

Traitor spit out blood and probed his upper teeth with a finger. "Just a split lip," he said, and spit more blood on the deck.

Arnett watched Toothless, still chuckling, move toward the door. "See if you can get her to my cabin and cleaned up without suffering any more injuries. I must go supervise the distribution of khat before these fools end up shooting one another."

Gaal trudged up the central stairwell with the woman over his shoulder, his arms clamped around her knees. She'd struggled at first, trying to raise herself off his shoulder. Her struggles had ceased when he'd rushed through the doorway into the stairwell, purposely clipping the back of her head on the metal door frame. All in all, she was being a pain in the ass.

Gaal exited the stairwell on D-deck and entered the captain's cabin, which Diriyi had claimed before Mukhtar even left the ship. He moved through the office into the bedroom to dump the woman on the bed. He collected the wastebasket from the corner and searched the bedroom and bathroom, scanning for anything that might be used as a weapon. Finding nothing, he moved back into the office and searched her desk and credenza, dumping a pair of scissors, a letter opener, and a heavy paperweight into the wastebasket. He moved to the door and set the wastebasket down in the passageway, and returned to the bedroom.

"I'm going to roll you onto your stomach and cut your hands free," he said to the woman. "If you so much as twitch, I'll shoot you. I've no doubt you'll get your legs free in short order. Clean yourself and tend to your wounds as best you can."

She glared up at him.

"If you don't like that arrangement, I'll leave you bound, cut your clothes off, and wash you myself. Now, will you cooperate?"

There was hatred in the woman's eyes, but she nodded.

"Good," Gaal said, as he rolled her onto her stomach. "I'll be back later with food. I saw a bottle of water in the bedside table. I'll bring more when I come back."

Gaal pulled out a knife and sliced the plastic tie binding the woman's wrists, and backed out the bedroom door, through the office, and into the passageway beyond. He closed the office door, and wrapped one end of a plastic tie around the doorknob before pulling the tie tight and securing the other end to the bulkhead storm rail. He moved down the passageway and repeated the process on the door from the captain's bedroom into the passageway. He moved back toward the central stairwell, collecting the wastebasket along the way, and descended to look for Diriyi.

Arnett's hunger and thirst had been niggling concerns during her near rape, blotted out by fear and rage. But the mere mention of food and water brought suppressed needs to the fore, and Arnett clawed her way across the bed to the bedside table. Lying on her stomach, she ripped the duct tape from her mouth and fished the water bottle from the drawer to drink in long, greedy gulps. Water leaked out the cracked corners of her mouth as she sucked the bottle dry.

It was soon gone, and she dropped the bottle and twisted on the bed to get her bound feet to the deck. Suddenly conscious of her nakedness, she pulled the shredded remains of her shirt together and stuffed shirttails into her waistband. She felt her rage rising again, and suppressed it. Food was the priority now, and who the hell knew if Traitor would be back with any, no matter what he said.

She pushed herself up and attempted to hop toward her office door, but dehydration and the rapid change in posture did her in. Head spinning, she crashed to the deck, to rise onto her hands and knees and move through the door to her desk like an inchworm, stretching forward and supporting her weight on her hands before dragging her knees up under her. Head still reeling, she hardly noticed when her shirttails pulled free and her tattered shirt fell open again.

She reached her objective and, still on the deck, pulled open a bottom desk drawer to reveal two boxes of protein bars. Ripping open wrapper after wrapper, she leaned back against the credenza and stuffed bars into her mouth, swallowing almost without chewing, as crumbs fell from her chin onto bare breasts. She finished and pulled herself to her knees, and rummaged in another drawer for a small pair of nail clippers to nibble at the thick plastic tie that bound her ankles. Soon she was free.

To do what?

Arnett dragged herself up into the desk chair, her mental fog lifted by the intake of calories. The respite from immediate personal danger allowed her to consider the bigger picture, and panic gripped her. She was responsible for the ship, but more importantly the crew, and she had no idea where they were being held or even how many were still alive. Gomez's frightened face rose in her mind's eye, and angrily she brushed tears from her cheeks with the back of her hand.

Since they'd separated her from the rest of the crew, she'd been reacting to her personal circumstances, but she had to reconnect and establish some sort of control. As much as she despised her captors, she knew she should try to defuse the situation.

She looked around at her cabin—now her cell—and rose to try the door from the office into the passageway. It was blocked closed from the outside, as she knew it would be. She moved to the bedroom and found that exit door blocked as well. Her eyes fell on her wardrobe closet, reminding her she was half naked. Despite her reluctance to comply with Traitor's orders, she knew she'd feel more confident and in control after a shower. Arnett walked to the bathroom, leaving a trail of sweaty, bloodstained clothes in her wake. One thought consumed her as she stepped into the shower—she'd see Traitor dead if it was the last thing she did.

Gaal's jaws moved in vigorous chewing motions, but he purposefully maneuvered the ball of khat leaves so few were crushed between his teeth to release their sap. It was a skill at which he'd become quite adept in the last months. He sat in an easy chair in the sitting area of the chief engineer's office, across a low coffee table from where Diriyi sat on a sofa.

"You're sure the whore can't get out?" asked Diriyi, his speech slurred a bit from the effects of his own wad of khat.

"Relax," Gaal said. "The doors are secured from outside, and the windows don't open. And even if they did, it's a twenty-meter drop to the main deck."

Diriyi nodded, then looked at his watch. He sat up straight, preparing to stand. "Come," he said. "She should be clean by now. I think it's time I kept my promise."

Gaal shrugged and made no move to rise. "If you think that wise."

Diriyi's eyes narrowed. "What do you mean?"

"I mean, the woman's face is already bruised, and now she has an ugly cut on her forehead from my teeth. She's had some training, and won't be easy to rape. I think it'll take more than you and I to hold her down, and we'll have to beat her into submission."

"What of it?" Diriyi asked.

"Think, Diriyi," Gaal said. "At some point the Americans will demand proof the crew's alive. They'll be insistent on seeing the woman, given their foolish tendency to place women in these positions and then agonize over what happens to them. Don't forget, I know how they think. Abuse of the woman will accelerate any rescue attempt." Gaal fixed Diriyi with a meaningful look. "And I think the idea's to delay that as long as possible, right?"

Diriyi tensed. "And what do you know of our plan, American?"

"I know your demands are impossible on their face and have no chance of being fulfilled," Gaal said. "I know Mukhtar has disappeared with all of the faithful and the cream of the crop of new recruits, leaving you and me here with this mob of rejects. I know you are promising these men an insane amount of money when the mission is over, and I suspect that's because you expect none to be alive to collect it." Gaal smiled. "Don't mistake me for one of these idiots, Diriyi."

Diriyi relaxed a bit and sank back on the sofa, studying Gaal.

"Perhaps I misjudged you, Gaal," he said at last. "What do you suggest?"

"Put the woman with the others. They'll all take comfort at being together, and each can confirm the safety of the others." Gaal paused, as if in thought. "When negotiations with the Americans get tense, let them talk to the woman if necessary. Perhaps at that point we can fit a few crew with collars and link the existing well-being of the crew with the immediate danger of their death, should we be attacked. That might buy a few days, or a week."

"You forget one thing," said Diriyi. "The men expect me to rape her then turn her over to them."

Gaal smiled. "But then you opened her legs in your cabin and found her diseased. The men will believe that, especially when I confirm it."

Diriyi returned his smile. "You're a clever fellow, Gaal. We'll do as you suggest." Then the smile faded, and his voice took on a hard edge. "But make no mistake. Before this is over I'll take her." He tongued the gap in his teeth. "And then I'll kill her."

CHAPTER NINE

M/T *Luther Hurd*
At anchor
Harardheere, Somalia

Gaal walked the length of the A-deck passageway, an assault rifle slung over his shoulder, stepping around a pirate squatting on the deck with thumbs flying as he sent a text message. Al-Shabaab had originally confiscated all phones, but with Mukhtar and the others safely away for over a week and the motley crew of bored pirates growing increasingly restless, Diriyi returned the phones to placate the men. Gaal smiled as he looked along the passageway and saw several other pirates engrossed with their phones. It was something he would never understand. Most of the country didn't even have running water or basic sanitation, yet every Somali seemed to have a cell phone and be addicted to using it.

The man he stepped around looked up and smiled, and Gaal returned the smile with a nod. He was accepted as second-in-command now; in fact, the pirates seemed to respect him more than they did Diriyi, a legacy perhaps of Diriyi's missing teeth and the manner of their extraction. But Gaal was careful not to encourage that, and had developed a wary rapport with Diriyi. The man didn't trust him, but Gaal had proven his worth in managing the unruly mob of pirates.

He glanced through the open door of the officers' mess room. The deck was littered with mattresses, on which several men were sprawled. The woman captain and several officers sat at a table, playing cards to pass the time before the next meal of goat meat and rice. The hijackers had concentrated the hostages for ease of surveillance, but at Gaal's suggestion they'd separated the officers. The unlicensed crew had similar communal arrangements in the crew mess room.

The days had a sameness, stitched together by routine. The hostages spent their days in languid monotony, punctuated by periods of terror and speculation when the pirates would fit crewmen with explosive collars and drag the captain out to speak on the phone. The pirates spent their days chewing khat, texting, and squabbling amongst themselves, watched over by Gaal.

Gaal watched the woman. Her cuts and bruises were healing, and she was looking increasingly attractive and obviously healthy. Soon it might be difficult to keep the men at bay, even with the story he'd spread that she was a petri dish of STDs. As if she felt his eyes, she looked up and glared. He smiled and moved down the passageway. She was a pain in the ass.

ARABIAN SEA
120 MILES FROM THE COAST OF OMAN

The Yemini fishing boat bobbed in the gentle swell as it chugged along at six knots, one of the scores of fishing boats ubiquitous to the area, a threat to no one. That was an image Mukhtar very much wanted to project, and he'd strolled the crowded wharf in Aden until he found just the right vessel.

The grateful captain hadn't asked questions when Mukhtar offered to charter his boat for several times the going rate, implying with a wink and a nod there may be a bit of smuggling involved. The poor man realized his mistake five miles outside the breakwater, when fast boats converged on his vessel and he was overrun by pirates. He'd little time to regret his action before Mukhtar shot him and his three-man crew and dumped their bodies over the side.

Mukhtar had no qualms about his actions. The fishing-boat captain was not one of the Faithful, or he wouldn't have accepted such an exorbitant sum nor been so eager to participate in illegal activity. And the crewmen were equally guilty, for what man would serve such a corrupt master if he weren't corrupt himself?

He raised the binoculars and studied the vessel in the distance. The tower of the drillship pointed to the heavens, like a great skeletal finger, and faint sounds of machinery and the ring of steel on steel carried across the water. Mukhtar forced himself to be patient.

DRILLSHIP OCEAN GOLIATH
ARABIAN SEA
120 MILES FROM THE COAST OF OMAN

The tool pusher stood on the centerline of the ship, staring down through the moon pool into the clear water, straining to catch a glimpse of the huge hydraulic grab. He cursed under his breath as the ascent of the drill pipe slowed, then stopped, and he heard the clang of steel on steel on the drill floor above. In his mind's eye, he envisioned the slips being placed and the tongs at work, unthreading a long stand of pipe to be moved aside so another could be lifted to bring the grab that much closer to the surface.

A roundtrip to the bottom—over eight thousand feet below—and back took hours. A pity the weight of the treasure and limited carrying capacity of the ROV forced them into this time-consuming process. But the remotely operated vehicle had proven its worth in other ways. Steering the little submersible to depths beyond the capacity of any human, the operator on the drillship had expertly placed explosive charges around the hull of the SS *John Barry*, ripping the old Liberty ship open and exposing her treasure for the first time in over sixty years.

The tool pusher fidgeted and shot a squirt of tobacco juice into the clear waters below. *Exposed* was still over eight thousand feet from *recovered*. He glanced at the immobile pipe. It was ingenious, really, the idea of turning a drillship into a giant version of the coin-operated claw arcade game. Of course, they expected their claw to pull up a hell of a lot more than a stuffed bunny.

He flinched at a sudden sound, then realized it was the massive thrusters kicking in, directed by the dynamic positioning system to keep the drillship precisely located over her target. He glanced once more at the unmoving pipe, checked his watch, and turned to head up to the drill floor to chew somebody's ass, just as there was a clank and a groan, and the pipe resumed its measured ascent.

When the massive hydraulic grab broke the surface an hour later, the moon pool was surrounded by crewmen and the excitement was palpable. Next to the tool pusher stood Sheik Mustafa and his American partners and the documentary film crew with their cameras at the ready. A hush fell over the crowd as the grab reached deck level and was maneuvered to its resting place. A hush broken by the tool pusher's gravelly voice.

"All right, all right! Get your thumbs out of your asses, and let's get her open."

At his command, crewmen jumped to hit the releases, and hydraulic cylinders groaned as they jacked open massive jaws to disgorge their contents. There was a rattle of metal on metal, not unlike a giant slot machine, as thousands of large silver coins hit the deck, mixed with mud and sand and bits of wooden packing crate. The rattle was replaced by cheers and screams of delight, and a grin was plastered on every face as the men thumped each other's backs in congratulation. But celebration soon yielded to practicality.

"There's more where that came from," the tool pusher yelled over the tumult. "Let's get her cleaned out and back in the water." He clapped his hands to get the attention of a few still celebrating. "Come on, come on, move it! Y'all can count your money later."

He smiled. He was already counting his.

M/T *Phoenix Lynx*
At anchor
Harardheere, Somalia

Zahra stood on the bridge wing of *Phoenix Lynx* and looked at the *Luther Hurd* in the distance, then turned his gaze seaward to the flotilla of naval vessels.

"So why's our friend Mukhtar so interested in this drilling vessel?" he asked, still looking seaward.

Beside him, Omar shrugged. "It's unclear. He's confiding in no one aboard the fishing boat. But I can't believe he intends to capture a drilling vessel so far from our waters."

Zahra nodded. "They're slow and conspicuous. Even the reduced naval forces would surround him long before he got to safe anchorage here. And if he meets Russians or Indians or South Koreans, he can't count on being handled with kid gloves. No, he wants something *on* the ship, and it's important enough to risk hijacking an American ship as a diversion." He shook his head. "I don't have a good feeling about this. We've had nothing but problems since the fanatics inserted themselves in our business."

"True," Omar said. "But at least the diversion is working in our favor as well. All the groups have men at sea or preparing to go, and this morning Wahid's group brought another captive to the anchorage at Garacad."

Zahra snorted. "Yes, I heard. An oceangoing tug with a four-man crew and no tow. Let's hope that the other groups bring home more worthy prizes. What of the negotiations?"

"Nothing," Omar said. "All the groups are reporting negotiations stalled."

Zahra sighed. "Very well. I suppose we can't delay without appearing weak. I'll call the other leaders and we'll start regular executions."

Omar hesitated, looking toward the naval vessels. "Are you sure, Zahra? Won't that invite attack?"

"That's why we'll start in the other ports with no naval presence. And the executions will be measured—shocking, but not wholesale slaughter. We'll release video on the Internet. An execution every few days should be enough, I think."

Omar nodded. "When should we start?"

Zahra pulled out his phone. "No time like the present."

USS *CARNEY* (*DDG-64*)
DRIFTING
HARARDHEERE, SOMALIA

Commander Frank Lorenzo, USN, Captain of the USS *Carney*, stood on the bridge and looked down at the group of sailors walking up the deck, led by Culinary Specialist 3 Jerry Harkness. The cook carried a pail full of meat scraps and other garbage, and was trailed by a half dozen off-watch sailors, all carrying cameras. Harkness waited for the would-be photographers to line the rail, then transferred the bail of the bucket to his left hand and put his right beneath the bottom to heave the contents overboard.

Nothing happened for a moment, and then the water boiled with heavy gray bodies and large triangular fins, as the cheering photographers snapped away.

"*Carcarinus Zambenzensis*, more commonly known as the Zambezi River Shark," the man beside Lorenzo said. "The most dangerous and aggressive of the shark family. They'll eat anything or anyone, and frequently do."

Lorenzo turned. "I didn't know you were a shark specialist, Lieutenant."

The man smiled. "I try to know a little about all the creatures I share the water with," he said. "Seals and sharks are old enemies." The smile faded. "But seriously, this is one of the worst areas in the world for those beasts. You won't find people frolicking in the surf in Somalia."

"I bet that's right," said Lorenzo. "I sure as hell—"

"Excuse me, Captain," the officer of the watch said from the opposite side of the bridge. "There's movement on the *Luther Hurd*. Looks like they're swapping out the hostage on display."

Ten minutes later, Lorenzo lowered his binoculars and watched the lieutenant note the date and time in a three-ring binder, right beside a picture of Jim Milam.

"OK, that's Jergens, the chief steward, up there now, and Milam, the chief engineer they just took down, right?" asked Lorenzo, continuing without awaiting an answer. "That's all the crew accounted for?"

The young SEAL looked up. "Affirmative, sir," he said. "They're rotating all the hostages on top of the wheelhouse. That's for our benefit. They want us to see the hostages are unharmed, but that any threatening move on our part will result in immediate deaths."

"But when the hell are we going to *do* something about it?" Lorenzo asked. "Every time I talk to that captain, I feel more helpless. I'm a sailor, not a hostage negotiator. Someone from your team should be handling this."

"Negative, sir," the SEAL said. "You're doing fine. You've been here from the beginning and have a rapport. We *want* them to get comfortable, because comfortable equals sloppy. Our whole mission is intelligence gathering to support planning and training. They're building a mockup back in Virginia, and our guys are training on possible scenarios. My orders are to go early only if the hostages are in immediate danger and there's no option."

Lorenzo nodded, and turned to stare across the water at *Luther Hurd*.

M/T *LUTHER HURD*
AT ANCHOR
HARARDHEERE, SOMALIA

Milam sat next to Arnett in a corner of the officers' mess room, watching Traitor fit a collar on Chief Mate Stan Jones. Jones tried to smile as he was led out to take his turn as the display hostage, but managed only a sickly grimace.

"I hate all of them," Arnett said under her breath. "But I hate that friggin' Traitor the worst."

"I can't argue with that," Milam replied. "Every time I hear that American voice coming out of his pie hole, I want to kill him. I think his name's Gaal, by the way, or something like that. Anyway, that's what these other assholes call him."

"Well, they'll be calling the bastard dead if I have my way," Arnett said.

Milam nodded as he looked around the room.

The pirates had him secure the air conditioning days before to conserve fuel, and the room was stifling. The sour smell of body odor and sweat-soaked mattresses assailed his nostrils, and out in the passageway he could hear Somali voices raised in anger. Probably an argument over khat. Such arguments were increasingly frequent now, and all the pirates were on a hair trigger. They ogled Arnett with undisguised lust, and for the life of him, Milam couldn't figure how she'd avoided gang rape. He turned back to Arnett, speaking softly.

"These assholes are getting restless. You picking up anything from your little chats with *Carney*?"

"Toothless or Traitor do most of the talking and then put the phone on speaker to prove I'm alive and kicking. Last time, before they could get it off speaker, the *Carney*'s captain asked for assurances there would be no more executions. I can't remember his exact words, but I got the impression he wasn't talking about our two guys. It was, I don't know, like he was talking about something more recent."

"You sure?" Milam asked.

She shook her head. "No, I'm not sure," she said, her voice cracking. She struggled to compose herself. "Look, Jim. If anything happens to me…"

"Shut up, Lynda. Nothing's going to happen to you."

She grabbed his hand and squeezed, her eyes blazing. "Listen to me. I've been thinking about this, and how these assholes think. I don't know how this is going to end, but I'm pretty sure there won't be any negotiated deal. The US Navy's going to be coming in here as soon as they can figure out a way to do it without killing too many of us. Politically, they can't afford to do anything else. We both know that, and so do the pirates." She shook her head. "What I can't figure out is why they haven't moved the crew ashore or split us up, at least me. Let's face it, an American woman captain has to be a high-value hostage for them. Leaving us all here aboard the ship is keeping all their eggs in the same basket, so I figure that means they want all eyes on the basket."

Milam nodded. "Makes sense, but so what? Where you going with this?"

"What happens when they finish whatever else they have going on?"

"I don't know, I guess… oh shit!"

"That's right," Arnett said. "If the navy hasn't rescued us by then, they may decide to spread out their eggs. We have to stop ignoring the elephant in the room. I'm the prize egg, and I suspect I'll be the first moved."

"So what're you saying?"

"I'm saying, if and when that happens, don't do something stupid and get yourself killed. Understood?"

Milam's jaw clenched. "We can surround you—put you in the middle. We're no good to them dead. They won't risk killing—"

Arnett squeezed his hand again. "Yes. They. Will," she said. "No heroics. OK?"

Milam looked unconvinced.

"Jim?" Arnett said. Milam didn't respond. "That's an order, Chief," Arnett said.

"I'll consider it," Milam said at last, relieved she seemed to accept that.

"There's something else," Arnett said. "The crew looks up to you, and if anything happens to me, I want you in charge."

"How the hell am I going to do that?" Milam asked. "If something happens to you, Jones becomes captain, and if something happens to him, it's Joe Silva."

"Yeah, technically," Arnett said, "and Stan Jones may be acting chief mate, but he's got five years' experience to your thirty—and as far as poor Joe goes…" She looked across the room to where Joe Silva was coiled on a bare mattress in the fetal position. "All he ever wanted to be is third mate, and he's practically catatonic since they murdered Gomez."

Milam followed her gaze and nodded sadly. "Well, you're right about Silva, poor bastard." He turned to face her. "But Stan may view things differently." Milam's voice softened. "After all, Lynda, he may be green, but he's got a year more sea time than you."

"Jesus! Don't you think I've thought of that? But I still don't think—"

"I'm not saying I disagree," Milam said. "But what do you expect me to do? Stage a mutiny and appoint myself captain?"

"Of course not. But… I don't know… guide him… offer advice…"

Milam sighed. "Well, it won't come to that, but if it does, I'll do my best." Milam turned around and smiled ruefully. "It's not like there'll be too many command decisions made here in the mess room."

"Maybe not," Arnett said, "but if there are, I'll feel a lot better knowing you're making them. Job one is getting as many of the crew home alive as you can."

"Well, hopefully the cavalry will arrive soon."

"Maybe," Arnett replied, the doubt obvious in her voice, "but my gut tells me something's up, and I wish I knew what it was."

CHAPTER TEN

DRILLSHIP *OCEAN GOLIATH*
ARABIAN SEA
120 MILES FROM THE COAST OF OMAN

Mukhtar sat in the Zodiac in the inky darkness three hours before dawn, relieved the wait was over. It wouldn't serve his purposes to capture the high-profile sheik and his American partners, and the two days of waiting for them to leave the drillship had seemed a lifetime. Finally, the helicopter lifted off the vessel and headed ashore, and his man aboard confirmed the sheik's departure.

Both the hour of the attack and the initial assault craft had been chosen with care. The security detail would be less alert at this hour, and looking outward at the sea. His man onboard was good with a knife and could silence each of the unsuspecting sentries with ease. The small inflatable had a minimal radar return and would show poorly or not at all on the drillship radar, supposing it was even being monitored. He'd had his men stop the outboard some minutes before, and they now paddled through the darkness, awaiting the signal.

And there it was—three short blinks followed by a pause, then repeated. He called softly to the men and they bent to the paddles. In minutes they found the rope ladder down the side of the drillship, right where he'd ordered. Mukhtar rushed aboard with seven men, and within five minutes they captured the surprised crew on watch and took control of communications. With the threat of a warning eliminated, Mukhtar pointed a flashlight into the night and flashed another signal. He was rewarded by the sound of powerful outboards awakening in the distance, and smiled as the sound drew closer.

Within fifteen minutes the deck of the drillship was swarming with pirates. Within twenty the entire crew of the drillship had been subdued. He watched as the pirates, most of them new recruits drawn by the promise of money, cavorted around the huge piles of silver coins on deck. He would give it all to the fools, for he was after something of far greater value, and now he had the means to obtain it.

Mukhtar smiled at the man sitting in the chair in the control room. "Now, my friend," he said, as he held the muzzle of his assault rifle inches from the man's forehead, "we're going to take a little trip. Not too far, just a few kilometers. Will you help, or do I need to retire you and find someone more helpful?"

"No. I mean, yes... I'll help," the tool pusher said. "But we can't move in this condition. There's too much pipe racked in the derrick. The stability is —"

Mukhtar jammed the muzzle of his weapon into the man's mouth, breaking a tooth and stifling the protest. "Enough of your tricks, infidel! Move the vessel or die! Those are your options. Do you understand?"

The terrified tool pusher tried to nod, his head held almost immobile by Mukhtar's weapon.

"Good," Mukhtar said, and withdrew his rifle.

The man looked up, blood running from his mouth. "I... I have a family. D-don't kill me. Please."

Mukhtar nodded and smiled. "Cooperate, and you've nothing to fear."

M/T *Marie Floyd*
Port Sultan Qaboos, Berth No. 1
Muscat, Sultanate of Oman

The three men stood on the main deck of the *Marie Floyd*, sweating in the noonday heat despite the shade of the bridge wing.

"I don't like it, Dugan," said the classification-society surveyor as he glared out at the deck, "not one little bit. This rust bucket was supposed to be headed to the Bangladesh breakers, and suddenly I get a call from Houston HQ telling me to get my ass down here from Dubai to expedite a *flag change*. Who changes the flag on a ship headed for the boneyard? And how the hell are you involved anyway? I thought you worked with Kairouz in London."

Dugan opened his mouth to speak, but Captain Vince Blake beat him to it.

"We're short superintendents," Blake said. "Mr. Dugan is a consultant."

The surveyor cocked an eyebrow. "So Hanley hires the *managing director* of a major competitor to babysit a flag change in the back of beyond?" The man turned and pointed across the open deck to where M/T *Pacific Endurance* floated at the next berth. "Where another of that major competitor's ships just happens to be berthed." He pointed down to the dock, where men unloaded steel plate, crates, and welding gear from a flatbed truck. "And I guess I'm not supposed to notice a newly arrived bunch of rednecks, looking suspiciously like a riding gang, loading material on both vessels. And I don't even want to know how that bunch of Russians fits into things or what's in those cases." He sighed. "Why me?"

"Look, it's just a flag change," Blake said. "The coast guard has no issue with it, so I don't see why it should be a problem for you."

"Why the hell *should* our USCG friends have heartburn?" the surveyor asked. "She's leaving US flag, and not their problem anymore. The only thing I got from my USCG counterpart was an email to the effect of 'be a pal and pull the Certificate of Inspection when you leave.' They're not even sending anyone to our little party. Which leaves me out on a limb all by myself, getting the bum's rush from HQ to do all the acceptance inspections on behalf of Liberia. But it's *my* signature that'll be on the new certificates and reports, and *my* ass on the line if whatever you screwballs are planning goes south and this bucket sinks."

Dugan stroked his chin. "Maybe we can keep everyone happy."

"That'd be a nice trick. How?" asked the surveyor.

"Your marching orders are to expedite the flag change, right?"

"Yeeeaaah."

"So do the flag change today with interim certificates. Defer all major inspections for a week and throw in as many 'outstanding recommendations to be cleared before leaving ports' as you want. Go back to Dubai on the afternoon flight, and come back next week before we sail to finish up the inspections and make sure everything is OK. That way you've expedited the flag change and covered your own ass at the same time." Dugan paused for emphasis. "Everybody's happy, and no very important people will be calling Houston to bitch about you."

The surveyor hesitated. "I guess that'll work, but I still don't like it!"

Blake took advantage of the opening. "Let's go up to my office. I'll pull the certificates for you," he said, leading the man into the deckhouse.

Ten minutes later Dugan stood at the rail, watching activity on the dock below. He turned at the sound of Blake's footsteps.

"He happy?" Dugan asked.

"Well, cooperative at least," Blake replied. "He's up to his neck in certificates and muttering to himself, but I think we'll officially be Liberian when he leaves. But what's this about sailing next week? I thought we were leaving tonight."

"He doesn't have to know that," Dugan said. "As long as we're officially Liberian, we're golden. All those outstanding recommendations he's going to saddle us with are meaningless since we don't intend to trade the ship, but they'll cover his ass and get him out of our hair."

Both men turned at the sound of a load being landed on the deck amidships by the ship's crane. Dugan noticed Blake wince at the sudden movement.

He fixed Blake with an appraising stare. "Pushing the envelope a bit on recovery time, aren't you?"

"Don't worry about me. It was laparoscopic surgery. I get a twinge now and then is all." His voice hardened. "And besides, *Luther Hurd* is my ship and those are my people. I may not be able to do anything for them, but I can do this."

"When we sail we can't turn back," Dugan said. "If there's any doubt—"

"I said I'm fine, Dugan. Drop it, OK?"

Dugan hesitated, then nodded and changed the subject. "Ever think you'd end up doing something like this?"

Blake grinned. "Can't say as I did. Maybe I should get an eye patch and a parrot to sit on my shoulder."

Dugan laughed. "Nah. He'd just crap down the back of your shirt."

His laughter was interrupted by angry voices, a distinctive Texas accent countered by another speaking—or rather, shouting—Russian-accented English.

"Crap," Dugan muttered, looking down at the dock. "Looks like there's a bit of friction between elements of our little band of swashbucklers." He started for the gangway, with Blake on his heels.

Dugan arrived on the dock to find two men toe to toe. The Texan was slender and of medium height. He was older, but appeared fit, and the well-muscled arm below the sleeve of his tee shirt was graced by a faded tattoo that read *USMC*. His Russian adversary was a head taller and decades younger, and neither was showing the slightest signs of backing down. A dozen men moved up in support of the Texan, as a similar number closed ranks behind the Russian, including a blond giant who towered above the others.

"Now hear this, Boris," said the Texan. "I don't give a damn who you are or what's in your little boxes." He punctuated his sentence by squirting tobacco juice on a stack of fiberglass cases. "I don't take orders from you. I got my own stuff to load, and when I finish, I'll load your crap if—and I do mean if—my boss tells me to. Got that?"

"My name is not Boris, little man. It is Andrei Borgdanov—*Major* Andrei Borgdanov. But you can call me *sir*. And if my equipment is not loaded on ship in—"

"All right, knock it off, both of you," said Dugan.

The Texan shot Dugan an irritated look, but brightened when he saw Blake.

"Cap'n," he said to Blake. "I was loading the gear like we agreed when this commie shows up and starts throwin' his weight—"

Borgdanov reddened. "I am Russian but not communist. Perhaps you should come into twenty-first century, *da*?"

"*Da* yourself, Ivan. You're all commies as far as I can tell."

"Cool it, Woody," Blake said.

The Texan nodded but seemed to think better of it, and sent another squirt of tobacco juice through the air to land inches from Borgdanov's foot. The big Russian got even redder and clenched massive fists. Dugan saw a smile flicker at the corners of Woody's mouth, as the smaller man clenched his own fists and set himself to take the Russian's charge.

"Enough!" Dugan yelled, as he stepped between them, facing Borgdanov as he pushed him back a step. "Captain Blake," Dugan said over his shoulder, "why don't you take Woody up the dock a ways and have a chat, while I discuss international cooperation with the major here."

No one moved at first, then Woody shot another squirt of tobacco juice onto the dock, well away from the Russian this time. He turned to the men behind him, as if seeing them for the first time. "What are y'all doing standing around!" he yelled. "Git back to work! This gear ain't gonna load itself."

Woody's men sprang back into action, as he watched a moment, then nodded to Blake. The two men walked off up the dock without looking back.

Borgdanov stared after them.

"OK, Andrei," Dugan said. "What's going on here?"

The major jerked his head in the direction of the retreating Texan. "This foreman is big pain in the ass," he said. "We wait here in sun two hours, and I order him *three* times"—the Russian held up three fingers for emphasis—"to load gear on ship so we can begin stowing properly. Two times, he ignores me, so last time I grab his arm to get attention." Borgdanov shrugged. "Then we have argument. I think maybe better you let me finish argument, then maybe he is no longer big pain is ass, *da*?"

"I think the *order* part is the problem," Dugan said.

"But *Dyed*," the Russian protested, "in Russia—"

Dugan reddened. "God damn it, Borgdanov, we're not in Russia! And I told you to stop calling me gramps!"

Despite the tension, the Russian grinned, as did the blond giant beside him.

"But Dugan," Borgdanov said, nodding toward his companion, Sergeant Ilya Denosovich, "as Ilya and I keep telling you, *dyed* is term of great respect."

"Yeah," Dugan said. "I can tell that by grin on the sergeant's face every time he hears it."

Both Russians laughed, the tension broken. Sensing the new dynamic, the other Russians moved away. Dugan lowered his voice.

"But understand you can't go ordering these guys around," Dugan said. "Woody and his boys have priority for the moment. Until they get the mods done, we can't proceed. Your work comes later." Dugan glanced at the other Russians. "For now, we need to cool things down a bit on all fronts. Why don't you leave a couple of guys to watch your gear and let the others wait in the crew mess? It's a lot cooler in the air conditioning."

Borgdanov considered that a moment. "*Da*," he said at last, before turning to the sergeant and spitting out a stream of Russian. The sergeant nodded and set about organizing the men, as Dugan and Borgdanov moved away a few steps and continued talking.

"But why do we even need these workers, *Dyed*?" Borgdanov asked. "Is easier to just make pirates disappear, *da*?"

"Don't call me… oh, to hell with it," Dugan said, knowing from experience he'd never win that contest. "We've been over this. We need the pirates alive."

The Russian shrugged. "OK, but seems a complicated plan. In Russia—"

Dugan sighed. "But we're not in Russia."

Borgdanov held up his hands, palms outward. "Yes, yes, I know. We are not in Russia. This you tell me many times," he smiled ruefully. "Not that I need you to tell me this. Anyway, since Istanbul, things have not been so wonderful for me in Russia."

Dugan paused, considering his next words. "You did everything you could in Istanbul, and saved thousands of lives. You should've been promoted."

"You do not get promoted when you lose eleven of thirteen men in operation, *Dyed*." Borgdanov looked away, and spoke almost as if speaking to himself. "Good men. *Spetsnaz*. The best," he said. He glanced over to where the blond sergeant was organizing the men, then turned back to Dugan.

"But my great regret is Ilya. I tried to have him transferred away from me, so he is not tarnished by my failure. But he is stubborn man, my Ilya. He refuses to go."

Borgdanov shook his head, as if to clear it of melancholy thoughts, and grinned.

"But now Ilya and I are, what is term? Ah yes, soldiers of fortune. And the pay from Mr. Alex Kairouz is very much like fortune to simple Russian soldier."

"You sure you're OK with this?" Dugan asked.

Borgdanov shrugged. "There is no future for me or Ilya in Russia, so I think this is not so bad. And the world is changing with many more opportunities for people with our training." He smiled again. "So we become, as you Americans say, private contractors. Just so long as we must do nothing against Russia."

"What about the others? What's their story?" Dugan asked.

"All different, yet all the same," Borgdanov said. "Things are not so good in Russia now. Putin is big asshole but powerful. Many people think there may be problems, and no soldier wants to shoot other Russians." He shrugged. "But any decision is dangerous, not only for soldier but family. Better to work outside Russia. This way, we don't have to choose side." He smiled again. "Is good opportunity, and for this we thank you, *Dyed*."

Dugan smiled back. "It's the least I could do since you saved my life."

"Yes," Borgdanov said. "Is like they say in India, karma."

"I didn't know you were a student of Indian philosophy."

"Even savages can have good ideas," Borgdanov said.

"I wouldn't call the Indians savages."

"Of course they are savages," Borgdanov said, then grinned. "They are not Russian! But don't worry, *Dyed*. You, we make honorary Russian."

CHAPTER ELEVEN

M/T PACIFIC ENDURANCE
ARABIAN SEA
50 MILES OFF OMAN

Dugan felt a slight vibration under his feet, as a fixed-tank washing machine blasted the underside of the deck. He watched crewmen move between the machines, checking remote indicators for nozzle angle and rotation, while he paced the main deck. And worried.

Bound for the scrapyard, *Marie Floyd*'s tanks were already clean and gas-free, allowing Blake to reduce her normal marine crew to the minimum necessary to sail. And Blake had taken over as captain of *Marie Floyd*, dropping the headcount even further to minimize noncombatants. Dugan's situation here on *Pacific Endurance* was a bit different. She'd been trading, and though empty, her tanks still had gasoline residue. She had to be clean before they could complete the mods, and to clean her, Dugan had to keep the whole crew. He paced the main deck and worried.

"You better mosey on down the deck a bit," said a voice behind him. "You're gonna wear a hole in this part. Reckon you're a worrier."

Dugan turned to see Joshua Woodley, aka Woody, grinning at him around the ever-present wad of tobacco in his cheek. Woody's coveralls were streaked with rust and mud and plastered to his body by sweat.

"Yeah, I guess I am at that," Dugan said.

Woody nodded. "Got no problems with worriers, long as they're doing something about what they're worrying about. I reckon you qualify."

"How's it coming?" Dugan asked.

"Well, we got the safe room rigged in the aft-peak tank and installed the controls. The biggest problem there was the mud, but we got 'er washed down all right," Woody said.

"Access?"

"We cut the engine-room bulkhead, but I got to thinkin' about it and just put in a plywood door instead of steel. All it has to do is stop the light. We painted it to match the bulkhead, and you can't hardly tell it's there even with the lights on. I don't reckon a pirate with a flashlight's likely to find it in the dark, even if he's brave enough to venture into a pitch-black engine room."

"What about—"

"Relax, Dugan. It's all in hand. Cameras, steering, sound-powered phones, jammers, everything. Just like you told me." Woody nodded at the men moving around the deck. "This here's the part that worries me. Edgar's already workin' on the tanks over on *Marie Floyd*, and we're still cleaning. When y'all gonna be finished?"

"Not a problem," Dugan said. "Tank mods don't have to be finished before we hunt. We'll work them along the way. When will everything else be finished?"

Woody looked at his watch again. "Long about noon I expect, give or take an hour." He paused. "Two days, start to finish. Not too shabby, if I do say so myself."

"Not too shabby at all," Dugan agreed, then added, "I'll tell the major."

The mention of the Russian earned him a scowl.

"What do you have against the Russians, Woody?"

Woody grunted. "Just don't like commies. My daddy died in Korea, and I fought the bastards in Vietnam. Kicked their asses, too."

Dugan hesitated. "I seem to recall we lost that one."

Woody cocked an eyebrow and turned his head to send a stream of tobacco juice over the rail. "Not the part I was in."

"You know they're not commies," Dugan said, changing his approach.

"Near enough. Just give it a rest, Dugan. Me and Ivan ain't never gonna be bass-fishin' buddies. Got it?"

"Loud and clear." Dugan turned to head for the deckhouse, as Woody fell in beside him. "I'll get Blake on the horn and see if he's ready to go hunting."

M/T *MARIE FLOYD*
ARABIAN SEA
125 MILES OFF OMAN

Blake peered down at the radar screen as the *Marie Floyd* steamed west at ten knots. She was ballasted deep and, for all appearances, a tempting target—a slow ship full of valuable cargo with her main deck near the waterline. He nodded at the blip showing *Pacific Endurance* running a parallel course on his port beam, well to the south. He and Dugan had agreed to run separately to avoid raising suspicions, but close enough to support each other if necessary. Otherwise, the radar screen was surprisingly clear except for a drillship he'd passed fifteen miles back, now showing on his starboard quarter. He wasn't too surprised, most ships were running farther to the north in the supposed safe lanes thinly patrolled by the warships of various nations. But for their plan to work, they had to steam into the heart of 'injun country,' as Dugan had called it.

As Blake started to move away from the radar, something caught his eye. A faint blip that, as he watched, changed from an intermittent to a steady target. Something small. He watched and waited, and positions at six-minute intervals showed the craft moving at twenty knots on a course taking it between his ship and *Pacific Endurance*. If it was a pirate, he'd turn toward whichever ship he saw first, and *Marie Floyd's* bridge was ten feet higher than that of *Pacific Endurance*.

As if reading Blake's mind, the blip changed course toward *Marie Floyd* and increased speed. Blake crossed to the phone on the bridge control console and dialed into the ship's public-address system. "Attention all hands. Pirates sighted on fast approach. All hands to their stations. All nonessential crew to safe room. Now! This is not a drill. Repeat. This is not a drill."

Blake hung up, moved to the VHF, and keyed the mike. "Big Brother, this is Little Sister. Do you copy? Over."

"We read you five by five, Little Sister" came Dugan's voice over the speaker. "And we have you on radar and understand your situation. Over."

"Roger that, bro," Blake said. "Going dark. Will call when we're done. Out."

"We'll be waiting, sis. Good Luck. Big Brother, out."

Blake was re-racking the mike when the console phone rang.

"Ready to switch steering to emergency local," said the chief engineer from the steering gear room.

"Take it, Chief," said Blake, and hung up. The phone rang again, this time from the engine room.

"Ready to switch engine to local control," said the first engineer.

"Take it, First," said Blake, and hung up again as the console alarms began to buzz discordantly, informing him that systems were in emergency override.

He silenced the alarms, and moved to a set of recently installed switches on the aft bulkhead, activating jammers to cancel all radio and cell-phone signals, making *Marie Floyd* a black hole communications-wise. He glanced around to ensure he'd missed nothing and then raced through the chart room to the central stairway, flying down the stairs two at a time. He stopped on A-deck to watch the dark-haired young Russian sergeant divide his men three and three between the officers' and crew mess rooms.

"Ready?" asked Blake.

The young Russian nodded. "*Da*," he said, and patted his gas mask before pointing through the door at the sound-powered phone on the bulkhead of the officers' mess. "We wait your order."

Blake nodded as the Russian stepped into the officers' mess and closed the door behind him. Blake opened the door to the machinery spaces and started down the stairs, the oppressive air wrapping him like hot, thick cotton, as the noise of the main engine and generators assaulted his ears. Bypassing the engine control room, he continued down to the generator platform level and aft to the rear bulkhead of the engine room. He swung open the almost-invisible plywood door and stepped into the jury-rigged safe room, closing the door behind him to block out at least a bit of the noise, if not the heat. The second mate sat in a folding chair tack-welded to the deck in front of a makeshift control panel facing the bulkhead. He was peering into one of two monitors mounted on the bulkhead in front of him, which displayed the sea ahead of the ship. In his hands was an oblong control box with a thick black cable running from it and up the bulkhead. He looked up as the captain entered.

"Everything OK?" Blake asked.

"Seems to be," the second mate said, glancing down at the control in his hand. "It takes a bit of getting used to. But it works fine as long as I remember that up is right rudder and down is left rudder."

Blake nodded, looking up to where the cable disappeared through the overhead into the steering gear room above. He smiled despite the tension. Trust an engineer to come up with the idea of wiring the spare crane control pigtail into the emergency steering servos. He looked over at the benches that lined the bulkhead, now occupied by his reduced crew and the Texans of the riding gang. He nodded at them and turned back to the second mate.

"Everybody accounted for?" Blake asked.

"Yes sir," the man responded. "Everyone is here except the Russians. The chief and the first engineer are at the engine-side controls."

Blake nodded and picked up the sound-powered phone mounted on the console, moved the selector switch, and turned the crank. Forty feet away, beside the big main engine, a light lit on a similar phone and the chief engineer answered.

"Engine side."

"All accounted for, Chief," said Blake. "Have the First kill the engine-room lights, then stand by to stop the engine. I'll call you when we're ready."

"Roger that," said the chief engineer, and he hung up and slipped the earmuff back over his ear. He nodded to the first engineer, who stood ready at the door to the plywood enclosure they'd built around the engine-side control station, and the first exited the little room and walked to a breaker box. They'd disabled the emergency-lighting circuits earlier, so as the First toggled breaker after breaker, the engine room was plunged into pitch darkness. The man looked around in the inky gloom, satisfied no pirate would brave the dark, and switched on his flashlight to make his way back to the little sanctuary.

When he opened the door to the little hut, the single 40-watt bulb was like a blazing sun. He stepped inside and closed the wooden door behind himself before releasing a rolled-up tarp, which fell over the door. Even if a pirate was brave enough to descend to their level, no light would leak out to reveal their position. The chief nodded his approval, and both engineers settled in to wait.

PIRATE LAUNCH
ARABIAN SEA
125 MILES OFF OMAN

Abdi grinned at his men as the Zodiac sped down the starboard side of the big ship fifty meters away. They'd been at the extreme end of their search pattern and ready to turn back when he'd spotted the tanker. He passed the ship's stern, then circled and cut speed to trail her, expecting evasive maneuvers. He read her name—M/T *Marie Floyd*—and below that, in strangely fresh-looking paint, her hailing port—Monrovia, Liberia. His smile broadened as the ship began the expected radical course changes to slew the stern from side to side and make boarding more difficult. But difficult was childishly easy for him, for he was Abdi, first among the first-boarders of the clan *Ali Saleeban*. He was already dreaming of his first-boarder bonus.

He signaled his best driver to take the tiller of the outboard, then moved through his men to the bow as the driver edged the inflatable closer to the ship, matching her maneuvers. Abdi pulled his sat-phone to alert the rest of the group far behind that he was about to begin an attack, and emitted an irritated grunt when he saw he had no signal. No matter, they'd know soon enough. He pocketed the phone and balanced himself in the bow of the boat, and motioned for the short ladder with hooks on the end.

His tiller man was good, and he didn't have to wait long. As the next course change started the ship's stern moving away from them, the launch shot forward against the ship side, and Abdi hooked the ladder over the bottom rail of the handrail and leaped onto it. He scampered up the ladder like a spider and jumped over the rail, unslinging his assault rifle, ready to ward off any counterattack. But there was none. He flashed a grin over the side and motioned his men up, and in seconds they joined him as the driver moved the Zodiac off a safe distance.

M/T *MARIE FLOYD*
SAFE ROOM

Blake stared at the monitor, swinging the stern from side to side as he watched the pirate launch close on the port quarter.

"Yes! There he is," Blake said. "First guy aboard. And here come the rest. I count five… six… seven aboard, one pulling the boat away."

Blake turned the selector on the sound-powered phone and cranked.

"*Da?*" said the young Russian.

"Seven pirates, repeat, seven papas aboard," Blake said. "One papa in boat."

"We are ready."

"Good. Get your masks on and stay on the phone," Blake said.

Blake watched the second monitor as the pirates moved out of sight. He switched to the camera in the A-deck passageway and waited. Within seconds the lead pirate burst through the door, gun at the ready, then called back to his men, who joined him in the passageway. The pirates moved toward the central stairwell, as beside Blake, the second mate counted. "… five… six… seven! They're all in, Cap!"

Blake threw a switch on the makeshift control panel and powerful magnets sucked home bolts in all the outside deckhouse doors and the doors to the stairwell on all the upper decks. He threw another switch and the lights went out in the deckhouse, plunging the pirates into darkness.

Blake picked up the phone. "Gas 'em," he said.

"*Da,*" answered the Russian, as Blake toggled on the night-vision camera just in time to see pre-constructed slots open in the doors from the officers' and crew mess rooms to disgorge tear-gas grenades, one after another. Trapped in the passageway and unable to see, the pirates were screaming and slamming into each other in their panic, which increased as the grenades clattered unseen on the deck and choking gas billowed around them. In seconds they began to fall, coughing and gagging.

"Five papas down in the passageway, two in the stairwell. Round 'em up, Sergeant," Blake said into the phone.

The doors from the mess rooms opened and the black-clad Russians emerged, the helmet-mounted night-vision goggles flipped down over their gas masks, giving them the appearance of large black insects. Within seconds they bound the pirates' hands with plastic cuffs and covered their eyes with duct tape. Blake watched as the Russians dragged the pirates back into the relatively fresher air of the officers' mess room and shut the door. The light on Blake's phone flashed, and he picked it up.

"All secure," the Russian said, his voice muffled by the mask.

"Acknowledged," Blake said. "Tell your guys to secure their night-vision glasses, and I'll turn the lights back on and start ventilation to clear out the deckhouse. The papa in the boat can't be allowed to escape. I'll try to draw him closer, but if you can't take him alive, make sure he doesn't get away. Clear?"

"Clear."

"OK, stand by," said Blake, as he turned the selector switch on the phone.

"Engine side, Chief speaking."

"Stop her, Chief," Blake said.

"Stop, aye" came the reply.

Blake heard and felt the big engine rumbling to a stop as he ordered the rudder amidships. He switched cameras again to gaze at the pirate launch, keeping station a hundred yards away on his port side. He willed the pirate closer to the ship.

Five minutes later, Blake watched in the monitor as the Russians crept up the starboard side of the main deck toward the midships pipe manifold. He switched the other monitor to the camera on the port bridge wing, which gave him a clear view of the port side of the ship, and watched the pirate, apparently encouraged by the ship's loss of speed, maneuver the boat closer until he was too close to see the main deck above him.

The Russians worked their way across the deck from starboard to port and stopped well short of the rail. The young sergeant crept forward alone, keeping low, until he was close enough to peek over the rail with a handheld periscope. He spotted the pirate and drew back, repositioning his men with a series of hand signals. When satisfied with their placement, he gave another signal, and six men charged the rail as one, spraying the Zodiac with automatic fire.

Three Russians concentrated on the idling outboard, and it coughed to a stop, riddled with holes and belching smoke. The remaining three men targeted the craft's starboard inflation tube and shredded it, as the terrified pirate crouched in what was left of his boat, clinging to the still-intact port side. Blake saw the man raise his head cautiously and then raise one hand over his head while he used his other to jettison weapons that lay awash in the boat. A line snaked out from the main deck and landed across the boat, and the pirate grabbed it and was hauled aboard and secured, none too gently. Blake heaved a sigh of relief and dialed the phone.

"Engine side, Chief speaking."

"We got 'em, Chief," Blake said. "I'm going back to the bridge and we'll switch back to normal running."

"Roger that. How many did we get?"

"Eight," Blake replied.

"It's a start," said the chief.

"That it is," said Blake. "That it is."

CHAPTER TWELVE

DRILLSHIP *OCEAN GOLIATH*
ARABIAN SEA
123 MILES FROM THE COAST OF OMAN

Mukhtar watched over the operator's shoulder as the man stared into the monitor and directed the little ROV over the seabed. It was cool in the air-conditioned control room, but sweat beaded the man's forehead and formed dark circles under the arms of his khaki shirt. Mukhtar rested his hand on the operator's shoulder and smiled as the man flinched.

"Move to the left," said Mukhtar, pointing on the monitor that displayed the camera feed from the ROV. "There."

Sure enough, as the ROV moved closer to the area he'd indicated, the objects came into focus: small gas cylinders half buried in silt.

"Good," Mukhtar said. "Gather them."

The operator nodded and engaged a joystick, and a robotic arm came into camera view, plucking cylinders from the silt to put them in the front basket on the ROV.

"Six," the operator said. "The basket's full. We'll have to bring her up."

"All right," said Mukhtar. "But get it back down as soon as possible. Gather as many of the cylinders as you can." The operator nodded, and Mukhtar left the control room, stopping on the way out to admonish his two men on duty to keep an eye on the infidels and summon him if anything looked suspicious.

He moved from the deckhouse to stand by the rail on the open deck, the outside temperature more to his liking. He gazed out to sea, assessing his situation. The prize was in reach, but it had been a long, hard path. One he'd hardly chosen.

Like others in the far-flung Somali diaspora, he'd left his afflicted land a student with high hopes of bettering himself. What he'd found in the UK, and later in Europe, was hatred and prejudice, both for the color of his skin and his religion. And though he'd never been there, by all accounts the US was even worse.

Oh, they spoke fine words of tolerance and equality, but eyes tracked him everywhere, even when he was in Western dress. Eyes that spoke eloquently, if silently. *What are you doing here? You're not one of us. Go back to where you belong.*

And so he had, but not before wandering Europe and working menial jobs, always the outsider. In time, he learned to become invisible. As a man, he was a foreign threat; as a fawning, obsequious servant, he was unremarkable and unthreatening.

He studied the ways of these people, so different from the clan system of his home. He met with others of the True Faith—some Somali, some not—in mosques and coffee shops, and they commiserated over their lives and the lack of respect for their faith and culture. He ended his European trek in Germany, becoming ever surer with each passing month that Islam could never coexist with the infidels. How ironic it was to reach that understanding in the country that had done so much to eradicate the hated Jews. Contrary to popular wisdom, the enemy of his enemy was not always his friend.

There in Germany, Allah had first set Mukhtar's feet on the true path. He'd worked as an orderly in a hospice—another job no one wanted—wiping the asses of the dying and listening to the drug-induced revelations of the medicated. The old man had been blind, just another lump of wasted flesh with no visitors, stubbornly refusing to die. But his rambling rants against the Jews had been interesting, as had the discovery this human husk had once been a doctor in the Waffen SS.

The real revelation had been a deathbed tale of regret, a story of a submarine going down with a cargo of nerve gas—a gas so potent it would have changed the course of that long-ago war. Intrigued, Mukhtar's research revealed *U-859* had indeed sunk after torpedoing an American ship. He speculated as to the value of such nerve gas to the jihad, but ultimately lost interest. What good was a weapon on the ocean bottom, over twenty-five hundred meters deep?

By the time he returned to Somalia, Mukhtar was a dedicated jihadist. He joined al-Shabaab and rose through its ranks, and daydreamed no more of *U-859* and her cargo of nerve gas. Until, that is, he saw the press release from the flamboyant and extravagantly rich playboy Sheik Mustafa of Oman announcing purchase of the salvage rights on the SS *John Barry*, the very ship sunk by *U-859*.

Historical accounts said *U-859* had been sunk after torpedoing the *John Barry*, so after *Ocean Goliath* located the Liberty ship, finding *U-859* had been child's play. And as he'd hoped, the sub had cracked open like an egg when she hit the bottom and littered the sea floor with her cargo. They found gas cylinders almost immediately. He sighed. If only the rest of it had been as easy.

He'd expected some deterioration, given the time involved, but he'd hoped for better results. When he'd dressed one of his men in the chemical suit and had him test the gas on a hostage, the results were hardly promising. Of the first six cylinders salvaged, five had been duds. His man had opened the gas in the hostage's face, and the first three cylinders produced a puff of white powder with no discernible impact. The gas was still potent in the fourth cylinder and the hostage died, but testing of the last two cylinders on a new victim produced the same white powder and no results. He'd thrown the live hostage back with the others and contemplated his next move.

He'd no choice but to salvage as many of the cylinders as possible. Once they got the cylinders to a lab, he could harvest and concentrate the gas that was still effective. But it was all going to take time—more time than he'd allotted. He had the tool pusher making daily reports, and to those ashore, the salvage operation appeared to be proceeding normally. However, he could never tell when the sheik might visit.

He had to scoop up all the cylinders quickly and move the drillship back over the *John Barry*. They'd then take the gas cylinders, loot the silver, kill the crew, and leave. Investigators would find a ship looted for her treasure. No one would know of the gas—until they found out about it in a most unpleasant manner.

Mukhtar sighed. One thing at a time. First, he had to collect all the cylinders.

CIA HEADQUARTERS
MARITIME THREAT ASSESSMENT
LANGLEY, VA

"You're sure about this?" Ward asked for the third time.

"As sure as I can be," the analyst replied. "He's used the phone twice. The message was scrambled, but it's definitely this guy Mukhtar's phone."

Ward fell silent for a moment and studied the chart on the conference table as he stroked his chin. "And what's he doing on a drillship?"

"More to the point," the analyst said, indicating two positions marked on the chart, "why did the drillship move after he got onboard?"

"What've you got on her?" Ward asked.

The analyst shuffled some papers. "Let's see. The *Ocean Goliath*. Owned by Emerald Offshore Drilling, Houston, Texas. Currently on charter to a consortium controlled by Sheik Ali Hassan Mustafa of Oman."

"What's the story with the sheik? Is he a radical? Any chance our friend Mukhtar is aboard as an invited guest?" Ward asked.

"Don't think so," the analyst said. "Sheik Mustafa is the stereotypical rich-playboy type, educated in the UK, hobnobs with the glitterati, the whole nine yards. All the financial checks come up clean as far as funding suspect charities and similar activities." He shrugged. "He's a rich dickhead, but an unlikely terrorist."

"So what's the connection then?" Ward persisted. "Our friend Mukhtar is hijacking a drilling operation? That doesn't make sense."

"It's more of a treasure hunt." The analyst slid a press release across the table. Ward picked it up and saw a picture of the smiling sheik holding up a model of a World War II Liberty ship. The press release ran several pages.

"Give me the high points," Ward said.

"The SS *John Barry* was en route to Iran with military supplies for Russia with a scheduled port call in Saudi Arabia, where she was to offload three million silver *riyals* minted in Philadelphia for the Saudi government. She never made it. On 28 August 1944, she was torpedoed by *U-859*, which was in turn sunk by a British fighter shadowing the *John Barry*. The sheik and his partners are after the silver."

Ward looked skeptical. "So how much are three million riyals worth today?"

"It's not the riyals, it's the silver. It was worth about half a million bucks in 1944, but silver was eighteen cents an ounce. Now, it's over thirty bucks an ounce, so the coins are worth between ninety and a hundred million for the silver content. But that's not the whole story. There were persistent rumors that *John Barry* was carrying a secret cargo of another twenty-six million dollars of uncoined silver bullion, and that's at 1944 silver prices."

Ward let out a low whistle. "How much is that worth?"

"At today's silver prices? Several billion—with a *b*—dollars."

"So let me get this straight," said Ward. "You're telling me the location of this wreck has been known for over sixty years, and no one's gone after it?"

"Too deep," the analyst replied. "It's in over eighty-five hundred feet of water, and silver's heavy. No one ever figured out how to salvage it before now. And it's not a cheap operation—the average day rate on a drillship like *Ocean Goliath* is almost a half million bucks. It took someone with deep pockets and an appetite for risk to even consider it. Remember, the only *verified* treasure is the coins."

"But an al-Shabaab connection still doesn't make sense," Ward said. "Even if there is a fortune in silver and this Mukhtar guy loots it, he's still got to turn it into something he can use to fund his operation, and I don't think converting that much silver to cash can be done under the radar." Ward stroked his chin and looked back down at the chart. "You said the ship moved sometime after Mukhtar went aboard. What do you make of that?"

The analyst shrugged. "Could be any number of legitimate reasons. The wreck might be in two or more pieces, or maybe they missed it on the first try and are trying another position."

"How long were they in the first position?" Ward asked.

The analyst shuffled through various satellite photos until he found the one he wanted. "Ten days."

"Sounds like they were already where they wanted to be," Ward said. "So what else could draw our friend Mukhtar's interest?"

"The only wreck that's even close is the sub."

"The submarine," Ward said. "Get me everything you can on this *U-859*."

Two hours later, Ward sat fidgeting at his desk, trying to get some work done as he stole glances at his phone. He answered it on the first ring.

"Ward."

"*U-859*. Keel laid in Bremen, Germany, in 1942. She was delivered to the *Kriegsmarine* in 1943 and assigned to the *Monsun Gruppe*, or 'Monsoon Group,' to operate in the Far East alongside the Imperial Japanese Navy. She was a Type IXD2 U-boat, fitted with a snorkel to enable extensive underwater operation during the passage from Kiel, Germany, to her Far East base at Penang, Malaysia."

"Thanks for the history lesson," said Ward. "Did you get anything that might be of actual use?"

"Look, Ward. There's not a lot there, OK?"

But there was more; Ward could sense it in the analyst's voice. He was just waiting for Ward to be properly appreciative.

Ward sighed. "OK, Joe. I know you're about to hit me with an 'oh, by the way.' I can hear it in your voice. Don't make me drag it out of you."

He could picture the analyst smiling.

"Oh, by the way," the man said. "There was one survivor from the sub."

"So what?" Ward replied. "I'm supposed to fly to Germany and interview a ninety-year-old Kraut, presuming he's even alive?"

"Japanese, actually," said the analyst. "He's ninety-four and lives in Frederick, Maryland. Would you like his address?"

IMAMURA RESIDENCE
112 SHADY OAK LANE
FREDERICK, MARYLAND

Jesse Ward drove down the quiet tree-lined street of well-maintained older homes set on large, immaculately landscaped lots—the American dream. The irritating mechanical voice of the GPS jarred him from his reverie.

"Arriving... at... one... twelve... Shady... Oak... Lane... on... right."

Ward pulled into the long drive and down toward a large detached garage set back some distance from the house. He stopped beside the house and got out, feigning an exaggerated stretch as he looked around. From his vantage point, he could see a manicured front lawn, complemented by an even larger area behind the house, dominated by a well-tended vegetable garden. He turned and started for the front door when he was hailed from the backyard.

"Agent Ward?"

He turned to see a small bespectacled man moving out of the vegetable garden, clad in a plaid work shirt with the sleeves rolled to the elbows. There was dirt on the knees of his well-worn jeans, and a straw hat was perched on his head, its broad brim hiding his face in shadow. He pulled off a pair of work gloves and dropped them to the ground at the edge of the garden as he continued toward Ward. He was bent with age and moved with arthritic slowness, leaning on a cane.

"Dr. Imamura?" asked Ward.

"Please, call me Yoshi," said the man, with the slightest trace of an accent. "I have not doctored anyone in some time." He smiled before gesturing to the garden. "Except, of course, my poor plants, who have no choice in the matter."

Ward followed the doctor's gaze. "It's a beautiful garden."

"My wife's passion." Imamura's smile turned wistful. "She got me interested in it after I retired. I lost her some years ago to cancer, but somehow, with my hands in the dirt I often feel she is still here, just out of sight in the next row. " He looked back at Ward. "But I don't think you came from Langley to listen to the maudlin ramblings of a very old man. Come. Let's sit on the patio and you can tell me what I can do for the CIA."

94

Imamura hobbled to a covered patio at the back of the house, with Ward in tow. They were met by a large black woman who looked to be in her sixties. She set a pitcher of lemonade and two glasses on a lawn table and fixed Ward with an inquisitive, none-too-friendly stare.

"Ahh… thank you, Mrs. Lomax," Imamura said. "Agent Ward, this is Mrs. Lomax. She does all the work around here and frees me to putter about in the garden. Mrs. Lomax, this is Agent Ward."

"Nice to meet you," Ward said. The woman nodded and turned to leave.

"I don't think she likes me," Ward said, as the back door closed.

Imamura chuckled. "Mrs. Lomax is quite reserved, but she is my rock. She's worked here for over twenty-five years, and her continued presence allows me my independence. My wife and I weren't blessed with children, so…" He shrugged. "I've enjoyed a full life, Agent Ward. I hope one day in the not-too-distant future Mrs. Lomax finds me in the garden, resting peacefully with a smile on my face."

Ward found himself warming to the little Japanese, despite what he suspected of the man's past. He nodded. "Sounds like a plan."

Imamura gestured Ward to a chair beside the lawn table as he took off his hat and placed it in another chair. He poured two glasses of lemonade, his hands shaking with the palsy of age, before taking a seat himself. "So tell me, Agent Ward. How may I help you?"

Ward scratched his head. "Well, to be honest, I'm not sure. Perhaps we can start with your own background and how you came to the US."

Imamura looked puzzled. "I hardly see how events of over sixty years ago can… oh, all right, I suppose it makes no difference. I was a doctor in Japan after the war, and I was offered the opportunity to come to the US in 1946. I was a young man, just married, and times in postwar Japan were extremely difficult. We were quite apprehensive because we did not know how *Japs* would be received in the US." He paused. "And it was hard at first. But we worked very hard at perfecting our English and fitting in. My new colleagues were very supportive, and my wife and I became citizens in 1955. We never returned to Japan."

"And by your 'new colleagues,' I assume you're referring to your co-workers at USAMRIID?" Ward asked, pronouncing it "U-sam-rid," the acronym for the US Army Medical Research Institute of Infectious Diseases.

"Yes," said Imamura, "though it was called the Biological Warfare Laboratories when I first joined it."

"One thing—no, make that several things puzzle me," Ward said. "War refugees were clamoring to enter the US at the time, but we were taking very few from Japan. Yet you were picked from the crowd, and as best I can tell from existing records—and there are damn few of those, by the way—you were fast-tracked straight to a good job in the US. Why is that?"

"Let us say that I had skills which were in demand."

"Such as?"

Imamura avoided eye contact, and lifted his glass to sip at the lemonade. The glass shook in his hand from a bit more than his normal palsy and ice cubes clinked in a steady rattle. "Agent Ward," Imamura said, "all details of my employment at USAMRIID and its predecessor are classified. You, of all people, should know that."

"You're right, Doctor. Forget I asked. My interest has nothing to do with USAMRIID, or your time here in the US."

"What interest is that?" Imamura asked over the rim of his glass.

"What were you doing on a German U-boat in the Arabian Sea in 1944?"

The sound of the glass shattering on the flagstone patio was like a gunshot. Lemonade splashed on both men's shoes and bits of glass and ice skittered across the patio, but neither man moved.

"Ho… how did you know that?"

"British war records," Ward replied. "Everything's being digitized now for historical purposes, and it's a lot easier than it used to be to make connections. Your name showed up as a POW with details of your capture and repatriation to Japan. It wasn't in the US records, and I doubt anyone would have thought to ask in 1946, or if they'd have even cared if they knew. But let's just say I've developed an interest. Now. What can you tell me?"

"It… it was long ago. Another world. I… I don't remember things well—"

"A sub sinks and you're the only survivor, and you don't even remember why you were there?" Ward fixed Imamura with a level gaze. "Somehow that seems unlikely."

Imamura had almost visibly shrunk as he slumped in his chair. He spoke not to Ward but to his own feet. "Please. Agent Ward. I… I am an old man—"

Ward cut him off. "Look, Doctor. Anything that happened is history. I'm not trying to root up bad memories, but I need—"

"I think you better go now!"

Ward looked up to see Mrs. Lomax standing in the back door. As he watched, she came out on the patio and started toward him.

"I just have to ask the doctor a few more questions."

"You're upsetting the doctor, Agent Ward. Please leave."

Ward ignored her. "Dr. Imamura, something's up with that sub, and I think lives may be at stake. I just need—"

"Now!" Mrs. Lomax said. "Or I'm calling the police."

Ward sighed and rose, dropping his card on the table before he turned to go. "Call me if you'd like to continue, Doctor."

"Go!" said Mrs. Lomax, pointing to his car.

Ward started for his car, trailed closely by the woman. She stood watching, arms folded, as he got in his car and pulled out of the drive.

Mrs. Lomax fussed about the patio, sweeping up the glass, the lemonade, and bits of melting ice, leaving wet streaks in the wake of her broom. She looked up, surprised, as Imamura leaned on his cane and struggled to his feet.

"Now don't you overdo it, Doctor," she said. "Just sit yourself back down. As soon as I get this cleaned up, I'll fix you some lunch. I got some of that soup you like simmerin' on the stove."

The doctor gave her a wan smile. "Thank you, Mrs. Lomax, but I'm not hungry. I think I'll finish my weeding."

"Now, you know the doctors said—"

Imamura waved a frail hand to cut her off. "I know, I know," he said. "But indulge me if you will. I have some thinking to do, and it's peaceful in the garden."

She opened her mouth to object further, then seemed to think better of it, and nodded. Imamura hobbled toward the garden, leaning on the cane. In a few minutes he was on his knees again, weeding around a row of tomato plants. The mindless work cast its usual spell, and he was soon moving more or less automatically, lost in his own thoughts. But much less-pleasant thoughts than usual.

Had it come to this after all these years? After working so hard to become thoroughly American? He'd been terrified at first that his role in the plan would be discovered. A plan so horrific that, even though never carried out, knowledge of his association would be sufficient to condemn him in the eyes of the world. Gradually he'd relaxed, increasingly sure that the past was buried and forgotten. And now this man Ward appeared from nowhere, asking questions. To what end? What did he want? *U-859* and its horrible cargo lay on the sea floor, over a mile deep, no threat to anyone. Imamura closed his eyes and his mind flashed back to a simple file folder, hand-lettered *Operation Minogame.*

What if it was true? What if, as impossible as it seemed, someone had found the secret and was going after the sub? Drops fell on Imamura's hands as he worked in the dirt. At first he thought it had begun to rain, despite the cloudless sky, but then he realized tears were rolling down his sunken cheeks. But the tears were not enough to relieve the stress of harboring a horrible secret for decades, and when the chest pain came, it was almost welcome—a sign that he could put down his burden at last and move on to whatever place in Heaven or Hell had been allotted him. He didn't cry out, but toppled over almost gently into the tomato plants, his last conscious thoughts of his wife and whether or not he would meet her.

CHAPTER THIRTEEN

Dugan stood on the main deck, braced against the slight motion of the ship as she drifted in a gentle swell, watching the M/T *Marie Floyd* drifting nearby. He turned his eyes from the ship to an inflatable roaring toward *Pacific Endurance*, a seaman at the outboard and carrying a single passenger. In minutes the roar died as the seaman cut power and expertly maneuvered the boat alongside the Jacob's ladder hanging down the side of *Pacific Endurance*. The passenger leaped onto the rope ladder and began to climb. Dugan met the man at the top.

"Welcome aboard, Vince. Glad you could make it," he said, extending his hand.

"Wouldn't have missed it for the world," Blake replied, shaking the offered hand. "Everything all ready?"

Dugan nodded as he led Blake across the deck. "Borgdanov's got them all lined up on the port side. He's going to flush out some translators first—all the gangs have English speakers to communicate with captive crews. After that, he'll go to work on confessions and clan connections."

"And what're we supposed to do?" Blake asked.

"Nothing," Dugan said. "It'll be more effective if they think it's a Russian operation. We just keep our mouths shut and try to look Russian."

"One thing I don't quite understand," Blake said. "Shouldn't we wait until we get more captives? Otherwise, we'll just have to do this all over again."

"Maybe not," said Dugan. "We've got thirty-four and you've got twenty-eight on *Marie Floyd*. If the Russians can convince these guys we mean business, we'll just toss any new captives we take in with them for a few days before we interrogate them. That may do the trick. I don't want to have to stop and go through this every few days unless we have to."

Blake nodded as the pair rounded the corner of the deckhouse and stopped to survey the scene on the port side of the main deck. The captive pirates were lined up with their backs against the deckhouse, their bare feet bound at the ankles with plastic ties and their wrists similarly restrained in front of them. All had duct tape across their mouths, and some were leaning back against the deckhouse to balance against the slight movement of the ship. Major Borgdanov and five of his black-clad Russians faced the prisoners, looking very much like the elite *spetsnaz* troops they formerly were. Each had a Russian tricolor flag patch on his shoulder. The major glanced over as the Americans arrived, and gave the briefest of nods before beginning to stalk up and down in front of the prisoners.

"I will need translator," the major yelled. "I am sure none of you savages is smart enough to speak *culturnyi* language like Russian. So! I think we must use English, *da*? So. If you speak English, raise hands. Now!"

His speech was met with a combination of uncomprehending stares and sullen glares, to which he responded with an exaggerated shrug.

"So. No translator? Is too bad. Without translator you are all useless to me." He spoke to Sergeant Ilya Denosovitch in Russian, who grinned and motioned to another Russian. The two men grabbed the first captive in line, carried him the few steps to the rail, and heaved him over, as effortlessly as if he were a feather. He fell out of sight and there was the sound of a splash. The sergeant unslung his automatic weapon and fired two three-round bursts down toward the water before turning back and saying something that caused the other Russians to convulse in laughter.

The major studied the remaining captives.

"Is too bad none of you speak English or Russian, so you cannot appreciate sergeant's little joke," said the major. "He said you savages are so skinny, you sink so fast he hardly has time to shoot you. But I am thinking about this. Maybe you are not useless after all. Maybe we have shooting competition and I give bottle of very good vodka to man who shoots most savages before they sink." He shrugged. "Not what I planned, but we should never pass up training opportunity, *da*?"

The major nodded toward the sergeant, who approached the next man in line. A dozen pairs of bound hands shot into the air.

The major held up his hand to stop the sergeant.

"What is this?" the major asked. "Could it be miracle? Some mysterious power that gives gift of tongues? Can I be so fortunate?" He walked to the first man with his hands raised and ripped the tape from his mouth. "Lower your hands and answer questions," he said, and the man nodded.

"What is your name?"

"Abukar."

"Abukar what?"

"Just Abukar."

"What is your clan?" the major asked.

"Ali Saleeban," the man replied.

"How long have you been a pirate?"

"I... I am not a pirate. I am a fisherman."

"Silence!" the major screamed, and the terrified Somali snapped his mouth shut.

The major re-taped the man's mouth with exaggerated gentleness, then patted his cheek as he stepped back and looked down the line at the other prisoners.

"Forgive me," said the Russian, "for not making myself clear. Is not quite enough to speak English, you must speak *truth* in English."

The major nodded to his men, who grabbed the would-be translator and tossed him over the side, followed by another burst of automatic fire.

The major moved to the next English speaker in line and untaped his mouth. "Maybe is more efficient if we start with hard question, *da*? How long have you been pirate?"

"Four years and three months," said the man without hesitation.

The Russian smiled and patted the man's cheek.

"Good! Very good! I think we have good translator, *da*?"

Joshua Woodley sat in the inflatable and cursed under his breath as the Somali plunged into the water ten feet away and soaked him with the splash. He looked up just in time to see the Russian sergeant step to the ship's rail and fire two short bursts down into the water, a good twenty feet from where the bound pirate struggled in the cargo net suspended loosely underwater between the inflatable and one of the ship's lifeboats. He had to admit, the commies were puttin' on a damn good show.

Woody gestured to Junior West, his companion in the inflatable, who reached out with a long boat hook and snagged the back of the struggling pirate's shirt to drag him to the boat. Together, they pulled the man onboard. The pirate flopped about in the bottom of the boat, his bare heels making a dull thump on the plywood floorboards, and Woody unholstered a Glock and dropped down beside him. He held the pistol to the man's head and put his finger to his own lips, the message clear. Wide-eyed, the pirate nodded enthusiastically and stopped making noise. Together, Woody and Junior dragged the pirate forward, out of the way.

They hardly had time to resume their positions before the second pirate splashed down. Junior pulled the man to the boat side, and wrinkled his nose in disgust.

"Woody," he whispered. "This one's done shit himself!"

"Jeees-us Christ," muttered Woody, as he unsheathed a Buck knife. "Here," he whispered, handing Junior the knife. "I'll hold the boat hook and you reach down and cut his pants off. Then we'll dunk him up and down until he's clean. Ain't nothin' in this deal about ridin' around in a boat fulla pirate shit."

He waited while Junior sawed through the pirate's belt. A man had to have standards, after all.

Dugan and Blake watched as one of the Russians put the video camera back in its case as the others taped the prisoners' eyes and cut their ankle restraints, so they could move back to the jury-rigged holding cells under their own power. Dugan looked down at the clipboard in his hand, and nodded.

"It's a damn good start," he said. "Of thirty-four prisoners, we've got good representation from ten of the twelve pirate clans, complete with video confessions. Hopefully, when we complete the same drill on your bunch, we'll pick up some members of the other two clans. If we can pick up at least that many more between here and Harardheere, we'll have made a real dent in their operation and be in a pretty good negotiating position."

"What about the 'dead' pirates?" Blake asked.

Dugan shrugged. "We'll keep them isolated from the rest. I doubt we'll have many more from *Marie Floyd* after Borgdanov finishes his little act."

"Yeah, well, I'm not real sure the Russians were acting," Blake said. "I suspect they'd do it for real in a heartbeat, and that's what made it convincing. And speaking of convincing, what about these confessions? I mean, we nailed them in the act, so there's no question of their guilt, but I doubt these confessions would hold up in court. It's pretty obvious they were coerced."

"Maybe not a US or UK court," he said, "but I don't think we'll have any problem in Liberia." He shrugged. "But it won't come to that. The confessions are just window-dressing for negotiations."

Blake nodded, then stared off in the distance with a troubled look on his face.

"What's up, Vince?" Dugan asked. "Things couldn't be going any better, and you look like someone just killed your puppy."

Blake looked back at Dugan with a wan smile. "Sorry. Just engaging in the time-honored tradition among captains of worrying about what's over the horizon. It's been easy so far. We've been at this less than a week and snapped up over sixty pirates. Sooner or later, the rest of them have to start worrying about all their buddies just disappearing. Then they may start getting cagey."

Dugan shrugged. "Maybe, but remember, these guys are pretty decentralized. I think realization is going to dawn gradually."

Blake looked doubtful. "I don't know, we may be pushing our luck. What happens if they stop sending out far-ranging scout-attack boats and keep operations closer to the mother ships? We might find ourselves up to our asses in more pirates than we can handle. If we lose the element of surprise, we're not in real good shape."

"Well, pal," Dugan said, "I guess we just have to hope that doesn't happen."

M/T PHOENIX LYNX
AT ANCHOR
HARARDHEERE, SOMALIA

"Silver? You're sure?" Zahra asked.

Omar nodded. "Great piles of it on deck, according to our man. At least a million of the old silver Saudi riyals. Worth much more than face value now."

"A fortune, no doubt," Zahra said. "But it still doesn't seem the sort of operation one would expect from the fanatics. And why hasn't Mukhtar looted the treasure and withdrawn? Surely he knows it's only a matter of time before he has company from the Omanis."

"I don't know, Zahra, but apparently he's promised the whole treasure will be divided among the men, and he's moved the ship to go after something else. Our man doesn't know what. Mukhtar allows no one but hard-core al-Shabaab followers in the control and operations areas. The speculation onboard is that he's going after an even richer treasure of gold or diamonds."

Zahra scoffed. "The speculation of fools. If there were such riches in the offing, the salvage operation would have brought those up first." He considered that a moment. "But still, Mukhtar is a fanatic, not a fool. If he's ignoring the treasure at hand to continue a search, then he's after something of immense value."

"What'll we do?" Omar asked.

"Nothing, for the moment. Have our man notify us the instant he discovers what Mukhtar's after. Then we'll decide."

"It will be done," Omar said, then hesitated.

"What is it, Omar?"

"These disappearances. Do you think they're somehow linked to Mukhtar?"

Zahra nodded. "It's crossed my mind. We've lost two boats and twelve men. The other bands are reporting similar strange disappearances, not so far from Mukhtar's drillship."

"A coincidence?"

"A bit too much of a coincidence," Zahra said. "I suspect he may have hunter boats of his own out to establish a perimeter."

"But surely, if he destroyed so many boats, a few of them would have gotten off a warning to their mother ships," Omar said.

Zahra shrugged. "Perhaps not. The turncoats that defected to al-Shabaab have no strong clan ties, and the lure of treasure is great. If they approached one of our boats, they'd be greeted as brothers. They could kill everyone in the boat before anyone got off a warning."

Omar nodded. "I suppose that explanation might fit."

"It's the only one that does," Zahra replied. "Warn our boats to be suspicious of any launches that approach them. I'll alert the other bands to the possibility."

Omar turned to go, but Zahra stopped him with an upraised hand.

"And Omar, I've been discussing the hostage executions with the other groups. It's clear they're having little impact. We've executed three so far, and still no owner has paid a ransom. We're going increase the rate of executions to one a day. Tomorrow's our turn to contribute a hostage. Pick one of the sick ones that might die anyway."

"It will be done," said Omar.

CHAPTER FOURTEEN

Jesse Ward closed the yellowed folder and pushed it away, almost as if he was afraid it might contaminate him. He looked across the conference table.

"Jesus Christ, Joe. *Logs*?"

The analyst nodded. "I'm not making it up. Apparently when they built their research facility in China in the 1930s, the Japanese claimed it was a lumber mill. I guess calling their human guinea pigs 'logs' was some sick bastard's idea of humor."

Ward looked shaken. "I'd heard of Unit 731 before, but I never checked out the specifics. These were some seriously bad people. What happened to them?"

"To most of them, nothing," said the analyst. "A lot of them, apparently including our friend Dr. Imamura, ended up working for us."

"That's disgusting!"

Joe shrugged. "Can't say I disagree. On the other hand, as nasty as these people were, they were the leading experts on chemical and biological warfare. The Cold War was upon us. We had the atomic bomb and the Soviets were looking for a counter. A lot of the 'logs' the Japs used were Soviet citizens kidnapped in cross-border raids from Manchuria, and the Soviets were demanding that all Unit 731 personnel be turned over to them for trial. Everyone was pretty sure they'd just fake executions and put these scientists to work on their own CBW program."

"So we just beat the Soviets to the punch and did the same thing, without fake executions," Ward finished. "Makes me proud to be an American."

"Well, at least for us they were working on defensive stuff, not weapons."

Ward scoffed. "Yeah, well. If you believe that, I've got a bridge to sell you."

"Look, Jesse. As long as other countries have—"

"I know, I know. You're right," Ward said. "I just have a problem with programs that make it hard to tell us from the bad guys."

The man nodded and changed the subject. "Any word on Imamura?"

"Still unconscious in the hospital. He may have had a stroke along with his heart attack. The guy's ninety-four with a do-not-resuscitate order. I suspect they're just checking him occasionally to see when to hang a toe tag." Ward sighed. "I doubt we'll get anything from him. Any luck connecting him to the sub?"

"None. What're we going to do?"

"What can we do?" Ward asked. "We have a hunch, no clue what was on the sub, and no idea if this guy Mukhtar is going after it. And our naval assets are all at least three days' steaming time away. I can't request repositioning on a hunch."

"So we…"

"So we wait and watch," Ward said. "And hope like hell nothing bad happens."

Dugan stood at the radar next to the captain in the early-morning light and watched the blip that was M/T *Marie Floyd*, well south of them. After much discussion, they'd decided to stay in the area for a few days, to continue to hunt at the edges of the pirates' normal range. They'd done well in this area, and as long as the pirate launches were ranging in front of the mother ships, they figured it safer to work the fringes. With luck, they could net enough captives to turn and head straight for the Somali coast and Harardheere. Running at full speed, they had more than enough fire power to discourage pirates from boarding, a much less-hazardous operation than offering themselves as bait.

The strategy had borne fruit. In the day since the interrogation of the prisoners, *Marie Floyd* had taken two more launches and *Pacific Endurance* had taken another, twenty more captives between the three boats. But it seemed a hollow victory when this morning's call to Alex had brought news of the murder of another of *Phoenix Lynx*'s crew, and the pirates' pledge to murder another seaman daily until payment of ransoms resumed. He swallowed his anger and wrestled with the idea of heading to Somalia with the hostages they had now, knowing every day's delay would cost another life.

"You got something, Cap?" asked Dugan.

"Possibly," said the captain, pointing at the screen. "She's on a reciprocal course and should pass us to starboard."

Dugan followed his finger and saw a faint blip. "Pirate?"

"Too soon to tell," the captain said, staring at the screen. "I don't think so. Too big and too slow. A fishing boat, if I had to guess. I'll keep an eye on her."

Twenty minutes later, the captain watched as the target seemed to split, with the smaller target on a direct course toward *Pacific Endurance* and moving fast.

"Trouble!" he said. "Looks like a mother ship, and she just launched an attack boat. They'll be on us in twenty minutes."

The captain moved to the console to dial in to the public-address system and order all hands to action stations. Dugan watched as the crew went through the transfer of steering and engine controls, and the captain moved back to Dugan's side at the radar for one final look before evacuating the bridge.

"Any chance *Marie Floyd* can close with us and present them two targets?" Dugan asked.

The captain moved the radar cursor to check the distance to their sister vessel. "Negative," he said, shaking his head. "The mother ship's slower, but she's too close. She'll be on us an hour before *Marie Floyd* can get close, even in the best of circumstances."

"Well," said Dugan, "not much we can do about it. I guess we just have to make sure we take care of the launch before momma shows up, and then play it by ear."

Dugan pulled out his sat-phone. "I'll let *Marie Floyd* know what's going on before we activate the jammers."

CIA HEADQUARTERS
MARITIME THREAT ASSESSMENT
LANGLEY, VA

Ward leaned back in his chair and stretched before looking at his watch. He'd lost track of time and missed dinner. Again. There'd be hell to pay from Dee Dee when he got home, if she wasn't already in bed when he got there. He turned off his computer and was locking his file cabinets when the phone rang. He considered not answering until he checked the caller ID.

"Ward," he said into the phone.

"Agent Ward, this is Dorothy Lomax."

"Yes, Mrs. Lomax. Thanks for returning my call."

"To be clear, Agent Ward, I'm not returning your call. I think you're a despicable person who has nothing better to do than harass a kind old man, even to the point of death. I could quite happily go to my grave having never spoken to you again."

"Ah… OK," Ward said. "Then suppose you tell me why you *did* call."

"Because despite my pleas, Dr. Imamura insists he must speak to you."

"He's awake?"

"He regained consciousness two hours ago."

"I'll be right there," Ward said.

Dorothy Lomax met Ward at the door to the hospital room and shooed him out into the hall. She glared at him.

"You're not to upset him. Is that clear?" she asked in a low voice.

"How is he?" Ward asked, ignoring her question.

"He's dying, Agent Ward," she said sadly, a gleam of moisture in her eye. "The doctor doesn't expect him to last the night." The glare returned. "And why he wants to spend even a second of what little time he has left talking to the likes of you, I have no idea. But I do know I'll not have you upsetting him."

"I'll try not to upset him," Ward said, moving around her toward the door.

"Oh, you'll do much more than try, Agent Ward," she said, following him into the room. "I'll see to it personally."

Imamura was a shriveled husk of a man, swallowed by the hospital bed. An IV tube was taped to one arm, and a multicolored display above the bed flashed the news to all who could interpret it that this was a man not long for the world. He turned his head on the pillow as Ward entered.

"Thank you for coming, Agent Ward," he said, his voice weak.

Ward nodded, as Imamura looked at Mrs. Lomax.

"Mrs. Lomax, you've been here constantly. Why don't you go get a bite to eat while I chat with Agent Ward?"

"I think I should stay, Doctor."

Imamura smiled weakly. "I know you do, my dear. But what I must discuss with Agent Ward involves my work, and you don't have the necessary security clearance. So as much as I would like to spend all my remaining hours in your company, I must ask you to leave us."

Mrs. Lomax opened her mouth to speak, then shut it and nodded. She left the room, closing the door behind her. Imamura turned back to Ward.

"A small deceit, Agent Ward. Mrs. Lomax is the last living person I care about and I hope to spare her details of my sordid past. But before I begin, perhaps you would share with me the nature of your interest in a German submarine sunk more than sixty years ago."

Ward shrugged. "I was hoping, as the only survivor of that sinking, you could tell me what my interest *should* be, especially since some very bad people seem intent on salvaging the sub."

"That... that's impossible," Imamura said. "*U-859* sank in over a mile and a half of water. Too deep to salvage."

"Perhaps it *was* impossible," Ward said. "But what was impossible yesterday is merely difficult and expensive today. The question is, what's there to salvage worth the cost and risk?"

"Perhaps you'd better sit, Agent Ward," Imamura said, his voice quaking. "It's rather a long story."

Ward shifted uncomfortably in the chair, his mind numb from Imamura's recitation. He struggled to get his mind around the horrific tale he'd just heard. "But that makes no sense," he said. "Just how did you even think Japan could survive this Operation Mi... Migoname?"

"*Minogame*," Imamura corrected. "The Minogame is a creature from Japanese folklore—a giant thousand-year-old turtle representing both longevity and protection. By withdrawing into the protection of his shell, Minogame lived one thousand years. That's how we intended to survive."

Ward looked puzzled, and Imamura continued.

"The virus was to be introduced in the European theater, as far from Japan as possible. The Germans were to deploy it in front-line weapons against both Allied and Soviet troops, but the incubation period was relatively long, up to a week before victims became symptomatic."

Imamura stopped and closed his eyes. Ward was afraid he'd lost consciousness, but the little man opened his eyes, took a labored breath, and continued. "However, we knew from our own experiments most were contagious within twenty-four hours of exposure. That would allow time for wounded men to rotate to the rear to aid stations, and visiting VIPs—who, of course, were always accorded priority air travel—to visit the field hospitals and carry the virus back to London, Washington, and Moscow. The long incubation period ensured the virus would be well established before the epidemic was even identified as such."

"But this… this engineered hantavirus. You claim it had a mortality rate of over seventy percent?"

"Seventy percent in an indigenous Chinese population that enjoyed some resistance to the original virus," corrected Imamura. "We projected a higher mortality rate in other populations, but we had no test data."

Ward wrestled with his disgust. "So back to my question. How could you hope to survive?"

"We anticipated we'd have time," Imamura said. "It would take several weeks or perhaps a month for the epidemic to become obvious. The first response would be denial, and the knee-jerk reaction would be to suppress the news to avoid panic. That, of course, is the exact opposite of what is needed to contain an epidemic. When we saw signs the epidemic was taking hold, we already had plans in place to begin a massive withdrawal of troops to the Japanese home islands, leaving twenty percent of our manpower in place facing the Allies. Those troops left in place would have firm orders to die where they stood, opposing an Allied breakthrough. They did not have to win, only sell their lives dearly to buy time for the virus to do its work."

"But when the Allies figured out they were the victims of biological warfare, they'd strike back hard, with massive air raids if nothing else," Ward said.

Imamura nodded. "We assumed as much, but who would they strike? Remember, all indications would point to the Germans, whose cities were already being pounded. At the time we initiated Operation Minogame, the Americans had limited ability to reach the Japanese home islands with land-based bombers. We hoped that, in their fury, the Allies would spend more of their resources striking the easiest targets, as the epidemic sapped their ability to strike at all."

"Which brings me to another part of this story I find a bit hard to swallow," Ward said. "I can't believe the Germans would go along with this."

"The Germans were duped, and I was part of that deception. They were shown a nerve toxin of Japanese origin to be used strategically in artillery shells. We—that is, the Japanese—were supposedly to use the toxin at the same time, with the stated purpose of demonstrating a united front to the Allies to prove that the Axis powers were willing to go to any lengths to stop them. The theory was, presented with the prospect of massive and unacceptable losses, the Allies would become amenable to a negotiated peace that would leave both Germany and Japan unoccupied."

Imamura drew a long, ragged breath. Ward reached for a glass of water on the bedside table, and held it while Imamura sucked from the bent straw.

He moved his mouth from the straw and water dribbled on his hospital gown.

"Thank you," he said, as Ward put the glass back on the table.

"I led a three-man team," Imamura said. "Our mission was to load the virus into the artillery shells, but approximately ten percent of the cylinders held nerve gas, should the Germans want to perform tests. Also, some of the artillery shells had to perform as advertised to ensure the Germans kept using them, at least for a time. Of course, a virus isn't a weapon one delivers with pinpoint accuracy. It was inevitable that the Germans would be infected as well."

"That means you..."

Imamura nodded. "I was sure to be infected, and if by some miracle I wasn't, I'm sure the enraged Germans would've killed me. I was to die for the emperor."

"Look, this is still nuts," Ward said. "How could Japan expect to survive?"

"Like Minogame, Agent Ward, inside a tight shell. The twenty percent of our forces still facing the Allies were to be only the first line of defense. There were to be three more concentric circles, with every ship or boat that floated and aircraft that flew prepared to hold the Allies at bay. They were to fight with what they had, with no more contact with Japan, and the home islands were to be isolated. As the epidemic took hold, it would, soon enough, spread from America to the troops facing Japan, attacking them from the rear, so to speak. On the US mainland, there'd be fewer Americans to build weapons, and no one to man the ships to bring the weapons to the front. In six months America would be fighting for its life, struggling to maintain any sort of civilization, as seventy to eighty percent of the world population perished. Japan would be the least of their worries."

"And then what?" asked Ward. "Japan's not self-sufficient, then or now."

"The people were already inured to hardship because of the war, a bit more was bearable. Rationing would be even more strictly enforced, and as military resistance against us collapsed, we'd plans to devote all the resources of the war effort into survival. We'd subsistence-farm every square meter of land, including rooftop gardens in the cities, and send out fishing fleets with navy escorts to ensure they came in contact with no one. We'd hoard every bit of fuel left over from the war effort to supply the fishing fleet and their escorts. Survival would be hard, but Japan would survive as a cohesive nation, and as such, the most powerful force on earth. When we did eventually emerge, we'd have the power to take what we needed, for there would be no one left to oppose us."

Ward bit back his anger. He was both repulsed and fascinated by what he was hearing. "And how'd you plan to 'emerge'? Did you have a vaccine?"

Imamura shook his head. "There was no vaccine—not that we didn't try to develop one. The virus defeated our every attempt. But every virus mutates with each generation as it spreads through a population, and the more successful it is—and by that I mean, the more virulent and deadly it is—the faster it seems to mutate to something weaker and more benign. A case in point is the Bubonic plague, the Black Death of the Middle Ages. Though a bacteria rather than a virus, there are parallels. Bubonic plague still exists today, but it's much less a threat than the form that wiped out a significant percentage of the world's population." Imamura drew another ragged breath. "Japanese are patient people. We planned to send out survey teams periodically, in contact by radio, to check on the mutation of the virus. They, of course, would never return to Japan, but set up monitoring enclaves. We were prepared to wait five, or even twenty-five, years for the virus to mutate into a less virulent form. Of course, we hoped it wouldn't take so long."

"Yeah, I'd have hated for you to be inconvenienced," Ward said, unable to contain himself any longer.

"I understand your anger, Agent Ward. And whether you believe me or not, you can't hate me more than I've hated myself for many years."

Ward nodded, calmer now. "I'd be much angrier if I didn't doubt the whole story. Something like you're describing would have required cooperation and coordination with a lot of people, and I've never even heard a hint of anything like it. I'm supposed to believe that you're the only one who knew?"

"The secret was closely guarded. Dr. Ishii's concept was—"

Ward interrupted. "That's Dr. Shiro Ishii, the head of Unit 731?"

"Correct," Imamura said. "Ishii was a powerful man with the emperor's ear. Less than fifty people knew of Operation Minogame, and as soon as surrender was announced, they all died or disappeared under mysterious circumstances, days before MacArthur ever set foot on Japanese soil. I was interned in a British POW camp in Oman and presumed dead, so no one was looking for me in the chaos of postwar Japan. The British knew nothing of my background and seemed indifferent. To them, I was just another Jap. When I was repatriated in 1946, my wife was terrified and told me of the deaths of all my former colleagues. The very next morning, we bundled up our few belongings and went to the American occupation authorities. I confessed I was a former member of Unit 731 and offered my services. By blind luck, I was interrogated by an OSS officer who recognized my potential usefulness. I didn't tell him of Operation Minogame, nor have I spoken to anyone about it until today, for the very reason you just confirmed. I knew no one would believe me. I'm telling you now because of what you've told me of this salvage operation." Imamura looked at Ward. *"You cannot let that happen!"*

Ward processed what he'd just learned. He didn't know quite what he'd expected, but certainly not the fantastic tale he'd just heard.

"Even assuming what you've told me is true, that was decades ago. You can't possibly imagine these weapons are still viable."

"Believe me, Agent Ward," Imamura said, "I've imagined little else for over sixty years. The containers were stainless steel of the finest grade, so corrosion will be minimal. Pressure will be extreme due to the depth—over thirty-five hundred pounds per square inch by my rough calculations—but the cylinders were thick-walled, with a small cross-sectional diameter. They may be crushed, but I doubt they ruptured."

"So what," Ward said. "Even if everything is intact, the nerve gas and virus would have degraded over time."

"Possibly, but it's very cold at that depth—a degree or two above freezing. I suspect there would be degradation of the nerve gas, though some of it's probably still lethal. But I'm most concerned about the virus. In our tests it was extremely hardy, and able to survive in all manner of environments. At extremely low temperatures, it almost seemed to hibernate, for want of a better word. I think, given the size of the shipment, some might survive. It takes only a tiny bit to begin replicating."

"Let me get this straight," Ward said. "You help engineer a deadly virus that can wipe out civilization as we know it, and thankfully, it gets sent to the bottom of the ocean. You then say nothing for over sixty years until you're on your deathbed. Don't you think it would have been a bit more useful to tell us about it a bit sooner—say, fifty-nine years ago—so we could have been working on a vaccine?"

"Did your investigation reveal my former position at USAMRIID?"

"Sure," Ward said. "Senior researcher in infectious diseases."

"And did it also," Imamura asked, "reveal my specialty?" He continued without waiting for an answer. "I was senior researcher for hantavirus and related viruses. I worked on nothing but finding a vaccine or cure for over forty years, but I was hampered by both inability and unwillingness to reproduce the actual strain we'd developed in Japan." He smiled wanly. "So condemn me as a monster if you will, Agent Ward, for I deserve that. But never doubt I labored mightily to put the genie back in the bottle. I regret that I failed."

The silence grew until Ward broke it. "If someone *is* trying to raise this virus, what do you recommend?"

"Do everything in your power to see that it doesn't surface," Imamura said, with a fierceness that belied his fragile condition. "If you fail, then redouble your efforts to destroy it. And most importantly, if it does come into your control, don't be swayed by those who will want to keep it to study for 'defensive purposes,' because that's the siren song. Unit 731 started with the noble aim of preventing disease, and ended cultivating those very diseases as weapons. Power corrupts, Agent Ward, as surely as the sun rises."

Imamura had risen onto one elbow as he spoke, gesturing at Ward with his hand for emphasis. The effort proved too much for him and he collapsed back on the bed with those last words, his breathing labored.

Ward stood. "Are you all right?"

A smile flickered at the corners of the old man's mouth. "As 'all right' as a dying man can be, I suppose."

"I... I meant..."

"I know what you meant, Agent Ward, and thank you. I'm fine, but if there's nothing else I can tell you..."

"No. I can't think of anything."

"Very well then," said Imamura. "Good luck in your operation."

"Thank you," Ward said, moving toward the door.

Mrs. Lomax was sitting in an uncomfortable-looking plastic chair in the hallway, clutching a well-worn Bible. She rose as soon as she saw Ward, and pushed past him before he could speak. He shrugged and headed for the elevator.

"Dr. Imamura?" Mrs. Lomax called.

Eyes flickered open and Imamura gave her a weak smile.

"Would you like me to read you some scripture, Doctor?"

"Why yes, Mrs. Lomax," Imamura said, "I'd like that very much."

CHAPTER FIFTEEN

Ward hadn't bothered to go home—he was already in the doghouse with Dee Dee. He'd just texted her he was working over and gone back to the office. He was still there after midnight, peering through a magnifying glass at satellite photos of *Ocean Goliath*, searching for some clue of a problem aboard. As far as he could tell, it was business as usual aboard the drillship, with Mukhtar's presence the only indication something might be wrong. And even that was circumstantial, revealed by the presence of a sat-phone signal, hardly conclusive. He didn't even know for sure the drillship was going after the damned sub. But what if it was? Imamura's nightmarish scenario replayed itself in his mind's eye.

He laid the magnifying glass on his desk and leaned back in his chair, pondering his options. How could he mount an operation against a perfectly legal and high-profile salvage operation taking place in international waters, funded by a rich Omani with American connections? Based on what? A *suspicion* there was a terrorist aboard? A *suspicion* that they were trying to salvage devastating bioweapons from a long-lost submarine? A *suspicion* based on no hard evidence whatsoever, but on the dying words of a ninety-four-year-old man who may or may not be delusional? No one above him in the food chain would authorize an operation based on what he had. But then, no one else had heard Imamura's story, and Ward knew in his gut the man had been telling the truth.

But he couldn't proceed without more intel, and collecting it without alerting the terrorists was a problem. He couldn't very well contact the company in Houston, since he didn't know who might be involved in an effort to salvage a bioweapon, or even if such an operation was underway. And even if no one ashore was involved, they might inadvertently let something slip during later communications with the drillship. No, he had to figure some way to gather intel independently, and it was pretty damn tough to sneak up on someone in the middle of the ocean. Unless you look like something they expect to see.

He thought of Dugan's nondescript tankers. According to his last unofficial report from Anna, the two ships were a day's run from the *Ocean Goliath*. What if one of those tankers could pass close to *Ocean Goliath* in the night? Nothing to cause alarm, just a tanker in innocent passage. And what if that tanker pumped a bit of oil overboard in the darkness? Not a lot, just enough to cause a sheen. Enough of a sheen to attract attention from shore to investigate the source of the pollution. His resources in Oman were limited, but he'd deal with that later—for now, he just needed to talk Dugan into a little side trip.

He looked at his watch—coming up on midmorning in the Arabian Sea. He dialed Dugan's sat-phone and got a recording, hung up without leaving a message, and tried again five minutes later with the same result. After three tries, he left Dugan a message to call him no matter what the time, and hung up.

He sat for a moment, weighing the benefits of going home. He'd have to be back in the office in four hours anyway, and the hour and a half round-trip to his house would have to come out of that time. He sighed and moved to his office sofa, and stretched out to wait for sleep that never came.

M/T *PACIFIC ENDURANCE*
ARABIAN SEA

Dugan watched on the safe-room monitor as the first pirate scrambled aboard, trailed by five more. Following what Dugan now knew was standard pirate operating procedure, one man remained in the boat and moved it away from the ship to starboard, maintaining his distance from the wildly swinging stern of *Pacific Endurance*. Dugan nodded, and cranked the sound-powered phone.

"*Da*," answered Borgdanov in the officers' mess room.

"Six, repeat, six papas onboard," Dugan said. "Stand by and I'll notify you when they're inside and locked down."

"Standing by," Borgdanov replied.

Dugan watched as the pirates left the field of vision of the deck cameras and waited for them to appear on the passageway cameras inside the house. He didn't have to wait long before he saw the outside door open and the pirates move into the passageway.

"Papas are in the house," he said into the phone. "I count one, two, three, four—damn! Four papas inside, repeat, four papas inside. I'll wait a bit on the other two before I lock down."

"Standing by," Borgdanov said.

As Dugan watched the monitor, the four pirates moved toward the centerline of the ship and began to file into the central stairwell. Dugan spoke into the phone.

"All four papas in stairwell, I am locking down before we lose what we have. You'll have to adjust," he said.

"OK," Borgdanov replied, and Dugan threw the switch that sucked the magnetic bolts home on all the exterior deckhouse doors and all the stairwell doors above A-Deck, trapping the pirates. Then he turned off the lights in the windowless passageway and stairwell, plunging the pirates into darkness.

"Locked and dark," he said into the phone. "All four papas in the stairwell but out of camera range. I have no visual."

"Do not worry, *Dyed*," Borgdanov said. "We will get them."

I sure as hell hope so, thought Dugan, as he watched Borgdanov and his men in the feed from the night-vision cameras as they moved into the darkened passageway, the combination of night-vision goggles over gas masks making them look strangely alien. They moved to the central stairwell and Borgdanov directed his men with hand signals, his silent commands revealing nothing to the pirates in the darkness. At his signal, one Russian held open the fire door and two more rushed into the stairwell, returning in seconds, each dragging a scrawny pirate they had clubbed senseless in the darkness. Two more Russians rushed into the breach with tear-gas grenades and they also returned in seconds, empty-handed, as the Russian holding the door pulled it closed. Dugan saw flashes of light around the edges of the stairwell fire door and Borgdanov making a wait signal, holding his men for what seemed like an eternity before sending them back into the stairwell. They emerged with one man with bound hands and taped eyes and another who appeared unconscious. Borgdanov waved his men and their captives back toward the officers' mess room, blocked open the fire door to the stairwell, and moved after his men to enter the door to the officers' mess and close it behind him. Dugan nodded and started the ventilation fans just as the light of the sound-powered phone flashed.

"I am sorry, *Dyed*," Borgdanov's voice came from the phone, "but we lost one. I hoped to take the last two with the gas, but I think the one highest up the stairs panicked when he heard his comrade behind him in the dark. Before the gas got him, he shot down stairs and killed his comrade." Borg-danov paused. "Where are other two papas?"

Dugan was flipping through the other monitor feeds as he listened to Borgdanov. He located the missing pirates just as the Russian finished speaking.

"They're both on the bridge, looking confused," Dugan said. "You think they heard the gunfire in the stairwell?"

"Is impossible that they did not," Borgdanov said. "What about papa in boat?"

Dugan pulled up the starboard bridge-wing camera feed in the second monitor.

"He's maintaining position. I don't think he's on to us, and I think he's close enough to still be inside our jammer range," Dugan said. "But it's close."

"OK," said Borgdanov. "I think these two on bridge are scared and will stay together now. We must take them without alerting comrade in boat. If he warns mother ship, we have big problem I think. I will take one man up stairwell to bridge deck and wait. I send Ilya and three men to port side, out of sight of man in boat. They will make distraction and draw papas to port side. When you see them react and rush to port, you throw switch and un-lock stairwell door. That will be my signal to rush out and take them from behind. I think they will surrender, but if not, we shoot first and our weap-ons are suppressed. If we are lucky, man in boat hears nothing. Then we make plan to take him."

"Why don't I just unlock the doors now? Maybe they'll come to you."

"No, *Dyed*. Stairwell smells of tear gas even with ventilation. They will not enter, I think. Also, magnetic locks make noise, and they will be already jumpy, as you say in English. Trust me, *Dyed*. These are not soldiers, only *piraty* and *prestupnikov*—pirates and criminals."

"OK, how do you want to time it?" Dugan asked.

"Is self-timing, *Dyed*. Ilya's diversion makes prestupnikov go to port side. You watch and unlock doors after they move to port. Door unlocking is my signal to spring trap. Simple plan is always best, *da*?"

"All right," Dugan said. "Make sure your guys have their night vision se-cured and I'll give you some light."

Korfa crouched on the port side, one deck below the bridge, tensing for his final charge. He took a deep breath and rushed up the steep stairs, his foot-steps ringing on the metal treads, and covered the distance from the top of the ladder to the wheelhouse door in seconds, his weapon at the ready. To find—Ghedi charging in from the starboard side.

The two pirates stared at each other in confusion.

"Where's the crew?" Ghedi asked.

Korfa said nothing, but tried to absorb what he was seeing. The big ship was plowing ahead, its bow swinging radically as the tanker made rapid and frequent course changes, the standard evasive technique to prevent pirate boarding.

Except no one was at the wheel, or on the bridge at all.

"It's a ghost ship," Ghedi whispered.

Korfa snorted. "Don't be a superstitious fool."

Both men flinched at the sound of gunfire.

"That was no ghost," Korfa said, nodding to the stairwell door and raising his weapon. "Go check it! I'll cover you."

"Perhaps you should check it, and I'll cover you," Ghedi replied.

"All right," Korfa said. "Perhaps we should both just cover the door and see who emerges."

Ghedi nodded, and the pirates took positions on either side of the chart table, weapons pointed at the stairwell door.

Dugan watched the pirates on the monitor and cursed the lack of communication. With the jammers activated and Borgdanov away from a sound-powered phone, there was no way to warn him that the pirates lay in wait outside the door. He switched the other monitor from the pirate in the boat and started cycling through the port-side camera feeds, hoping to catch a glimpse of the other Russians who were preparing the diversion. There was a flash of black as one of the Russians moved into view on the port-side exterior stairway, and Dugan's mind raced as he tried to figure out what to do. If the pirates *didn't* take the bait and move to the port bridge wing, there was no way he was releasing the magnetic lock and sending Borgdanov into a trap. Then what? Perhaps "simple plan" was *not* always the best.

Sergeant Ilya Denosovitch stood on A-deck and debated whether to space his men out on the charge up the outside stairway or to group them together. Any way he spaced them, they would be sitting ducks for even a halfway-competent marksman firing down on them from the bridge wing. But that wasn't likely, given what he'd seen of the *piraty's* competence, coupled with the fact that the major would be attacking them from the rear as soon as they rushed to port. Presuming, of course, *Dyed* got the door unlocked promptly. The sergeant decided to rush the ladder as a group and nodded, sending his men clamoring up the ladder, each man pounding the rail with a free hand as he climbed, multiplying the sound of their approach. Both pirates jerked at the din coming from the port side.

"What's that?" asked Ghedi.

"Go check," said Korfa, and after a slight hesitation, Ghedi moved to the port door and onto the bridge wing.

Korfa heard a burst of automatic fire to port, and Ghedi was back on the bridge. "Soldiers," he yelled. "Coming up the port stairway."

"How many?" Korfa demanded.

"At least a dozen," Ghedi gasped, moving toward the starboard door. "I didn't stay to count."

Korfa took a last look at the closed stairwell door, and turned to flee to starboard with Ghedi.

Dugan watched, racked with indecision, as one pirate moved to port and the other maintained his watch on the stairwell door. The pirate to port fired a burst down the outside stairway, and then rushed back across the bridge, shouting at the other pirate. The man at the stairwell door gave the door one last look, and then joined his companion, both headed for the outside starboard stairway. So much for the plan. Dugan released the lock on the stairwell door.

Borgdanov heard the magnetic bolt release and burst onto the bridge, his weapon at the ready. Instead of seeing the *piraty* to port as he expected, they were fleeing to starboard, and had almost reached the door to the starboard bridge wing. He fired a short burst ahead of them, in an attempt to contain but not kill them, spider-webbing the thick glass of the bridge window. The *piraty* didn't even slow down. They were through the door to the bridge wing and starting down the open stairway on the starboard side before he even reached the door to the bridge wing.

He turned as Denosovitch and his men rushed onto the bridge.

"Ilya," Borgdanov said. "Send your men down the central stairwell to keep the pirates from entering the deckhouse from below. I will keep pressure on them from above. It will be easier to hunt them on the open deck without so much cover. You set up here on the bridge wing. You know what to do."

"*Da,*" Denosovitch said, and deployed his men as ordered.

Dugan watched the scene unfold on the bridge, and switched the second monitor to the pirate launch. The boat driver was staring toward the ship, aware something was wrong. The cat was out of the bag.

Erasto kept an eye on the ship and matched her movements expertly, as the vessel maintained her foolish evasive maneuvers. Didn't they know his brothers were already aboard? He jerked at the sound of gunfire from the bridge. He saw two Somalis emerge and rush down the outside stairway. He couldn't make out their features, but he recognized his cousin Korfa from his red shirt. The men were halfway down the ladder when a large soldier in a black uniform appeared above them, chasing them and loosing an occasional burst of gunfire as he came.

He maintained station, unsure what to do, and as he watched, the Somalis reached the main deck. He heard them scream his name just before they leaped over the starboard side, and he turned the Zodiac toward them, intent on rescue.

Dugan watched the pirates jump. *Idiots!*

"Stop the engine!" he said, and the captain cranked furiously on the sound-powered phone to alert the chief engineer beside the engine.

But it wasn't a finely tuned control system, and Dugan knew it was over before it started. *Pacific Endurance* was halfway through a hard turn to port when the pirates jumped, with her stern slewing to starboard. The pirates slipped under the stern and through the big propeller before the chief engineer even touched the engine control.

Erasto knew it was too late, even as his friends hit the water. Their heads surfaced less than a meter from the ship's hull, and then it was moving over them and toward Erasto, a giant steel wall rushing forward with the combined speed of the ship's swing added to the speed of his own boat. He shoved the outboard tiller hard to starboard, and the Zodiac veered to port, slamming the starboard side of the little craft hard against the advancing steel wall of the hull. For one terrible moment he thought the boat would turn over, but it was pushed along by the swinging hull, trapped by the force of the water, the bow of the little Zodiac pointing toward the stern of the ship.

The ship began to slow, loosening its hold on the Zodiac, and Erasto gave the outboard full throttle to shoot down the hull, under the ship's stern and away from her. Astern of the ship, water stained red with his comrades blood still roiled from the slowing propeller. He circled far to starboard of the tanker, intent on getting back to the mother ship. He'd be back, and he wouldn't be alone.

The steel deck was hot on the sergeant's chest and stomach as he lay prone on the rear of the bridge wing, even through the body armor and uniform. He wished he'd had something to lie on. Denosovitch put his eye to the scope of the Dragunov sniper rifle and zeroed in on the passing pirate launch. It'd be easier now that the ship had stopped turning and was drifting through the calm water. The shooting platform grew more stable by the second.

He zeroed in on the outboard motor, leading a bit to compensate, and placed two shots into it in quick succession. He was rewarded by an almost-instant cessation of the noise drifting across the water and a thick smoke billowing out of the outboard, as the Zodiac drifted to a stop. Now to collect Mr. Pirate. He sighed as he saw the man dig in his pocket.

The sat-phone wasn't quite to the pirate's ear when the man's head exploded.

The sergeant shrugged. Some *piraty* just had a death wish.

CHAPTER SIXTEEN

M/T *Pacific Endurance*
Arabian Sea

"We can outrun them," Dugan said, as he peered into the radar.

"*Da*," Borgdanov said. "The mother ship we can outrun. But her attack boats? How many does she have? This we do not know. And remember, *Dyed*, we just took out attack boat from this mother ship while she is in radar range. *This* mother ship will know we either have comrades aboard or that we killed them. She will trail us, I think, sending out attack boats to harass us, and call others to join the hunt. And if we, how you say... ziggy... ziggy..."

"Zigzag," Dugan said.

"*Da*. Zigzag. If we zigzag to help hold off attack from chase boats, I think we cannot even outrun mother ship. To escape, we must first at least cripple them so we can break contact."

"And just how do we do that?" Dugan asked.

"They will be cautious, but also confused. If we outrun her, she will send attack boats. But if we drift..." Borgdanov shrugged. "I think maybe she is curious and will come close enough for us to damage mother ship and attack boats. Then we run."

"If that's a mother ship, they've got a lot of men aboard. You've got six men."

"Make that twelve," said a voice behind him. Dugan turned to find Woody and his five-man crew just coming onto the bridge.

"Goddammit, Woody," Dugan said. "What're you doing here? I told you all to stay in the safe room."

"Reckoned y'all could use a hand," said Woody. "And if you think I'm gonna be stuck down in some hidey hole waiting for a bunch of friggin' pirates to overrun the ship and capture my ass, you got another think coming, Dugan."

"Look, Woody," Dugan said, "you're not trained—"

"Screw you, Dugan. I was in the Corps." He nodded at the older man beside him. "And so was Dave here. He was in Hue while I was at Khe Sanh." Woody glared at Dugan. "And Junior here was at Fallujah. Maybe you heard of 'em all?" Woody kept his eyes on Dugan and spoke back over his shoulder. "How 'bout you other boys?"

"Fallujah. Both times."

"Nasiriyah."

"Najaf."

Woody smiled at Dugan. "Ole Ray Hanley likes us vets," he said. "And I expect we got enough training to take on a buncha raggedy-ass pirates."

"Maybe so," Dugan said. "But you'd have to use the captured guns, and there's not much ammo for them."

Woody's smile broadened. "Nice thing about those private jets, the security ain't quite so tight. You didn't think all those crates we brought aboard were tools, did you?" Woody extended his arm toward Junior West, who produced an M-4 carbine from behind his back and handed it to Woody.

Dugan opened his mouth to say something, then seemed to think better of it. He turned to Borgdanov. "What do you say, Major?"

The Russian stared at the Americans, then nodded, looking straight at Woody. "I think is good thing, so long as you understand there can be but one leader. You agree to follow my orders?"

Woody nodded back. "I reckon I can live with that. Provided you're open to a suggestion from an old sergeant now and again."

Dugan stood on the starboard bridge wing of the drifting *Pacific Endurance*, clad in one of the captain's extra uniform shirts with four-stripe epaulettes, with his hands raised in the universal sign of surrender, watching the approaching mother ship. Of course, *ship* was a bit of a misnomer. She looked to be a fishing boat, about eighty feet long, hard-used and rust-streaked. The name *Kyung Yang No. 173* on her battered bow confirmed her to be Korean—no doubt hijacked and pressed into service by the pirates. But the most prominent feature of the approaching vessel was not hardware but humans.

"Christ!" Dugan said under his breath. "She's crawling with friggin' pirates! There must be fifty of them."

"Weapons?" asked Borgdanov from where he crouched out of sight behind the wind dodger.

"Assault rifles. Some RPGs. I count six—no, seven RPGs. Nothing heavier."

"Boats?" asked the Russian.

"Three," Dugan said. "All rigid inflatables. Two towed along their starboard side and one on the aft deck. So far, so good. No one in the boats. Looks like they're going to check us out from the mother ship before they send anyone over."

"That is good," said Borgdanov. "How are they approaching?"

"They're coming alongside with their starboard side to ours and their bow pointed at our stern," Dugan said. "The boat on deck will be below you and to your left when you stand where I am now. You should have a clear shot at it, leaving the other two for your guys."

"What about the others?"

Dugan looked down the length of the main deck. "They're ready," he said.

Borgdanov's black-clad Russians were all hidden from sight in the pump room or behind machinery, but Woody's men were hidden in plain sight. Four were sprawled on the deck from the stern to the midship manifold, apparent victims of the pirate attack. Woody and Junior were draped across the rail, as if they'd been killed trying to repel boarders. Liberal use of blood from the pirate slain in the stairwell completed the illusion. Each of the 'victims' was within a few steps of the cover of a mooring winch or tank hatch, where their M-4 assault rifles waited. The theory was that with the ship dead in the water, littered with bodies, and the captain on the bridge making an obvious gesture of surrender, the pirates would be less suspicious. Dugan looked back toward the approaching vessel. That was the theory. He sure as hell hoped it would work.

"Remember, *Dyed*," said Borgdanov's voice below him, "the closer they come, the better. They must be within fifty meters for me to have the best chance to take out the boat with the RPG. My shot will also be signal for others to open fire."

"How could I forget?" Dugan said out of the side of his mouth. "That's about the tenth time you've told me."

Borgdanov said nothing, and Dugan watched the pirate approach at dead slow. The boat pulled even with him, a bit beyond Borgdanov's specified fifty meters, and Dugan saw the water roil at the stern of the boat as she reversed engine to stop her forward motion.

"We got a couple of little problems," said Dugan, trying to keep his mouth from moving.

"What problems?" asked the Russian.

"They're a bit farther away than fifty meters, but I figure we have to take what we can get. The bigger problem is, about twenty of the assholes have me in their sights and look like they'd really like to pull their triggers."

"Just drop straight to the deck very fast. You will be out of sight before they can react."

"I'm not worried about *me*, genius. What happens when you pop up in the same exact spot seconds later? They'll blow you away in a heartbeat. We should've thought this through a little more."

"Where are my men?" yelled a pirate across the gap.

Oops! Dugan hadn't figured on a speaking part.

"Como?" he yelled back. "No hablo Ingles."

Even over the distance, Dugan could read the confused body language of the head pirate as he conferred with the man next to him.

"Look," Dugan said out of the side of his mouth. "I'm going to drop, then try to draw their fire away. Don't pop up until you hear them shooting at me. Got it?"

Silence.

"God damn it, Borgdanov. Got it?"

"*Da*, but be careful, *Dyed*," the Russian said.

Dugan dropped straight down to the deck, out of sight of the pirates in their lower position. He heard indignant shouts, and a hail of automatic fire filled the area where he'd previously stood, the bullets smashing into the thick glass of the side bridge windows behind him. He crawled across the deck on elbows and knees, the hot steel burning his unprotected forearms as the anti-skid surface scraped his elbows. He stopped fifteen feet from the rear of the wheelhouse and got into a runner's starting stance, higher than he was before but still low enough to be out of the line of sight of the pirates in the lower vessel. He counted to three and then bolted upright, his upper body in full view of the pirates, covering the distance to the back of the wheelhouse in four long strides. He slipped out of sight around the corner of the wheelhouse as bullets slammed into the structure where he'd been, whining off into the distance. He leaned back against the wheelhouse bulkhead, his heart pounding, as he heard the explosion of the major's RPG. Then all hell broke loose.

Borgdanov was up as soon as Dugan disappeared from sight around the corner of the wheelhouse. He found his target exactly where Dugan had said it would be, and fired the RPG as he heard cries of alarm from the *piraty* that spotted him. Even without looking, he saw them in his mind's eye turning their weapons toward him, and he dropped out of sight just before a tsunami of automatic fire engulfed the bridge of *Pacific Endurance*, the din magnified as the hail of fire smashed the side windows of the bridge or ricocheted off steel bulkheads. He heard two more explosions, distinct even in the cacophony of noise, and crawled on his stomach to peek down over the edge of the deck. There was nothing but smoking debris where the two launches had previously floated alongside the pirate vessel, proof his men's RPGs had been successful as well.

There was bedlam on the pirate ship as the surprised *piraty* fell from covering fire laid down by his remaining men and the Americans. The *piraty* dived for cover and responded with wild, undisciplined fire at the ship itself, as if they thought they could sink the huge vessel with small-arms fire. Then he saw a man rise with an RPG, and turned and crawled for all he was worth away from his former firing position. He had no doubt where that RPG would be aimed.

Woody hung over the rail, playing possum with one eye open. As soon as Borgdanov's RPG took out the boat on the aft deck of the pirate vessel, he bolted from the rail.

"Cover," he yelled to Junior. "Pass it on!"

On the pirate ship all eyes were on *Pacific Endurance*'s bridge, and the Americans were under cover and armed in seconds, well before any of the pirates noticed. Woody yelled for his men to lay down covering fire as two more Russians leaped from their hiding places with RPGs to take out the boats tied to the mother ship.

He watched as the raggedy-ass pirates scrambled for cover, some dropping along the way. Their return fire, when it came, was furious but inaccurate. Their AKs weren't much in the accuracy department to begin with, and the dumbasses were keeping them on full automatic, pretty much making hitting anything a matter of luck. But even dumbasses can get lucky, Woody reminded himself, and glanced along the deck to make sure all his boys were staying under cover.

When he glanced back, he saw a pirate rising with an RPG hit by at least two rounds, but not before he fired his weapon. Woody flinched as the starboard bridge wing was enveloped in an explosion, and hoped no one was on the receiving end.

"Take out the RPGs!" Woody shouted, and the order was relayed from man to man.

The next pirate that tried to fire was hit before he could aim, but the rocket leaped across the distance between the two vessels and slammed into the hull of *Pacific Endurance* to explode in a fireball, well above the waterline. Another pirate died before he even raised the tube of the weapon, and taking note, the four remaining RPG men fired from cover without aiming, in the general direction of *Pacific Endurance*. Two rockets flew over the ship, missing her completely, as one obliterated the starboard lifeboat. But in keeping with Woody's observation that even dumbasses get lucky, the fourth slammed into the hull at the waterline, in way of the aft-peak tank.

The captain sat at the makeshift control console in the safe room jury-rigged in the aft-peak tank, feeling neither in control or safe as he'd watched the pirate vessel approach via the feed from the starboard-bridge-wing camera. His functions were to be ready to pass engine orders to the chief engineer at the local controls of the main engine and to steer the ship away from the pirate vessel when the time came.

Well, at least he could see what was going on. The pirate vessel moved alongside and stopped. He saw the pirates pointing and shooting and the boat on the deck of the pirate ship disappear in a fire ball just before a rocket leaped from the pirate vessel and seemed, for an instant, to be coming straight at him in the camera. The monitor flashed black at the same time he felt, rather than heard, a terrific explosion high above him. He cycled the feed through all the rest of the cameras and confirmed them operable. He was blind on the starboard side, which, of course, was where he needed to see.

There was another terrific concussion forward of him—how far forward he couldn't tell—and then something struck the ship's side below him to starboard. The hull rang with the impact, and it was like being inside a giant bell. The concussion lifted him from his chair and unseated the rest of the noncombatants from their benches, throwing them all to the deck in a jumble of tangled bodies and limbs. The temporary lights blinked out and the space filled with smoke and steam.

The captain struggled to his feet in the darkness, shaking his head in an attempt to clear the ringing in his ears. As his hearing returned, he heard the sound of rushing water in the tank below him.

"Anybody hurt?" he called into the darkness, as here and there a flashlight winked on. Scattered voices responded, confirming no serious injuries.

"I have to stay at the console," he said to the chief mate. "Count heads and get everyone into the engine room, then come back and go down to see how much water we're taking on."

The light blinked on the sound-powered phone.

"Everybody OK?" Dugan asked before the captain could speak.

"No one's hurt," the captain said, attempting to cycle through the camera feeds as he talked. "But we got no lights and they blew a hole in the hull at or below the waterline. I can hear water coming in. I don't know how bad. We'll check it."

"OK," Dugan said. "Stand by to get us out of here."

"That's going to be a pretty good trick," the captain replied, looking at the blank monitors. "That last impact shook up the monitors. I got no visual to steer by!"

CHAPTER SEVENTEEN

M/T *Pacific Endurance*
Arabian Sea

Borgdanov crept to the edge of what was left of the starboard bridge wing and looked down with a worried frown. His men and the Americans had the *piraty* pinned down for now, but they were starting to recover from their surprise and to fire more economically and more accurately. He mentally willed his two men with the RPGs to hurry, and was rewarded by the sight of a rocket leaping from below him, stabbing toward the mother ship and exploding at her waterline, followed by another, which detonated three meters farther aft.

He raised his own RPG and took aim at the wheelhouse of the fishing vessel.

"No!" said a voice behind him. He snapped his head around to see Dugan crouched in the door to the wheelhouse.

"What is problem, *Dyed*?" Borgdanov said. "*Piraty* are in range of our jammers now, but if we move out of jammer range and leave them with communications, they will call other pirates. One RPG in wheelhouse will knock out radios."

"And kill some innocent fishermen in the bargain," Dugan said. "You know they make hostages of the crews of the vessels they hijack as mother ships."

Borgdanov shrugged. "This may be true, but we cannot leave them with communications."

"There are probably half a dozen sat-phones on that boat in addition to the radios," Dugan said. "Even if you take out the radios, we can't cut their communications, short of boarding and destroying their individual sat-phones. Do you think that's likely to happen without at least some of your guys taking a bullet?"

The Russian looked down at the fishing boat, where the pirates still outnumbered his combined force at least three to one.

"*Nyet*, but what will we do?"

"Do you think they've used up all their RPGs?"

"*Da*, otherwise I think they would still be using them."

Dugan crept up beside the Russian, keeping his head down as he approached the edge of the deck. "Then I think we should just sit tight, stay close with our heads down, and wait until they're ready for us to rescue them," he said.

Borgdanov looked skeptical. "That was not plan."

"Plans change," Dugan said, leaning over to peek at the fishing boat, already listing to starboard as water gushed into the holes in her hull. "Besides, we can't be sure of knocking out all communications without unacceptable risks, so dealing with this bunch here and now is the best option, even if it does cost us time. If we leave them behind and they *do* sic other pirates on us, losing time may be the least of our problems. Let's bag this bunch as quickly as possible and head for the coast."

Borgdanov followed his gaze. "Maybe you are right, *Dyed*."

Dugan gave a resigned nod. The delay from being right might cost another innocent seaman his life.

M/T *PACIFIC ENDURANCE*
ARABIAN SEA

"Well, they're stubborn, I'll give them that," Dugan said to Borgdanov. "I figured when we put *Marie Floyd* up close and personal on the opposite side of them, they'd get the message and give up."

Marie Floyd had arrived an hour or so after the gunfight with the pirates. Unable to communicate because of the jamming, Blake had come aboard *Pacific Endurance* via Zodiac to confer with Dugan and Borgdanov. They'd attempted to intimidate the pirates by having Blake move *Marie Floyd* to the other side of the crippled *Kyung Yang No. 173*, boxing her in and towering over her, but too far away for the pirates to attempt a boarding of either tanker.

The fishing boat was listing badly to starboard, her engine room flooded. But her condition had stabilized, and she appeared in no immediate danger of sinking. Far from surrendering, the pirates were using the captive crewmen of the *Kyung Yang No. 173* as human shields. The helpless South Koreans were tied to the handrails, four on each side of the fishing boat, with a pirate under cover in the house behind them, ready to fire from his protected position and kill the hostages at the first sign of attack from either tanker.

"These *piraty* think they are untouchable as long as they have hostages," said Borgdanov. "And everyone plays their game. Is for this reason they become so strong, *da*? Maybe better we just sink them with grenades and RPGs. Is bad to lose these eight fishermen, but how many more fishermen do we save if we kill so many pirates?"

"Christ! So we just bomb the hell out them, sink them, and leave? Is that your idea of a friggin' plan?" Dugan asked.

"This is big delay, and we have primary mission. But"—Borgdanov shrugged—"you are boss. If you say wait, we wait."

"Maybe I can negotiate—"

"*Dyed*, I'm sorry, but this is bad idea. Is obvious you are American."

"So what?" asked Dugan.

"So they know you are concerned about hostages and they will drag out negotiation forever, hoping their comrades will come looking for them. I think is better if I negotiate."

It was Dugan's turn to shrug. "Well, I can't deny you seem to be pretty good at dealing with these assholes. What do you have in mind?"

Borgdanov grinned. "Nothing complicated. Simple plan is always best, *da*?"

Borgdanov moved to the handrail at the edge of A-deck, the lowest deck on *Pacific Endurance* where he still enjoyed a height advantage over any place on the fishing vessel. He appeared to those below him like a man looking down on them from the edge of a cliff, a commanding figure despite the white flag in his hand.

"I want to talk," Borgdanov called down. "Summon your leader."

A thin Somali of medium height stepped out of the wheelhouse and looked up.

"I am the leader. What do you want?" shouted the man.

Borgdanov shrugged. "I want you to surrender. Lay down arms and you will be treated fairly and your wounded will get medical attention."

"I don't think so," the pirate replied in British-accented English, nodding to the South Koreans tied to the rail. "Perhaps you've noticed we have hostages. It will go badly for them if you attack us, but you can save them all if you're prepared to be reasonable and let us go."

Borgdanov snorted. "Well, you are big comedian, I think. How do you suppose that will happen?"

"Give us one of your ships and six crewmen to run it. Move everyone else to the other ship. We will give you two hostages as a show of good faith as soon as we see you moving your men to the second ship. After we've boarded the ship and confirmed the six crewmen you leave behind can run it and that no one else is hiding aboard, we'll release the remaining six hostages. Then we go our separate ways."

"And if I refuse?" Borgdanov asked.

"Then we will begin executing the hostages," the pirate said, making a show of looking at his watch. "You have one hour."

Borgdanov stroked his chin, as if considering the proposal, then responded. "Thank you for generous offer of one hour to consider, but is not necessary. Ilya!" he called back over his shoulder, never taking his eyes off the pirate.

Sergeant Ilya Denosovitch and three other Russians herded two dozen Somalis to the rail, including the three captured earlier in the day. All were naked, with duct tape over their eyes and mouths and hands bound before them with plastic ties.

Borgdanov suppressed a smile at the look of shock on the head pirate's face.

"You see," he said, "I think you have good idea to shoot hostages. Is very clear what you intend. Anybody can understand. So. I think I do the same, *da*? But I am more generous. You have eight, so I decided twenty-four—three to one. Is bargain, *da*? And by the way, these *piraty* are spares. I have plenty more. So please"—Borgdanov gestured to the pirate leader—"you go first. I insist."

The pirate stood motionless and speechless until Borgdanov continued. "OK. OK. I know is difficult to start sometime. I go first."

Borgdanov grabbed the pirate nearest him at the rail and threw him to the deck. The pirate fell out of sight of the fishing boat and the Russian unholstered a Makarov pistol and fired down at the deck three times. There was an angry cry from the pirates on the fishing boat and weapons rose, stopped halfway up by an urgent order from the pirate leader as he stared at the guns of the other Russians, all targeting him.

Borgdanov nodded to the Russian sergeant, who helped him lift the executed captive and hurl his body over the rail, into the sea. The body splashed down face-up and floated a moment before slipping below the clear water, staring up at the world he was leaving behind.

"Now please. Go ahead," called Borgdanov. "Execute hostage. We do not have all day, I am afraid. Ahh, but where are my manners? You were so nice to tell me your plan, so I should tell you mine before we continue, *da*? Is very simple. You kill those hostages and I kill all the rest of these fellows here, and then we get this silly kill-the-hostage game out of way, *da*? Then we finish blowing up your ship with RPGs and we pick up whoever can swim. Then we kill them. Not fast like bullet, but slow like hot steel rod in ass and things like that. Not everybody, of course. Maybe two or three we leave alive to tell others is not good thing to fuck with Russians." Borgdanov shook his head, feigning sadness. "But you, my friend, I am sorry to say, will not be one who lives. You are leader, so leader must become example. You I will sit on steel deck naked and stomp your balls flat with my heel, then I will tear off your head and piss in the hole." Borgdanov smiled. "Is quite easy to tear off head, especially skinny little fellow like you. Now—any questions?"

The pirate leader licked his lips. He tried to speak twice before anything came out of his mouth. "If… if we surrender, how do we know you won't do that anyway?"

Borgdanov inclined his head toward the Somali captives that lined the rail. "You do not. But if I executed captives, why are these fellows still alive? I will turn you over to proper authorities unless something forces me to do otherwise, like problem we have here."

"Do we have your word?"

"No," said Borgdanov. "But I will give you my word that if you don't surrender within sixty seconds and stop wasting my time, I will kill you."

The pirate leader swallowed hard, then laid his assault rifle on the deck and raised his hands.

Dugan stood with Woody out of sight of the pirates and watched the Russians push the Somalis to the rail. He flinched when Borgdanov unexpectedly threw a pirate to the deck beside the corpse of the man that had died earlier in the stairwell and then put three bullets in the dead man. The corpse was flying over the side before he figured it out. He was still scratching his head when the pirates surrendered minutes later.

"Sure didn't see that one coming," he said.

Beside him, Woody was equally impressed. "I'll be damned if I ain't getting to kinda like the commie bastard."

"One hundred and sixteen," Dugan said, looking down at the list. "With at least a half dozen from every major pirate clan. We'll divide them up evenly, and as soon as Woody can get us patched up, I think we're ready to head for Somalia."

"How are the four wounded pirates doing?" Blake asked.

Borgdanov shrugged. "Not so bad. Ilya is cross-trained as combat medic and is very good. He says no problem. All wounds are in arms or legs. I think these *piraty* were shot by Woody's men. My men never miss kill shot."

Beside him, Woody bristled. "Screw you, Ivan. My boys—"

Borgdanov laughed. "Is joke, little man. I think you must… how do you say… lighten up, *da*?"

Woody looked somewhat mollified and was about to speak when Dugan changed the subject. "What about repairs, Woody? When can we get underway?"

Woody shot a stream of tobacco juice over the rail and into the sea, and looked up as if he were envisioning the repair process.

"Let's see," he said. "Nothing much we can do about the starboard lifeboat or the bridge wing. The RPG took out the starboard navigation light, but I got Junior riggin' up a temporary. Doubt it'll meet regulations, but at least she'll show a green light. One of the RPGs blowed a hole in number-five starboard ballast tank, but she's way above the waterline and hit between frames. That ain't much of a problem—most of the steel just peeled back, but it's still attached. We can close up the hole by heating and hammering it back in place, then we'll throw a doubler plate on the inside and weld it up. It'll be a beat-to-fit, paint-to-match homeward-bound job, but it'll do." Woody paused. "The biggest delay's gonna be the after peak tank. A hit right at the waterline took out a chunk of one of the frames. That ain't quite as easy to fix with what we got onboard. Lucky the water didn't quite make it up to the safe room."

"So where do we stand on that?" Dugan asked.

Woody shrugged. "The captain's ballasting to give us a port list so we can get the hole on the starboard side out of the water and have a better look at it. I'm thinking the quickest way is to just weld a light plate over the outside and box around the hole on the inside of the tank. We can put a bunch of scrap metal in the box for reinforcement and tack-weld it all together, then fill the whole damn thing with concrete." Woody looked over at Blake. "I called Edgar over on *Marie Floyd*. He told me there's a bunch of sacks of Speed Crete up in the foc'sle storeroom." Woody smiled. "I figured there would be. If Ray Hanley's gettin' ready to scrap a ship, I reckon a good supply of cement has been standard supply onboard a few years."

"No comment," Blake said, and Woody laughed.

"What about the monitors?" Dugan asked. "We're out of the pirate-hunting business for now, but that doesn't mean we won't run into some. If so, I'd still like to be able to steer from the safe room."

"The fiber optics is OK," Woody said. "The monitors themselves got a shaking—more than they could tolerate, I reckon. I got the boys stealing the TVs out of the officer and crew lounges. I think we can jury-rig somethin' up."

"Good," Dugan said. "Which brings me back to, how long?"

"I got Edgar and his boys coming over to give us a hand," Woody said. "I figure twelve, maybe fourteen hours." He looked past Dugan at an approaching figure who stopped several feet away, intent on catching Woody's eye but seemingly reluctant to intrude on the conversation. Woody shifted his stance so the man was no longer in his line of sight and lowered his voice.

"That is," he said, "if you can keep that damn Korean off my ass. Somehow he figured out I'm the go-to guy for repairs, and he's been followin' me all over the damn ship. I can't seem to shake him."

Dugan took a quick glance at the Korean, then turned back to Woody.

"What's he want?"

"Best I can tell, he wants me to patch up the *Ding Dong 173*, or whatever he calls that tub, so he can go back to fishing." Woody gave Dugan a hard look. "I take it you ain't told him he's now officially a passenger."

Dugan smiled. "Captain Kwok's understanding of English seems to deteriorate rapidly when the discussion turns to something he doesn't want to hear. Just keep politely ignoring him. I'm sure it will sink in sooner or later."

"For the last time, Jesse, no!" Dugan said into the sat-phone, so forcefully Ward figured he might have been able to hear him even without a phone. "I got guys working over the side in the dark with flashlights, trying to get out of here as soon as possible for Somalia. I'm sure as hell not going to burn a day going in the opposite direction and then a day coming back to do a drive-by oil spill in the middle of the night. You'll have to think of something else."

"I have no one else," Ward said.

"You've got navy ships, and helicopters, and jets, and all sorts of resources you could use for—"

"All the ships are too far away and way too obvious, as is a military chopper. I told you, I can't risk alerting the terrorists. If there *is* something going on and they think we're on to them, they could scramble with—" Ward caught himself. "Well, it would just be very bad, that's all. I need you to do this for me. Trust me, OK?"

"Two days' delay means two more dead hostages," Dugan said. "I'm sorry, pal, but I need more than 'trust me' if I'm going to carry that on my conscience."

"Tom," Ward said, "if I don't get some intel on this drillship, and soon, we both might have a lot more than *two* lives on our consciences."

"What are you talking about?"

Ward hesitated. The story was so fantastic he was having trouble convincing any of his own superiors it was anything but a fairy tale. He hoped he could be more convincing with Dugan. He took a deep breath and began.

Five minutes later Dugan had stopped pacing the main deck and stood motionless, the phone pressed to his ear.

"Jesus Christ!" he whispered into the phone. "That... that can't be true, Jesse. How could anyone... I mean... do you believe this?"

"I don't know what I believe, but I don't think Imamura was lying, if that's what you mean. We have to at least check it out."

"But why us?" Dugan asked. "We're a day away, and even if you don't have any navy ships close enough, a chopper from a navy ship or ashore would —"

"Make them suspicious as hell," Ward said. "I can't put a chopper over them until I'm ready to set it down on her helideck with an assault force, and I've got no grounds to board her at the moment. Not without further confirmation." Ward hesitated. "But it goes beyond that, Tom. The few people above me in the food chain I've talked to about this think I'm nuts, but they didn't sit there with Imamura. I need more proof before I'm likely to get much support for going after an American drillship chartered by a well-connected foreign ally, engaged in an outwardly legal activity in international waters. And the satellite imagery of the drillship pretty much shows business as usual. I need an excuse for getting closer—one that won't make al-Shabaab take the virus, assuming they have it, and run."

"For all you know, they already have," Dugan said.

"I don't think so. We've had the drillship under constant satellite surveillance. There have been no boats or chopper flights from the drillship since then. There's a fishing boat tied up alongside, which is a bit suspicious in itself, but not illegal. We think that's how Mukhtar got there, but it hasn't left the side of the drillship. Whatever was there is still there."

Dugan fell silent, considering what he'd just learned.

"Tom?"

"Oh! Sorry, Jesse," Dugan said. "I was just trying to come up with a plan. We have a few hours before we finish here. Let me think things over and get back to you."

"All right. But call me as soon as you can."

"Will do, pal," Dugan replied, and hung up to resume pacing the deck.

CHAPTER EIGHTEEN

Dugan picked his way across the canted upper deck of the engine room by the light of his headlamp, trailed by Woody and the Korean chief engineer. They moved cautiously over the tilted grating, watching their footing and holding on to piping and equipment to steady themselves. Dugan started down a stairway to the next level, the descent made difficult by the heavy starboard list tilting the already steep stairway at a crazy angle. He stepped off the stairway at the next level down and illuminated the ladder treads for Woody and the Korean to descend.

"Ain't as bad as I figured," Woody said to Dugan when all three were at the bottom. "The generator flat is above the water, and"—he examined the space below in the light of his headlamp—"only the lower level flooded above the deck plates, and just on the starboard side." He played his light over the partially submerged electric motors of two pumps and turned to the Korean. *"What those pumps?"* he shouted.

The little Korean frowned, then seemed to understand. *"They are bilge pumps,"* he yelled back. *"And I am Korean, not deaf."*

Dugan suppressed a smile and interjected himself into the conversation. "What else is under, Chief?"

The Korean played his light over the water below, where the tops of electric motors showed in scattered places like small islands. "Both bilge pumps, ballast pump, sanitary pumps, cooling-water pump, refrigeration plant for fish hold"—he ticked them off on his fingers—"motors all gone."

"Well, we won't get any motors out here. How about work-arounds?" Dugan asked.

The chief nodded as he considered the possibilities. "General-service pump has bilge suction and crossover to ballast system. Can maybe make temporary hookup and use fire pump for cooling water, sanitary, and ballast. Reefer plant..." He shrugged.

"Yeah, I don't reckon y'all will be needing the reefer plant since the first RPG went into the fish hold," Woody said.

"What about the main engine?" Dugan asked. "Did the water rise high enough to get into the sump?"

The Korean shook his head. "I check before. Water not rise to shaft seal. I pull oil sample already. No water."

Dugan nodded. "Then it's just a matter of getting her patched up and pumped out. What do you think, Woody?"

Woody scratched his chin. "Well, best not to run them generators with this kind of list. We need to get her back up a bit straighter first. I saw two or three Wilden pumps in the foc'sle store on *Marie Floyd*, and y'all have some on your ship too. We can bring both ships right up alongside and drop air hoses down to run the pumps. We'll rig a couple of mattresses over the holes on the outside of the hull to slow down the water." He looked down at the water. "Ain't that much volume, so she should pump out pretty fast. We'll list her to port and get the holes out of the water and patch 'em best we can—doublers or cement boxes, or both. Won't be pretty, but she'll be tight."

"How long?" Dugan asked.

Woody sighed. "It's still the middle of the damn night and we ain't even finished with *Pacific Endurance*, so which one do you want first?"

"I want them both first," Dugan said.

"Yeah, that's what I figured," Woody said. He looked at the Korean. "Can your men tend the pumps and rig the piping crossovers?"

"Yes, yes," he said.

Woody turned back to Dugan. "OK, we'll see what we can do. Maybe noon."

M/T *Marie Floyd*
Arabian Sea

"You told me noon," Dugan said, looking at his watch.

"I told you *maybe* noon," Woody replied. "And now I'm tellin' you fifteen hundred for sure. And you're damned lucky to get that."

"All right, all right," Dugan said. "Sorry to lean on you, but we need to get moving as soon as possible."

"Get moving *where*, is the question." Blake stared across the mess-room table at Dugan. "Why the hell are you taking off for parts unknown in a Korean fishing boat?"

"I can't tell you," Dugan said. "It's something I have to do and this was the only way I could figure to do it without slowing our operation down. As soon as you show up off Harardheere, you can demand that they stop executing hostages or threaten to match the executions man for man, but they won't believe it until they see what you've got. It's going to take you four and a half days to get there as it is, and I don't want to add any time to that."

"I understand that part," Blake said. "What I don't understand is why you're going and how you intend to join back up with us."

"And the answers are, I can't tell you and I don't know," Dugan said. "And if I don't get to Harardheere, it doesn't matter. You know the plan. Start without me. Getting our captives there and setting up the deal is the important thing." Dugan looked at Woody. "And speaking of that, you know what you have left to do, right?"

"Well, I thought I did until you explained it to me ten times, but now I'm all fucked-up," Woody said.

Dugan turned red and Woody raised his hands in a calm-down gesture. "Yes, I got it down. The tank mods are already finished on *Marie Floyd*, so I can put everybody on finishing up *Pacific Endurance*. Don't worry."

Dugan nodded, mollified, and Woody continued. "But I'll tell you something else, for whatever it's worth. I don't know where the hell you're headed, but I'll be damned if I'd sail off with those Koreans without someone to watch my back. That chief's OK, but I think Captain Kwok just wants to get the hell out of Dodge, and if you think he's gonna cooperate when it's just you and him and his crew, you might want to rethink that. As soon as you have a difference of opinion, I reckon you're either gonna become a passenger or be dumped over the side."

Dugan nodded. "I was thinking the same thing myself."

Vince Blake stood on the port bridge wing of the *Marie Floyd* staring down at the *Kyung Yang No. 173* as she got underway. Dugan and the three Russians waved up at him from the afterdeck and Blake returned the wave, as the fishing boat slipped from between the two ships and headed east.

Blake waved across to the captain of *Pacific Endurance* and got a nod in reply, then started the agreed upon separation maneuver.

"Dead slow ahead," he called into the wheelhouse.

"Dead slow ahead, aye," parroted the third mate.

"Rudder amidships," he called.

"Rudder amidships, aye," the helmsman confirmed.

He stood watching on the bridge wing until he was well clear of the other ship, then set the new course and began to gradually increase speed, knowing *Pacific Endurance* would soon fall in a mile away on his port beam. There would be no intentional slow steaming now, not that it mattered much. Two tired old tankers near the end of their economic life weren't greyhounds of the sea, but he hoped they could maintain thirteen knots. Four and a half days at that speed—and five lives.

An hour later and at full sea speed, he let his mind wander to the *Luther Hurd*, and Lynda Arnett, and Jim Milam, and the rest of the crew. He wondered again if he was doing the right thing, and then suppressed those doubts. If he could do nothing for his own crew, at least he could help others. He glanced at the digital readout of the speed log and nodded. Thirteen-point-two knots. Not bad.

On a whim, he walked to the console, picked up the phone, and hit a pre-select.

"Engine Room, Chief speaking," a voice answered.

"This is the old girl's last run, Chief," Blake said. "I'd like all she's got."

Blake listened patiently to a long tale about exhaust temperatures, overload protector settings, and a variety of other things about which he knew little as he awaited the words he knew were coming.

"... but I'll see what I can do," the chief said.

"Thanks, Chief. I appreciate it," Blake said, before cradling the phone.

Five minutes later, he smiled as he watched the RPM indicator creep up, and the speed log output move to thirteen-point-eight knots. If they could pick up a favorable current, they might beat his ETA. Four lives lost was better than five.

M/T *LUTHER HURD*
AT ANCHOR
HARARDHEERE, SOMALIA

Gaal adjusted the explosive collar around the chief engineer's neck, preparing him for his turn as display hostage. Milam glared at him, his hatred palpable. Gaal had insisted that he and Diriyi take over the tasks of changing the collars, citing his concern that the rest of the holders were so perpetually stoned on khat that they risked blowing themselves and the hostages up. Diriyi had acquiesced reluctantly, feeling the task was beneath him. Sensing that, Gaal had assumed most of the work himself, and the hostages grew to hate him even more.

Gaal pulled the last strap tight and nodded to a waiting pirate, who came over and jerked his head toward the door. The chief engineer started his trek up to the flying bridge, the exercise now routine. Gaal ignored the glares of the other hostages and fell in behind the chief and his guard, and followed them into the passageway and up the central stairs. He exited the stairwell at D-deck and walked a dozen steps down the passageway to the captain's office, and entered without knocking.

Diriyi was on the sofa, staring at his sat-phone on the coffee table in front of him. He looked up as Gaal entered. "I think something is wrong," he said. "Mukhtar should have called hours ago."

Gaal shrugged and dropped into the easy chair across from Diriyi. "It's probably nothing," he said. "Maybe he's having trouble with his phone."

"No. There are other phones, and he's eager to confirm the naval vessels are still in place watching us," Diriyi said. "Also, he knows I'm eager to know when he's done, so we may finish our business and leave. Things have been greatly complicated by Zahra and those other fools and their executions."

"Don't worry, Diriyi," Gaal said. "I know the Americans. They're single-minded and focused on us. They'll do nothing unless we provoke them by executing *our* hostages. They care nothing for the others."

Diriyi looked unconvinced. "Perhaps," he said. "But all the same, I wish Zahra and those other idiots had not complicated the situation. What can they be thinking?"

M/T *PHOENIX LYNX*
AT ANCHOR
HARARDHEERE, SOMALIA

"A mother ship?" Zahra asked. "You're sure? Maybe it's just late checking in."

"I don't think so," Omar said. "No one has heard from them in over two days. And she vanished in the same area as all the rest."

"How many now?"

"All the bands are reporting disappearances. Over a hundred now, I think," Omar said. "Do you think it's the work of Mukhtar and his fanatics?"

"Who else? The naval forces are eager to show the world how effective they are. If they'd done it, they'd trumpet the news." Zahra shook his head.

"No. The only ones who might do this secretly are the fanatics. What's our man on the drillship say? If Mukhtar is targeting us, he should know."

"His report is long overdue," Omar said. "I fear he's been discovered. What should we do?"

Zahra said nothing for a moment. "How close is our remaining mother ship?"

Omar shrugged. "At her speed, perhaps three days from the drillship. Less, of course, for the launches she supports."

"And the other bands?" Zahra asked.

"More or less all at the same distance, but some have faster mother ships. Why? What're you thinking?"

"That there's little point in wandering around aimlessly to be picked off by Mukhtar at his leisure," Zahra said. "If we combine forces, perhaps we can end his interference once and for all."

Omar stroked his beard, then nodded. "It might work. We could rendezvous at sea and pick the two fastest mother ships to carry the men, then use them to support a larger force of attack boats. It'll take a little time to organize, but we could strike by surprise and overwhelm him."

Zahra smiled and reached for his phone. "I know it'll work. I'll confer with the leaders of the other bands. I think it's time we pay Mukhtar a little visit. And while we're at it, we can relieve him of his treasure."

CHAPTER NINETEEN

"You same pirate, Dugan," Captain Kwok said, glaring across the small wheelhouse of *Kyung Yang No. 173*. "Pirates take ship. You take ship." He shifted his gaze to include Borgdanov. "Somalis. You. Commie friends. All same. All pirate."

"I am not Communist. I am independent contractor," Borgdanov said, earning himself an even harder glare from the Korean.

"We *did* salvage your vessel, Captain Kwok," Dugan said.

That seemed to stoke the fires of the little Korean's anger even hotter.

"YOU SHOOT HOLES IN SHIP! NO HOLES! NO NEED SALVAGE!" he shouted, before spitting out a stream of Korean that Dugan was just as glad he didn't understand. Kwok returned to English. "First port, you see! I file charges. You big pirate!"

Dugan lost it. "File whatever you damn please. You looked plenty happy for our help when we untied you from that handrail, as I recall."

Kwok clamped his mouth shut and ignored Dugan to stare out at the sun-lit sea. Sergeant Denosovitch came up the interior stairway and into the wheelhouse to relieve Borgdanov, and Dugan motioned for the major to follow and headed out of the wheelhouse to the aft deck of the fishing boat.

"Thank you for agreeing to come, Andrei," Dugan said. "I know it's not what you signed on for."

Borgdanov shrugged. "After you explained situation, I cannot let you go off alone." He grinned. "Ilya and I must keep you from trouble, *da*? And Corporal Anisimov, he likes the bonus. Besides, seems most difficult part is to get there."

"Yeah, Woody sure called that one right," Dugan said. "Captain Kwok's not a real happy camper."

Borgdanov nodded. "He is not so cooperative. But makes no difference, I think. We are four, and one of us can stay in wheelhouse to make sure boat stays on GPS track." He looked out at the sea. "And weather is fine. How long do you think?"

Dugan snorted. "Our tankers are speedboats next to this thing. I doubt she'll make more than eight knots, maybe less with all the jury-rigging in the engine room. It'll take us the better part of two days to get there."

"Good," Borgdanov said. "Maybe we use time to figure out what we do when we arrive. You have plan?"

Dugan shrugged. "Nothing firm. Plan A is to pretend to fish and get as close as we can without drawing attention. If we see anything suspicious, we pass it to Ward so he can convince people the threat is real. Assuming we *don't* see anything Ward can use, plan B is to pump a bit of oil over in the middle of the night so it drifts down around the drillship, and then we'll haul ass. Ward can use investigation of the oil spill as a pretext to get agents aboard for a closer look. Either way, when we're done, we head back toward the tankers. Ward promised me to start a navy ship in this direction, and get close enough to meet us with a chopper en route. With a bit of luck, we should get to Harardheere not long after the tankers arrive."

Borgdanov nodded. "Do you think this virus is real, *Dyed*? It seems like fantastic story."

"Not a clue, but Ward is certainly taking it seriously."

DRILLSHIP *OCEAN GOLIATH*
ARABIAN SEA

Mukhtar ignored his throbbing head as he watched the little ROV surface beside the ship. His men were working with the drillship crew now to supplement the work force and help hoist the craft back onboard. The men's movements were dull and lethargic, almost as if they were moving in slow motion. Half the regular ship's crew lay dead or dying in the crew lounge, and four of Mukhtar's men lay with them.

They all realized they were dying, but some undefinable will to live kept them moving, just as fear of Mukhtar drove them to their tasks. Just to be sure, he had two loyal men stationed on the fishing boat. No one was leaving until he'd brought up all the cylinders, a task made more difficult as men dropped of the disease hourly.

The revelation had come to him as the drillship crew began to sicken and die, starting with those who had survived the nerve-gas exposure. It was a miracle. In His great wisdom, Allah, blessed be His Name, had transformed the nerve gas into a deadly plague. *Yawm ad-Din*, the Day of Judgment, was at hand, and Allah had chosen Mukhtar as his instrument. The honor and responsibility were almost more than he could bear, but he would not fail!

His initial actions had been correct. He'd isolated the infected men in the crew's lounge, not realizing it was already too late, and spent the next four days scouring the sea floor to bring up every cylinder he could find. For what seemed the hundredth time, he debated leaving with what he had, and for the hundredth time he ignored the urge. He knew nothing about this new weapon, but sensed more was better than less, and he was determined to have it all.

He watched impatiently as the ROV was hoisted aboard, and his dwindling work force started to transfer cylinders from the ROV into a half-filled cargo basket on deck. Another full basket sat nearby. When he was sure he had all the cylinders, he would hoist the baskets aboard the fishing boat with the ship's crane. And then he would get God's great cleansing plague ashore somewhere, Inshallah.

M/T *Luther Hurd*
At anchor
Harardheere, Somalia

Gaal's eyes flew open as he heard the key in the lock of his cabin door. He feigned sleep as his hand sought the grip of the Glock beneath his pillow. He heard his door open and his hand tightened on the Glock.

"Gaal," called Diriyi's voice. Gaal opened one eye and saw the Somali's form silhouetted against the light of the passageway. He looked at his watch.

"What do you want? It's one o'clock in the morning."

"Take the spare collars to the top of the wheelhouse, then join me in the officers' mess room."

"Why?"

"Never mind why," said Diriyi. "Just do as I say." He closed the door before Gaal could respond.

Gaal got up and dressed before going to the spare room, where he kept the extra explosive collars. He carried them to the top of the wheelhouse and laid them on the deck not far from where the bosun dozed in a lounge chair, fatigue having overcome his anxiety at being shackled to the handrail with two pounds of explosive wrapped around his neck.

The bosun started awake, wild-eyed in the light of the small penlight, as Gaal bent over him. The man jerked away and tried to stand, but Gaal pushed him back down in the chair.

"Relax," Gaal said. "I'm not going to harm you. Do you understand?"

The bosun nodded, distrust in his eyes, as Gaal held the light in his mouth and lifted the explosive collar to poke around beneath it. Terrified, the bosun tried to force his chin down to see what Gaal was doing, but Gaal pushed the collar up harder to keep the bosun looking straight up at the stars. Then Gaal pressed the collar back in place, straightened, and walked off, his progress marked by the faint glow of the penlight lighting his way.

He made his way down the central stairwell to A-deck, and found Diriyi waiting outside the officers' mess staring down in disgust at the man supposedly guarding the hostages. The pirate sat on the deck snoring, his back against the bulkhead, an AK draped across his outstretched legs.

Diriyi sneered. "This rabble now seems to look to you as a leader, Gaal. I'm happy to see you command such a disciplined group."

Gaal grimaced and kicked the sleeping man hard. The man jerked awake and scrambled to his feet in a flurry of elbows and knees.

"Sorry to disturb your nap," Gaal said, as the man stood blinking, his head swiveling between Gaal and Diriyi.

"Leave him," Diriyi said, and motioned for Gaal to come closer. When he did so, Diriyi lowered his voice. "Something is wrong," he said. "We will go in and bring out the woman and three other hostages one at a time. Bind their hands and tape their eyes here in the passageway, and then shackle them with the other one on top of the wheelhouse."

"There are only three extra collars," Gaal said.

"I know that," Diriyi said. "Have this fool"—he nodded at the guard —"take the woman to my cabin."

"But why?"

"I will explain later, in my cabin. For now, just do as I say."

Gaal hesitated, then nodded and followed Diriyi into the mess room.

Something was definitely wrong. Diriyi seemed agitated and nervous, and for the first time in days, he followed Gaal to the flying bridge and assisted in collaring the hostages. Diriyi handed Gaal each collar, and then held a penlight as Gaal fitted it. Gaal felt Diriyi's eyes on him as he worked. He finished and stepped back. The third mate, the chief mate, and the chief engineer now stood with the bosun, each fastened to a corner of the flying bridge.

"Good," Diriyi said, and moved toward the bosun.

"Where are you going?" Gaal asked.

"To check his collar," Diriyi said.

"I checked it when I brought the other collars up," Gaal said. "It's fine. Do you think I'm not competent to fit a simple collar?"

Diriyi hesitated. "Very well," he said. "Let's go down."

Gaal nodded and followed Diriyi down the stairs.

"What's going on?" Gaal asked minutes later in the captain's cabin.

"Mukhtar called and he sounded crazy," said Diriyi. "He was raving about Yawm ad-Din, the Day of Judgment, and saying something about a cleansing plague. None of it made sense, but it's clear the operation is coming to an end and now's the time to leave."

"I don't understand," Gaal said. "What about the woman? Why's she here?"

Diriyi smiled a gap-tooth smile. "I'm keeping my promise, but since I plan to take my time, I'm taking her ashore. After that..." He shrugged and pointed to where Arnett sat on the sofa, duct tape over her eyes and binding her wrists together behind her back. An oversized duffel lay on the sofa beside her.

"I need help getting her in the bag," Diriyi said.

Gaal smiled back, with a composure he didn't feel. "You'll need help taping her feet as well," he said. "Else you might be missing a few more teeth."

Diriyi frowned and extracted something from his pocket and moved to the sofa. He pressed the stun gun to Arnett's bare neck and held it there as she jerked and spasmed before toppling over.

Diriyi looked back and smiled again, as he slipped the stun gun into his pocket and reached down to pick up a roll of duct tape from the coffee table. He tossed it to Gaal. "That should hold her awhile. Tape the bitch's ankles."

Gaal did as instructed, uneasy as he watched Diriyi grab the big duffel and open the heavy zipper that ran its length. Diriyi spread the bag open on the deck, then came over and grabbed Arnett under the armpits and gestured for Gaal to take her feet. In seconds, they had her in the duffel and zipped up. A tight fit, but Diriyi didn't seem concerned with the woman's comfort.

"So what now?" Gaal asked.

"We take her ashore," Diriyi said, "and leave these fools to face the Americans when they come."

"They may be watching us with night-vision equipment."

"They'll see two men leave with a bag. Hardly enough to trigger action." He smiled. "And besides, I'm counting on their night vision, because they'll also notice the new hostages on display." He held up a remote actuator. "And when we're far enough away, they'll see those hostages lose their heads. I'm sure that will bring the attack."

Diriyi laughed. "It's a pity I didn't think of this earlier. We could've made collars for the whole crew." He sighed. "I guess we just have to do the best we can under the circumstances—Beard of the Prophet." Diriyi looked toward the cabin door. "What's that?"

Gaal turned to follow Diriyi's gaze, then felt the electrodes on his neck. *Dumb, dumb, dumb* was his last conscious thought before he fell to the deck. When his brain started functioning five minutes later, he was lying on his side with his wrists and ankles bound with duct tape. His mouth was untaped, but the last thing Gaal wanted to do at the moment was call for help from another pirate. He moved his bound wrists to the knife he wore on his belt, but the sheath was empty. He lifted his wrists to his mouth and began to gnaw at the tape.

CHAPTER TWENTY

M/T *Luther Hurd*
At anchor
Harardheere, Somalia

Jim Milam stood trying to assess the situation as the pirates' footsteps faded on the steel treads of the ladder. He heard the rattle of steel chain on the deck.

"This is Milam. Who's there?" he called into the dark.

"Me, Chief. Johnson."

"Boats," Milam said to the bosun. "Are we on the flying bridge? Can you see? How many others—"

"I'm here. Jones," called Stan Jones.

"M-me too. Silva," added Joe Silva.

"I can see," said the bosun. "We're on the flying bridge." The bosun looked around, his eyes accustomed to the moonlight. "I'm chained as usual, but it looks like y'all are pulled up short on the handrail. They left y'all's hands tied and no piss bucket or water bottles, so I'm thinkin' they ain't figuring on y'all being around too long." He paused. "That asshole Traitor was up here earlier, messing around with my collar. I don't know what that was about either."

"OK," Milam said. "Is everyone all right?"

"You mean other than being chained to a handrail with a friggin' bomb strapped to my neck?" Jones asked. "Yeah, other than that, I'm just peachy."

"What about you, Joe?" Milam asked.

"I… I'm OK, Chief," Silva replied. "But I wish they hadn't left us blind. It makes it all worse somehow."

"Yeah, I know," Milam said, as chains rattled on the deck to his right.

"I got some slack in my chain and my hands are free," the bosun said. "Move toward me, Chief, and I might be able to get that tape off your eyes."

Milam's hands were bound behind his back, his wrists chained to the handrail. He moved toward the sound of the bosun's voice until his short chain was taut.

He heard chain rattling on the deck as the bosun moved, then "Crap! That's as far as I can go. Can you bend toward me, Chief? Maybe I can reach your head with one hand."

Milam's shoulders were burning from being twisted in directions they weren't intended to flex, but he gritted his teeth and inched his head farther and lower, to be rewarded with a tentative touch to the crown of his head.

"Oof. Almost," the bosun said, strain in his voice. "Just a bit more and I might be able to hook my fingers under the tape."

Milam willed the pain away and surged forward. A half inch.

He heard a snort from the bosun's direction and felt the fingers slipping down the side of his face, and then—

"Got it!" the bosun said, and Milam clamped his eyes shut to a new pain as the ring of duct tape was torn from his head, taking a substantial wad of hair along with it.

Milam staggered back against the rail. "Christ, Boats! I think you friggin' scalped me!"

The bosun peered down at the hairy ring in his hand. "Sorry, Chief."

"That's OK, Boats. Thanks," Milam said.

"Can either of you reach us?" asked Stan Jones.

"Sorry, Stan," Milam said. "Both of you are too far away."

"Wonderful," Jones said.

"Well, if it's any consolation," Milam said, "things don't look any better with my eyes open."

The woman squirmed unexpectedly halfway down the sloping accommodation ladder, almost causing Diriyi to drop her over the side. It would serve the bitch right if her unseemly stubbornness resulted in her going to a watery grave. He managed to balance the moving bag on his shoulder the rest of the way down to the bottom landing, and then bent at the waist to drop the bag onto the floorboards of the Zodiac. It hit with a satisfying thump and stopped moving. Diriyi smiled his gap-tooth smile and jumped into the boat, untying the craft and cranking the outboard. He looked at the second inflatable tied to the accommodation ladder and considered sinking it, then discounted the idea. He was no doubt being watched from the infidel ship, and he didn't want to draw undue attention.

He turned the little boat toward shore, and increased speed. Not too fast, he must make sure Gaal had time to free himself and collect his weapons.

He certainly didn't want the infidels to find Gaal all tied up and think him a victim. Diriyi laughed aloud, pleased with himself, as he slipped a phone battery from his pocket and tossed it over the side. It had puzzled him at first when his mole on the *Phoenix Lynx* had reported that Zahra seemed to know a great deal about Mukhtar's operation against the drilling vessel, but it soon became clear. Only he and Gaal had been privy to that information. Of course, there could be a mole on the drilling vessel itself, but Gaal was the more likely spy. He'd already proven his readiness to turn his coat at the first opportunity. And besides, Gaal was such a convenient scapegoat. The Americans were sure to take some of that rabble alive, and they would all claim Gaal as their leader. And if the Americans captured a leader, they'd be less inclined to look for him.

Gaal ripped at the last stubborn strand of tape with his teeth and it parted. He separated his wrists and tore the clinging remnants of the tape away, as he hawked and spit on the deck, trying to rid himself of the foul taste of the adhesive. His hands free, he made short work of the ankle binding, then leaped to his feet and rushed into the passageway. He stopped, surprised to see his knife and Glock on the passageway deck.

He collected his weapons and then rushed out of the deckhouse, onto the exterior staircase zigzagging up the starboard side, and looked overboard. There, at the edge of the circle of light around the bottom of the accommodation ladder, he saw a Zodiac moving away from the ship, and knew he was too late to save Arnett. He pounded up the stairs.

The guard inside the bridge heard his heavy tread and met him as he came up the stairway, onto the bridge wing.

"Quickly," Gaal said. "I think we'll be attacked. Go reinforce the guard on the hostages. I'll take care of things here."

The man nodded, and rushed down the stairs, as Gaal moved into the wheelhouse to a lighting panel. Without hesitation, he threw on the deck lights, and the main deck and the exterior of the deckhouse lit up like high noon, providing any force attacking from the dark a decided advantage. He dug in his pocket for his sat-phone—and found it dead. He mashed the power button repeatedly, then gave up and rushed back to the bridge wing and up the steel stairway to the flying bridge.

Milam clamped his eyes shut and then opened them cautiously, blinking in the harsh glare of the deck lights. He heard steps and turned to see Traitor top the open stairs from the bridge deck below.

"I'm Sergeant Al Ahmed, US Army Special Forces," Traitor said. "I'm going to get you out of here, but you have to do exactly as I say."

And I'm the friggin' Easter Bunny, thought Milam, as his mind raced, trying to figure out what Traitor was up to. He watched the pirate rush to a cringing Joe Silva and probe under the third mate's explosive collar. Stan Jones, blind like Joe Silva, was next, and the pirate was on him before he could react. Milam had no clue what the bastard was doing, but sensed the end was near and vowed not to die without at least getting in his licks.

He tensed as Traitor approached. One good one in the family jewels might bring the pirate down between him and Boats. If they could stomp the son of a bitch to death, maybe Boats could find the key on him. A lot of friggin' maybes, but it was the only plan he had.

Traitor was moving toward him now, holding something in his right hand. Milam turned toward him, and when Traitor was close enough, aimed a savage kick at the pirate's groin. But Traitor was fast, deflecting the kick with a forearm block that sent the wire cutters in his hand flying over the rail.

"You stupid son of a bitch!" Traitor said. "I'm trying to help you!"

"Yeah, right. Screw you," Milam said, and braced himself against the handrail, ready to kick again.

Traitor pulled a knife from his belt and started toward Milam.

"There is no time for this, you idiot," Traitor screamed, threatening Milam with the knife. He raised the knife high as he approached and Milam tracked it with his eyes. Milam was surprised by the side kick, and Traitor's heel slammed into his solar plexus like a jackhammer, driving the air from his lungs. Milam began to collapse, but Traitor was on him in an instant, driving his shoulder into Milam's chest to pin him upright against the rail. The knife flashed in Gaal's hand, slashing the straps that secured the collar under Milam's armpits. Then Traitor stepped back, and as Milam sagged to the deck, Traitor dropped the knife and grasped the collar with both hands in one fluid motion, ripping it over Milam's head. He continued in a whirling motion, like an Olympian throwing a discus, and released the collar.

Diriyi mashed the button and felt a rush of exhilaration as a fireball bloomed in the distance, followed by the delayed rumble of an explosion. The thrill faded as he realized there was one fireball, not four. Something was very wrong. First, the lights had come on, making the *Luther Hurd* an island of light on the dark surface of the surrounding sea. Then the movement on top of the wheelhouse. He cursed himself for not thinking to bring binoculars, then twisted the throttle on the outboard and roared toward shore.

"Jesus Christ!" Captain Frank Lorenzo said, as he peered through the binoculars toward *Luther Hurd*. "That was definitely Ahmed. Are they all down?"

"Can't tell," the SEAL beside him said. "But what the hell's he doing? He was supposed to give us at least thirty minutes' warning when he was ready for us."

"Well, that didn't happen, Lieutenant," Lorenzo said. "Are your SEALs ready to rock-and-roll?"

"The bird's warming up now," the SEAL said. "And I have two more waterborne teams ready to go when we give the word."

"That would be now, Lieutenant!" Lorenzo said, but he was already talking to the SEAL's back.

Gaal, aka Sergeant Al Ahmed, struggled to his feet and took inventory. The collar had barely cleared the bridge wing when it detonated with an earshattering crash, driving him to the deck. The chief engineer was on his knees, his arms tethered to the top rail, twisted up painfully behind him. He'd recovered enough of his wind to moan as he put a foot on the deck and struggled to his feet. The two blindfolded men appeared to be terrified. They stood chained and alone in their darkness, begging someone to tell them what had happened. The bosun was. least effected, having seen what was coming and thrown himself to the deck. As he struggled to his feet, Ahmed started toward him, when he felt as well as heard the pounding footsteps of men on the steel stairway below.

"Can you hear me?" asked Ahmed, letting out a relieved sigh when the bosun nodded. Ahmed handed the bosun a set of keys.

"Unshackle yourself and help the chief," Ahmed said. "Get him to lie down on the deck where he can't be seen from below and tell him to be very quiet. Then return to your position, but stand up so you can be seen by any pirates who look up from below. We have to fool them a bit longer. I'll be back as soon as I can. Understand?"

The bosun nodded and Ahmed turned to rush down the stairs to the bridge deck. He got to the starboard bridge wing as three pirates topped the stairs from below.

"Gaal! What's happening? What was the explosion?" the first man asked.

"One of the hostages lost his head," Gaal-Ahmed said. "There's no time to explain. The infidels will attack very soon, and we must be ready. Go below and get everyone to take defensive positions on the main deck, both sides, from bow to stern. They could approach from any direction, and we can't let them get aboard."

"But what of the hostages?" asked the man.

Ahmed looked up at the flying bridge, relieved to see the bosun standing there, the collar around his neck and chains draped around his wrists to give the impression he was restrained. "We still have three collared hostages to discourage the infidels. Move all the rest into the officers' mess before you disperse on the main deck, then block the doors from the outside. Leave one guard."

The pirates looked confused.

"*Move!*" Ahmed shouted, and the three took off down the stairway.

CHAPTER TWENTY-ONE

Ahmed waited until the pirates were two decks below before he raced back up the stairs to the flying bridge.

"Release the others," he said to the bosun. "I'll help the chief."

Milam was steadying himself on the handrail as he climbed to his feet. Ahmed grabbed his other arm to assist him. Milam jerked away.

"Special Forces, huh. You took your own sweet time gettin' in the game," Milam snarled. "Don't you think you could have let us know?"

Ahmed shook his head. "I was already suspect because I'm American. Having you all hate me was the best cover. But things are about to get very interesting, so make up your mind if you believe me or not. If you won't let me save you, I'm sure as hell going to save myself."

Milam glared at Ahmed, then nodded, as the bosun and his newly freed shipmates gathered round.

"Where's the captain?" Milam asked.

"Diriyi, the one you call Toothless, zapped me with a stun gun and took her ashore," Ahmed said. "I couldn't stop him. When you're all safe, I'll go after her."

"What's your plan?"

"I expect a SEAL team from the *Carney* will be arriving soon," Ahmed said. "But the original plan won't work. I've decoyed the pirates away for the moment. I'll free the rest of the crew, and I want you to take them and escape in the free-fall lifeboat. The pirates are all watching out at sea, awaiting attack. They won't be looking up. If you board quietly, the launch will catch them by surprise. You should meet SEALs coming over water. Tell them there are no hostages left aboard."

"What about you?" Milam asked.

"I can take care of myself," Ahmed said.

"Why trust this son of a bitch?" Stan Jones demanded. "All we have is his word the captain's not onboard. I say we search for her before we take off in a lifeboat."

"Look, Stan," Milam said, "Lynda and I talked about this. I don't think—"

"Sorry, Chief," Jones said, taking a step toward him. "It's not your call. With Lynda gone, I'm the acting captain, and I—"

The sap came out of Ahmed's pocket and struck the back of Jones's head so fast it was almost a blur, toppling him. On Ahmed's right, he caught movement from the corner of his eye and ducked a retaliatory swing from the bosun, the big man's fist striking air where Ahmed's head had been. Ahmed danced away, his hand on his Glock as a warning.

"What the hell did you do that for?" Milam demanded.

"Because we don't have time for a debate," Ahmed said. "Decide if you're in or out. Right now. Or I go my own way."

Milam looked at the others, then nodded. "OK, we're in. What should we do?"

"Go to the lifeboat, as quietly as possible. Get it ready to drop, and wait. I'll take care of the guard and lead the rest of the crew to the boat."

"They won't trust you," Milam said. "I'll come with you." He turned. "Joe, can you and Boats get Stan to the boat while I go with Traito—the sergeant."

The two nodded, and Ahmed watched as they began to help a now-conscious Jones to his feet. Ahmed motioned for Milam to follow and moved to the stairs.

Ahmed stopped at his cabin on C-deck, then raced down to A-deck, Milam in tow. He left Milam in the central stairwell and walked down the passageway to the officers' mess. The single guard in the passageway glanced at the pillow wrapped around Ahmed's right hand, held there with his left.

"Did you injure yourself—"

The Glock spoke twice, its bark reduced to dull thuds by the pillow. The guard collapsed, his AK clattering to the deck. Ahmed picked up the assault rifle and called down the passageway to Milam.

With the whole crew together for the first time since capture, the atmosphere in the crowded officers' mess was tense. Milam was besieged with questions—faster than he could answer them, each louder than the last.

"Quiet!" he yelled, repeating the order several times before it took. "I don't have time to explain, but we're getting out of here. Right now I need everyone to just shut the hell up and listen to me. Got that?"

There were murmurs and nods of assent as he continued.

"First, I need a headcount," he said, looking around until he spotted Dave Jergens, the chief steward. "Dave?"

"I did a count when they put us together, Chief," he said. "Eighteen. Everyone's here, except the four of y'all they pulled out of here earlier and the bosun."

Milam nodded. "All of those are accounted for. Now listen, we're going to the lifeboat and everyone has to—"

"Why are you doing this? Where's Captain Arnett?" the steward asked.

Milam hesitated. "They took her ashore."

His announcement was met with shocked silence, and he continued before the crew had time to digest the news. "But there's nothing we can do about that. We got one chance to get out of here, and not much time to do it. We're going to move out of here and back to the lifeboat. No talking. No noise. We'll launch the boat and head toward the navy ships."

"How?" a seaman asked. "There's friggin' pirates all over the ship. Even if we get the boat in the water, it ain't exactly a speedboat. They'll blow the hell out of us before we get a hundred yards."

"We'll have a little help," Milam said, opening the door and motioning to Ahmed.

There was a low collective snarl. "That friggin' Traitor," said someone.

"Not exactly," Milam said. "Meet Sergeant Ahmed, US Army Special Forces."

At Ahmed's suggestion, the men left their shoes in the mess room, and followed Milam single file up the stairwell to D-deck. The elevated exterior catwalk to the top of the machinery casing was exposed, in full view of the pirates on the main deck below should they look up. Milam crept across in stocking feet, hoping like hell they wouldn't.

On the top of the machinery casing, he peeked over the starboard rail. Two pirates sat on a set of mooring bits, AKs across their knees, as they chewed khat and chatted, the alarm of a few minutes before seemingly forgotten. Milam turned and motioned to Ahmed, crouched out of sight across the catwalk, and the next man started across.

Milam had half the crew crouching out of sight on the machinery casing when a young seaman's sock snagged in the catwalk grating. The man finished the crossing in a stumbling run, his first unbalanced step on to the top of the machinery casing producing a dull but audible thump.

Milam took a quick peek over the rail. The pirates were looking up.

Ahmed crouched in the shadows of D-deck, listening to the pirates below.

"I tell you, I heard something."

"Bah! You're an old woman, jumping at shadows. Sit back down and have some khat."

"Maybe you're right. I can't see a thing with these bloody lights glaring in my eyes anyway," the first pirate said.

Ahmed crept to the edge of the deck and peeked over, seeing the pirate shading his eyes with his hand and peering upward. He watched as the man dropped his hand and returned to his seat on the mooring bit. The man looked around.

"I don't like these lights. We're exposed," the pirate said.

"Relax," the other pirate said. "The lights also show the hostages ready to lose their heads. The Americans won't attack. Otherwise, they'd have come long ago."

Ahmed moved back to his position, signaled Milam, and sent the next man across the catwalk. The rest followed at ten-second intervals, then Ahmed joined them. Getting into the free-fall lifeboat was a repeat of the catwalk exercise, requiring transit of another exposed walkway while pirates sat in plain sight on the stern two decks below. Milam stayed back this time, sending the men to the open rear door of the enclosed boat, where a recovered Stan Jones counted heads and ushered them into the boat. Milam sent the last man across and turned to Ahmed.

"The fools will be surprised," Ahmed whispered. "But they'll recover quickly. I'll cover your escape, then go after the woman. I must find her soon, or she's dead."

Ahmed saw Milam swallow and extend his hand.

Ahmed took the offered hand and felt Milam's hand tighten on his. "Get her back," Milam said, his voice cracking.

"With the help of Allah, I will," Ahmed replied. "But now you must go." He glanced toward the lifeboat, where Jones stood in the open door beckoning Milam to come. "Tell Mr. Jones I'm sorry I struck him, and also to keep the boat going straight away from the ship. You need to get out of the light cast by the ship quickly."

Milam nodded and gave Ahmed's hand a final squeeze.

Ahmed watched Milam move into the lifeboat and swing the stern door shut quietly. He waited, knowing it would take a moment before Milam settled himself into a rear-facing seat and strapped himself in for the sudden deceleration when the lifeboat hit the water.

He surveyed the pirates on the main deck below while he waited. There were four on the stern, and the pair he'd overheard farther forward on the starboard side. No doubt there were more on the port side out of his direct line of sight, but that didn't matter. They'd have to move into his field of fire to target the lifeboat and he'd have the advantage of surprise. He decided to let his first target be self-selecting. The pirate with the quickest reflexes would be the first to die. It seemed fair.

He'd no sooner made the decision than the lifeboat began to move, plunging over the side bow first. It struck the water at a sharp angle, submerged, then broke the surface some distance from the ship, the momentum of the dive carrying it away even before the engine cranked to hasten the progress. The pirate directly below Ahmed won the reaction-time lottery. His rifle was at his shoulder before Ahmed drilled him with a three-round burst in the back.

Ahmed shifted his aim to take out the second pirate of the pair, also before the man got off a shot, just as the second pair of pirates on the stern opened up on the lifeboat. But the boat was a moving target, and both pirates had their AKs on full automatic—noisy but inaccurate. Few of their bullets found a mark before their fusillade was cut short by two three-round bursts from Ahmed.

He ducked as a hail of fire ricocheted off the side of the machinery casing, well above his head, and realized he was taking fire from the two pirates on the starboard side. They were firing blind into the lights above them, and Ahmed fought his urge to flee and finished them with two aimed bursts.

He heard shouts coming from below him to starboard and spun, just as two more pirates rounded the machinery casing and rushed onto the stern. They froze, confused at the sight of their dead comrades, and Ahmed shot them down before they recovered. He looked out and saw the lifeboat, a dim patch of orange in the gloom now, and he turned to the deckhouse. Time to get the hell out of Dodge.

US NAVY SH-60 SEA HAWK
AIRBORNE NEAR *LUTHER HURD*
HARARDHEERE, SOMALIA

The SEAL lieutenant watched from the chopper as the free-fall lifeboat dived off the stern of *Luther Hurd*, followed by the flash of gunfire. He cursed under his breath as he saw what little was left of his rescue plan evaporate, along with plans B and C. All the plans called for Ahmed to get the hostages centralized in one room and the explosive collars neutralized before calling in a request for rescue along with the hostage location. Now, at least some of the hostages had escaped in the lifeboat. Or was it all of them? If not, where were the rest? And where the hell was Ahmed and why hadn't he called? This was turning into a grade-A clusterfuck! He looked at the screen in front of him and the symbols of his two waterborne teams now closing on *Luther Hurd*. He keyed his mike and ordered one to hold its position and vectored the other toward the lifeboat. No way in hell was he going to charge in without at least some idea of what was going on.

LIFEBOAT
HARARDHEERE, SOMALIA

Milam braced for impact as the boat dropped bow first into the sea. He felt the strange sensation as the boat plunged underwater before surfacing, followed by the rumble of the diesel as Stan Jones hit the electric start. He heard the rattle of gunfire and a sharp knock as something hit the fiberglass canopy.

He looked up to Jones in the elevated seat, with its glass ports to provide visibility for the coxswain. "You better get down lower, Stan," he said. "You're a sitting duck up there, and it doesn't much matter where we're going until we get away from the ship. Sit on the deck and reach up and hold the bottom of the wheel."

Jones didn't respond for a moment, then turned and gave Milam a strange look as he reached his left hand across his chest and felt behind his right shoulder. He pulled back a bloody hand. "Thanks for the advice, Chief, but I think you're a little friggin' late."

"Christ," Milam said, and began to unbuckle his harness, as beside him the bosun did the same. Both men were up and beside Jones seconds before he slumped in his harness.

"I'll hold him, Boats. You unfasten his harness," Milam said.

The bosun did as instructed, and between them, they maneuvered Jones to the seat just vacated by Milam.

"You steer, Boats," Milam said. "Just take a quick look to make sure we're still headed away from the damn ship and then stay down and hold on to the bottom of the wheel. We'll take care of Stan."

The bosun nodded and moved to the wheel, as Milam tried to get Jones's shirt off so he could see the wound. Frustrated, he tore it, just as the chief steward made his way up the aisle with the first-aid kit.

"Let me help, Chief," said the steward, as footfalls sounded at the rear of the boat, followed by rapping on the stern door.

"US Navy. Open up," said a voice on the other side of the door.

"Thank God," Milam said, leaving Jones in the steward's care and moving aft. "Boats, get on back in the coxswain's seat and let me by."

He moved aft and threw open the stern door.

"We've got an injured man—"

"Hands on your head and don't move!" said a black-clad figure, his face obscured by goggles, unlike the assault rifle pointed at Milam, which was quite visible.

Milam hesitated, confused.

"Hands on your head! Now!" the man shouted again. "And have someone open the forward door."

"Christ on a crutch," Milam said, putting his hands on his head. "Somebody open the bow door before this moron shoots me," he called over his shoulder.

He heard the bow door open, and after a moment a voice from the bow called to the SEAL holding him at gunpoint. "Clear. No bad guys inside."

The SEAL lowered his weapon. "Sorry," he said. "It could've been a trap. What's your situation?"

Milam's anger vanished. "We got an injured man. Gunshot wound. Everybody else is OK."

The SEAL nodded. "We'll leave our medic with you. *Carney*'s sending out another boat. Any hostages left aboard the ship?"

"No," said Milam. "But they took the captain ashore. And there's a US Army guy aboard, but he looks like a pirate."

"We know," the SEAL said, and keyed his mike.

M/T LUTHER HURD
AT ANCHOR
HARARDHEERE, SOMALIA

Ahmed raced down the stairwell, feeling strangely exhilarated. It was good to have a taste of his own identity, but now he had to be Gaal again, if only for a few moments. He reached main-deck level and ran out the starboard door of the deckhouse, and into a confused melee of pirates. He ran up the starboard side of the main deck toward the accommodation ladder, shouting as he ran to gain attention.

"Everyone listen!" he yelled, as he stopped on the main deck and pointed back toward the deckhouse. "The hostages overpowered me and escaped, and the Americans will attack any minute. Everyone back to the deckhouse. It's more defensible. We can hold them off long enough for boats to rescue us from shore."

Ahmed turned to the nearest pirate. "The infidels took my phone," he said. "Give me yours so I can call and arrange the boats!"

The pirate hesitated.

"Now! You idiot," Ahmed yelled, and the man pulled a phone from his pocket and handed it over. Ahmed pocketed it and turned back to the milling crowd.

"What are you waiting for?" he screamed, and fired a burst from his AK near the feet of the nearest group, sending bullets whining off the steel deck and into the darkness. "Go now, or by the Beard of the Prophet, I will shoot you down myself."

The startled pirates started running toward the deckhouse, and as soon as they were all in motion, Ahmed turned and ran for the accommodation ladder. As he started down the sloping aluminum stairway, his heart sank as he heard an outboard crank and saw a man in the remaining Zodiac untying the boat from the ladder. One of the pirates was a bit smarter than the rest.

"Stop!" Ahmed screamed, and brought up his AK, but the pirate twisted the throttle and the boat roared off. Ahmed's burst hit him in the back and he toppled out of the boat, which slowed abruptly and veered against the hull, thirty feet away from the bottom landing of the accommodation ladder.

Ahmed slung his AK on his back and flew down the ladder, hardly hesitating at the bottom before diving in. He reached the boat in half a dozen strong strokes, and pulled himself aboard as angry shouts reached him from the main deck above. Their attention drawn by his gunfire, even the dullest pirate understood Ahmed was abandoning them.

He twisted the throttle and veered away from the ship in a series of erratic turns to avoid the fire of two dozen assault rifles on full automatic.

AIRBORNE OVER *LUTHER HURD*
HARARDHEERE, SOMALIA

"Christ! I think that's our guy they're shooting at," the SEAL lieutenant said.

"What should I do?" the pilot asked.

"Fire a burst over their heads," the SEAL said, picking up the mike.

"Roger that," the pilot said. The chopper swooped down, gun blazing, to hover just off the ship.

"This is the United States Navy," the speaker boomed. "Lay down your weapons and raise your hands."

Weapons clattered to the deck below and hands shot in the air.

"Well, that was tough," the pilot said. "Ah, what do we do now?"

"Damned if I know," the SEAL said. "I guess we hold them here until the guys in the boats arrive."

"What about our guy in the Zodiac?"

"They didn't hit him, and he can see what's going on. I figure if he needs help, he'll either circle back or call."

Ahmed looked back over his shoulder at the chopper hovering beside the ship. He considered going back for help, but dismissed the idea. If he had any chance of finding the woman at all, he must act now. If he returned, he knew he'd be forced into a planned, structured mission, and there wasn't time. He reached over in the darkness to feel the firmness of the starboard inflation tube. It had been hit, but the leak wasn't too bad. He'd be ashore long before it was a problem.

Halfway to shore, he was no longer as confident. The starboard tube had lost over half its buoyancy and the little craft was listing. The strange trim was causing the boat to track to starboard as well, so to compensate and maintain course, he had to steer continually farther to port. The maneuver cut his forward speed by half, and the scattered lights of the harbor didn't seem to be getting any closer. That's when he noticed the port tube was leaking as well.

Reflexively, Ahmed reached into the pocket of his sodden pants and pulled out the pirate's phone, hoping by some miracle it had survived the dunking. The screen was dark and resisted all efforts to revive it. He cursed and tossed the phone over the side and stared ahead at the lights, willing the boat forward.

A half mile from shore, he figured he could still make it, even as the tubes lost most of their buoyancy and let the transom sag to the point of drowning out the outboard. There was still air left in pockets and he could ride in the collapsed mess, propelling himself with the paddle.

Unfortunately, he neglected to think about the weight of the outboard until it was too late to jettison it, and the motor pulled the whole mass from beneath him, leaving him treading water. No worries. He was a strong swimmer.

A hundred yards away, a dark fin broke the water.

CHAPTER TWENTY-TWO

DRILLSHIP *OCEAN GOLIATH*
ARABIAN SEA

Mukhtar stood swaying at the control panel, clutching the storm rail to steady himself, as he stared at the bank of brightly lit displays and bewildering profusion of controls. He concentrated, trying to remember why he was standing here, and it came to him. He was the only one left, far too weak to transfer the cylinders or man the fishing boat alone, even if he'd had the strength to throw off the lines.

That's why he was here, staring down at the controls of the dynamic positioning system, watching it work its magic unattended. He didn't understand it, but knew it contained powerful computers. Computers that monitored a satellite, then automatically adjusted the vessel's thrusters to keep her rock steady over her chosen work area more precisely than any human hand.

And somewhere in his fever-racked brain, he knew the thrusters that held the ship steady also moved her. If only he'd paid more attention when he watched the drillship crew do it. He fingered the joystick and sent up a prayer for Allah to guide him. He must get the Great Cleansing Plague ashore!

KYUNG YANG NO. 173
ARABIAN SEA

"Piece of shit!" Dugan said, as the screen of the ancient radar went black for the fourth time in the last hour. He gave the cabinet a hard whack with the flat of his hand, and nodded when the screen jumped back to life.

"You break my new radar! Radar OK till you come! I say Phoenix replace."

Dugan sighed and cursed his own stupidity. Ever since he'd attempted to shut Captain Kwok up by offering to charter the fishing boat on behalf of Phoenix, the little Korean had been compiling a massive repair list, which, through some tortured logic, he had deduced was the charterer's responsibility.

"Look, Kwok," he said. "This friggin' radar was *new* about twenty years—"

He was interrupted by the trill of his sat-phone. He fished it out of a pocket.

"Dugan."

"Tom. This is Jesse."

"I'm glad you called. We're almost at the location you gave us and—"

"And the drillship's not there," Ward finished his sentence.

"That's right," Dugan said. "What's up?"

"I wish I knew," Ward said. "An earlier sat photo showed her off location, but I wanted to get a follow-up on another pass to confirm. She's moving. Looks to be ten or twelve miles north of you, moving northeast at two knots."

Dugan looked back at the blinking radar, and suppressed an urge to kick it.

"I see her now. I saw that target earlier but didn't realize it was her," Dugan said. "Ah... this kind of shoots our hang-around-and-pretend-to-fish plan in the head. What do you want me to do, Jesse?"

"I don't see we have a choice," Ward said. "Just pretend you're on the same course, overtake her, and get as good a look as possible."

"Roger that," Dugan said, as he caught Kwok's eye and pointed to the radar screen. Kwok leaned over from the wheel and looked, and Dugan mimed turning. Kwok nodded and made the course change.

"We're turning for her now," Dugan said.

"ETA?"

"If she's doing two knots, we should be able to overtake her in a couple of hours if the weather holds." Dugan eyed a building thunderhead on the horizon. "But I can't guarantee that. It looks like we have a storm building to the south."

"OK. Let me know," Ward said, and hung up.

"Son of a bitch," Dugan said, as the little fishing boat overtook the drillship and moved even with her port side. The larger vessel wallowed in the moderate swells, and the top of her towering derrick cut a regular arc through the air. She was typical of her class, with an engine room aft and deckhouse and navigation bridge forward, topped with a cantilevered helipad that jutted out over her bow. But the ship design wasn't the cause of Dugan's concern.

"Sea is not so bad. Why is ship rolling so much?" Borgdanov asked.

Dugan raised his glasses and studied the ship.

"Christ," he said. "There's a lot of pipe racked back in the derrick. She's got to be top-heavy as hell. With the swell, that's got her rolling pretty good."

"What do you mean?" Borgdanov asked.

Dugan pointed. "You see that dark vertical shape inside the derrick? That's drill pipe, and it's heavy. When they're putting pipe down, it's faster if they keep sections screwed together into what they call a stand. They keep a few stands stored vertically in the derrick. But that's when they're sitting in one place. They normally lay everything flat on deck when they're moving. And she's got way more racked back in the derrick than I've ever seen." Dugan glanced over his shoulder to the south. "When this storm hits, she may capsize."

He raised the glasses again, studying the drillship as they grew closer. He started at the bow and moved aft, lingering on the fishing boat tied to the port side. The smaller vessel was bobbing erratically as it was dragged along, straining at the thick hawsers that secured it, as the two vessels intermittently banged together with hollow booms. He spotted a pile of rags on the open aft deck of the drillship, and adjusted the binoculars until the pile jumped into focus—a dead man, between two large gray mounds. There were other, smaller mounds scattered on the deck, and as he examined them more closely, Dugan realized he was looking at piles of silver coins. Coins slid from the piles as the big ship rolled, covering the deck with a fortune in silver. A fatal temptation moving toward the Omani coast, the derrick top swinging through the sky like a gigantic metronome of death.

Dugan's hand trembled as he reached for his phone.

Ward answered on the first ring.

"We got a little problem here," Dugan said.

Ward studied the latest satellite imagery. The front was more defined now, moving toward Dugan's position, but the more imminent threat was to the west. He was reaching for the phone when it rang.

"We got a little problem here," Dugan said. "From the looks of it, everyone is dead, and I'd say the virus is definitely onboard, along with a huge pile of silver." He paused. "But on the positive side, given the condition the ship's in, this storm will probably sink her within a few hours at most."

"You don't have that long," Ward said. "We've picked up what we think are two pirate mother ships west of you, on a course for the last position of the drillship. I don't know if they're al-Shabaab or garden-variety pirates, but they're headed your way. As soon as they pick up the drillship on radar, they'll figure out it's moving and launch their high-speed attack boats."

"It doesn't matter who they are," Dugan said. "If they're after the virus, all they have to do is grab a few bodies and haul ass, and if they're after the silver, I don't think they're going to let a few bodies slow them down. It's just too damn tempting. Intentional or otherwise, these guys are going to end up carrying the virus ashore. I can send you pictures via my phone. Is that enough evidence to get a strike to sink this thing before the pirates get here?"

"Maybe," Ward said. "But that's not the problem. Even if we sink her with a missile or air strike, we can't get anyone else there quickly enough to police the wreckage. There'll be debris and infected bodies floating around when the pirates arrive. If your visitors are al-Shabaab, they may harvest a few. And no matter who they are, chances are they'll pick up any floating bodies to take them ashore for a proper Muslim burial." Ward sighed. "Either way, we're screwed. If the virus gets off the ship, there's no way we'll ever be able to contain it. According to Imamura, the only way to kill the virus is to burn the bodies."

"At least you might have some time to start distributing a vaccine," Dugan said.

Ward said nothing.

"Jesse? Are you there?" Dugan asked.

"Yeah," Ward said. "I'm still here, but, ahh... there is no vaccine, Tom. Imamura worked on one for over fifty years and came up dry."

"Holy Mother of God!" Dugan said. "What's the mortality rate?"

"A minimum of seventy percent," Ward said. "Imamura speculated it would be much higher. If everyone on the drillship is dead, that would make it a hundred percent." Ward paused. "Tom, if this isn't contained…"

"Yeah, I can figure that part out, Jesse."

Ward said nothing, and the silence grew. Dugan broke it at last. "Look, Jesse, we're not equipped to deal with this. I wouldn't know where to start. Aren't there any other naval forces nearby?"

"Sure, a few. Chinese, Indian, Russian. Take your pick. They all have ships in the area as part of the anti-piracy effort. Do you really want any of those guys getting access to this bug? Hell, I don't even want our side to get it. Everyone will pay lip service to destroying it, but the temptation to keep 'just a little for research purposes' will be great."

Dugan cursed, then lapsed into silence again.

Ward waited a bit, then asked, "What are you going to do, Tom?"

"Not a clue," Dugan said. "But I guess I better figure something out. And by the way, Jesse, thanks for dropping me in the crapper again."

Ward heard a click.

Kyung Yang No. 173
Arabian Sea

"You don't have to go," Dugan said.

Borgdanov shrugged. "I am Russian, so I am fatalist. And if what Ward says is true, we will all die in few months anyway. If I must die, I prefer to die trying to prevent epidemic." He smiled at Sergeant Denosovitch, who was nodding in agreement. "And besides, without us, who will look after you, *Dyed*?"

"Well, thanks anyway," Dugan said.

The corporal said something in Russian and the others laughed, as Dugan looked on, a question on his face.

"Corporal Anisimov says Ilya and I must go with you to keep you alive to sign bonus check at end of mission. He has already picked out nice car," Borgdanov said.

Dugan smiled wanly and bent to apply more duct tape to the juncture between his survival suit and rubber boot. He, Borgdanov, and Denosovitch were dressed in bulky bright-orange cold-water survival suits they'd pilfered from the emergency-gear locker of the *Kyung Yang No. 173*. They were the typical Gumby suits with integral mittens and booties, designed to be donned over clothing. At least they *had* sported integral mittens and booties until Dugan had cut off the clumsy appendages at the ankle and wrist, enduring outraged screams from Captain Kwok as he did so.

"You cut survival suit!" Kwok screamed. "This no good. Suits very expensive. Phoenix pay, I tell you."

The look on Dugan's face and the knife in his hand had forestalled further protests, and the little Korean had hurried back to the wheelhouse to record this latest outrage on his growing list of expenses.

The initial roominess of the suits and Dugan's impromptu modifications meant that, stripped to their underwear, Dugan and the two much larger Russians could fit in the suits sized for the much smaller Korean crewmen. For all of that, the suits were tight, snug on Dugan and approaching skin-tight on the Russians, and all three looked like gangly teenage boys after growth spurts, with wrists and ankles exposed.

The foul-weather-gear locker yielded three pairs of rubber boots they could squeeze their feet into and some long rubber gloves that would provide much better manual dexterity than the clumsy mittens Dugan cut off the suits. The trio had donned the boots and gloves and then slipped the sleeves and legs of the survival suits down over them before taping the resultant seams with duct tape. With the tight-fitting hoods of the survival suits in place and the full-faced tear-gas masks the Russians had in their gear, the trio would be about as microbe-proof as was possible, considering the circumstances.

And hot as hell. Suits designed to prevent hypothermia in arctic waters were not the most comfortable apparel in near-equatorial heat. Dugan could already feel the sweat puddling in his boots. He pressed the last piece of tape into place and straightened, finding Borgdanov holding a gas mask and eyeing it skeptically.

"Do you think masks will do any good, *Dyed*?" he asked. "They are for tear gas. I think not so good for biologicals."

"Ward says the main mode of transmission is contact, except when the stuff's embedded in a powder medium and intentionally delivered as an aerosol. If the masks will filter out the powder, we should be OK." Dugan grimaced. "And it's not like we have anything else."

Borgdanov nodded, and Dugan continued. "Christ," he said. "We better get this done before we die of heat stroke. Get the corporal here up in the wheelhouse to keep an eye on Kwok. When we're ready to leave, I want to make sure our ride's still around."

Borgdanov nodded and spoke to the corporal in Russian. The man moved toward the wheelhouse as Dugan and the two other Russians pulled on their hoods, donned their gas masks, and moved to the bow of the fishing boat. The pocketless survival suits complicated things a bit, so the trio had improvised. The big sergeant had an assault rifle slung across his body in one direction and a coil of rope in the other, almost like crossed bandoliers. Borgdanov and Dugan both carried small backpacks. The Russian's holding a radio, a Glock, flash-bang grenades, and spare ammunition for both the assault rifle and the Glock. They didn't anticipate resistance, but they could hardly go into the unknown unarmed. Dugan's backpack held tools and other things he'd pilfered from the fishing boat—anything he anticipated he might need for his half-formed plan.

They'd spotted the rope ladder earlier, trailing down the starboard side just forward of the after house. Dugan surmised it was how the pirates had come aboard initially. They hadn't bothered to pull it in. A lucky break, because boarding the rolling drillship would be tough, even if they weren't covered from head to toe in rubber.

Dugan watched the ladder now as Kwok inched the fishing boat toward it. As the drillship rolled toward them, the bottom of the ladder swung away from the hull, only to reverse course and slam back against the hull as the big ship rolled away. Far too soon, they were alongside the ladder, and as it swung toward the fishing vessel, Sergeant Denosovitch scampered over the rail and stepped on the bottom tread, grasping the vertical ropes of the ladder in each hand. As Dugan had advised him, he kept only his toes on the ladder rungs and his hands on the ropes, not the wooden rungs—advice that served him well when the ladder slammed back against the hull.

On the next out-swing, the sergeant climbed two rungs before he had to brace himself for the swing into the hull, and on the out-swing after that, he managed four. The higher he got, the closer the ladder stayed to the ship's side. Dugan watched from below as the Russian scaled the ladder with ease. *Frigging showoff.*

In no time the sergeant peered down at them from the deck of the drillship. He slipped the coil of rope from his shoulder and lowered the end to where Dugan and Borgdanov waited. Borgdanov grabbed the dangling rope and threaded it through the straps of the backpacks as Dugan held them up. Borgdanov tied a knot expertly and signaled the sergeant, who hoisted the backpacks aboard. As the backpacks ascended, Dugan crawled over the rail.

He stood facing outward, his feet on the gunwale, gripping the waist-high rail at his back with one hand, sweat pooling in his boots not just from the heat. The end of the rope came down again, this time with a loop tied in it, and Dugan grabbed it with one hand. In a brief moment of machismo, he considered refusing the safety line. A very brief moment. He dragged the loop over his head and under his arms. Moments later he felt the rope snug up across his chest, as above, the sergeant took a turn around the handrail and took slack out of the line.

Dugan watched the ladder swing back toward him and tensed to make the step, but at the last second his nerve failed. He clung to the rail of the fishing boat, just as Kwok overcorrected to pull a bit away from the drillship. As the vessels separated and the drillship rolled away, the rope bit into Dugan's chest to rip him from the rail, and he saw the black expanse of the hull rushing toward him.

50 YARDS FROM THE BEACH
HARARDHEERE, SOMALIA

Ahmed saw the fin again from the corner of his eye and murmured a silent prayer to Allah. From what he could see in the moonlight, it wasn't a huge shark, perhaps five or six feet, but it was plenty big enough to kill a defenseless swimmer. And he was, for all intents and purposes, defenseless. He'd jettisoned his AK when the boat sank, and though he still had the Glock stuck in his waistband, he knew the shark would strike from the dark depths before he ever saw it. Once he was crippled, he'd no doubt other sharks would join the feeding frenzy. As if confirming that grim thought, he spotted a second fin to his left as he turned his head to breathe. Ahmed banished such thoughts and focused on the distant shore. *There is no God but Allah, and Muhammad is the Messenger of Allah,* he repeated to hold dark thoughts at bay.

First contact was a brush against his leg, filling him with terror. A terror unabated as he stroked even harder for shore and felt the brush of a large body against his side. They were toying with him, like a cat with a mouse before the kill. He felt hard contact to his chest as he was lifted clear of the water, and clutched at the gray mass below him, shocked and bewildered. A blast of air and water erupted in his face.

Ahmed wiped his eyes with the back of a hand and blinked down at what he realized was a dolphin's blowhole inches below his face. The dolphin submerged, and Ahmed treaded water as elation replaced terror.

"*Allahu Akbar,*" he shouted into the night sky, then turned to stroke hard for the beach. Around him, dolphins rolled and leaped from the water, shedding droplets that gleamed silver in the moonlight.

HARARDHEERE, SOMALIA

Arnett felt the bag shift on the man's shoulder, followed by a short sensation of weightlessness—too short for her to prepare herself for the landing. She grunted as she landed flat on her back and air rushed from her lungs, and then struggled with the horrible feeling of being unable to take a breath. She heard the zipper an inch from her nose and smelled the khat on Toothless's breath as he leaned over to unzip the bag. Dim light leaked around the edges of the duct tape over her eyes, and the canvas shifted beneath her as Toothless upended the open bag and turned her out face-down on the floor. Rough concrete scraped Arnett's cheek and she smelled animal dung, just before rough hands rolled her onto her back.

"Where is your smart mouth now, whore?" Toothless asked.

Arnett sucked in air until she was able to respond.

"You... your brea... breath smells worse than the goat shit on this floor, asshole. Don't you own a toothbrush? Oh, that's right. You don't have many teeth left, do you?"

The savage kick landed in her side, and she was unable to suppress a moan at the unseen assault. Then she sensed Toothless leaning over her again, his closeness confirmed by his fetid breath and spittle spraying on her face as he spoke.

"That's right, whore. Moan," Toothless said. "Soon you'll have even more reason to moan as I fill your holes with my manhood."

Her head was jerked to the left by a vicious openhanded slap.

"Lie here and think about that," Toothless said. "I must gather supplies before the infidels decide to strike our safe house. And perhaps I'll have a cup of tea and a bite to eat. Whore-training is hard work, and I must keep my strength up."

She heard Toothless laughing as he moved away from her. The light leaking around her blindfold lessened—Toothless was apparently taking the light source with him. Moments later, she heard the complaining squeak of an un-oiled hinge followed by the rattle of a chain. Then an engine started and faded, and all was quiet.

Arnett rolled onto her stomach and inched her knees forward, elevating her butt and grinding her face into the foul-smelling concrete. She pushed her bound wrists toward her butt, trying to get her butt through the circle of her bound arms to get her hands in front of her. The first attempt wasn't close—nor was the twenty-first. She was sweating now, her panic rising at the thought of Toothless's return. She made herself relax and imagined her body was rubber, stretchable at her whim. She focused on her shoulders, willing muscles to relax, glorying in each fractional gain, until her wrists were below her butt and she was—stuck!

She was a tortured pretzel, her shoulders burning now, unable to continue or to return her hands to their previous position behind her back. Her right cheek was scraped raw on the rough concrete. Arnett threw her weight to the right and rolled up on her butt, her hands partially pinned beneath her. She took a deep breath, drew her knees to her chin, and pulled up on her arms with all her might to slide her bound wrists past her butt. Something tore in her left shoulder and she felt blinding pain, and then her wrists were under her knees. Arnett collapsed onto her right side, gasping at the pain in her shoulder, on the verge of passing out. She fought down nausea and forced herself to bring her knees to her chest once again, and worked her feet out of the circle of her bound arms.

Her shoulder throbbed and her left arm was useless. She tried raising her bound hands to loosen the tape around her eyes, but the required movement was too painful. She had to separate her hands first so she could immobilize the left one. She tried rolling onto her left side to support her left arm on the floor, as she lowered her head and gnawed at the tape binding her wrists. The adhesive tasted bitter in her mouth, and bits of tape stuck to her lips, but finally, the tape parted.

She moaned as she sat back up, holding her left arm tight against her side and picking at the tape circling her head with her good right hand. Her fingers found the end and picked it free. She unwound the tape quickly until she got to the last round stuck to her hair, then squeezed her eyes shut and gave one final jerk, hardly flinching as the tape tore at her hair.

Arnett blinked in the dim light. She was in some sort of dilapidated outbuilding, one that had housed livestock from the smell. It was poorly constructed and cracks in the plank walls let in moonlight that striped the rough floor. She reached down with her good hand to free her ankles. It was a matter of feel versus sight in the dim light, but her fingers found the tiny ridge that marked the end of the tape and picked it free. It unwound in one long strip.

Her first thought was escape, and she struggled to her feet and found the door in the dark. It yielded a half inch, then stopped with a metallic rattle, chained shut from the outside. She took a step back and the movement sent a stabbing pain down her left arm. She had to attend to that.

Arnett retraced her steps, kneeling and groping for the discarded tape with her good hand. She found it and fashioned a large loop with part of the tape, then tore the rest of the strip away by holding it in her teeth and tearing with her good hand. She slipped the loop over her head as a sling to support the weight of her useless left arm, then used the rest of the tape to circle her slight torso twice, immobilizing her now-supported arm against her body. Crude but effective.

Hurting and exhausted, Arnett leaned against the wall and tried to figure out what to do next.

A half-hour later, she clutched the handle she'd broken off an old rake found in the corner of the shed behind a stack of mud bricks. It had taken what seemed like forever to carry the bricks to the duffel bag, one at a time in her good hand. When the bag would hold no more, she'd managed to zip it. It was barely visible on the dim moonlight-striped floor.

She knew she had to kill Diriyi. Her guess was he'd brought her here on the spur of the moment and no one knew he'd done so; otherwise, there'd be a crowd, eager to participate in her rape. If his body was found, his death would be a mystery. If found alive, he'd raise the alarm.

Arnett pressed the end of the short rake handle against her useless left arm, testing the sharpness of the jagged point at the broken end. It wasn't much of a weapon, wielded by an exhausted and brutalized woman with a wrecked shoulder against an armed adversary. However, the odds seemed a bit better when you considered she was Lynda Arnett, five times Isshinyru Karate National Champion in the Black Belt Weapons Division. Her weapon of choice was the traditional Okinawan short sword, the *sai*.

Arnett closed her eyes and centered herself, visualizing Toothless in her mind's eye and mentally walking through her strike a half dozen times, each time changing Toothless's reaction and the necessary response on her part. When she'd covered the possibilities mentally, she practiced them physically in slow motion, testing every footfall, feeling the wooden rod in her hand. She'd reached the point of trying them full speed with her eyes closed when her heart leaped into her throat. A car engine!

Diriyi smiled to himself as he parked the SUV. The town was abuzz with the news of the American attack, and the few occupants of the al-Shabaab safe house had fled, fearing an American retaliatory strike ashore. That the cowards had left in haste had been obvious, and they left plenty of food and provisions.

It was strange how these things worked out. Mukhtar's gamble on the drillship had gone wrong, and Diriyi's gut told him he would never see the man again. The fool had risked everything to get the nerve gas, and for what? Fame as the most effective fighter of the jihad? Notoriety as the favored of Allah who had slain the most infidels? Such delusions of grandeur were invariably costly. Now there'd be few of al-Shabaab left, and Diriyi was the most visible. He'd no intention of becoming the recipient of the Americans' wrath. He'd lay low awhile, then return to a life of piracy. After, of course, he'd enjoyed and killed the woman. Who knows, perhaps in a year or so he could claim a reward for leading the Americans to her grave. His smile widened.

Diriyi glanced in the back of the SUV before he got out. He'd enough provisions for several weeks. He'd have to cut some brush to camouflage the SUV, but that could wait. It hadn't yet begun to lighten in the east. Time for a little romp with the whore. He grew hard at the thought, and reached down to touch himself through his trousers.

He picked his way down the path to the goat shed in the light of the battery-powered lantern. The key turned in the padlock, and the chain rattled as he pulled it through the door handle. The dry hinge squealed its lament as he pushed the door inward. Time for some fun.

"Are you ready for some fun, whore?" he asked. He held the lantern high and moved into the shed, the complaining door swinging shut behind him.

Diriyi stopped, puzzled. The duffel bag, obviously full, was just visible at the edge of the circle of light cast by the lantern, but he couldn't see the woman. Then he understood and laughed.

"So you think you can hide from me in the bag, like an ostrich with its head in the sand? You are truly a stupid bitch. Giving me pleasure is going to be the only thing of value you will ever accomplish in your short life."

Diriyi held the lantern high and covered the short distance in a few long strides, aiming a savage kick at where he figured the woman's stomach would be.

Arnett stood with her back to the wall on the hinge side of the door as the door swung shut behind Toothless, revealing his back. She heard his derisive words, and nodded as he moved forward and drew his leg back to kick the bag. It was the response she'd hoped for, and she was moving even before the toe of his running shoe contacted the pile of bricks.

Toothless screamed as the toes of his right foot shattered, and he stumbled back, dropping the lantern, which flickered but didn't go out.

"Toothless!" yelled Arnett, and the pirate turned toward her, reaching for the Glock in his waistband. Too late.

"Kiii… aiii!" screamed Arnett, just as the jagged end of the rake handle contacted the man's Adam's apple and she threw her hip to put all her body weight and momentum into the blow. The wood ripped through voice box, jugular vein, and esophagus, and impacted the pirate's cervical vertebrae, forcing him backward even as he sank to the ground. Arnett drew her makeshift weapon back sharply, and arterial blood gushed from the gaping wound, spraying her before she could jump away.

Toothless lay on his back on top of the bag of bricks, blood pumping from the hole where his throat had been, moving his lips in wordless comprehension. His eyes fluttered shut and his lips stopped moving, and the air in the shed became even more foul as he lost sphincter control. Arnett stood motionless, staring down at him in the soft glow of the overturned lantern.

The trembling started in her good right hand and got increasingly violent. The bloodied stake slipped from her grasp, and the palsy spread to her legs, which buckled. She fell to her knees and retched, adding the stench of her own vomit to the miasma of death and goat dung. She felt an urgent need to flee and dragged herself toward the door on her three functioning limbs, the rough concrete punishing her hand and shredding her pants at the knees.

The door squeaked as she clawed it open and crawled into the moonlight, collapsing against the rough plank wall. She was suddenly very cold, even in the equatorial night, and she shivered uncontrollably. Shivers turned to sobs—whimpers at first, then growing to deep, wracking cries of anguish and freely flowing tears. Tears of sorrow for Gomez and the other dead crewman, tears of relief that she'd escaped Toothless, and finally tears of rage at the murderers that had done this to her and her crew. She hugged herself with her good arm and let her emotions out, crying until she was drained and exhausted.

Arnett jerked awake with the sun in her eyes, enraged at herself for falling asleep. She struggled to her feet. All her joints were stiff and her left arm and shoulder throbbed. She saw the SUV parked fifty yards away beside a dirt track, at the end of a narrow footpath through low brush and small boulders. There wasn't a house in sight.

She moved back into the shed, breathing through her mouth to avoid the stench, and knelt to pull the Glock from the dead pirate's waistband. A search of his pockets yielded another full magazine, a sat-phone, and car keys. She stuck the Glock in her waistband and pocketed the other things before she turned toward the shed door.

Arnett froze at a sound from outside, then bolted to the wall seconds before the door flew open and banged against her. The door swung closed to reveal Traitor, gun in hand, kneeling over Toothless with his back to Arnett. She raised the Glock in her right hand and drew a bead on the back of Traitor's head. Her hand trembled not at all as her finger tightened on the trigger.

CHAPTER TWENTY-THREE

M/T *MARIE FLOYD*
ARABIAN SEA
EN ROUTE TO HARARDHEERE, SOMALIA

Captain Vince Blake paced the bridge, glancing at the speed log each time he passed. A building south wind on the beam steadily increased the swell, and the old tanker had a pronounced roll now—and a speed of 13.5 knots, despite the chief engineer's best efforts to coax more from the tired old engine.

Blake's pacing was interrupted by the buzz of the sat-phone.

"*Marie Floyd*, Captain speaking," he answered.

"Captain Blake, this is Ray Hanley. The navy boys took back the *Luther Hurd* last night—"

"How's the crew? Everyone all right?"

"Just the two guys we already knew about," Hanley said. "Jones, the acting captain, was injured, but not seriously."

"Don't you mean acting chief mate? Arnett's the capt..." Blake's voice trailed off. "You... you said there were no more deaths. Why is Stan Jones acting captain? What about Lynda?" Blake asked at last.

"Truth is, we don't know," Hanley said. "They took her ashore just before the attack. All we can do at this point is hold a good thought for her."

Blake didn't trust himself to respond. He composed himself, then changed the subject. "How about the other ships? Any more executions?"

"Two days, two dead seamen," Hanley said. "Just like the bastards threatened."

Blake glanced at the speed log and resisted an impulse to punch the control console.

"Maybe we should tell them we're coming with hostages of our own," Blake said. "And tell them to hold off executions until we get there."

"Except we don't know where all their boats are," Hanley said. "If they figure out where all their missing buddies are before you get under the protection of the USS *Carney* and the other navy ships off Somalia, you can bet they'll swarm you. Don't forget, this little operation of ours is totally off the books. We can pull up next to the navy boys and the pirates will *think* we're under their protection, but the truth is, none of the Western governments want to touch our little privateering operation with a ten-foot pole. They'll help us by ignoring us, but that's as far as it goes. Tough as it is, we have to stick with the plan."

Blake sighed. "I understand. We're almost ready."

"What do you mean, *almost*? You should be done."

"We are here," Blake replied. "Woody has the whole gang finishing up *Pacific Endurance*." Blake turned as he spoke and looked across at where *Pacific Endurance* was keeping station with him, a mile away.

"Hey, Junior. Get your ass up here," Woody called down into the tank.

Seconds later, Junior West's head and shoulders emerged from the open expansion trunk of number-one starboard cargo tank, a welding hood tilted back and a cap worn backward under the hood soaked with sweat.

"Whatcha need, Woody?" asked Junior. "You're holding up progress."

"Where are you?"

"Last seam. Maybe three feet," Junior said. "Course, that's just the first pass. I figure I ought to give 'em all at least one more."

"No need," said Woody. "Just seal all the seams with epoxy. It ain't like it's a permanent job."

Junior nodded. "Whatever you say. You think this is gonna work?"

"Don't see why not," Woody replied. "All any pirate opening the tank cover or the ullage hatch is gonna see is gasoline. They won't know they're looking at a six-foot-square box with a couple of tons at most and that the rest of the tank is full of seawater. The digital readout in the cargo control room will show the tanks all full."

Woody shrugged. "And even if they're suspicious enough to gauge the tanks by hand, those funnels and capped pipes we have rigged to line up under the ullage hatches will let the tape go all the way to the tank bottom and show gasoline all the way." Woody smiled. "I gotta admit, that Dugan's smart."

Junior nodded, and started back down into the tank.

"Junior," Woody said, and Junior stopped and looked over. "Don't forget to cut a couple of little holes in the tops of the walls of the false tanks so the inert gas can equalize. Put 'em way up at the top, right below the main deck where nobody can see 'em. I don't know how savvy these pirates are, but I don't want any of them getting suspicious 'cause there's no inert-gas blanket on the cargo."

Junior nodded again and disappeared into the tank.

DRILLSHIP *OCEAN GOLIATH*
ARABIAN SEA

The black hull rushed toward Dugan as he threw his weight to the side, attempting to spin on the rope. At the last moment, he twisted in flight and his back slapped against the hull, snapping his head against the steel with a dull thud, cushioned by the thick neoprene of the survival-suit hood. The impact drove the air from his lungs. He clung to the rope and saw stars and fought to retain consciousness.

He saw Borgdanov at the rail of the fishing boat, screaming up at the deck of the drillship and gesturing wildly. Then Dugan was moving again, almost in slow motion at first, then rushing toward Borgdanov as the drillship rolled and Kwok overcorrected again, sending the fishing boat charging at the drillship. Dugan dipped into the water to his knees, staring up helplessly at Borgdanov as the bow of the fishing boat towered above him on the crest of an approaching swell. He squeezed his eyes shut in anticipation of being crushed between the steel hulls.

Then the rope bit his chest even harder, and he was jerked upward as the drillship reached the end of her roll and started back in the opposite direction. Dugan opened his eyes to see Borgdanov flash by, as if Dugan was ascending past him on an express elevator. A strong hand grabbed his leg, and he heard a thunderous crash and the screech of steel on steel as the rope slackened its grip on his chest and he felt himself falling—not swinging now, but straight down.

Dugan landed on top of Borgdanov, driving him to the deck of the fishing boat some feet back from the mangled handrail. He heard muffled Russian curses below him, as Borgdanov rolled him off and got to his feet before reaching down to help Dugan. Dugan took the offered hand and pulled himself up.

Borgdanov put his facemask against Dugan's so he could be heard over the engine. "Are you injured, *Dyed*?"

"Ju-just my pride," Dugan said, as his breath returned. "Thanks."

The Russian gestured up toward the drillship. "Is thanks to Ilya. He pulled very hard when you were in water, and then released rope at just right moment so I can pull you in. We are very lucky, I think."

Dugan stepped back and nodded before waving up at the sergeant, who returned his wave. He took in the situation. Kwok was maintaining station next to the drillship, and Dugan could make out a steady stream of abuse in English and Korean coming through the open window of the wheelhouse, even with the noise and the mask. He had no doubt the little Korean was tallying repair expenses mentally, even as he maneuvered his boat. There was a sizable dent in the hull of the drillship, and the gunwale of *Kyung Yang No. 173* was set in a good eighteen inches, with the attached handrail mangled. Dugan had a fleeting thought about Woody's cement-box patches and put it out of his mind. First things first. He put his facemask against Borgdanov's.

"OK. Let's try this again. Do you think you should remind Ilya to make damn sure I'm on the ladder before he snubs up the safety line?"

Borgdanov smiled through the mask. "*Nyet*. I think he remembers now."

Dugan nodded and moved to the side of the boat. He jumped on the ladder without hesitation this time, and ten terrifying seconds later, he crawled over the handrail onto the deck of the drillship. Borgdanov was on the ladder and starting up as soon as Dugan cleared the rail, and the *Kyung Yang No. 173* moved away to trail the drillship.

As previously agreed, the Russians armed themselves and took the lead, communicating with long-familiar hand signals. The ship's movement was different than the fishing boat's, more extreme due to the weight of the pipe in the derrick but less erratic. Dugan cast a worried look at the storm clouds to the south. The seas were coming from the starboard quarter now, striking the vessel diagonally on the stern. If the wind and waves shifted to the beam, things could deteriorate quickly. He pushed the thought from his mind and fell in behind the Russians.

Besides the single body they'd already spotted on the open deck, they found several more in the deckhouse passageways. When they pushed open the crew lounge, Dugan almost lost it. Bodies were everywhere, leaking blood and fluids. It was all he could do to keep from vomiting in his mask. He closed the door, and they began a room-by-room search of the rest of the quarters, faster now, sure they would encounter no armed resistance.

They found two more bodies in upper-deck rooms and encountered the last one on the bridge, lying in a pool of his own blood and vomit on the deck next to the dynamic positioning console. Dugan studied the bank of flashing video monitors on the DP console and considered trying to bring the vessel's bow into the weather. One look at the controls dissuaded him.

He didn't know the system, and this wasn't the time for on-the-job training. He could make things worse.

Instead, he gestured the two Russians close. Without the noise of the fishing boat engine, they could hear each other better now, but they still had to yell to communicate through the masks and hoods.

"I think that's all of them," Dugan yelled. "We need to get all the bodies into the crew lounge with the rest so we can burn them." He looked at Borgdanov. "If the sergeant can do that, I need to show you something."

The two Russians nodded, and the sergeant moved toward the body, but Dugan caught his arm. "Don't touch them directly," Dugan said, and pointed to the curtain between the chart room and the main area of the bridge. "Throw a curtain or shower curtain over the bodies and then roll them over onto it. Then you can drag them down the stairs or into the elevator without touching them any more than you have to. After you get the bodies taken care of, find the laundry and look for some bleach. Slosh it over any body fluids on the deck."

The sergeant looked confused. "Bletch?" he said.

"*Klornogo otbelivatelya*," the major said, and the sergeant nodded his understanding before moving to tear down the chart-room curtain.

Dugan motioned Borgdanov to follow, and led him out the bridge door and up the external stairway to the helideck perched high over the bow of the drillship. He found the nearest fire station, freed the fire monitor, and swiveled it to point overboard before opening the valve wide to send a stream of water arcing over the ship's side. He left it there, and with the Russian in tow, crossed the helideck to the fire station on the opposite side of the ship and repeated the operation.

"These monitors will spray water until I stop the fire pump and drain the line," Dugan said. "That may take a few minutes. While that's happening and Ilya is moving the bodies, I want you to look for the gas cylinders. According to Ward, they look something like scuba tanks. When you find them, put them with the bodies in the crew lounge. Get the sergeant to help you when he finishes with the bodies."

Borgdanov nodded, and Dugan continued. "But remember, while you're doing that, keep an eye up here on these monitors. If you see diesel shooting over the side, one of you needs to get up here quick and close the valves. Got it?"

"*Da*. As you explained on the boat, I understand."

Dugan nodded and headed for the stairs.

Sweat squished between Dugan's toes as he raced down the external stairs on the port side of the deckhouse. Only the fact that the boots were tight kept his feet from slipping around inside them. He hit the main deck and moved aft toward the machinery casing, his footing made even more treacherous by the loose layer of silver coins shifting across the open deck with each roll of the ship.

He slipped twice, the second time falling to his hands and knees as the ship took a hard roll to port. He froze at the metallic clang of drill pipe shifting in the towering derrick beside him, then breathed a sigh of relief as the vessel began to right herself. His relief was short-lived.

There was a thunderous boom, and he felt the steel deck vibrate through his gloves as the pirates' fishing vessel once again lost its fight with the mooring lines holding it captive and surged back against the side of the drillship. Dugan struggled to his feet on the tilting deck. *Christ!* How the hell did he get into this mess? He swallowed his fear and pressed aft to the machinery casing, hoping the layout wasn't too different from what he was used to.

He found the main fire pumps on a lower level, turned off the one that was running, and closed the discharge valve before dropping into the bilge to trace the system piping. He found the drain valve a few feet away. Water gushed over his legs and into the bilge when he opened it, cooling him a bit. He was tempted to linger, but he had no time. Truth be told, not even enough time to drain the system properly—there would be water trapped in branch lines unless he opened the valves on every single fire station—but that didn't matter. Opening the two monitors at the very top of the system would allow enough air into the system to drain the main line and allow it to vent when he refilled it. That would have to do. Reluctantly, Dugan climbed out of the cool bilge in pursuit of his next objective.

He spotted the centrifugal purifiers first, and found the diesel-oil transfer pump not far away. He traced the pump discharge piping until he found what he needed—a branch line about the same size as a fire hose—then traced the system farther, closing valves as he found them, isolating the branch line.

The hacksaw he'd taken from the Korean boat was old and dull. Undoubtedly, there were better tools aboard the drillship, but he had little time to find them and figured they might be under lock and key. His hands were sweating in the clumsy rubber gloves, and he almost lost his grip on the saw several times before it began to bite into the pipe. When he penetrated the top of the pipe, diesel gushed out, covering his hands and making the pipe and saw slick under his rubber gloves.

Dugan bore down hard on the saw and his right arm ached with the effort, as the dull blade sank through the pipe with glacial slowness. The pipe finally parted with a snap, and Dugan lurched forward as the hacksaw slipped from his grasp and clattered in the bilge below. *Good riddance!* He moved to the nearest fire station.

He cut the fitting off the end of the hose with a knife from his backpack and dragged the hose to the severed diesel line. The hose slipped over the end of the pipe easily. It was a bit bigger than the pipe, and it might leak, but he prayed it would hold long enough. Five minutes later, the hose was clamped securely to the pipe with a half dozen stainless-steel hose clamps scavenged from the fishing boat.

Water dribbled from the fire-system drain valve in a feeble stream, intermittently petering out then increasing with each roll of the ship. Close enough. Dugan shut the drain valve, lined up the other valves in his jury-rigged system, and started the diesel-oil transfer pump. The pump growled to life and the flat fire hose ballooned to a cylindrical shape as diesel gushed through it to fill the fire main. *So far, so good.* He rushed up a steep stairway to the engine control room.

The ballast control console was straightforward, and the mimic board allowed him to understand the system immediately. He started a single ballast pump, opened and closed several remotely operated valves, and then left the engine room to dash up the stairs and pick his way forward over the shifting silver carpet of the open deck. The ship took another bad roll, accompanied by the thunderous boom of the fishing boat against the side and a sound like a huge slot machine disgorging a jackpot, as coins spilled from the last intact pile to skitter across the deck.

He spotted the Russians on the starboard side, each with a cylinder on their shoulder, and worked his way across the pitching deck.

"Are the monitors—"

"Do not worry, *Dyed*," Borgdanov said. "Ilya closed monitor valves."

Dugan glanced at the sergeant and saw confirmation in the stain on his legs where diesel had splashed him.

"And I found cylinders," Borgdanov said. "Thirty-seven in two cargo baskets near crane. These are the last two."

Dugan nodded and fell in behind the Russians, just as the captive fishing boat banged against the hull again.

The Yemeni fishing boat Mukhtar had hijacked had seen better days when her previous—recently deceased—owner had acquired her a decade earlier. Maintenance since had been as needed, leaving her thinning hull a patchwork of steel of various thicknesses, held together by welds of indifferent quality. It was a miracle she had survived pounding against the stronger hull of the drillship as long as she had.

But even miracles have limits, and the repeated hammer blows took their toll. Steel bent and welds cracked, spreading through hull plating and frames as well. Water wept through the hull in a dozen places. Then the weeps became trickles; the trickles, streams; and the boat, heavy with water, moved more ponderously as it wallowed low in the water beside the drillship, straining on the lines that held it there.

CHAPTER TWENTY-FOUR

Ahmed squatted beside Diriyi's lifeless body. The ripped throat, blood pool, and stench left no doubt the man was dead. He wasn't surprised that he'd found Diriyi—Harardheere was spread out, but still easily covered on foot by a man fit enough to run at a steady pace. And Diriyi hadn't been popular. The few people that had seen his tricked-out SUV pass were only too happy to share that information with Ahmed. That same SUV on the side of the road led Ahmed to the shed.

He was surprised, however, to find Diriyi dead and the woman missing, and that complicated things. Known now as a man of shifting loyalties, his alter ego, Gaal, was undoubtedly unpopular with the various pirate gangs that called Harardheere home. He'd no doubt that the same people so eager to point out Diriyi would be equally happy to point him out to anyone interested. His best option was to rescue the woman and call for extraction. There were two problems with that, of course—he couldn't find the woman and he had no means to call anyone. Ahmed held the Glock in his right hand and began to search Diriyi's pockets with his left. Diriyi's cell phone would solve at least one of those problems.

The sound behind him was less than a whisper, but enough. He dived to the right as a bullet whistled past his ear. He landed on his shoulder and followed through in a tumbling roll, ending up with his Glock trained on—the woman!

"Don't shoot!" Ahmed said. "I'm on your side. Sergeant Al Ahmed, US Army Special Forces."

The woman's own gun was trained on Ahmed's forehead from less than five feet away, and it didn't waver. "Pleased to meet you," she said. "I'm Queen Elizabeth. Drop the gun! Now!"

Ahmed considered the situation. He couldn't shoot the woman, so holding a gun on her was rather pointless. He bent, keeping both hands in sight, and laid the gun on the concrete floor.

"I've been undercover the whole time," Ahmed said. "I helped the chief engineer and the others escape, and then I came after you."

"Really?" the woman said. "Seems like the last thing I recall was you coming up to the captain's quarters to help Toothless here stuff me in a duffel bag."

"He zapped me with the stun gun too," Ahmed said. "That's why I couldn't stop him from taking you."

"I guess I missed that part, though I do remember you holding a gun to my head and pulling the trigger."

"An empty gun," Ahmed said.

"That would carry a bit more weight with me if we hadn't both found out it was empty at the same time," the woman said.

Ahmed shrugged. "I suspected. The terrorists disarmed me when I came aboard. They were unlikely to hand me a loaded gun before I proved my loyalty. Then Mukhtar turned away from me when he racked the slide to fake chambering a round, and when he did hand me the gun, it felt light, like the magazine was empty. And besides, if they planned to test me, I didn't think they'd waste a high-value hostage like you. So I was pretty sure."

"Pretty sure?" she asked, her face reddening. "Did you say *PRETTY SURE*?"

Ahmed shrugged again. "It was a calculated risk."

Her hand twitched and the gun barked. Ahmed's hand flew to where his left earlobe had been.

"You stupid bitch!" he screamed. "You could've killed me!"

She stared at him with ice-cold eyes as he clutched his bleeding ear. "A calculated risk," she replied. "And if I wanted to kill you, there'd be a hole between your eyes. But as you've probably figured out, I don't believe your little fairy tale. That is, I'm ninety-nine percent sure it's a lie. That one percent is keeping you alive, so here's what we're going to do. If you're who you say you are, you must have a contact. Someone who can convince me you're legit. So you're going to call them now and let me talk to them. Got it?"

"My phone was trashed when I went in the water," Ahmed said. "I was about to take Diriyi's when you shot at me."

"I already took his phone." She grimaced in obvious pain as she worked her left arm out of a makeshift sling and free of tape wrappings to dig in her front pocket. She produced a phone and held it out with a shaky left hand, all the while keeping him covered with the Glock in her right.

"Call whoever you need to," she said, "but don't say a word. I don't want you warning anyone or giving away our position. You hand it back to me as soon as it starts ringing, and so help me God, if I hear as much as a peep out of you, you'll get a bullet in the head. Is that clear?"

"Very clear," Ahmed said, as he dialed.

A moment later he held the phone out, and the woman took it with her left hand and held it to her ear.

Arnett glared at Traitor and listened to the phone ring, her finger on the Glock's trigger. She was about to hang up when a man answered, his accent distinctly American.

"482-5555," he said.

"Who is this?" asked Arnett.

There was a long silence, then the voice asked, "Who're you calling?"

"I'm calling anyone who can verify there's a guy in Somalia pretending to be a pirate when he's actually a sergeant in the US Army Special Forces," Arnett said. "And you better talk fast, because I'm about to put a bullet in his head."

There was a long pause. "Captain Arnett?" asked the voice.

Arnett's heart jumped, but she caught herself. It could still be a trick. "That's me," she said. "Who's this?"

"Agent Jesse Ward, Central Intelligence Agency, ma'am. And I must ask you, are you having a storm there?"

Storm? What was he talking about? Then she remembered.

"No, Agent Ward. I believe *good weather* are the words you're waiting for."

"They are indeed, Captain," Ward replied. "I take it you've met Sergeant Ahmed. Please don't shoot him. He's one of my most valuable assets."

Arnett realized she was still pointing the Glock at Ahmed and lowered it as Ward continued. "Hold one, ma'am. There's someone I know wants to talk to you."

Arnett listened as she heard connection noises, then a phone ringing.

"*Marie Floyd*, Captain Blake speaking."

Relief washed over Arnett in waves, and for the first time in days, she believed she was going home.

DRILLSHIP *OCEAN GOLIATH*
ARABIAN SEA

Dugan stood on the open deck and braced himself against the roll of the ship as he nodded to Borgdanov.

"All of them," he said. "We need to get as much oxygen to the fire as possible."

Borgdanov nodded back and opened fire, rounds from his assault rifle stitching holes in the thick shatterproof glass of the crew-lounge windows. He worked his way down the row, stopping to pop in a fresh magazine, and Dugan followed behind him, beating the remnants of the shattered glass out with a fire extinguisher. When they'd finished, Dugan moved to the two fire hoses stretched out on deck, and bent to double-check the nozzles. He'd opened both to *fog* position, and wrapped the levers with wire from his backpack to prevent accidental closure. Satisfied, he nodded to Borgdanov, grabbed one of the hoses, and fed it through a glassless window, nozzle first, as the Russian did the same with the second hose farther down the row of windows.

"I don't know how much they're going to dance around when we pressurize them, and we don't want them popping out," Dugan said, "so feed in plenty."

Borgdanov nodded, as Dugan finished and duct-taped his own hose to the storm rail just below the ruined window. He used half a roll, wrapping the hose and rail repeatedly. Ugly but strong, at least strong enough to help prevent the hose from backing out of the broken window. He moved to Borgdanov's hose and repeated the procedure, then looked out at the building seas. The ship had a perceptible port list now, as Dugan's ballast adjustment began to manifest itself—perhaps a little too soon. He gave the ocean a last worried look, and hurried into the deckhouse with Borgdanov at his heels, fighting their way uphill as the ship took a roll.

They found the sergeant outside the crew lounge using the safety line to lash oxygen and acetylene cylinders to the passageway storm rail. Dugan looked into the open door of the crew lounge and nodded. Dead crewmen and pirates covered the deck, and trapped between the bodies were the gas cylinders. Scattered about the large room were cans of various shapes and sizes—paint thinner, alcohol, cooking oil, anything and everything flammable. Zigzagging across the room was a fire hose leading through the open door and arranged over the bodies. The nozzle at the end of the hose was wired shut and firmly secured to a table pedestal. Visible along the length of the hose were punctures Dugan had made with his knife. Not bad for a jury-rigged crematorium.

"I do not see why we need torch, *Dyed*," Borgdanov said. "I think alcohol and other things are enough."

Dugan shook his head. "All that stuff will burn fast. We need the diesel to keep feeding the fire, and diesel's not like gasoline—it's damned hard to get going. The torch is our insurance." Dugan glanced over at the sergeant. "Looks like Ilya's finished. Let's get it done."

Borgdanov nodded and spoke to the sergeant in Russian, as Dugan opened the valves on the oxygen and acetylene cylinders and plucked a friction striker from where it hung on a loop over one of the valves. The Russians moved up the passageway to the fire station that served the perforated fire hose.

Dugan stepped through the door and followed the oxygen and acetylene hoses down a narrow path through the bodies to the center of the room. The hoses terminated at a cutting torch taped to the leg of a coffee table inches away from a five-gallon can of cooking oil. Dugan squatted, opened the valves, and then struck a spark at the head of the torch. A flame flared to life against the silver side of the oil can. Dugan adjusted the valves on the torch to maximize the heat, dropped the striker, and raced from the room. He nodded down the passageway to Borgdanov, who opened the valve on the fire station a single turn, just enough to send diesel coursing through the hose to leak through the perforations over the pile of bodies. They fled the deckhouse.

"I think something is wrong, *Dyed*," said Borgdanov five minutes later, as Dugan and the two Russians balanced on the pitching deck some distance from the broken windows of the lounge.

"Give it a minute more," Dugan said. "When the cooking oil ignites, flames will spread to the rest of the more volatile stuff fast, then we'll see result—"

They all flinched at a loud explosion, and a ball of flame rolled out the farthest of the broken windows of the crew lounge. In seconds, flames were licking out of all the windows.

"There we go," Dugan said. "Time to add a little more fuel to the fire. Remember, open the valve wide."

Borgdanov nodded and rushed to the far fire station, while Dugan manned the nearer one. He twisted the valve open and diesel rushed into the flat hose, inflating it like a thick white snake, and Dugan watched the bulge at the leading edge travel down the hose and through the broken window into the lounge. In moments, there was a loud *whomp*, as diesel misted from the fog nozzle and ignited in a violent burst, followed by another as the spray from the second nozzle ignited. Flames boiled from the windows, topped by smoke that rose in a thick black cloud, caught and ripped away by the increasingly violent wind.

The fire was roaring now, and Dugan had to once again shout to make himself heard through the suits and masks. "That should do it. Let's get the hell off this thing."

Dugan started aft along the pitching main deck, starting down the port side, then changing course to traverse to starboard. There was a definite port list now, with the vessel rolling more to port than starboard, and the layer of silver coins had started to shift across the open deck, leaving surer footing to starboard. Even as Dugan rushed aft, he knew something was wrong. When he reached the stern, he moved across the ship and looked down the port side.

He cursed as the two Russians joined him.

"What is wrong?" Borgdanov asked.

"I wanted to give the fire plenty of time to burn," Dugan said. "So I set the ballast system up to slowly give her a port list. I figured that, being top-heavy, she'd capsize in an hour or so."

Dugan pointed to the Yemeni fishing boat, awash to its main deck and tight against the side of the larger vessel, hanging off half a dozen thick mooring hawsers. "I didn't figure on this. That friggin' boat's sinking, and she's heavy enough to increase the list, at least until those mooring lines part. Now it's a crapshoot."

The Russian looked confused. "What means 'crapshoot'?"

"It means we got to get the hell out of here. Now!" Dugan said, turning to look out at the increasingly violent sea. "Where the hell is Kwok?"

He swiveled his head, and a moment later, spotted the *Kyung Yang No. 173* in the distance, listing to starboard and headed away from the drillship. Dugan looked at Borgdanov and started to speak, but the Russian was already digging the radio from his backpack. His hands in the thick gloves were clumsy, but he pressed the radio to his hood near his ear and shouted through the facemask. After several attempts, he lowered the radio.

"Anisimov does not answer," Borgdanov said. "I think is big problem."

Dugan stared at the distant boat in disbelief. "Wonderful. The son of a bitch is abandoning us. Can it get any worse?"

The sergeant pointed into the distance, in the opposite direction from the *Kyung Yang No. 173*. Dugan saw a flash of white on the crest of a wave, and recognized it as a small craft headed their way, fast. As he watched, there were more flashes, until he'd counted eight, all undoubtedly loaded with pirates.

CHAPTER TWENTY-FIVE

Kwok looked out across the building seas at the drillship and cursed Dugan. He glanced back down at his radar and cursed again, as the flickering display went black, and he slapped the side of the cabinet with his open hand. The display blinked back to life and Kwok stared in disbelief, then rubbed his eyes and looked again.

Eight targets were closing on his position, not more than ten miles away, and closing fast. They were small and fast, their radar signatures indistinct. He had no doubt who they were. He turned to the impassive black-clad Russian, who watched from the rear of the small wheelhouse.

"Many pirates come!" Kwok said. "We must leave. Now!"

The Russian stepped forward and studied the display, then spoke into the radio mike clipped to his web gear. After several attempts, it was obvious he'd received no response. He looked at Kwok and shrugged.

"Major does not answer. I think maybe he is in noisy place and cannot hear radio in backpack," he said. "So. We must wait. He will call soon, I think."

Kwok looked across at the drillship. She was rolling more now, but also seemed to be developing a port list. He spotted faint traces of smoke rising from the deckhouse.

"We cannot wait! If we stay, pirates will catch us too." Kwok spoke to the helmsman in Korean, and the man began to turn the wheel.

"*Nyet!*" The Russian leveled his rifle. "We wait for others. Stay here."

Kwok raised his hands in surrender, and spoke over his shoulder to countermand the order. *Kyung Yang No. 173* returned to her previous course, creeping along in the lee of *Ocean Goliath* at two knots. She'd hardly settled back on course when the chief engineer rushed up the short stairway and into the wheelhouse.

"We're taking on water," he said to Kwok in Korean. "A lot of water!"

"What? How? Where?" Kwok asked.

The engineer shook his head. "I can't tell yet," he said. "But I think when you struck the drillship you disturbed one of the concrete patches. I'm pumping most of it out, but the pump can't keep up. We're already developing a starboard list."

"Can you repair it?" Kwok asked.

"Possibly," the engineer said. "If I can find it."

"Show me." Kwok started to follow the engineer down the stairs.

"Where you go?" the Russian demanded, stepping in front of Kwok.

"Hole in hull. Ship sinking," Kwok said. "I go look. You get out of way now."

The Russian stepped aside, confused, then fell in behind the Koreans.

Kwok turned over the situation in his mind, even as he raced downstairs after the engineer. He'd been with the Americans and the Russians when many pirates had been killed, and now he was—for all the pirates knew—voluntarily helping them. Eventually the pirates would find out about their dead colleagues and figure out who killed them. It wouldn't go well for him if he was their prisoner when that happened. Kwok reached that conclusion just as he stepped into the engine room, and the stench of diesel filled his nose and the engine assaulted his ears. He knew what he had to do.

Kwok followed the chief down the starboard side, and nodded as the man played the beam of his flashlight over the rising water in the bilge. Kwok turned to the Russian and motioned for him to stoop down, then spoke into the man's ear.

"Much water," Kwok shouted, to make himself understood over the engine. "We have leak. There." He pointed to a random place in the bilge. "You look. You see. You must bend down and look under that pipe."

Kwok motioned for the chief to shine his flashlight on the place where he pointed. Confused, the engineer did as ordered.

As the Russian bent to peer into the bilge, Kwok slipped a wheel wrench from a holder along the handrail and cracked him in the back of the head. The Russian collapsed, unconscious, and Kwok shouted in the chief's ear.

"Get two men to bind him and carry him to the wheelhouse, where I can keep my eye on him," Kwok said.

"Are you crazy?" the chief shouted back. "The other Russians will kill us!"

"And if we wait around for those fools, the pirates will kill us instead. We're getting out of here, so do as you're told. And I want full power from the engine when I ask for it. Now, take care of the Russian and find that leak. Understood?"

Kwok had just reached the wheelhouse when he saw a fireball rise from the deckhouse on the drillship. He ordered the helmsman to point the boat's bow southwest and increased speed to full power before he moved to the radar. The pirates would be on the drillship in less than ten minutes, but he figured their initial reaction would center on the silver, and he hoped to slip away in the confusion. Even if that miserable engineer couldn't get the leak fixed, floating around in a life raft awaiting rescue was a better alternative than being killed by pirates.

Kwok decided to improve his odds. He twisted the dial on the VHF to channel sixteen and keyed the mike.

"Mayday, mayday, mayday," he said, then repeated the name of his vessel and location. "Ship sinking. Many pirates come. Mayday, mayday, mayday."

He was on his fourth repetition when two crewmen dragged the Russian up the stairs and dumped him on the deck. The Russian moaned, and Kwok looked down at him, momentarily distracted. His head snapped back up as the VHF squawked.

"*Kyung Yang No. 173*," said an accented voice. "This is Russian naval vessel *Admiral Vinogradov*. We acknowledge your mayday and are coming to assist. Over."

Kwok looked back at the bound Russian, and blood drained from his face.

DRILLSHIP *OCEAN GOLIATH*
ARABIAN SEA

"We have assault rifle," Borgdanov said. "But most of ammunition I use to break windows. I have part of magazine left. Also the Glock with three magazines. But eight boats means twenty or thirty *piraty* at least. I think we have big problem, *Dyed*."

"Agreed," Dugan said. "But I'll be damned if I'm going to surrender just yet. Maybe we can—Jesus Christ!"

Dugan lost his footing and slammed into a mooring winch as the *Ocean Goliath* rolled to port on a particularly large wave. This time she lingered at the bottom of the roll, as if deciding between righting herself and lying on her side on the storm-tossed surface. Dugan held his breath at metallic clanging from the derrick as the drill pipe shifted, then let it out as the big vessel shuddered and rolled upright. But just upright, she was hardly rolling to starboard now. He regained his balance and moved back to where the Russians gripped a set of mooring bitts, bracing themselves against the roll.

"This baby's going over anytime," Dugan said. "The pirates might not recognize that right away, or realize everyone is dead. They'll come at us from the port side because it's lower and they can board easier. Then they'll either get distracted by all that silver or they'll head forward to the bridge and quarters to seize control of the ship. Either way, I don't think they'll head back aft, at least not initially. I figure we squat out of sight back here behind the machinery casing and see what develops." He looked up at the darkening sky. "There's bound to be a lot of confusion, and this storm will hit anytime. Maybe we use that to our advantage."

As if responding to Dugan's words, a raindrop hit his facemask, and in seconds, they were in a downpour. He looked forward at the smoke and flames billowing from the starboard-side lounge windows. Strangely enough, the wind was decreasing, and the smoke was rising in a black, greasy column. He turned away, reassured. No rainstorm, no matter how fierce, would quench the diesel-fed fire now, and when the ship went over, the lounge would be on the high side. She'd burn right up until she sank.

Dugan moved to the port side, and squatted out of sight behind the machinery casing. The Russians followed suit as the rain came down in sheets and collected on the pitching deck to form small waves on its way to the deck scuppers and overboard. The water accumulated on the exposed top deck of the machinery casing as well, faster than it could drain. Running to port because of the list, the water spilled over the edge of the upper deck like a minor waterfall, surging stronger with each roll of the ship.

"We can flush off under that water," Dugan shouted to Borgdanov over the noise of the downpour. "Then we can take these damned masks off. I doubt there's any airborne dust floating around in this mess. Remember to flush your gloves and boots well too—just in case—and don't touch your face. Tell Ilya."

Borgdanov nodded and turned to the sergeant, as Dugan crawled under the powerful stream. He turned his face up, staying there through several surges, as the water gushed over him from head to toe. Then he held his gloved hands under the flood, rubbing them vigorously to flush any residue off their slick surface. He looked to his right and saw the Russians similarly engaged, then stripped off his gas mask and closed his eyes before turning his bare face back into the stream. He crawled out of the direct stream and opened his eyes, blinking furiously and fighting an urge to wipe his eyes. He'd been in the suit less than two hours, but it seemed like two days, and the cool water on his face was comforting, even under the circumstances.

His respite was cut short by the sound of approaching outboards, and Dugan shouted for the others to get down.

The pirates approached like a band of howling Comanches, their swift boats speeding up swells and crashing down the other side. The first boats drew close and cut their speed to match that of the wallowing drillship, and the more daring of the pirates balanced in their boats, timing the movement of the big ship. At the bottom of *Ocean Goliath*'s port roll, several leaped to catch the bottom handrail and hauled themselves aboard.

Dugan's guess the pirates would be distracted by the silver was correct, and the first aboard screamed through the rain to their brethren, alerting them to their great good fortune. Here and there, pirates in the boats fired celebratory shots into the air.

Waabberi balanced on the shifting layer of silver as the big ship rolled, his initial exuberance at discovering the treasure mitigated by sudden terror as the port rail dipped toward the water and metallic clanging filled the air from the derrick. Something was very wrong. There was no evidence of Mukhtar or anyone, and the ship was close to capsizing. They couldn't stay here long, but—he looked down at his feet—he wouldn't abandon this treasure. He turned to the men beside him.

"You," he said, "position four men halfway between here and the deckhouse. If Mukhtar and his fanatics are about, I don't want to be taken by surprise." The man nodded and rushed to do as ordered, and Waabberi turned to the second man.

"We don't have long," he said, "and we must save the silver. Have the men scoop it up and dump it in the boats."

The man looked out at the seas. "The silver's heavy. We can't load the boats so heavily in these seas."

"The mother ships will be here in an hour, maybe two," said Waabberi. "Load the boats and shelter in the lee of the drillship until they arrive. Her hull is breaking the waves a bit. Even if she rolls over, she'll float awhile. We'll be all right as long as no one is in the shadow of the derrick when she goes over."

The man looked doubtful, and Waabberi lost his patience.

"Don't question me!" he screamed. "Get moving! Now!"

The man glanced at Waabberi's hand moving toward the pistol in his waistband, and turned away.

"At once, Waabberi," he said over his shoulder, and began to shout orders.

Soon pirates swarmed aboard with empty backpacks, having hastily emptied ammunition bags and anything else that could hold coins. Those without containers spread their shirts on deck and piled coins to be gathered into bundles. The drivers stayed in the boats, circling on the stormy seas, waiting their turn to nose up to the ship to take on silver.

Dugan squatted at the corner of the machinery casing and peered through the pouring rain at the controlled chaos. He felt Borgdanov beside him.

"What do you think, *Dyed*?"

"They're pretty occupied. If we had a boat, we could slip away. But I'll be damned if I can figure out how to get one."

"Lifeboats?"

"They'll all be forward near the quarters. There are life rafts back here, but I don't think we can slip away from these guys in a raft. And besides. We'll never catch Kwok in a raft."

As they spoke, the first boat moved away from the side to make room for the next. It was a semirigid inflatable, visible through the driving rain as it wallowed up a swell and circled close in the relatively calmer waters beside the rolling drillship.

"That's it!" Dugan said, pointing to the boat. "He's loaded and staying in the lee of the hull. My bet is he'll wait for the others back here beside the stern. He'll be by himself until another boat is loaded. That's our shot."

Borgdanov nodded and motioned Dugan back out of sight behind the machinery-casing bulkhead. The Russians conversed in hush tones, the sergeant looking doubtful, then nodding in reluctant concurrence. Borgdanov turned to Dugan.

"Ilya will go first without weapon," he said. "He must take out pirate without attracting attention, or we have little chance. After Ilya captures boat, you and I jump and he picks us up. If we are lucky, we sneak away in rain without being seen."

"And if we aren't lucky?" Dugan asked.

Borgdanov shrugged. "You and I will have weapons. We empty them at pirates to keep their heads down and maybe make them a little cautious. Then we jump and hope for best." He looked at the sergeant, then turned back to Dugan. "This you should know, *Dyed*. Ilya and I do not surrender, no matter what. Russian military is not so kind to *piraty*, so I think they will not be so kind to us."

"You're out of uniform, how will they know?"

Borgdanov shrugged. "We both have unit tattoos. Sooner or later, they will figure it out. Then it will not go so well with us. But you are American. You, I think, they hold for ransom."

"Thanks for the thought," Dugan said. "But apart from the Fruit of the Loom label in my underwear, I suspect we're all going to look alike to these guys."

Borgdanov smiled and clapped Dugan on the shoulder. "Is true, and also I now remember I make you honorary Russian. So, *tovarishch*, do you want rifle or Glock?"

Dugan shrugged. "I doubt I'll hit anything anyway, but I have a better chance with the rifle."

The sergeant passed Dugan the assault rifle, as Borgdanov dug in his backpack for the Glock, the spare magazines, and a roll of duct tape he used to tape the magazines to his thigh. Dugan held the unfamiliar weapon and looked back and forth at the Russians, then down at himself and his bright orange suit, and wondered if this was how the redcoats felt.

He heard the muted mutter of the outboard now as the pirate boat crept along beside the ship at two knots. Borgdanov dug in his backpack again and pulled out a small mirror on a collapsible extension, and then discarded the backpack on the deck. He pulled the extension out full length, and then crouched low and crept near the port side, examining the water near the ship. He nodded and motioned the others to join him.

"Is good," Borgdanov said. "He is very close. And he looks forward, at the others, not up. I think we can make nice surprise for him, *da*?"

Dugan nodded, and Borgdanov spoke to the sergeant. On the next roll upright, both Russians stood and moved to the rail, and Dugan followed suit. The sergeant scampered over the rail and stood with his heels on the deck edge, holding the rail behind him.

Dugan looked down and saw the pirate in the boat below him, just as Borgdanov had described, oblivious to their presence. The ship rolled back to port, and the sergeant timed his drop perfectly at the lowest point of the roll, a mere ten feet above the pirate's head. He entered the water feet first beside the boat, close enough to grab the side as he flashed by the startled pirate. His head submerged, but he kept his hands on the edge of the boat, and heaved himself upward, propelled by both his tremendous arm strength and the additional buoyancy of the survival suit.

The Russian shot out of the water like an orange porpoise, and flopped far enough into the boat to wrap his massive right hand around the pirate's bicep. He fell back into the water, attempting to drag the pirate with him, but the terrified man clung to the tiller of the outboard, pulling it hard over and sending the boat into a tight circle, as he found his voice and began to scream. Desperate to silence the pirate, the sergeant gave a mighty heave and pulled the man into the water, then clung to the boat with his left hand as he held the now-thrashing pirate underwater with his right.

Dugan and Borgdanov watched as the tightly circling boat slipped astern, no longer matching the drillship's speed. Dugan looked forward, relieved no one seemed to have heard the pirate's cries.

"I must help Ilya," Borgdanov said. "Stay here, *Dyed*. We will be back with boat." Without waiting for Dugan's concurrence, he slipped over the rail and dropped into the sea.

Terrific. Dugan looked after the boat, alone on a sinking ship with three dozen bloodthirsty pirates. He was moving back to the shelter of the machinery casing when they spotted him. He saw one of the pirates shout, then point, and several moved down the deck toward him. His first instinct was to run, but there was nowhere to go, and if he jumped overboard, he'd draw attention to the Russians and the boat, and both he and the Russians would make nice orange targets for pirates shooting off the stern. No, the best option was to keep them forward awhile. If they didn't *see* him jump overboard, they might be cautious about charging aft. And every second they delayed, the drillship would move away, increasing the range.

Dugan raised the assault rifle and opened fire, sending pirates scrambling for cover. His fire was indiscriminate—he had no illusions about his own marksmanship—and he emptied the magazine in seconds before moving to the cover of the machinery casing. Out of sight, he moved aft, keeping the bulk of the machinery casing between him and any approaching pirates. At the stern rail, he dropped the now-useless rifle overboard and crawled over the rail to drop feet first into the water.

"Is it one of Mukhtar's fanatics?" Waabberi asked.

"I don't think so. He was a big white man in orange coveralls with a hood."

Waabberi scratched his chin. "One of the crew then. But where did he get the weapon? Crews aren't normally armed."

His underling shrugged. "Perhaps he took it from one of the fanatics."

"It doesn't matter," Waabberi said, looking up at the derrick as the ship started another roll to port. "Put one man on guard in case he returns, and get everyone else back to the silver. We don't have time to waste on—"

He ducked at the crack of a gunshot, then realized it wasn't a shot at all, but the forward mooring line on the doomed Yemeni fishing boat parting at last. Deprived of this last crucial bit of support, the boat's bow dipped below a swell, and the forward motion of the drillship drove it deeper still, increasing the load on the remaining forward lines that, stretched to the limit of their elasticity, snapped in quick succession. Attached to the drillship now by only her stern lines, the bow of the boat swung away from the hull, and for one critical moment, the sinking boat acted as a rudder.

The big ship veered to port, at the very bottom of her port roll, and never recovered. The rest of the drill pipe in the derrick broke free to join the loose single string that had been producing the doleful clanging, and the ship pitched on her side, spilling pirates and silver into the storm-tossed sea. Despite Waabberi's warning, two of the boats were caught in the shadow of the derrick and disappeared, while the rest sped away from the ship in panic, then returned to circle the sinking ship, like flies disturbed from a dead carcass.

Dugan plunged through the water, turned end over end in the powerful prop wash from the drillship's thrusters. He felt a moment of disorientation and panic, but then he was free of the turbulence and the buoyancy of the survival suit carried him to the surface. He panicked again when his head broke the water, and he looked around in the driving rain. His visual range in the water was considerably less than it had been from the higher vantage point on the ship, and it was reduced even further as he bobbed up and down in the waves. How would he find the Russians? Even the huge ship was becoming a blur as it moved through the rain away from him and intermittently disappeared as he got caught in wave troughs.

A massive groan reached him, like the death rattle of some great beast, and he rode up on the crest of a wave in time to see the dim outline of *Ocean Goliath* rolling over. Then things went quiet, the only sound the hiss of the rain on the water.

And Dugan felt very, very alone.

CHAPTER TWENTY-SIX

Kwok looked aft and eyed the edge of the rainsquall, now stretched across the near horizon like a gray-white curtain, obscuring his view of the threat he was trying so desperately to escape. The storm front had passed with remarkable speed, and *Kyung Yang No. 173* had run out of it, into clear skies and troubled but calming seas. She struggled over a big wave as Kwok turned to watch the helmsman fight the wheel, compensating for the increasing starboard list.

Kwok dropped his gaze to the Russian bound on the deck, blood dried on the side of his head, glaring up at Kwok with hate in his eyes. Kwok ignored him and looked back out to sea, as he mentally parsed the possible outcomes of his current situation. His reverie was disturbed by hurried footsteps on the stairs, and moments later the chief engineer burst into the wheelhouse, soaking wet and dripping water on the deck.

"I found the leak!" the chief said in Korean, "but we must—"

"Is it fixed?" Kwok asked.

The engineer shook his head and tried to speak, but Kwok cut him off.

"Why not? Can you do it?"

The chief nodded. "Yes, but I must—"

Kwok exploded. "Then don't stand here talking to me! Repair it at once! Why'd you even come here?"

"That's what I'm trying to tell you," the chief said. "It's the most forward of the concrete patches the Americans placed. They left some materials onboard, so I think I can make the repair, but the force of the water against the hull is making the leak worse. I must slow it down a lot before I can hope to patch it. We must reduce speed until I can get it patched and the concrete sets."

Kwok looked back, as if trying to peer through the curtain of rain.

"Out of the question," he said. "The pirates could overtake us and capture us before the Russians arrive. We must get as far away from them as possible."

"And if the boat sinks?" the chief asked.

"Then we take to the raft," Kwok said. "The Russians should be here anytime to rescue us."

"And how do you intend to explain abandoning their countrymen, or the fact that we're floating around in a raft with a bound Russian?"

Kwok shrugged. "Dugan and the other two fools won't survive the pirates, so no one will know we abandoned anyone, and as far as our friend here goes"—he looked down at the Russian—"I don't think he'll be joining us in the raft. I suspect he'll drown if the ship sinks, or perhaps fall over the side before then."

The chief glared at Kwok. "*We* didn't abandon anyone, Captain. You're the one who ran away."

"And saved your neck in the process, you ungrateful fool," Kwok said.

"I doubt it was *my* neck you were concerned with," the chief said. "And it remains to be seen whether you saved any of us. Besides, running away is one thing; murder to cover it up is quite another."

"I'll deal with the Russian as I see fit," Kwok said. "Now stop your insubordination and get below and fix the leak. Without stopping the engine. Is that clear?"

"But I can't—"

"I said, is that *CLEAR*?" Kwok screamed.

The chief fixed Kwok with a silent glare. "I'll try," he said at last, and turned to the stairs.

ARABIAN SEA
ASTERN OF CAPSIZED *OCEAN GOLIATH*

Dugan bobbed in the water and fought rising panic. Staying afloat was no problem in the suit, but that was about the only positive. He imagined a slow death, floating around without food or water—unless, of course, a shark happened along. He compartmentalized his fear and tried to concentrate on the task at hand.

Visibility was awful. The raindrops whipped the sea into a fine mist a few inches above the water—inconsequential if you were in a boat, but blinding if the only thing above water was your head. Each time a wave lifted him, Dugan fought to lift his head higher and swiveled it frantically, hoping to catch sight of the Russians. He slipped back into each trough disappointed.

Then he heard it—the muted mutter of an idling outboard. On the next crest, he looked toward the sound and glimpsed a flash of orange before he tumbled back between the waves.

"Help! I'm here," he cried on the next crest.

"I hear you, *Dyed*," came the reply. "Keep shouting!"

Moments later, the boat almost ran over him as it crested a wave and crashed down toward him. It sheared away at the last minute, and then it was beside him, and Borgdanov pulled him in. Dugan lay with his back against a mound of coins.

"It's good to see you guys," he said, looking around. "Wherever the hell we are. I think I drifted quite a ways after the ship went over."

Borgdanov pointed through the rain. "Ship is there. Maybe five hundred meters away. We were closer just before she turned over, but still, we could barely see ship. But we heard gunfire and saw flash of orange and think maybe you jump in water. We have been searching."

Dugan nodded. "Thanks," he said, as he looked around.

The boat was heavy, plowing through the confused seas rather than riding over them, and the sergeant was fighting the tiller of the outboard to keep her from broaching sideways to the swell. Dugan turned to Borgdanov.

"What's our situation?"

"I lost Glock when I jumped" Borgdanov said. "But some *piraty* left weapons in boat when they go to take silver. We have two AKs and one RPG." He shrugged. "Fuel, not so much, but I think we have enough to catch Kwok. Anyway, we must try, *da*? You remember which way he goes?"

"Looked like southwest," said Dugan, looking around in the rain. "Wherever the hell that is."

Borgdanov smiled and said something to the sergeant, who patted a wooden case at his feet.

"*Piraty* left us nice compass," Borgdanov said. "So we go southwest. But *Dyed*, I think you should drive. Ilya and I keep watch with guns."

Dugan nodded, and moved to change places with the sergeant.

"I suggest one of you keep watch and the other start dumping the silver," Dugan said, as he pointed the boat southwest. "Loaded like this in these seas, we'll be lucky not to sink. Much less overtake anything."

The Russians stared at the pile, reluctant to jettison the treasure.

"Don't forget," Dugan said, "some of the dead men on the ship may have handled this stuff. I doubt viruses prefer to live on silver, and it's had a hell of a lot of water flushed over it, but make sure to keep your gloves on."

The idea the silver might be contaminated ended the Russians' reluctance, and Borgdanov jettisoned silver while the sergeant kept watch. As the boat lightened, Dugan increased speed, and the boat labored through the seas to the growl of the outboard.

ARABIAN SEA
BESIDE CAPSIZED *OCEAN GOLIATH*

"I warned the fools to stay out of the shadow of the derrick," Waabberi said to no one in particular, as he studied his band of bedraggled survivors. Miraculously, all of his men had survived the capsizing, except the drivers of the boats caught under the derrick. The survivors filled the five remaining boats to capacity, and floated together in a group in the lee of the overturned drillship, clustered around Waabberi's boat.

"Beard of the Prophet," Waabberi said. "If we were so unfortunate as to lose three boats, why did one of them have to be loaded with silver?"

"But Waabberi," a pirate said, "only two boats perished under the derrick. The silver boat was farther aft. The strange men took it."

"Strange men? What are you talking about, you fool? What strange men?"

"Big white men, dressed in orange," the pirate said. "I looked up and saw—"

"And you're telling me this now!" Waabberi screamed. "Why didn't you tell me at the time?"

"I tried," the man said. "But I was farthest away from the ship and I couldn't get your attention. Then the gunfire from the ship drowned out my shouts, and the ship capsized. Then I was rescuing our brothers—"

"Enough," Waabberi said. "Which way did they go?"

"I... I don't know. I lost of them in the rain."

Waabberi nodded and sat thinking to the combined soft muttering of the outboards, as the boats maintained station against wind and waves in the lee of the stricken drillship. Who were these strange men? Crewmen, no doubt; but where could they go? They didn't have enough fuel to go far. They must be close by, even now.

"Stop the motors!" he shouted, and the five outboards sputtered to silence. "Now," Waabberi said, "everyone listen. They can't be far."

Several men pointed at once, then Waabberi heard it himself—the distant sound of a straining outboard. He turned to his driver. "What direction is that?"

The man looked at his compass. "Southwest," he said.

Waabberi nodded and took quick inventory of his little flotilla, grateful now that some of his men had ignored orders and left their weapons in the boats when they boarded the ship to load silver.

"Quickly," he said, motioning over the fastest boat of the five and jumping aboard. "Three men here with me in the chase boat. The rest of you spread yourselves evenly among the other boats and follow. Unarmed men, get in the boat with the silver." Waabberi looked at the driver of the boat loaded with silver. "You'll be slow, so bring up the rear. Don't take risks in these seas. We've little enough to show for our efforts, and I don't want to lose any more silver. Is that clear?"

The man nodded as all the outboards roared to life, and Waabberi squatted in his own boat and pointed southwest.

ARABIAN SEA
5 MILES SOUTHWEST OF *OCEAN GOLIATH*

Dugan raised his free hand to shade his eyes from the bright sun reflecting off the water. They'd run out of the rainsquall a mile back, and it had been like switching on a light in a darkened room. The wind had calmed as well, and the sea was settling but still choppy, marked here and there with white-caps. He shot a worried glance over his shoulder at the gray-white curtain of rain and took a chance on increasing speed.

The sun was a mixed blessing. No longer deluged by cooling rain, Dugan once again broiled in the survival suit, and saw sweat running down the Russians' faces as well. He was contemplating stripping off the suit when a shout rang out in front of him.

"*Dyed!* There!" Borgdanov cried, just as the boat crested a wave. Dugan squinted into the distance in the direction of the Russian's pointing finger.

He smiled as he made out the unmistakable profile of the *Kyung Yang No. 173*. His smile faded.

"She's listing badly," Dugan said.

"No matter," Borgdanov replied. "I think is better to be on listing fishing boat than in middle of ocean on Zodiac with little fuel and no food and water, *da*?"

"I can't argue with that," Dugan said.

"How long before we catch her?" Borgdanov asked.

"Hard to say. She's not making full speed, but neither are we. I'd guess maybe half an hour—less if the seas cooperate."

Borgdanov nodded. "Is good—"

The sergeant yelled something to Borgdanov and pointed aft, and Dugan swiveled his head to see a pirate boat emerging from the rainsquall. As he watched, three more boats appeared out of the curtain of rain in quick succession. He looked forward to find the Russians checking their weapons.

"Can we beat *piraty* to fishing boat, *Dyed*?" Borgdanov asked.

"Doubtful," Dugan said. "Not that it'll make much difference."

"Will make big difference," Borgdanov said. "Is better platform to defend, and we add Anisimov's gun to our firepower."

"I'll do my best." Dugan increased speed, capsizing now the lesser risk.

Ten minutes later, it was obvious Dugan's initial doubts were justified. For every yard they had gained on the fishing boat, the lead pirate seemed to gain a yard and a half on them, and the rest of the pirate boats weren't far behind. Dugan noticed a fifth boat now, breaking the rain curtain and moving more slowly than the others. The pirates in the lead boat began a sporadic, if wildly inaccurate, fire in Dugan's direction. He took no comfort in the poor marksmanship; when they got closer, it wouldn't matter.

"I don't think we're going to make it to Kwok's boat," Dugan said. "And at this speed, we're burning a lot of—"

The outboard began to sputter and cough, then stopped.

"—fuel," Dugan finished, as his boat lost power and coasted down a wave.

Dugan tried unsuccessfully to restart the outboard, then threw a worried glance back at the pirates. He moved to the collapsible fuel bladder and opened the fill cap. There was a slight hiss as air rushed into the collapsed container, and Dugan released it from its securing straps, lifting and tilting it so that every last bit of fuel could drain through the attached hose to the outboard. He motioned the sergeant to take his place.

"Hold this up," Dugan said. "Not much there, but we'll go as far as we can."

He returned to the outboard. It started on the second attempt.

The chief engineer kneeled in the bilge, shoulder deep in oily water as he groped beneath the water's surface, searching by feel for the crack in the concrete patch. There! He'd found it again, and felt the rush of water on his fingertips. It was about 150 millimeters long from the feel of it. The thin wooden wedges he'd made should plug it enough for the bilge pump to catch up, then he could work on a more durable repair—if he could get one of the damn things tapped into the crack to stay this time. Broken remnants of half a dozen wedges floated on the water sloshing around him, testimony to his failure so far.

He closed his eyes and held his breath in anticipation as the boat rolled to starboard, and the water rose over his head. He grabbed a grating support with his left hand to steady himself, but kept his right hand firmly pressed to the crack—he wasn't going to lose contact with it again.

The boat rolled back almost upright, and as his head broke water, the chief braced his knees against the tank top and threw up his left hand. The crewman assisting him on the deck plates above leaned down to press a wooden wedge into it.

"Last one, Chief," the man yelled over the engine noise.

The chief nodded. He couldn't afford to lose this one, there was no time to make more. He lowered the wedge beneath the water and worked the thin edge into the crack by feel, using both hands. Once started, he then held it there against the incoming rush of water with his left hand as he reached up his right toward the deck plates. He was coated head to toe from the oil floating in the bilge, and he felt a rag in his open palm as his assistant above tried to wipe the oil away to improve his grip. Then came the firm slap in his palm, and he gripped the hammer handle.

He drew in another deep breath and closed his eyes as the boat rolled and the bilge water enveloped him again, and he groped underwater with the hammer until he felt the top of the thin wedge. He tapped tentatively and felt the wedge ease through the fingers of his left hand, deeper into the crack. He tapped again, just enough to seat the plug but not break the thin wood, as he had on his previous attempts. It only had to hold long enough to get the bilge pumped; he mustn't overdo it again.

He made a final light tap, his left fingers on the wood telling him the wedge was no longer moving into the crack, then he let go of it, just as the boat rolled back upright and his oily head broke the water.

"Got it!" he shouted to his helper, and started to climb out of the bilge. No sooner were the words out of his mouth than the wedge popped to the surface, borne away into a maze of piping on the wave of water rolling through the bilge. He considered trying to find it, but knew it was futile. He grimaced and started for the wheelhouse. He had to convince Kwok to stop the boat.

As he exited the engine room onto the open deck, he looked aft and saw the parade following his own boat. There was no mistaking the orange-clad figures in the lead boat. He rushed up to the wheelhouse, finding Kwok staring aft.

"Dugan and the Russians are—"

"I can see them, you fool," Kwok said. "And they're leading the damned pirates right to us! But what're you doing here? Is the leak fixed?"

"No. Our speed's making the leak worse. I can't repair it unless we stop."

Kwok looked aft again. "In ten minutes it'll be over, I think. We must maintain our speed until then. After that, it'll be safe to stop."

"Wha... what do you mean?"

Kwok pointed and the engineer squinted. The rainsquall had moved farther north, revealing the capsized drillship. Hovering over it was a black dot.

"That'll be a Russian helicopter," Kwok said. "If we can maintain our distance, I think they'll take care of our pirate friends. But if the pirates get here first, I'm sure we'll become human shields again."

"But Dugan and—"

"Screw Dugan!" Kwok shouted. "He's the one that put us in danger to start with. Now he's leading the pirates right back to us, so I think it only fair he helps us for a change. When the pirates catch him, they'll slow down to deal with him and the Russians. If he and those crazy Russians resist, all the better—it'll slow the pirates even more. And if the Russian chopper arrives while they are all mixed together and kills them all"—Kwok shrugged—"so be it. It's none of our affair."

The chief looked down at the bound Russian.

"That chopper is undoubtedly attached to a Russian ship, probably on the way here now. How do you intend to explain him?" The chief nodded at the Russian.

Kwok shrugged again. "If by some miracle Dugan and his crazy Russians survive, we'll just release the corporal here, claim it was a misunderstanding, and apologize. They'll be angry, but I doubt much will happen. But if Dugan and his companions perish, no one knows the corporal's here. I doubt the helicopter has fuel to stay for a prolonged period, so we'll have some time after they leave before the Russian ship arrives. We'll just wrap our friend here in chains and slip him over the side, as if he never existed."

Kwok smiled at the chief, pleased with his own cleverness. "When the Russians arrive, we are simply a poor fishing boat that was attacked by pirates. If you can get the leak repaired, we will continue to port. If not, we ask the Russians for help. Either way, we can forget we ever met Dugan and his crazy Russians."

"Yo... you're insane! I won't be involved with murder!" the chief said.

Kwok narrowed his eyes. "I suggest you rethink that position," he said. "Or you'll go over the side with your new Russian friend. Now get below where you belong and keep us afloat. I'll tell you when you can stop the engine."

RUSSIAN KA-29TB HELICOPTER
1 NORTHEAST OF *OCEAN GOLIATH*
ARABIAN SEA

The pilot stayed in the clear air behind the rapidly moving front, wary of any developments that might endanger his craft. He dropped low to the water and moved toward the plume of black, greasy smoke. The drillship was lying port side down, her hull awash, and as the pilot reached the ship and hovered over her, she lost her fight with gravity and slipped below the waves. The pilot circled and keyed his mike.

"Momma Bear, this is Baby Bear. How do you copy? Over."

One hundred nautical miles to the east, the comm center on the Russian naval vessel *Admiral Vinogradov* answered. "Baby Bear, this is Momma Bear. We read you five by five. What is your situation? Over."

"We had to divert to avoid weather," the pilot said. "We're presently over the site of a large drillship that burned and sank. No apparent survivors. Request you come to this position to extend search. Do you copy? Over."

"Baby Bear, we copy and confirm we're en route to your present position. What of your original mission? Over."

"There is activity to my southwest. En route to investigate. Over," the pilot said.

"Acknowledged, Baby Bear. Keep us informed. Momma Bear, out."

ARABIAN SEA
300 YARDS ASTERN OF
KYUNG YANG NO. 173

Dugan flinched as a bullet whizzed by his ear.

"Not to be critical," Dugan yelled to Borgdanov over the roar of the outboard, "but maybe you should start shooting back at these assholes."

"*Nyet*," said Borgdanov. "Is waste of ammunition. Do not worry, *Dyed*. We open fire when they get closer."

The outboard coughed to a halt just as he finished speaking.

"Well, that'll be anytime now," Dugan said. "We just ran out of fuel. Tell me when to start worrying."

ARABIAN SEA
700 YARDS ASTERN OF
KYUNG YANG NO. 173

Waabberi raised the binoculars and fiddled with the focus until the distant dot revealed itself as a Russian chopper. He shifted his gaze to the following boats, and watched them break pursuit and turn to run for the protection of the rainsquall as each identified the threat. Being caught on the open sea by a Russian chopper was a pirate's worst nightmare. It was survivable with hostages as shields, but when they caught a boat manned solely by pirates, the Russians were merciless.

He looked after the fleeing boats. The fools would never make the protection of the squall line. The chopper was too fast.

But how had the Russians found them? He turned back to study the orange men's boat. Someone must have called for help, but who? It couldn't be the fishing boat—they'd been chasing it only a few minutes, far too short a time for anyone to respond to a distress call. But the orange men came from the drillship, and they must have a radio. And if the Russians were coming to rescue the orange men, the way to avoid immediate and violent death at the muzzles of Russian guns was to get as close to the orange men as possible, whoever they might be.

He turned back to his quarry, just as the orange men's boat died.

"Faster," he said to his driver.

"But Waabberi," the driver said, "we should follow the others—"

"Silence, fool!" Waabberi said. "Our only hope is hostages, and the hostages are there. Keep at least one of them alive," he yelled above the outboard.

KYUNG YANG NO. 173
ARABIAN SEA

The chief engineer stared down at the water sloshing in the bilge. They were listing over ten degrees, and each roll of the boat brought water up to the deck plates on the starboard side of the engine room, dangerously close to shorting out the electric motor of the general-service pump, his last remaining way to pump bilges. This was lunacy and Kwok was an idiot. He touched his pocketknife through the cloth of his sodden coveralls, and made a decision.

He climbed from the engine room to the wheelhouse, taking the steps two at a time. His knife was open in his hand as he burst through the wheelhouse door.

Kwok turned, his scowl turning to concern as he saw the knife. "Yo... you dare attack me?" he shouted, as he moved to where the Russian's assault rifle lay on deck against the wheelhouse bulkhead.

The chief ignored Kwok and stooped to slice the tape at the Russian's wrists and ankles. The Russian sprang up, covering the distance to Kwok in two long strides.

He looked at Kwok with contempt. "To shoot, Kwok," he said as he disarmed the Korean, "you must first move safety selector."

"I... I meant no harm," Kwok said. "I left the drillship to save us all. You too. Bu... but I was wrong. It was a misunderstanding. I am very sorry."

The Russian smiled at Kwok, then shrugged. Kwok visibly relaxed seconds before a great ham of a fist smashed him in the face.

"Apology accepted," the Russian said, looking down to where Kwok lay on the deck, his face already purpling. He aimed a savage kick into the little Korean's midsection, and then turned back to the chief.

"You," he said. "Tie this bastard up, then tell me what is happening."

"We are sinking, and your countrymen are coming," the chief said, as he fished a roll of duct tape from his pocket and tossed it to the Russian. "And tie him up yourself. I have to stop us from sinking."

The chief turned on his heel and rushed to the engine room.

Arabian Sea
250 yards astern of
Kyung Yang No. 173

Unarmed, Dugan crouched as low as he could in the boat, then realized how stupid it was to expect an inflatable boat to provide any protection from a bullet. He scooted over to put as much of the outboard as possible between himself and the pirates. Borgdanov and the sergeant knelt on either side of him, calmly firing an occasional three-round burst back at the pirates. Dugan looked up at Borgdanov.

"For Christ's sake," Dugan said. "There's only one left. Use the RPG!"

"*Nyet*," Borgdanov replied without looking down. "He is still too far for RPG. We must be sure of kill shot. Anyway, chopper is coming soon, and the *piraty* are terrible shots. At this distance, it would be accident if they hit anything."

Just as the Russian finished speaking, bullets stitched the starboard tube of the inflatable, followed by the hiss of escaping air. Borgdanov looked down and shrugged. "Even *piraty* get lucky sometime," he said. "But maybe you are right. We are not moving and they are coming fast." He glanced over. "Ilya, the RPG."

Arabian Sea
Kyung Yang No. 173

Anisimov balanced himself on the canted open deck of the listing fishing boat, holding his assault rifle and looking for an opportunity to add his fire to that of his comrades. But it wasn't to be. Without her forward motion to maintain rudder control, the *Kyung Yang No. 173* was wallowing in the remaining swell, making her a very unstable firing platform. Given the range to the pirate boat and the fact that he would be firing past his comrades, he stood as much chance of hitting them as he did the pirates. He lowered his weapon and glanced up at the approaching chopper.

He did a double take. The chopper had stopped its approach and was hovering. What's wrong? Surely they can see the situation. They should be closing on the *piraty* with their mini-gun to provide cover for the major and—

Then it hit him, and he rushed for the wheelhouse and the radio.

ARABIAN SEA
250 YARDS ASTERN OF
KYUNG YANG NO. 173

Dugan peeked around the outboard and watched the pirate boat go airborne as it topped a swell fifty yards behind them, moving at full throttle now. He glanced at the sergeant on his knees beside him, the RPG to his shoulder, and willed him to pull the trigger. There was a muffled thump, and he watched the round fly from the weapon and plunge into the sea, thirty feet from their own boat.

"*Mat' ublyudkek,*" the sergeant muttered, as he tossed the now-useless weapon over the side and reached for his assault rifle.

"What the hell?" Dugan said.

"RPG is dud," Borgdanov said from Dugan's opposite side, continuing to stare aft as he fired at the pirates. "Where is chopper, *Dyed*? We could use help now."

Dugan rolled on his back and searched the sky. He spotted the chopper just as it went into a hover, and watched, waiting for it to charge forward and take out the pirates. *What's he waiting for?*

"Ahh… Andrei. This guy's not acting too friendly. If you have any secret hey-I'm-a-Russian-too signals, now would be the time to trot them out."

RUSSIAN KA-29TB HELICOPTER
OVER *KYUNG YANG NO. 173*
ARABIAN SEA

The co-pilot peered through the sight. The heat-seeker would do the work, but the range was relatively short and he had to ensure he got the weapon close enough to acquire the target. He was intent on his task, undistracted by the sudden chatter on the radio. Only slowly did it penetrate.

"Russian chopper! Abort! Abort!" a frantic voice screamed in Russian. "You are targeting friendlies!"

But he'd already launched.

CHAPTER TWENTY-SEVEN

Dugan sensed something was wrong and was rising even before the flame bloomed from the chopper.

"Get *DOWN*, *Dyed*," screamed Borgdanov, as Dugan rose between the two Russians firing at the advancing pirate boat.

Dugan, with no time to explain, placed a hand on the shoulder of each Russian and shoved with all his strength. The surprised Russians cursed as they tumbled into the water, and Dugan threw himself backward over the outboard. He was still in midair when the missile struck. The concussion drove the air from his lungs, and he plunged beneath the surface of the water just as a fireball rolled over it.

Disoriented, he surfaced seconds later, more from the buoyancy of the survival suit than from his own efforts. He felt a strong hand on his arm, and turned his head to find the sergeant towing him toward the charred remains of their deflating Zodiac. Soon, he was clinging to the side of the damaged craft with the two Russians, looking at a debris field where the pirate boat had been.

"Wh… what happened?" Dugan asked. "I was sure he was aiming for us."

"Maybe he was, *Dyed*," Borgdanov said. "But *piraty* boat was very near with engine at full power. Our own motor was cooling. So. I think heat-seeker made targeting correction." He looked at the smoldering remains of the Zodiac. "Even so, was very close. Being underwater and in suits saved us, I think."

Dugan looked up, searching the sky.

"Let's hope the chopper doesn't come back to finish the job," he said.

Kᴜᴜɴɢ Yᴀɴɢ Nᴏ. 173
Aʀᴀʙɪᴀɴ Sᴇᴀ

Oblivious to the VHF squawking demands that he identify himself, Anisimov watched in horror through the wheelhouse window as the fireball erupted on the sea behind him. Then as the fire dissipated, he saw an orange head bob to the surface, then two more, and all three moved to the charred remains of the first Zodiac. Relief flooded over him, and he heard the radio for the first time.

"—demand you identify yourself at once. Over."

Anisimov started to key the mike, then stopped. He looked down at his black utilities, devoid of rank markings but clearly Russian Special Forces. Instinctively, he touched the Russian tricolor flag patch on his shoulder. The Russian government didn't particularly like it when their elite soldiers resigned to become private contractors, and Anisimov and the others had done so under assumed names. And he was quite sure that Russian officials would like it even less if they knew that private contractors were impersonating active-duty Russian personnel. When Major Borgdanov accepted the assignment, the clear understanding was that there would be no possible contact with regular Russian forces. This could be tricky.

Anisimov stared at the mike. What did the major always say? Ah yes, when your back was to the wall, attack! Surprise assault is always the best defense. He walked to the wheelhouse window, where his uniform was visible to the hovering chopper and keyed the mike.

"Russian helicopter over my position! Identify yourself at once! Over," he said.

"This is flight Bravo Three from Russian naval vessel *Admiral Vinogradov*. I say again. Identify *yourself*," came the reply.

Anisimov ignored the request. "What is your name and rank?" he demanded.

"*Identify yourself at once.* Over," the chopper pilot said.

"Very well," Anisimov said. "This is Colonel Alexei Vetrov, Federal Security Service, Special Operations Group Alpha. Now. What is *your* name and rank? Over."

There was a long pause before the pilot responded, his voice tentative.

"Th... this is Captain Lieutenant Ivan Demidov," the pilot said. "Wh... what are you doing here, Colonel, if I might ask?"

"*Nyet!* You may *not* ask," Anisimov replied. "We are on classified mission, involving something you may have seen on way here. Beyond that, I cannot discuss on open radio. Is this clear, Captain Lieutenant Demidov?"

"*Da*, Colonel," Demidov said. "Do... do you require assistance? Would you like us to pick up the three men in the water?"

Anisimov hesitated and looked back at the charred Zodiac, and then around the fishing boat. Major Borgdanov and company seemed to be all right. The fishing boat was in bad shape, but if it sank, the Russians were nearby and he could always put out a distress call before taking to the raft. Better to get the chopper away for now.

"*Nyet*, Captain Lieutenant. Not at this time," Anisimov said. "What is your mission?"

"To rescue Korean fishing boat and arrest *piraty*," the pilot replied.

"Consider the first part of your mission successful," Anisimov said. "But I believe most of the *piraty* are escaping as we speak."

"We'll catch them, Colonel," said the pilot. "Though I suspect they'll all be killed resisting arrest."

Anisimov paused. He had no idea what had transpired on the drillship, nor if any of the pirates had been exposed to the virus. If they had, the results could be catastrophic. If they hadn't—well, they were still murdering pirates, weren't they?

"That outcome would be... helpful to our mission, Captain Lieutenant," Anisimov said. "In fact, it would be most helpful if these *piraty* disappeared without a trace. Is my meaning clear?"

"What *piraty*, Colonel?" the pilot asked. "Now, if there is nothing more, we'll undertake routine patrol to north and return to ship."

Thirty minutes later, Dugan and the two Russians sat in the charred, half-deflated Zodiac alongside the listing *Kyung Yang No. 173*. The seas had abated to a slight swell, and the two stricken vessels drifted side by side, tethered by a single thin line. Anisimov stood on the canting deck of the fishing boat and tossed Sergeant Denosovitch a plastic jug, as Dugan and Borgdanov opened cans and sloshed clear liquid around the crippled inflatable.

"That ought to do it," Dugan said. "We'll leave the rest of the stuff in the cans. It'll go up quick enough when it all starts burning."

He surveyed their handiwork. The air was thick with the pungent smell of paint thinner, mineral spirits, and whatever other flammables Anisimov had scrounged from the paint locker. They'd splashed it all over the boat until it puddled on the floorboards, and then stacked open cans of the liquid that remained in the middle of the boat.

"You got the bleach, Sergeant?" Dugan asked.

"*Da*," the sergeant said, and held up a large plastic jug in each hand.

"Let's get to it then," Dugan said, reaching for one of the jugs.

The three took turns helping each other douse the outsides of their survival suits with bleach. When all the suits were thoroughly wetted, Dugan nodded, and the men stripped the suits off and tossed them over the cans in the middle of the boat. Their underwear joined the pile, and they leaped, naked, to the deck of the fishing boat.

Anisimov had things prepared—buckets with a solution of strong soap and water, brushes, and sponges. One man stood still while the other two scrubbed him and flushed him with seawater. When they were done with that, each stepped under the powerful flow of the temporary shower Anisimov had rigged by securing a fire-hose nozzle to the handrail of the upper deck.

"That should do it," Dugan said, as he stepped from beneath the torrent and signaled Anisimov to turn off the water. He walked to the rail and untied the line holding the crippled Zodiac. Anisimov appeared with a flare gun, the other two Russians close behind. Dugan waited until the Zodiac was twenty feet away.

"Do it, Corporal," Dugan said. Anisimov nodded and fired, and the Zodiac burst into flames.

ISOLATION UNIT
SICKBAY
USS *BUNKER HILL* (*CG-52*)
ARABIAN SEA

"Christ, I'll be glad to get out of here," Dugan said to Borgdanov across the tiny room they shared with the other two Russians.

Borgdanov shrugged. "Is not so bad," he said. "Is only three more days, and is much better than the two days we spend on fishing boat, *da*? For sure food here is better." He shuddered. "I am not so fond of kimchi."

Dugan nodded. He was glad to be off the fishing boat, however impatient he was with the current situation. With his help, the Korean chief engineer managed to get the leak stopped. A call to Ward had done the rest. They set a westerly course for Aden to get them out of the Russians' immediate operating area, while Ward arranged an extraction. Two days later, a Sea Hawk helicopter had lowered biohazard suits for Dugan and the Russians, not to protect them but to isolate them from contact with others.

They'd been winched aboard the chopper one by one, with Dugan the last to leave. Before going, he'd read the newly cooperative Kwok the riot act, reminding him of the realities. He would be shadowed by satellites and air-craft all the way to Aden, and if he changed course or attempted in any way to contact another vessel, he would be sunk without warning by a cruise missile. Ward's superiors had been much less reticent about authorizing de-cisive action after they'd learned what they were dealing with.

Given the speed of the fishing boat, the incubation period for the virus would elapse before the vessel reached Aden, and there she would be met by a medical team to assess the crew's health before releasing them.

"What about charter and repairs, Dugan?" Kwok had asked. "You prom-ised."

Dugan had handed Kwok a card. "Mail your bill for the charter and *rea-sonable* expenses here, and it will get paid, Kwok," Dugan said, glancing at the chief engineer. "As long as it's accompanied by a signed statement from the chief here that you didn't retaliate against him and the other crewmen that helped us."

"This is blackmail!" Kwok said.

"Your call, Kwok. Money or revenge," Dugan countered, leaving the little Korean sputtering on deck as the chopper hoisted him skyward.

"Do not worry so, *Dyed*," Borgdanov said, pulling Dugan back to reality. "We will be finished incubation period soon, and by that time we arrive in Harardheere. Blake says executions have stopped since *piraty* now know about our hostages, and I think it is not bad thing to give them time to think. Like you say in English, give them time to boil, *da*?"

Dugan smiled, despite his mood. "I think you mean, give them time to stew," he said.

Borgdanov shrugged. "Boil. Stew. Whatever. How you cook *piraty*'s ass is not so important, I think—as long as you cook it."

CHAPTER TWENTY-EIGHT

"*QUIET!*" Zahra shouted for the third time, slapping his open hand on the conference table.

Eleven faces snapped toward him, surprised and quieted by the explosive sound. Surprised looks turned to scowls as the men glared down the long table.

"And just who're you to give orders, Zahra," one said. "We're all equals here."

"Even among equals someone must maintain order," Zahra said.

The man sneered. "So you've appointed yourself. Is that it?" There were grumbles of agreement.

"I appointed myself to nothing," Zahra said evenly. "When these ships full of our brothers arrived, their captors contacted me. These people made it clear they'll only deal with a single point of contact. I didn't seek them. As soon as the situation became clear to me, I called you all here to Harardheere."

Zahra kept his face impassive and watched reactions as he spoke. In truth, he was elated the new arrivals contacted him first. As the possibilities had occurred to him over the last week, he'd become giddy with anticipation. If only he could pull it off. He sighed inwardly. But first he had to leash this pack of hyenas.

"And now that we're here, Zahra," asked another man, "just what would you have us do? We've come the length of the Somali coast to gather, and now you propose giving up all of our captives and half the ships. That's ridiculous. If they give us two ships and a hundred or so captives, we should give them back the same."

"I've been dealing with them for over a week," Zahra said. "This American Blake is a tough negotiator, and this fellow Dugan who arrived yesterday is worse. He threatens to take all the men to Liberia. He even joked that for ten thousand dollars he could ensure they all get the death penalty."

"Savages," muttered a man down the table.

"He's bluffing," the first man scoffed. "Western governments will never permit that. Many European governments won't even turn our captured brothers over to *any* country with the death penalty."

"But we aren't dealing with Europeans," Zahra said. "At least not in name. They showed me papers documenting themselves to be Liberians, but in truth I don't know who they are. There are both Americans and Russians among them, but I suspect the Russians are mercenaries. It doesn't matter. As long as Liberia is willing to provide them cover, I doubt any of the Western powers will make a fuss. In fact, I'm quite sure they're secretly happy they don't have to deal with the problem themselves. Make no mistake, my brothers, these Liberians are serious people. They allowed me to speak with a few of the prisoners, who told me the Russians murdered quite freely and laughed in the process."

"But their offer is outrageous! We can get more ransom—"

"Can we?" Zahra asked, cutting the man off. "Thanks to the al-Shabaab fanatics and their lunacy with the American ship, there's now a UN moratorium on the payment of ransoms. One which hasn't been broken despite the fact that we've executed over twenty hostages. That means even if owners and insurers are willing to deal with us, as these Liberians seem to be, it's now impossible for them to process the necessary transactions through their banks. I doubt we see another cent in ransom money, at least until things cool down, and that may take months, or even longer." Zahra stopped and stared down the table. "That makes the offer of two ships full of gasoline very attractive. The asset is already here; no government can stop its delivery. Together, they carry over one hundred and fifty million dollars' worth of petrol, even if we sell it below market price."

A man down the table looked doubtful. "So you say. But we're warriors, not merchants. We already have other tankers, and we've always ransomed them in the past. What's so special about these?"

Idiot! Zahra struggled to hide his contempt.

"Those are crude tankers," he said. "Their cargo is useless to anyone lacking the means to refine the crude. These are product tankers, full of premium gasoline. It's as good as cash."

"The ships and captives are here, within easy reach," said one of the others. "We greatly outnumber these Liberians. Why negotiate at all? Why not just take the hostages *and* the ships?"

Zahra could no longer hide his exasperation. "With what? A collection of khat-chewing holders? These Liberians have over a hundred of our best attackers, and the Russian assault after the drillship sinking wiped out over forty more. Must I remind you that only one mother ship survived that attack with a few men left alive? We hardly have enough experienced men left to conduct normal operations against single unarmed ships, and only then if we combine forces. We have nowhere near the necessary firepower to successfully attack targets defended by armed Russians!"

"I still say they're bluffing," came a reply from down the table, and the group once again dissolved in chaos, each man shouting his opinion to be heard above the melee. Zahra shook his head in disgust.

"Have you confirmed the cargos, Zahra?"

The voice was hardly above normal speaking level, yet it was heard through the commotion. The others fell silent and turned to the speaker. Gutaale was at least a decade older than the others, and universally respected—and feared.

"Have you confirmed the cargos, Zahra?" he repeated.

"Yes, Gutaale," Zahra said. "Several of my men have lived in Europe and worked as seamen on tankers, and the Liberians allowed us to inspect the ships. My men confirm that they are both full of gasoline."

"And whoever these Liberians are, doesn't it seem strange they have such a fortune in gasoline to trade? Something doesn't seem right to me," Gutaale said.

Zahra suppressed a smile. If he could win Gutaale over, the others would fall in line, and the man was asking the very questions he'd asked himself.

"Nor to me, Gutaale. At least at first. But things became clear during negotiations. Blake wouldn't answer that question, but this Dugan isn't quite so clever. He let a few things slip and Omar, my interpreter, was able to pick up on them. Between us, we pieced things together," Zahra said. "The tankers are both old, near the end of their lives. The cargoes belong to major oil companies, and the oil majors self-insure their cargo. I think these Liberians just diverted the tankers here to use the cargo as trade goods. They will, of course, claim that they were hijacked by pirates and that they were only able to negotiate the release of the crews. The ship insurers will be happy to get off by paying scrap value for the two old tankers, and the oil companies will be stuck with the bill for the gasoline." Zahra paused, his admiration obvious. "It's quite clever."

"And quite obvious," Gutaale said. "There'll be repercussions."

"Ah, but that's the beauty of it," Zahra said. "Repercussions from whom?"

He ticked off points on his fingers.

"All our captives will be released, so the great humanitarian issue is solved. With the captives out of the equation, pressure will be off the various governments. Maintaining the anti-pirate force is expensive, and I suspect they'll all jump at the chance to reduce their naval presence. Will the insurers complain? I don't think so. No hostages reduces the pressure on everyone. They'll let things calm down a bit, and in a few months start very low-key talks about payments to release the remaining ships.

"This is not a bad deal," Zahra continued. "Everyone is a winner except the oil companies, and how much sympathy can they expect? In three months' time, everyone will go back to ignoring poor, benighted, lawless Somalia. Then we do what we want."

Gutaale stared at Zahra. Zahra held his breath, then heaved an inward sigh as the corners of the older man's mouth twitched upward in a smile.

"You have it all figured out, Zahra," Gutaale said. "Exactly what is it that 'we' want to do?"

Zahra smiled back. "Organize, innovate, train, upgrade our equipment, and a dozen other things!" His voice grew excited as he warmed to the subject. "Just think of it Gutaale," he said. "This is the first time we will have such a sum all together. We have a chance to combine forces and use it wisely. Night-vision equipment. Remote-controlled drones to extend our search areas. Better, bigger, faster boats with better radar and evasion capabilities. Training to teach us to use it all. Intelligence assets in the world's shipping centers. The list is long," Zahra said, "and all possible with this influx of money."

"We've made good money in the past," Gutaale said.

"Yes. A million here, five million there," Zahra said. "All divided and spent foolishly. How many times have you seen the fools we employ crowd the khat market, waving fistfuls of hundred-dollar bills? We can do better. We must."

"What do you propose?" Gutaale asked.

"To make the deal," Zahra said. "I say we give them all the captive seamen, and negotiate for the remaining ships. We may get something for the ships from the insurers in a few months when things calm down a bit. In the meantime, we do nothing but acquire new equipment, train, and put our intelligence assets in place. The men we get back from the Liberians will be the core of our force, and they'll know how they were captured and how to develop countermeasures. When we launch again in six or eight months, we'll use our intelligence nets to select our targets carefully. Rather than scooping up every poxy fishing boat or rusty Greek freighter carrying cement, we'll focus on high-value targets—loaded tankers and container ships, or perhaps passenger vessels." Zahra paused, as if thinking. "Yes," he said, "particularly passenger vessels. We can use the fanatics' trick and get people onboard ahead of time. If we make the very first capture of our new venture a passenger vessel, we'll have tremendous leverage. Think of having over a thousand European hostages!"

"Which it seems to me," Gutaale said, "would eventually bring back the warships and put us in a situation very similar to where we are now."

"Agreed," Zahra said. "But the key word is *eventually*. It'll take a year or more before we get to that point, and by that time, we'll have bought our way into what passes for a government here." He smiled and looked around the table. "We can all be ministers of something or other, and work diligently to free the hostages from the horrible pirates—in exchange, of course, for a sizable aid package from the Western powers."

Gutaale leaned back in his chair and nodded. "All right, Zahra," he said. "You've convinced me." He looked around the table. "Does anyone disagree?"

No one spoke.

"Very well, Zahra," Gutaale said. "Make your deal with these Liberians."

M/T *MARIE FLOYD*
AT ANCHOR
HARARDHEERE, SOMALIA

Dugan walked across the main deck to where Blake stood staring out at the M/T *Luther Hurd*, anchored in the shadow of USS *Carney*.

"How are your people, Vince?" he asked.

"Looks like they're both going to be OK," Blake said. "The navy's evacuating them to Bahrain for further evaluation, then they'll fly them home. Looks like Stan may heal faster than Lynda, but the doc on the *Carney* said she might be able to avoid surgery and get by with physical therapy."

Dugan nodded. "How about you? What're your plans?"

"I'll take the *Luther Hurd* on to Diego Garcia," Blake said. "Hanley leaned on some politicians who leaned on the navy, and they're flying some replacement crew out via Bahrain also. We'll tag along a few hours behind *Carney* until we get in chopper range." Blake looked a question at Dugan. "But I don't think you came up here to discuss my travel plans. What's up?"

Dugan grinned. "I just got off the phone with our new buddy Omar. Hook, line, and friggin' sinker! They bought the whole story."

"Terrific! You were smart to let them keep some of the ships. They think they got the best end of the deal. The crews are the issue."

Farther down the deck, Woody emerged from a ballast tank manhole and began to pull a cutting-torch hose from the tank and coil it on deck. He was finished by the time Dugan and Blake reached him.

"What's up?" Woody asked.

"You tell me," Dugan said. "How are the ballast-tank bulkheads coming?"

"Finished," Woody said.

"And the engine room?"

"Let's just cut to the chase, Dugan," Woody said. "I said 'finished.' That means every damn watertight bulkhead on this ship is like Swiss cheese."

"OK. How about the jammers and the li—"

"Jesus H. Christ on a crutch, Dugan! You sure you ain't related to Hanley? You could be twins separated at birth."

Dugan opened his mouth to protest, but Woody cut him off. "Every single thing on your list is finished. Here on *Marie Floyd*, and over on *Pacific Endurance* too."

Blake laughed, reducing Dugan's indignation to a sheepish grin.

"OK, OK," Dugan said. "Pack up and get your boys over to the *Carney*."

"If it's all the same to you," Woody said, "me and the boys will ride on *Luther Hurd* with Andrei and his guys till Bahrain."

"*Andrei*? You mean Borgdanov? The same guy you said you'd never be bass-fishing buddies with?"

"He ain't half bad," Woody said grudgingly. "For a foreigner, I mean."

Dugan laughed, then stroked his chin. "Not a bad idea. We'll have the Russians with us here on *Marie Floyd* right up to the last minute, but if Zahra gets any cute ideas, having you and your boys with your M-4s close by will be good backup."

M/T *Marie Floyd*
At anchor
Harardheere, Somalia

Dugan stood with Blake near the accommodation ladder. Borgdanov and his black-clad Russians surrounded them facing outward, a threatening counterbalance to the fifty-strong contingent of the twelve clan leaders farther down the deck. The pirate presence was growing, as pirates released from their holding cells joined their leaders on deck.

But quantity didn't trump quality. Only the pirates who boarded with the clan leaders were armed, and even if they outnumbered the Russians more than four to one, the result of any firefight was far from certain. The Russians' superior weapons, body armor, and fire discipline made them formidable adversaries, and no pirate was eager to deal with them, despite the numerical imbalance.

By agreement, Dugan and Blake stayed aboard—hostages until the exchange was complete. It had begun early in the morning, starting with the release of *Phoenix Lynx* and her surviving crew, followed by release of the captive ships in the out ports. The freed vessels carried not only their own crews but those of ships Dugan allowed the pirates to keep. Each vessel released was met by a warship from the Western powers, and the identity of each hostage confirmed against a master list. When all the hostages were verified safe, *Carney* relayed the news to Dugan and escorted *Phoenix Lynx* a safe distance away. They waited now, out of sight just over the horizon.

Blake glanced nervously over the side, to where *Luther Hurd* rode at anchor, a half mile away. "I feel a bit naked without *Carney* in sight."

Dugan shook his head. "I had to lean on Ward to get them to leave in the first place. If we can't see them, they can't see us. Plausible deniability. Besides, *Carney*'s skipper already has his neck stretched out a bit by talking the SEALs into forgetting those boats."

Blake nodded and glanced down over the rail at two big high-speed Zodiacs tethered to the small landing at the bottom of the accommodation ladder. They rode there among half a dozen empty pirate launches of assorted shapes and sizes, clustered around the little landing like nursing piglets.

Dugan turned. "Well, we always knew this would be the tricky part," he said to Borgdanov. "Recommendations?"

"They will not attack until after we go down, I think," Borgdanov said. "I stay on top with six men while Ilya takes six more down ladder and prepares boats, *da*? *Dyed*, you and Captain Blake go with Ilya. When all is ready in the boats, Ilya signals me and we come down very fast, while Ilya and his men keep weapons pointed up at edge of the main deck. If any *piraty* leans over the main deck to shoot, Ilya's men kill him. Then we escape. Simple plan, *da?*"

"*Sounds* simple," Dugan said, hoping it would be.

"Good," Borgdanov said, and barked orders. The sergeant nodded and motioned Dugan and Blake to the ladder, then followed with his six men. Dugan moved down the sloping aluminum steps and into the first Zodiac, and Blake moved into the second. They fired up the outboards, as the Russians divided themselves between the two boats and trained their assault rifles up at the rail. The sergeant gave a sharp whistle and the remaining Russians rushed down, Borgdanov in the rear. By prearrangement, the second group also divided, filling both boats to capacity. The last Russian to board each boat cast off the lines, and Dugan and Blake backed the boats out of the cluster. Dugan looked up at the sergeant's shout.

Half a dozen pirates reached the rail, forced back by Russian fire. All the Russians targeted the rail, except Borgdanov and the sergeant, who were pulling the pins on grenades and tossing them into the pirate boats.

"*GO! GO! GO! Dyed!*" screamed Borgdanov, as he and the sergeant finished and raised their weapons to target the rail.

"*HANG ON!*" Dugan screamed, as he spun the boat around and hit full throttle, and Blake followed suit. Heavily loaded, the boats bucked in the water and bogged down as the propellers cavitated, but almost simultaneously Dugan and Blake realized their mistake and backed off the throttles a bit. In seconds, the boats were up and planing across the water, as Dugan felt the concussion of the grenade blasts on his back and heard the earsplitting explosions.

The pirates aboard *Marie Floyd* rushed back to the rail, pouring wild, undisciplined fire after the boats, joined by freed pirates on the deck of the nearby *Pacific Endurance*. But the boats were already difficult targets—too difficult for the marksmanship of the pirates.

Borgdanov pointed to the *Marie Floyd*, where three pirate launches clustered unharmed at the bottom of her accommodation ladder. Dugan shrugged.

"We'll just have to let those go," Dugan yelled over the noise of the outboard. "They're all stirred up now. If we go back to toss grenades in those boats, someone might get killed."

Borgdanov smiled. "We do not have to return," he yelled back. "Just because *piraty* are terrible shots, does not mean we are. Stop. I think we are safe here."

Dugan cut power to an idle, and the boat drifted to a stop. Blake did the same and the boats drifted together, the powerful outboards muttering.

"Just as well," Dugan said. "I wasn't going to go much farther anyway. I'm not totally sure of the range of the remotes."

Borgdanov nodded, then shouted orders to his men. The Russians opened fire on the distant boats, a steady *rat-tat-tat* of aimed three-round bursts from a dozen weapons. In minutes, the three pirate boats were riddled with holes and sinking. Dugan opened his mouth to congratulate Borgdanov on his men's marksmanship, but was distracted by an unexpected vibration from his pocket.

M/T *Marie Floyd*
At anchor
Harardheere, Somalia

Omar stayed to one side and tried to make himself small as Zahra paced the deck and screamed curses after the fleeing Liberians.

"Those steaming piles of goat dung have the effrontery to betray me?" Zahra screamed. "To shoot my men and destroy my boats? They've reneged on the agreement, and we'll bring boats from ashore and hunt down this *Luther Hurd*! She can't outrun us! We'll blow them up and sink them all, and if the navy ships come back, we'll claim it has nothing to do with us! Tankers blow up all the time."

Omar didn't think it wise to point out that their men had been shooting at the Russians first.

"Omar!" Zahra screamed, and Omar scurried over.

"Call this Dugan on the cell phone you gave him for the negotiations. I want to let him know he's about to die so he can enjoy the anticipation," Zahra said.

"But Zahra—"

"*DO IT!*" Zahra screamed, and Omar pulled out his phone and hit a preset.

After a moment, Omar took the phone from his ear and spoke. "I have him, Zahra," he said.

"Good," Zahra said. "Tell him that he'll soon be dead."

Omar nodded and spoke into the phone, then looked back at Zahra.

"And now ask him if he knows what I'll soon be doing," Zahra commanded, preparing to launch into a long description of the slow torture he intended to inflict on Dugan and all his men.

Omar translated Zahra's words, and listened to the phone a moment. His face took on a strange expression, then morphed into a fearful look as Zahra continued.

"Tell him I'll—"

"I... I can't tell him anything, Zahra. He hung up."

"*WHAT*? He just hung up? What did he say?"

"Well, after I asked him if he knew what you'd be doing, he said... he said..."

"Out with it, you fool! What did he say!"

Omar was trembling now. "He... he said, 'I suggest the backstroke,' and then he hung up," Omar said.

ZODIACS
HARARDHEERE, SOMALIA

"—suggest the backstroke," Dugan said, then tossed the phone over the side. "Let's do it," he shouted across to Blake in the next boat.

Blake fished a small electronic device from his pocket and flipped up the guard over the single button. He thumbed the button and multiple explosions bloomed along the hulls of both *Marie Floyd* and *Pacific Endurance*, well below their waterlines. They caused small but obvious boils of white water, sending spray into the air as dull thumps echoed across the sea.

Dugan nodded and pulled a remote from his own pocket. He stared at the device a long moment, then looked back at the ships.

"These are very bad people, *Dyed*," Borgdanov said. "I think you should not worry about their fate. Whatever chance they have is better than chance they give people they burn to death and shoot in head, *da*?"

Dugan nodded and hit the button, sending a single signal to turn on half a dozen battery-powered jammers hidden on each ship. It was a one-time thing. As soon as the jammers came online, they blocked the signal that had activated them. Along with everything else.

The deck vibrated under Zahra's feet from a series of muffled explosions, and he looked across the water to see the water roiled by a similar series of explosions along the hull of the *Pacific Endurance*.

"They've sabotaged us," Zahra said, his mind racing. "Very well. Forget the Liberians for now, Omar. Organize the seamen among our men. We'll ground the ships in shallow water to save the cargo. Get them started, then call all available boats from ashore, just in case."

Zahra actually had good cause for optimism. Contrary to popular perception, tankers typically have a great deal of reserve buoyancy and can survive significant damage, given calm water and fair weather.

But this wasn't a casualty. This was destruction orchestrated by a man who spent his life keeping tankers floating, and who sure as hell knew how to sink one. So as much as Woody had griped as he crawled through tank after tank watching Dugan mark places to cut with a can of spray paint, he'd followed instructions to the letter. As had the Russians when Dugan showed them where to place the shaped charges for maximum effect.

The ships were going down, and they were going down fast.

Omar rushed from the deckhouse to where Zahra stood, watching the main deck a foot above the water.

"Zahra," he said. "The engine room is flooded. We can't move the ship!"

Zahra nodded, never taking his eyes off the water. "Have you managed to reach anyone ashore?"

"No," Omar said. "No phones. No radio. No nothing. We're being jammed."

Zahra looked up. Pirates boiled out of the deckhouse, alerted to the fact the engine room was flooded and that sinking was imminent.

"We must escape," he said, quiet urgency in his voice. "There aren't enough lifeboats. It'll be every man for himself when this mob realizes that. Go get them started launching the boats, then pick four of our most loyal men and sneak away to meet me on the stern. I saw a small life raft near there. We'll launch it and escape while the rest of these fools kill themselves over a place in the boats. Go now!"

"At once, Zahra," Omar said, and scurried away.

Zahra moved calmly, reassuring men as he met them. Telling them that tankers took a long time to sink, and that boats were on the way from shore, and that they were readying the lifeboats as a last resort.

He lied his way aft, then slipped from sight into the alleyway between the deckhouse and the machinery casing. He waited there impatiently until Omar arrived with four men in tow.

"Here," Zahra called, and motioned them aft to where the life-raft canister rested in its cradle near the ship's rail. "Quickly now," Zahra said. "Two men on each end. Lift the canister and toss it into the sea on my count of three. Omar, hold the rope, and don't let go!"

The men positioned themselves as instructed and prepared to heave.

"One. Two. Three. Heave!" Zahra shouted.

The men heaved on command, and an almost-weightless fiberglass canister shot ten feet in the air and plunged the short distance to the sea, splitting in two halves and revealing—nothing.

"It… it's empty," Omar said, holding a rope attached to nothing.

Zahra looked farther up the deck, where two other pirates intent on survival had attempted to launch another life-raft canister. It too was empty.

"They've sabotaged all the rafts," Zahra said. "That leaves only the lifeboats. Listen to me, all of you. We'll go to the nearest lifeboat. As soon as it's launched, shoot down anyone who gets in our way and get aboard. Is that clear?"

The men nodded, and Zahra led them up the port side to the lifeboat station. But they soon found they had no cause to use their weapons.

"It's welded!" Zahra heard a man cry as he neared the lifeboat. "The lifeboat davit is welded together! We can't launch the boat!"

Zahra looked around. The main deck was awash now and the tank vents were starting to go under, water boiling around them as the last pockets of air were forced from the tanks. He raced up the exterior stairway to the bridge wing, his underlings close behind. They gained the bridge wing and flew across it to the stairway up to the flying bridge above the wheelhouse, the highest spot on the ship.

And there they stopped.

Soon they were joined by others, and the small space was an island of humanity, its population staring down at the sea rushing to claim them, each knowing there was no escape.

ZODIACS
HARARDHEERE, SOMALIA

Dugan watched the main deck of the *Marie Floyd* dip below the water, with that of the *Pacific Endurance* not far behind. He did his best to ignore the masses of humanity collecting above the bridge on both vessels.

"Seen enough?" he yelled over to Blake.

Blake nodded, and headed toward the *Luther Hurd*, undoubtedly thinking of dead shipmates. Dugan gritted his teeth and fell in behind.

Halfway back to the *Luther Hurd* he saw them, two large black triangles cutting the water. He turned as the sharks swam past, and looked out over the water at a dozen fins converging on the sinking ships.

Dugan closed his eyes and thought of Bosun Luna, flaming tire around his neck, his agonizing death recorded to brutalize his family. He thought of other families in the Philippines, India, Europe, and the US—and victims yet to be. And his heart grew hard. *What goes around, comes around.*

"Bon appétit, boys," he whispered, and turned toward *Luther Hurd* without looking back.

Author's Notes
The Facts behind the Fiction

A novelist never lets the facts get in the way of a good story, but I firmly believe the strategic use of facts make a tale more compelling. Given that truth is often stranger than fiction, I thought a review of the facts behind *Deadly Coast* might be of interest.

UNIT 731
EPIDEMIC PREVENTION RESEARCH LAB
HYGIENE CORP
JAPANESE IMPERIAL ARMY

I've visited Japan many times, and found the Japanese to be gracious and friendly. So much so, it's often difficult to believe the events of the Second World War and the period leading up to it. Horrifying human experimentation carried out by Unit 731 was rumored for some time, and in the last fifteen years, well documented. The Dr. Ishii Shiro mentioned in the book was a real person. Under his leadership, Unit 731 committed atrocities that are almost beyond belief.

None of the perpetrators of these atrocities were brought to justice. At the war's end, members of Unit 731 were the world's foremost experts on chemical and biological warfare (largely as a result of their inhuman experimentation). Much documentation was destroyed before it was captured by occupying forces, and the world in 1945 was still a dangerous place. In that context, Ishii Shiro and his colleagues, a group unknown to the world at large, traded expertise for immunity. The rank and file of Unit 731 were sworn to secrecy and melted back into the general population, while higher-ranking members became advisors to classified US chemical- and biological-warfare programs. The official position was that Unit 731 never existed.

The Japanese government never changed that stance, but a decade or more ago, something extraordinary happened. Former members of the rank and file of Unit 731 began to tell their individual stories. Local governments, assisted by volunteers, many of whom were academics, set up exhibitions in sixty-one locations across Japan. In the course of eighteen months, the truth was told. Many of those testimonies are chronicled in a book by Hal Gold, titled *Unit 731 Testimony*. It isn't reading for the faint of heart.

While Mr. Gold's book provided the historical background, I did take license. None of the dialogue or actions attributed Ishii Shiro in *Deadly Coast* are factual, and the relationship with his Nazi counterparts is also my invention, as is Dr. Imamura. There was never an Operation Minogame, but there was an operation conceived by Dr. Ishii for a last-ditch biological attack against the US mainland.

Operation PX was finalized on March 26, 1945. It was to be a suicide attack against the US West Coast by the *I-400*, the largest Japanese submarine and one of only three vessels of its class. *I-400* carried three seaplanes in watertight hangars, and the sub's range was to be extended by converting ballast tanks to fuel tanks. She was to launch a seaplane attack against West Coast population centers with plague, cholera, and perhaps hantavirus. The crew was then to run the vessel aground and carry other pathogens ashore.

Ishii's plan was scrapped just prior to launch by General Umezu Yoshijiro, Chief of the General Staff. Umezu reportedly stated, "If bacteriological warfare is conducted, it will grow from the dimension of war between Japan and America to an endless battle of humanity against bacteria. Japan will earn the derision of the world." Umezu remained steadfast against the plan through the last five months of the war, even as the US bombed Tokyo to rubble. He faced violent opposition for his reticence.

General Umezu was given the inglorious duty of representing the Japanese Imperial Army at the surrender aboard the USS *Missouri*, and later was tried as a war criminal. He received a life sentence and died in Sugamo Prison in 1949. Dr. Ishii never served a day in prison, and died of throat cancer in 1959. Go figure. One can only hope Ishii's demise was a painful one.

THE LIBERTY SHIP
SS *JOHN BARRY*

Every good pirate tale needs a treasure ship, and I was pleased to find a real one in the neighborhood. Owned by the US War Shipping Administration and operated by Lykes Brothers Steamship Company of New Orleans, Louisiana, the SS *John Barry* sailed from Norfolk, Virginia, on July 24, 1944. She was bound for Iran with war materiel, with an intermediate stop in Saudi Arabia to deliver three million newly minted silver *riyal* coins. She never made it.

On the night of August 28, 1944, the *John Barry* was torpedoed by the German submarine *U-859*, and sank in over 8,500 feet of water, 127 nautical miles off the coast of Oman. Two seamen died in the attack, and the rest took to lifeboats. These survivors' tales placed the *John Barry* solidly in the ranks of history's lost treasure ships.

According to the captain's statement, there was an additional secret cargo of $26 million (at 1944 silver prices) in silver bullion aboard the *John Barry*. The captain's statement was backed by anecdotal evidence from other crewmen, and cryptic, if inconclusive, references scattered throughout official records. The existence of the additional silver was never established. Clearly out of reach over a mile and a half deep, the *John Barry* and her cargo became another legend in the pantheon of lost treasures.

And so it remained until 1992, when an unlikely alliance of American treasure hunters and an Omani sheik employed a British salvage expert and a French drilling vessel in an ambitious attempt to wrest treasure from the depths. Using an unmanned remotely operated vehicle to place explosives, the operators of the drillship *Flex LD* blew open the *John Barry's* hull and used a mechanical grab of their own invention to scoop up the exposed silver coins. The salvors managed to raise 1.8 million of the confirmed cargo of 3 million silver riyals.

Unfortunately, the silver bullion (if it exists) couldn't be identified in the jumbled wreckage, and the rest of the silver coins were too mixed in the wreckage to allow easy extraction. The salvors terminated operations with a stated intention of making another attempt. To date, the remaining riches of the *John Barry* remain unrecovered.

I took obvious liberties with the story, but the methods employed by my fictional drillship, *Ocean Goliath*, closely parallel those used by the very real drillship *Flex LD*. Most importantly, the *U-859* was not sunk immediately after her attack on the *John Barry* as indicated in the story, but sailed on to make some very interesting history of her own.

U-859

Contrary to the portrayal in the novel, the real *U-859* was outward-bound from Germany to the German-Japanese submarine base in Malaysia when she encountered and sank the *John Barry*. *U-859* was a type IXD2 boat, the latest class of submarine in the *Kriegsmarine*, and on her maiden voyage. Class IXD2 boats were large, with a range of 30,000 miles, and charged with the increasingly perilous task of maintaining a sea link between the Third Reich and the Empire of Japan. By 1944, the subs provided the only remaining method for sharing technology and scarce resources. *U-859*, like many eastbound subs, carried a cargo of mercury, in perpetual short supply in Japan and vital in the manufacture of munitions. Other boats carried not only mercury but also parts and drawings for the Messerschmitt ME163, an early jet fighter. Drawings the Japanese used to develop the Mitsubishi J8M1. Five of these advanced planes were captured when the Japanese surrendered in 1945. Records show that radar technology, optical instruments, and parts for V-2 rockets, along with German technicians, all made the long undersea voyage in the bellies of German U-boats. Reading of the technology transfer from Germany to Japan, I wondered what Germany might have received in return, and the idea of Unit 731 transferring biological-warfare expertise was born.

Before encountering the *John Barry*, the real *U-859* had already sunk two Allied ships and survived an air attack from a British Catalina off South Africa. She managed to shoot down the British plane, but was depth-charged and damaged in the fight. By the time she found and sank the *John Barry*, the limping U-boat was the subject of a search by British forces, which the loss of the *Barry* intensified. Undeterred, three days later Korvettenkapitän Jan Jebsen, the skipper of *U-859*, attacked and sank the M/V *Troilus* of the Blue Funnel Line. *U-859* sailed on, evading all British attempts to locate her.

But all was not well aboard *U-859*. Her snorkel was damaged in the earlier depth-charging and was only partially effective. Forced to remain submerged almost constantly by British patrols, the atmosphere inside the boat was increasingly toxic. It was with great relief that Jebsen surfaced on the night of 16 September and received radio orders to proceed to base at Penang, Malaysia.

A week later, on the morning of 23 September, *U-859* was approximately twenty nautical miles northwest of the base at Penang. Confident he'd finally shaken pursuit, Jebsen was cruising on the surface and allowing his weary men the luxury of coming topside in shifts to suck in lungfuls of fresh sea air. He was a bit more than an hour from the safety of the port. At Swettenham Pier in Penang, garlands of flowers were prepared for *U-859*'s crew and a Japanese naval band was tuning up. A crowd of Japanese and German naval personnel stood ready to welcome *U-859*, giving the base a carnival air.

Much closer to *U-859*, HMS *Trenchant* slipped beneath the azure waters of the Malacca Straits as her captain, Commander Arthur Hezlet, RN, studied the approaching U-boat in his periscope—the Royal Navy had found *U-859* at last. Or more accurately, the U-boat found the Royal Navy, since the British had intercepted the Germans' signals to base and broken the code. Commander Hezlet had been in position for thirty-six hours, awaiting *U-859*'s arrival.

HMS *Trenchant* fired a spread of three torpedoes from her stern tubes, with the middle torpedo striking the German sub just astern of the conning tower. *U-859* broke in half and sank immediately. Of the sixty-seven men aboard, nineteen survivors were in the water, including seven who made an astonishing escape from inside the sinking boat. Among the seven was the only officer to survive, twenty-two-year-old Oberleutnant Horst Klatt, the sub's first engineer. Much like my fictional Japanese, Dr. Imamura, Oberleutnant Klatt was in the toilet at the time. I based my description of Imamura's escape on Klatt's firsthand account of his own harrowing and miraculous experience.

Though perilously close to Japanese forces, Commander Hezlet ordered HMS *Trenchant* to surface and rescue survivors. Minutes into that exercise, Japanese ships appeared on the horizon and a Japanese fighter appeared overhead. Hezlett managed to pick up eight survivors, including Oberleutnant Klatt, before the attack forced him to submerge and evade. The remaining eleven Germans were rescued by the Japanese.

The story doesn't quite end there, for *U-859* did indeed contain a biological hazard and she was salvaged years later. After researchers turned up the fact that the submarine sank with some thirty-one tons of toxic mercury aboard, there were wide-spread concerns the flasks would eventually leak, poisoning the seafood chain. After diplomatic discussions between West Germany and Malaysia, the West German government launched a salvage operation in the winter of 1973.

There were ethical as well as environmental concerns. Containing the bodies of almost fifty German submariners, the wreck had long since been designated a burial site by the German War Graves Commission. As *U-859's* only surviving officer and the individual most familiar with the sub, Horst Klatt, then fifty-one years old, was asked to lead the expedition. And lead it he did, eventually recovering some thirty of the estimated thirty-one tons of mercury.

THE PIRATES

The world has a romanticized view of piracy; but with apologies to Johnny Depp and Captain Hook, there's nothing romantic about it. As I write these words on September 2, 2012, Somali pirate gangs hold eleven ships and 178 hostages of various nationalities. Yesterday, pirates in Haradheere murdered a crewman from the *M/V Orna* in cold blood and wounded another, announcing in a phone call to the press "More killings will follow if the owners continue to lie to us—we have lost patience with them." To most folks, those numbers and events mean little, but they represent a threat all too real to those who make their living on the world's oceans and their friends and families.

The total number of hostages at any given time is a moving target, with hostages being ransomed as new hostages are captured. The International

Maritime Bureau reports that last year (2011), a total of 1,206 seamen were held hostage at some point during the year, including some held for more than two years. Hostages are forced to live in deplorable conditions and subjected to constant physical and psychological abuse. Based on interviews with freed hostages, over half report being beaten and approximately ten percent suffered severe abuse, including being tied up in the sun for hours, being locked in freezers, or having fingernails pulled out with pliers. Thirty-five hostages died in 2011, nineteen of whom died while used as human shields.

Deadly Coast is fiction, and none of the characters or their actions is real. As much as I might like to play God and wrap up the Somali pirate problem so neatly, I'm afraid the solution offered exists only between the covers of this book. But though the story is fiction, I did attempt to sketch the scenes in Somalia with some authenticity. I was greatly assisted in that effort by the book *The Pirates of Somalia* by Jay Bahadur. Mr. Bahadur is a Canadian journalist who spent time in Somalia interacting with the pirates. The result is a compelling narrative that is obligatory reading for anyone interested in learning about Somali pirates. I will add that Mr. Bahadur went to great lengths to present a balanced view and his book is wonderfully objective. As a novelist rather than a journalist, I labored under no such obligation, and my pirates are considerably nastier than Mr. Bahadur's. I leave it to the reader to decide which portrayal they find more compelling.

So there you have it—the threads unraveled from the fabric of history and woven around current events to produce *Deadly Coast*. I hope you enjoyed reading the story as much as I enjoyed writing it.

Fair Winds and Following Seas,
R.E. (Bob) McDermott

Postscript on the Somali pirate situation - October 2014 - It's been two years since I penned *Deadly Coast*, and I'm pleased to say that during that period the Somali pirate situation has changed for the better. Aggressive use of private marine security (i.e. armed guards) by shipowners coupled with more aggressive anti-piracy operations by the world's navies have reduced Somali pirate attacks to a seven year low. As portrayed in *Deadly Coast*, the pirates view the whole sordid thing as a 'business,' and when you increase the cost of doing that business, the smart money goes elsewhere. That's the good news. The bad news is that piracy is increasing off the West Coast of Africa, where both the motivations and methods of operation differ greatly. So piracy continues as it has for hundreds of years, with the sporadic efforts at eradication resembling nothing so much as a giant global game of Whack-a Mole.

Thank You

Time is a precious commodity. None of us truly knows quite how much we'll have, and most of us are compelled to spend large blocks of it earning a living, making our leisure time more precious still. I am honored that you've chosen to spend some of your precious leisure time reading my work, and sincerely hope you found it enjoyable.

If you enjoyed this book, I do hope you'll spread the word to friends and family. I also hope you'll consider writing a review on Amazon, Goodreads, or one of the many sites dedicated to book reviews. A review need not be lengthy, and it will be most appreciated. Honest reader reviews are the single most effective means for a new author to build a following, and I need all I can get.

I invite you to try the other books of the Dugan series listed on the following page, and if you're a fan of post-apocalyptic fiction, I hope you'll also consider my *Disruption* series, beginning with *Under a Tell-Tale Sky* and available on Amazon.

And finally, on a more personal note, I'd love to hear your feedback on my books, good or bad. If you're interested, I'd also like to add you to my notification list, so I can alert you when each new book is available. You can reach me on my website at **www.remcdermott.com**. I respond personally to all emails and would really like to hear from you.

Fair Winds and Following Seas,

R.E. (Bob) McDermott

More Books by R.E. McDermott

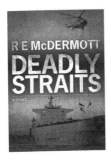

Deadly Straits - When marine engineer and very part-time spook Tom Dugan becomes collateral damage in the War on Terror, he's not about to take it lying down. Falsely implicated in a hijacking, he's offered a chance to clear himself by helping the CIA snare their real prey, Dugan's best friend, London ship owner Alex Kairouz. But Dugan has some plans of his own. Available in paperback on both Amazon and Barnes & Noble.

Deadly Coast - Dugan thought Somali pirates were bad news, then it got worse. As Tom Dugan and Alex Kairouz, his partner and best friend, struggle to ransom their ship and crew from murderous Somali pirates, things take a turn for the worse. A US Navy contracted tanker with a full load of jet fuel is also hijacked, not by garden variety pirates, but by terrorists with links to Al Qaeda, changing the playing field completely. Available in paperback on both Amazon and Barnes & Noble.

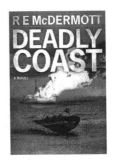

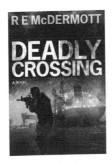

Deadly Crossing - Dugan's attempts to help his friends rescue an innocent girl from the Russian mob plunge him into a world he'd scarcely imagined, endangering him and everyone he holds dear. A world of modern day slavery and unspeakable cruelty, from which no one will escape, unless Dugan can weather a Deadly Crossing. Available in paperback on both Amazon and Barnes & Noble.